OPEN DOOR

JUDY BALDWIN LORD

ISBN 978-1-64191-554-0 (paperback)
ISBN 978-1-64191-555-7 (digital)

Christian Faith Publishing, Inc.
832 Park Avenue
Meadville, PA 16335
www.christianfaithpublishing.com

Grateful acknowledgement is made to the following: Author Photo: Kristi Gnyp. The CFP Staff, you have been wonderful! CHIP CHRISTY, songwriter/singer and author of the song "Hometown Girl." LAUREN FINLING, writer of "Bedtime for Baby Star." The poem was written for the CRIMINAL MINDS episode entitled, "There's No Place Like Home." Published 10/11/12.

I would like to recognize the following for "making the world a prettier place." Author's hair stylist, Nadine Girvan, author's make up artist, Trudy Kowalski, and "Ryder's" groomer, Joan Lamborn.

Printed in the United States of America

This book is dedicated to my one and only Savior, Jesus Christ. When he invited me to join him on this special journey, he asked me to bring only blank sheets of paper and a few pens. We shared many private moments as the landscape changed and the words were written while finding ourselves walking through valleys and climbing mountains. Hours were spent stopping to rest by streams of still water and sitting on porch swings. We experienced many sunrises that came dancing over the trees, and we watched the rain refresh their leaves. Yes, it is true that God never sleeps. I can attest to that, as he awakened me in the wee hours of morning to write yet another chapter by a night light. We made friends with neighborhood dogs while walking my own little Ryder—the one he had brought to me in the early days of my grief as I suffered the loss of my late husband. Yes, his presence is assured. He is in everything—big, small, and in between. Count on it.

Now we have reached the end of this journey, the goal has been achieved. The outcome in the lives of those who choose to read the story we have written together remains to be seen. I pray his kingdom will be expanded as well as my very own boundaries. I pray that hearts have been prepared long before the words were written. I pray that the soil these words fall upon will be fertile and soft. I pray that doors will be opened and seeds that have been planted will bear fruit and flourish. I pray the pebble he gave me to toss into the water will cause ripples that will change a life. I pray that his glory and his glory alone will shine through for all to see. I pray that people will place their very own Ebenezer stones and continue their journey clothed in his grace.

This is a book about love and second chances. May the reader follow in the footsteps that God and I have trod. I invite you to step into this journey as you walk through these chapters and hold tightly to the hem of his garment as you travel. Healing will surely find you with the mere touch of his hand.

I am so grateful God asked me to walk alongside him in this endeavor. I have enjoyed the ride...

ACKNOWLEDGMENTS

So many people have encouraged me in the writing of this book, and I thank them all. Many thanks to Brad Havens for his belief in me. It was with Brad that the idea was born one spring night in the Woodside Farmington Hills, Michigan church office. Heartfelt thanks to my good friend, Sue Robinson, who has been my biggest cheerleader since the day we met. I am blessed that God chose to have the two of us walk the same path on our earthly journey. To Joan Lamborn and Kathie Laper for continually nudging me to go on our girls "getaways" during a time when I didn't really know what I was doing or where I was going. Those trips refreshed me and gave me a calmness in spirit. To Toni Olson, who has touched my heart in so many ways, too numerable to mention. To Rosa Lee Gazette, with whom I have shared many memories, both happy and sad. To Debbie Pinn whose endearing relationship with her husband, Paul, led to the creation of a love story that will live on. To my late husband, Richard Baldwin, who assured my eternity when God used his hand to guide me back to Christ. To my dear daughter, Mandi Yaris, and my son-in-law, Steve, who have given me two wonderful grandchildren, Madison and Cole, the very loves of my life. To all my church friends both at Woodside Bible Church and Ward Evangelical Presbyterian Church, all of you are a blessing to me, forever to be cherished. To Ryder, my little yorkie who came to me when I needed him most. My little four-legged friend who sat beside me with every stroke of the pen, even in the midnight hour. To my husband, Ron, who led the cheers to the finish line. And last but not least, to the cowboys out there—you know who you are—love will always find you no matter how far you run.

"Ask and it will be given to you; seek and you will find; knock and the door will be opened to you. For everyone who asks receives; he who seeks finds; and to him who knocks, the door will be opened."
—Matthew 7:7–8

PART I

The Decision

Kate

She couldn't breathe. She knew it was happening again. She couldn't escape anxiety no matter how hard she tried. Another attack loomed. Her heartbeat was becoming more rapid. It was no wonder. She had lost her mother and her child. She had lost her love, the man she had trusted; the one she had adored. The man who had promised to never let her down. But the trust was unmerited, the adoration was built on sand that shifted suddenly, and the promise had been broken. Never again.

She took what little strength she had, gathered herself together, and walked to the garage. She had to find them. She had to dispose of them. It hurt too much to look at them. The paint brushes were there, all in a bucket. She took the bucket by the handle and walked to the edge of the driveway where she threw both bucket and paint-brushes into the waste can. The nursery she and her mother had painted together was no longer a room of welcome for a baby that never came home.

"I am done." She vowed to herself, and then she fell to the ground.

Zack

That is where Zack found her. He had always described her as a fragile little thing. Now he knew how fragile she really was. He was just the old man, the neighbor who had watched her for so many years. He had watched her as a toddler. He had seen her take her tumbles and get back up. He had observed how she and her mother ploughed through the grief of losing her dad. He had watched her graduate from high school. Totally unobserved, he had watched.

She seemed a little bit of a mystery to Zack, especially when she disappeared for some time after her mom died due to an untimely car accident. There had been no lights in her house when darkness fell and no sign of activity during the day. He had finally reached the conclusion that grief had taken her to another family member to live and make a fresh start.

But then a few weeks had passed, and she was back. As he walked his exercise route, he noticed the windows were open, the car was in the open garage, and Kate could be seen sitting on the porch swing in early morning where she and her mom had sat not so many months ago.

He had waved to her as he passed by that first morning of her return. She had smiled and waved back. He was glad she was home. For how long, he didn't know. He only knew that she had endured much in her nineteen years. He didn't realize at the time how much she had suffered.

Yes, the old man who lived at the end of the street, the one whose exercise route always led him to walk by her house every morning, saw her crumbled on the ground.

He dug in his pocket for his phone as he ran to her side. He quickly dialed 911.

Kate, Zack, and Brenda

The next morning, Zack arrived standing in the doorway of her hospital room with a handful of helium balloons and a teddy bear.

"I know you," Kate said.

He nodded as he placed the balloons on the table next to the bed and handed her the teddy bear.

"I've heard it said that a lady never outgrows teddy bears," Zack said to her.

She took the bear and replied, "You're Zack who whittles under that tree in your front yard and keeps his TV too loud."

He looked at her, smiled, nodded, and replied, "That would be me."

"You're the reason I'm here," Kate continued.

"No, I'm not the reason you're here, but I am the reason you're alive," Zack replied.

"Well, I don't want to be," Kate replied.

"Here or alive?" Zack questioned.

"Both," she replied.

Zack sat down in the chair next to the bed, looked her straight in the eye, and said, "You've got a lot of life to live, little missy, and I'm going to be here to help you—like it or not."

Just then, the nurse walked in. "You got that right, little missy," the nurse began. "You sure scared everybody. You're okay, but you're goin' to be with us for a while."

"Why?" Kate asked.

The nurse replied, "Why, why, she asks? Well, let me put it to you plain and simple. I've learned a little bit about you since you arrived, and anyone who has gone through what you have gone through needs help and a lot of it, that's why!"

Zack looked at Kate and said, "Yes, I told her. I told the doctors, and I told anyone who would listen. You've been to hell and back, and the time has come for someone to take care of you. While you're here, they will." He pointed to the nurse and then continued, "When you get home and out of here, I will."

Zack made his testimonial so adamantly while looking her straight in the eye, she knew better than to protest. Maybe she did need some help. Maybe he was more than just the old man who played his TV too loud. Nobody knew much about him. He had kept to himself most of the time. He was old enough to be her father. Maybe that's exactly what she needed, a father who could be her strength, at least, until she gained it back for herself.

These were Kate's thoughts as the nurse kept scurrying around the room doing whatever nurses do at times such as these. The nurse kept looking at Kate out of the corner of her eye, and Zack kept staring at her too. He was expecting her to protest his offer of taking care of her.

Finally, the nurse interjected, "I'm not leavin' this room until I have my say! This man"—she pointed to Zack—"is your angel in disguise. He found you in a little heap on the ground, so don't question him! He's your lifeline right now, and you better allow him to let you lean on him!"

The nurse walked to the doorway, turned, and said as she left, "By the way, my name is Brenda."

She left the room, saying something to herself that neither Kate nor Zack could decipher.

Kate looked at Zack as if to protest, but before she could utter a word, Zack exclaimed as he stood from the chair, "Are we clear?"

After fidgeting a bit, she placed the teddy bear beside her on the pillow and answered, "We're clear."

And that was the beginning.

2

Zack and Kate

They grew to simply adore one another. Zack did become her "father," and he looked upon her as a daughter. Spring turned to summer and fall into winter. The seasons came and went as their trust grew stronger and stronger.

One of those unusually hot July days, they were sitting on the swing of Kate's front porch, drinking sweet tea.

"You know, I just can't force myself to like this stuff," Zack exclaimed, "but because of you, I'm trying. It just needs a little something more. Pass me the sugar."

He stirred it into his glass and took another swallow before speaking.

"I've always thought you were an exceptional person, having gone through everything you have had to endure, being so young and all. I know how hard it must have been for you when your mom died," Zack said, looking at Kate.

Kate had always flinched when her mother's death was mentioned. News of the car accident had come at her like an ocean wave, knocking her down and taking her out into the deep against her will. Her mom had been the only person she had left in this world, and then she was taken away from her abruptly. It was a time she chose not to remember, or even talk about. It was too painful. She did not want to scratch that scab and leave the wound open and have to start the healing process all over again. Yes, she still had scabs, not scars. But she had learned that Zack was completely safe, and she trusted him beyond measure. She surmised that's what you do when someone saves your life. There had never been any "flenching" with Zack. Trusting him had been easy, and he came to her when she thought she would never trust another man again.

"It was hard," Kate answered.

"Well, you were barely nineteen years old when it happened," Zack responded.

Kate nodded.

"And you had no brothers or sisters," he continued.

Again, she nodded.

"You must have felt pretty alone back then," he said.

"I did," she confessed.

"I wondered how in the world a girl of nineteen was going to take care of a house. But you did, and you still do. You've survived tragedies that would have killed some, Kate," Zack almost whispered.

"I will always remember that day as if it were yesterday," Kate replied, "the day the rug was pulled out from under me. That was the day everything changed in an instant."

She looked out into the distance.

"There wasn't much I had to do to keep up with the house. Mom had pretty much taken care of everything before she died. She believed in planning ahead."

Zack smiled.

Kate continued, "And somehow the house was paid for."

"Maybe you have a long-lost relative somewhere," Zack replied.

"Oh, sure! Or maybe that man who was on that show, *The Millionaire*, went to my bank and paid off the mortgage!" Kate exclaimed.

Kate laughed and shrugged her shoulders. "Nope, no long-lost relatives. No millionaires. Like I said, my mom planned ahead. I'm sure she did something that assured me a future. This house was one of them."

Zack took her hand and said, "You've always looked so fragile but have proven yourself to be very strong, Kate. I've always admired your resiliency."

"Funny, that's what my mom used to tell me," she replied.

Zack noticed the far-off look in her eyes.

He took a sip of the sweet tea and asked, "What is it, Kate?"

She took a deep breath before answering. She trusted him. She kept saying that over and over to herself—how very much she trusted Zack. She had never told anyone. Only her mom knew her secret. Perhaps it was time to bring it out into the light. Perhaps it was time to let it go…to a man who never pointed fingers…

It was over a bowl of popcorn and a small glass of amaretto on the rocks when Kate told Zack her complete story. When she had finished, she agreed with Zack.

"You were very right when you said I had lost much in my lifetime. You just didn't know how much until tonight."

It was winter, and the night was cold. He took her hand.

"My dear Kate, nothing you have ever done or nothing you have ever said would ever make me turn my back on you. What's past is past. What's done is done. And I love you like a daughter unconditionally."

A soft fire was burning in the fireplace when he turned to face her directly.

"Kate, one thing all the people in this neighborhood are right about is that I am an old man."

"And you live at the end of the street," Kate interjected.

Zack nodded his head and mimicked how the neighbors had stereotyped him.

"Oh, he's just an old man who lives at the end of the street. Be polite. Be cool. He bothers no one."

He looked at Kate, becoming very serious.

"One day, I am going to be gone, not of my own choice, mind you. That's just the way it is. We live, we try to help out where we can, we love Jesus, and then we die. We go home. One day, that is going to happen to me."

"But," Kate began, "surely God knows I've lost too much in my lifetime. I can't lose you too."

"But you will. I only hope that in the time we have shared, I have taught you to be even stronger than you have been before. I know you have taught me a lot about being young. We've had a lot of laughs, haven't we, Kate?"

"Yes, we have. You brought laughter back into my life, and I am so very grateful," Kate replied.

"I'm glad to know that," Zack said as he began to smile.

"I know what you're thinking." Kate began to laugh.

"Oh, you do, do you?" Zack questioned.

"Yes, I do!" Kate exclaimed.

"What, what am I thinking, little missy?"

"You're thinking of the night we were going through those old pictures of you and your late wife. Honestly, Zack, you were so skinny and, I'm sorry, ugly next to your gorgeous wife," Kate began.

"I remember what you said, girlie," Zack said.

Kate continued, "You were in a bathing suit with those little skinny legs of yours, and your wife was standing beside you, all dark hair flowing down around her shoulders, smiling a beautiful smile, and you were just standing there looking like, 'Why did this beautiful woman choose me?' So I couldn't help but ask you the question you were merely thinking that day the photographer snapped that picture, remember?"

Zack replied, "Yes, I do, missy, go on."

"Remember what you answered?" Kate questioned again.

"I do," Zack replied.

"Answer again, Zack," Kate said and playfully hit him on the shoulder.

He looked Kate straight in the eyes and said, "My wife always told me she was not attracted to my skinny legs, and it certainly was not my face, all rugged, just look at it!" Zack began as he walked across the room to stand in front of the wall mirror. "No, what she was attracted to was my humor. I made her laugh. And in time, I grew somewhat handsome and filled out with her cooking." He walked back to the couch and sat down.

Kate smiled. "You and she had a lot of laughter in your life, didn't you, Zack?"

"Oh, yes, we did. We were both doozies," Zack said, laughing. "And one day you will too. You look for a man with skinny legs, little missy, you'll be happy! Just you wait and see!"

"I love you, Zack. I don't know what I would have done if you hadn't scooped me up," Kate exclaimed.

Zack added, "And acquired a taste for sweet tea." He quickly added, "Well, kind of—you drink more sweet tea than anyone I have ever known!"

He hugged her as he stood to walk to the door and said, "Your secrets are safe with me, Kate."

She watched him from the window and waited for him to flash the porch light, signaling his safe return home. As she walked into the kitchen, she knew that yet another piece of her would die when Zack did. The laughter would once again be gone. And the snow continued to fall.

The next morning, Zack showed up on her front porch with a box of Krispy Kreme doughnuts. He held up the box and said, "To go with the sweet tea this fine morning, missy."

She laughed when she saw him, invited him in, and brewed a fresh pot of coffee instead of tea.

"Oh, thank you, Lord," he said as she poured him a cup of coffee. He pointed to the doughnut with chocolate frosting, inviting her to take it. She didn't hesitate.

"Kate, I have something to show you," he said as he took a glazed doughnut for himself. He continued, "Are you up for a ride after our little breakfast?" he asked.

She nodded while licking her fingers. "I love these doughnuts," she exclaimed.

"I know you do," Zack answered. "I remember you always saying if you're going to eat calories, it's going to be the best-tasting, caloric, and gooey thing in the world."

She reached for another doughnut. "Cinnamon sugar this time," she said, quickly adding, "variety."

When she had finished the very last crumb, they walked to the end of the street to Zack's car.

"Where are we going, Zack?"

"To the bank," he answered.

"What? Why?" Kate questioned.

"I'm going to share something with you that I have never told anyone else before."

"Oh, secrets from your past?" Kate laughingly questioned. "I thought I was the only one with secrets."

He replied, "Nope, I have them too. And it is now time to let you in on a few of them—well, one big one."

Zack continued to drive, looking straight ahead, and then said, "You know, Kate, I haven't caused much of a stir in our little neighborhood. Not yet, anyway. As we've said before, everybody around here just knows me as the 'old man at the end of the street.'" He laughed and continued, "Yes, I'm the old man that sits under that tree in my front yard next to the road and whittles."

"I've seen you whittling, but I never wanted to disturb you," Kate replied. "You always seemed very deep in thought out there sitting under that tree. Do you make things?"

"Oh no, I just whittle," Zack began. "It calms me, it's therapeutic."

She nodded.

He continued, "I'm the whacky old man that goes to the old farmland store in town and feeds the caged squirrels when I have nothing else to do."

"Well, I must be crazy too," Kate added, "because I go with you now to do that too! In fact, I would love to go there after you tell me your big secret." Kate laughed.

"Want to get that cage opened today and let them out?" Zack questioned.

"I'm ready!" Kate exclaimed.

"Seriously, Kate, I need to share something with you with no interruptions," Zack said.

Kate nodded, making the motion to zip her mouth closed.

"I don't bother anybody, and I keep pretty much to myself. That is, until I found you in a heap on the ground."

She smiled as he patted her hand.

"Mighty glad I did too," he said. "Anyway, people say I'm just someone who minds his own business, keeps his heat turned up to eighty degrees in the winter because my feet stay cold, and I'm a man who plays his TV too loud because I can't hear real good. That's okay. I don't mind that kind of talk. People tolerate me. It doesn't hurt me one iota. But what I'm saying is they only know the surface, on-top-of-the-skin things, about me."

He took a deep breath before continuing, "It takes a long time to gain my trust, Kate, but, you've managed to do that. I've discovered as the years have gone by that hurting hearts are always drawn to one another. And, I saw you hurting from a mile away. When I picked you up, just a little fragile heap on the ground and put you in that ambulance myself, I knew my life was going to be changed from that second on." Zack continued, "You are very special to me, Kate, and I trust you. That is why we are taking this little ride downtown today."

Zack pulled into a parking place at the local bank. He looked at her and said, "*Kadima.*"

Kate questioned, "What did you say?"

"I said *kadima.* It means 'Let's go.'"

3

They walked into the bank with no one looking up, affirming he was basically an "unknown" in town. Zack requested a form, gave it to Kate to sign, had the paper notarized, took a key, and walked into the vault. Kate stood beside him as he opened the box. He took her hand, looked around for cameras, and, seeing none, said, "When I die, you come to this box. Everything in it is yours. Don't be shocked, for this is the 'me' nobody took the time to know until you literally fell at my feet."

He took the papers out of the safety deposit box one at a time and laid them on the table. He took Kate's hands in his own and said, "My wife and I could never have children, as I have told you before. All these years when people have driven past and have witnessed me sitting in my chair under that tree whittling—well, let me tell you what I was always thinking—I was wondering what a child of my wife and I would have been like now after all these years. I got my answer when I found you. You are the daughter I never had, Kate. God brought me you, and I thank him every day. I want to thank you now. I'm leaving all this to you," he said as he held up the documents.

Kate stared at him in disbelief. She was speechless.

"No need to say anything," Zack began as he put the documents back in the deposit box. "And before you ask, I will answer, yes, I am the one, the one who paid off your mortgage all those years ago."

Still speechless, Kate allowed Zack to take her by the arm as they returned to the car. He turned the ignition, looked at her, and said, "What you are being given is more money than you will ever need. When I'm gone, you go find your dream. You go in search of that man with skinny legs, laugh a lot, and I command you to be happy."

Kate continued to stare out the windshield. Zack turned to her and said, "I have one more piece of advice for you. Get out of this town before the folks here discover who I really was. When money is involved, seemingly long-lost relatives and friends will be coming out of the woodwork. They will be impostors. So put that house of yours up for sale as well as mine. Take what you need, leave the rest, and go."

Kate found her voice and whispered, "*Kadima* ?"

"Yes, *kadima*, my child, *kadima*," Zack replied.

He backed out of the parking space and asked, "Shall we go home now and eat the rest of those doughnuts?"

"Don't we have a stop to make first?" Kate questioned.

Zack looked at her as if to ask where.

Kate continued, "You know, the squirrels."

Zack laughed and replied, "Oh, missy, that is an adventure that needs to be done in the dark of night!"

He sped toward Kate's house, finishing his thought, *And we need the right tools to cut that lock on the cage.*

After a brief silence, Kate looked at Zack and asked, "We will do it, though, right, Zack?"

"Oh yes, we will do it."

That night, Zack sat in his living room thinking of what Kate had shared just two nights before.

"Oh, the crooked paths we sometimes have to travel," he said to himself.

He wanted the best for her and her future. She deserved it after all she had been through. He also wanted what time they had left together to be days of laughter. That's why he could not, would not, tell her he was, indeed, dying.

"This ticker of mine is just giving out," he said to himself, placing his hand over his heart.

He prayed she had not noticed the times he was out of breath or the times he had steadied himself on the railing while stepping off her porch.

He walked downstairs to his workroom, taking deep breaths as he went, and picked up a piece of wood he had found on one of his walks through the woods. He knew it was perfect for what he was going to whittle into a special shape just for Kate. She had asked him once if he "made things" with all that whittling. Well, he hadn't made anything until now. This would be special. She would understand.

It was in the dark of night when Kate heard a knock on her door. Looking out the peephole, she saw Zack. She opened the door and looked at the big grin on his face as he held up a tool big enough to break a lock. Her hand quickly went up to her mouth to stifle a laugh, thinking the neighbors would hear and know what they were up to.

"It's time?" she questioned as she grabbed her coat and ran to the car before realizing Zack was still on the porch.

"You okay?" she questioned.

"Yes, yes! Get in the car! I'm coming!"

He struggled to go down the porch steps, but Kate didn't notice. She had leaned over to start the car engine.

They arrived at the old farmland store and rejoiced when they saw no cars in the parking lot. Everything had been locked up for the night, especially those two squirrels that would soon be free.

"Zack, we can't just cut the lock and let them run. We have to take them somewhere."

"I know that, missy. Look in the trunk," Zack replied.

She walked to the back of the car as he popped the lid to the trunk. Snuggly, in one of the corners of the trunk sat a cage big enough for two squirrels.

Zack said, "We're goin' to take them to the woods, and they're goin' to love it!"

Kate almost shouted out loud as Zack motioned for her to hush.

"How are we going to catch them and put them in that cage?" Kate whispered.

"Watch how the master works," Zack replied.

He took the cage from the trunk, filled it with unshelled peanuts, and walked over to the squirrels. He took a few of the nuts and held them up to the squirrels.

"Gotta gain their trust, but I'm certain they know us by now from all our visits, don't you think?"

Kate nodded.

The squirrels took the nuts and began to eat. Zack got to work. It was only a matter of minutes for that lock to come loose. Kate took the cage as he opened the door where the squirrels had been held captive. Within what seemed only seconds, those squirrels scurried into that cage filled with peanuts. Kate shut the cage door, Zack grabbed the cage, and Kate began to run to the car.

"Hurry!" she yelled to Zack.

He was doing the best he could, and he finally made it to the car. He was glad Kate was too excited to ask any questions about why he was so out of breath.

When safely in the car with the squirrels, they both began to laugh while the squirrels munched happily in the backseat inside Zack's homemade cage. As they approached the woods, they looked at each other mischievously.

"Shall we?" Zack asked.

"Oh yes, let's set them free!" Kate replied.

"You do the honors, missy. I need to sit here for a while and watch."

It was then Kate turned and looked at Zack; she saw how flushed he was.

"Are you okay?" she asked.

He patted her hand and motioned for her to go. She gave his hand a playful squeeze, took the cage from the backseat, walked to the corner of the woods, opened that cage door, and set those squirrels free.

"Run!" she exclaimed. "Run!"

And they did. Not once did they look back.

On the way home, Zack said, "Don't you look back either, Kate. Memories are fine, but you can never go back. It's never quite the same. Loving relationships can never be replicated, but there can always be room for new ones if you allow it to happen. Look for the adventure ahead and pray the path straightens out a bit around every turn. You're goin' to be just fine whatever the road may bring."

"My resiliency?" Kate questioned.

"Oh yes," Zack replied.

And with that, he patted her hand once again. Kate could not help but fear something was wrong, very wrong. And she had already begun bracing herself for yet another rug to be pulled out beneath her. Another long journey into the deep…

"Dying is a wild night and a new road."
(Emily Dickenson)

Kate heard the sirens before her feet hit the floor that early April morning. She sat straight up in bed and ran downstairs. The noise was too loud. The blaring sound was on her street; she knew it.

She, quickly, threw her robe around her shoulders and ran outside. Her first glance was at Zack's house. That's where the ambulance had stopped.

"No!" she shouted.

She ran barefoot down the street and saw him as he was being carried out on the stretcher. She rushed up to him, grabbing his hand.

"No, Zack, no!"

He squeezed her hand and said; "Missy, do you realize you have your robe on?"

She looked at him, aghast.

"Zack, you are scaring me to death! What is going on here? What happened?"

"I just had a bad breathing spell, that's all. Needed a little boost of oxygen."

"I'm going with you to the hospital!" Kate exclaimed.

"Get some clothes on, missy, and meet me there, okay?"

The attendants nodded.

"Is he going to be all right?" she asked them.

"He's okay for now, but we need to get him to the hospital. Meet us there."

Kate slowly let go of Zack's hand.

"I'll be right behind you!" she shouted as she ran back to her house.

She found Zack laying on a gurney in the emergency room, a curtain partially surrounding his bed for privacy.

"What is going on?" Kate nearly shouted.

"Well, you see, I have this condition I have failed to tell you about on purpose. But now it seems the cat is out of the bag, so to speak," Zack began.

"And exactly what is this condition?" Kate asked.

"Oh, just a little trouble with my ticker here," he replied as he pointed to his chest. "But missy, listen to me, the doctor has given me my ticket home. That's the way I look at it. Don't look at this as a bad thing, do you hear me?" Zack answered.

"But it is! Oh, it is! I can't bear this, Zack!" Kate exclaimed.

"But you will bear it! And you will bear it like you have all the other things that have happened to you in your life that you questioned in your weakest moments. You will bear it, and you will move on like you always have," Zack said as he took a laborious breath.

He continued, "You remember everything I have ever told you, do you hear me? You are strong. You are beautiful. You will find joy regardless of your circumstances, and you will find that man God has prepared for you."

Before continuing, he took her hand in his. "And I repeat, preferably one with skinny legs and a goofy look on his face, as to why you chose him."

Zack forced a laugh.

"Don't try to be funny at a time like this!" Kate forced herself to sit in the chair next to the hospital gurney.

"Oh, but I have to, missy, it's my second nature." He tried to reassure her. Again, he gasped for a breath before continuing, "Now they're going to be putting me in a room soon, and I will call you to come back and hold my hand. You go home until I call. Mind me now, missy! I mean it."

Zack pointed to the nurse standing nearby. "You remember Brenda?" he questioned.

For the first time, Kate looked up to see someone other than Zack.

"I do remember Brenda," Kate replied, "and she's scurrying around this cubicle just like she did when you had brought me to this same hospital."

Brenda nodded, saying nothing.

"Brenda, you're going to allow me to stay, aren't you?" Kate looked at her pleadingly.

Zack interceded before Brenda could answer, "No, it could take hours before they get me into a room." He took another breath.

"Now run along. I'll call you when I'm cozied into my room—and bring me a doughnut when you come back."

Brenda blurted out, "Now, Mr. Zack, you know you can't have a doughnut!"

Zack looked at Kate, smiled, and said, "Go, sweet girl, I'll call you."

Brenda nodded, keeping her promise to agree with him. She didn't want to, but she did.

Kate looked at Zack and said, "Okay, but you call me the minute you get into a room."

Zack nodded.

Kate gave him a kiss on the forehead and slowly walked from the room. Looking over her shoulder, she saw Zack give her a thumbs-up. She also heard him say, "Brenda, give me some ice chips!"

He wanted to leave this world, knowing Kate was smiling because he was still giving orders.

Kate turned and walked back to his bedside.

"I'm coming back with doughnuts and my pajamas because while you're here, I'm going to take care of you, and so is Brenda."

Brenda smiled. "I remember when he said similar words to you, Miss Kate."

Kate looked Zack straight in the eye and questioned, "Are we clear?"

Again, Brenda smiled. "Yes, sir, I remember him sayin' that to you way back when."

"And what was my answer?" Kate asked.

Zack replied, "We're clear."

As Kate walked through the door, she walked with determination to her car.

"This time I'm taking charge, Zack. Now it's up to me."

After Kate had left, Brenda looked at Zack and said, "The first time I met you was when you brought that sweet girl into this very hospital."

She busied herself, walking swiftly around the area where Zack was. She pulled the privacy curtain and said, "You two became fast friends that very night, didn't you?"

"Yes, we did." He could barely reply.

"Well, don't you think you should have leveled with her? Told her the truth? I know you know it. You don't have much longer on this earth!" Brenda exclaimed out of pure exasperation.

"I know that," Zack replied.

"Well, why didn't you ask her to stay?" Brenda asked.

"I want her to remember the way we were. I watched my wife die. That image stayed with me for years. I don't want Kate to watch me die, I don't want her to live with that image, and I do not want her to be called until I do die, is that clear?"

Brenda looked at him, saying nothing. She only shook her head from side to side.

"Now don't go shakin' your head at me. I know what I'm doing!"

"No, you don't. You can barely breathe. I don't understand how you cannot call her back here!"

"Sometimes love has to steer you in another direction, my dear. I know I'm not going to make it to a room, and so do you. I repeat, are we clear?"

"Are we clear? Are we clear? Is that all you can say? Are we clear?" Brenda mumbled more to herself than Zack.

Brenda looked at him. He was trying so hard to take a breath.

Zack continued, "The pain has been too severe this time. I can't walk, and I can barely breathe."

Brenda found her voice and said, "Okay, I'm not going to argue with you. You need to save your energy. We're clear." Again, she scurried around the room for lack of anything better to do.

"And one more thing," Zack managed to say, "break it to her gently. She is such a gentle, fragile soul."

Brenda turned to him and asked one more time, "Are you sure you don't want me to call her back?"

"Brenda, my dear, I've heard that dying can be a wild night, and I've had some 'wild' angels around me all my life. It's only fitting they're with me now. I don't need Kate here, I am absolutely sure. I want her to remember me laughing," Zack said with a wave of his hand.

Brenda took his hand, kissed it, and turned to get the wet sponge that had been placed on the small table next to the bed.

"You knew you couldn't have ice chips, much less doughnuts, for gracious' sake," Brenda was saying as she turned to face Zack. He did not answer her. There was a smile on his face, but he was gone.

4

"Oh, lordy mercy, lordy mercy!" Brenda just kept saying over and over as she pushed the emergency warning for the doctor. "Oh, Mr. Zack, you were bigger than life. Oh, dear, oh, dear!" she kept repeating as she kept looking at him.

"Now you just sit right up out of that bed and tell me what you want me to say to that girl! Are we clear? You just open that mouth of yours and give me some orders like you always do on what you want me to tell her! Just exactly how do I break something like this gently?"

He made no sound.

"I remember that precious girl when you brought her in here all those years ago. You were her world, Mr. Zack! She came back to life because of you!" Brenda was near hysterics.

All Brenda could think of was that she had to call her.

"Oh my, oh my, sorry seems to be a sorry word for a time like this!" she exclaimed to no one. "What indeed do I say to her?"

It was then the doctor pulled the curtain back and walked over to Zack.

"I will tell her," he said. "You just get her here."

Brenda looked at him, tears beginning to fall.

"I got too close to this one, Doctor," was all she could say.

"We all do sometimes," he replied.

As Brenda turned to leave, the doctor continued, "After you call her, why don't you take some time and go home? I'll explain that you had to leave."

Gratefully, she dabbed her eyes and left the room to call Kate.

With a sense of urgency, Kate walked from her car through the hospital door. The emergency room was empty except for the nurse that had been stationed at the receiving desk. She walked quickly to the desk and said, "I was called back to the hospital in reference to a patient admitted a few hours ago."

"Patient's name?" the nurse asked.

"Zack, Zack Morris," Kate replied.

The nurse looked at the files on the desk, opened a folder with Zack's name on it, looked up, and said, "Could you wait here, please? I need to get the doctor."

"Doctor? Why? Can't I just go to Zack's room? I'm sure he has a room by now," Kate exclaimed.

"Please just wait here," the nurse insisted and scurried off, carrying the manila folder.

Kate's stomach began to churn. It took mere minutes for the doctor to appear.

"Are you alone?" he asked Kate.

"Yes, why?" Kate asked.

He asked Kate to follow him as he led the way into a private room.

"What's going on?" Kate nearly screamed.

"I'm so sorry," the doctor began. "There was nothing we could really do. Zack had been ill for a very long time. I don't know if you knew that or not. He insisted on complete privacy in the matter and wanted no one to know just how desperate his situation was."

Kate became more horrified with each word.

"Wait, wait, wait!" Kate exclaimed as she threw her hands in the air. "Are you trying to tell me that my Zack died?"

The doctor could only nod. He had witnessed this look on many faces during his career. One would think he could find the right words, but even to this day, all he could manage was to nod. He always thought at times like these that his mother had been right. He should have been a professor that did not have to deal with death—someone who only taught about it. He would never grow accustomed to this one-on-one news he was forced to give loved ones so many times. Never.

Kate stared at him in disbelief.

He led Kate to a nearby chair and said, "Zack shared with me at his regular checkups that you would be in charge of things when his time came. I know how very deeply he cared for you."

He looked at Kate with so much sympathy she knew if she started crying she would never stop. The doctor continued, "He was adamant that you not know, exactly, what he was going through. Are you going to be okay?"

Just then, Brenda stepped into the room. She walked over to Kate and put her arms around her.

"I thought I sent you home," the doctor said.

"Oh, I was goin', I was goin', but then I turned around. I just couldn't leave this sweet child alone at a time like this! So I turned around. I'm just too close to this one, Doctor, I'm just too close."

The doctor nodded in understanding, placed his hand on Brenda's shoulder, took one more sympathizing look at Kate, and left the two women alone.

"Women need women at times like these," he murmured to himself.

He passed the nurses' station on the way to his private office.

"Staying all night again tonight, Doctor?" the nurse asked.

"No, tonight I'm sending myself home," he answered.

"Good for you," she replied. "Good for you."

Kate looked at Brenda and said, "I want to see him. Can I please see him?"

Brenda hesitated as she remembered what Zack had said, "I want her to remember me laughing."

Well, Brenda thought to herself, *a smile was close enough.*

She took Kate by the hand and led her to a room where Zack had been moved. Kate waited in the hallway until Brenda motioned her to enter.

"I'll give you some privacy," Brenda said.

"Please stay," was all Kate could reply.

She walked to the bed and looked at the man who had been her world for nearly thirteen years. She sat down in the chair next to the bed and reached out her hand to touch his. She kissed his one hand and then the other.

Brenda watched, with tears streaming down her face.

"This was the hand that held mine when I needed to be put back on solid ground," she said to Brenda. Looking up, she met Brenda's eyes.

Kate whispered, "I trusted him. I shared everything with him, my deepest secrets, my biggest dreams."

"Oh, missy," Brenda began, "I know you would bring that man back to life with just the warmth of your own hand, if you could! I know how much he loved you and what he meant to you! He talked to me about you all the time."

Kate looked up, once again, tearing her eyes away from Zack's hand that she still held so tightly. She said, "I know. He talked about you, too. He said you were his 'go-to' source when he needed an ally. I know how special you were to him. That's why I asked you to stay with me in this room."

"Lordy mercy, missy, I can still see that big hulk of a man standing in your hospital room that day with all those balloons in one hand and a teddy bear in the other." Brenda was almost weeping.

"And you were scurrying around that room trying to be busy and speaking your own mind at the same time." Kate smiled.

Brenda reached for a tissue, retrieving it from her pocket, and dabbed her eyes.

Looking at Zack, Kate continued, "Oh yes, this man was going to take care of me whether I liked it or not. He made that perfectly clear, didn't he, Brenda?"

"Oh yes, he did, missy—he sure enough did," Brenda replied.

"You did too, if I remember correctly," Kate added.

Brenda merely nodded. She walked over to Kate and placed her own hand on Zack's shoulder while holding Kate's hand with the other.

Kate whispered, "I do believe he has a smile on his face."

"Oh yes, he does, missy, yes, he does," Brenda whispered back.

It was an hour before those two left that room. Eventually, Kate stood, kissed Zack's forehead, and hugged Brenda. Saying nothing more to anyone, she left. She had arrangements to make. She had a friend to bury. Then and only then would she allow herself to cry.

Kate left the hospital that night, remembering Zack the way he had always wanted her to remember him—with a smile on his face.

"The path to peace is paved with knee prints."
(Beth Moore)

Kate was on her knees when the final decision was made. She was leaving. One foot was tugging at her to remain in the past, the other was pulling her toward the future without Zack. There was nothing for her here—not anymore. She had always been a "runner." She knew how to do that. And soon after the funeral, she would be running again. No more Zack to encourage her to slow down, smell the roses, and reach toward hope.

The loss of Zack had devastated her. She kept looking to the end of the street toward his house. She could see him sitting under that tree in his front yard, whittling. She knew she had to go in his house eventually, and she knew it had to be before his funeral. He had told her, "*There's something there I want you to have, missy. I want to make you laugh before you leave town.*"

She had always listened to him, and she was not going to start disobeying him now. She would honor him as always, especially in death. She smiled as she remembered how much he loved giving orders.

"Okay," she said to herself, "I've made the decision. Once upon a time, Zack told me to leave. He's made it possible for me to do so. I am leaving."

Over and over she kept convincing herself this was not the same as "running." She was merely leaving. She rose to her feet and walked out the front door.

It was as if her heart kept breaking with every step she took, but she finally made it to his doorway. She searched for the hidden key, secured it in her hand, and unlocked the front door. She stepped into its familiar surroundings and walked around the living room, touching everything that had been Zack's.

Then her eyes fell upon something that made her laugh out loud. She walked over to the shelf and picked it up—two carved replicas of the squirrels they had set free in the dark of night.

"I wonder where those squirrels are right now?" she questioned with a smile on her face. What would Zack tell her?

In his own way, he would probably say, "*Oh, missy, those squirrels are runnin' free in the woods now. Probably have had some babies. They're busy eating out of people's bird feeders and bathing in their bird baths, driving bird lovers crazy!*"

She put the two tiny carved squirrels in her pocket and walked through the front door she had left open. She had a funeral to attend.

Some neighbors came to pay their respects. Kate sat with the only person that truly understood the depth of her loss, Brenda. Both sat in silence. Both understood. Both wanted no intrusions to their thoughts and their memories.

When the memorial was over, Brenda looked at Kate and said, "I know you're leaving, and I wish you the best. I'll pray you all the way to peace and safety, dear child. Don't ever forget me, but don't look back. Just take your good memories and leave the rest behind."

Kate smiled, embraced her, and said, "I will never ever forget you."

Then as if in a daze, Kate walked to her car, started the engine, and followed the hearse to the cemetery. When she said her final farewell to Zack, there was only one stop she had to make before leaving. She looked at the empty tissue box beside her in the front seat of her car. She had used that last tissue to wipe the cemetery mud from her shoes.

Within a few miles, she had reached her destination—the home she was leaving behind. The "For Sale" sign was in the front yard. She lingered in the car, looking at the past as if through a microscopic lens. These days she had to 'compartmentalize.' The future in panoramic vision seemed too large to comprehend.

She walked to the porch and sat on the swing where her mother and she had planned a nursery. She walked into the living room, remembering the soft firelight where she had shared her secret with Zack. The kitchen table held the pitcher where most of the sweet tea had been tolerated by Zack. She walked into her bedroom and over to the dresser. She opened the bottom drawer and pulled out a package, tucking it under her arm as she walked back to the porch swing. It was there on that small table next to the swing she placed the now empty tissue box. She had cried many tears there. Now it was over. She turned to leave.

All she took with her were the clothes on her back, her inheritance, two tiny carved squirrels in her pocket, and that very special package that was tucked safely and protectively under her left arm right next to her heart.

6

Kate didn't know where she was going. She just knew she was on the road.

I'll know when I find it, she said to herself.

Familiar scenery disappeared, and new terrain came before her eyes.

All my life I've waited for phone calls that never came. Phone calls from a man who only gave me broken promises and secrets only confessed to Zack and my mom, she thought. *I'm tired of it*, she continued talking to absolutely no one but herself.

"Time to move on," she said out loud

She pulled the car onto an exit offering fast food. "Quick off, quick on," the sign read. She chose Burger King and went inside, visiting the restroom first.

She looked in the mirror. "Oh, look at that face, would you?" She spoke out loud. "It holds all the lines of all the roads I've traveled down and all the curves I've gone around on two wheels."

It was then that another woman came out of one of the stalls, looked at her, and said, "Honey, you're still young. This is what you have to look forward to," pointing to her own full figure. The lady washed her hands, gave Kate a quick smile, and walked through the door, swinging her hips.

Kate merely looked in the mirror again and said, "Time for a makeover. Time for a mulligan. A mani/pedi. A new 'do.'"

She wanted peace. She craved a quietness of spirit she had known so many years before her world stood still.

After eating her fast food, she walked back to the car, vowing to eat healthier at the next stop. With a click of the remote, her car engine roared to life.

"Time to pull up my big girl britches," she said to no one in particular. She was tired. She had run away from too many heartaches. No more! This was the last. No more painting herself in corners. The footprints she left behind in all that paint when she tried to get herself out of those corners proved too messy to even try to clean up. Time again to throw away the brushes. Just like she had literally done that morning Zack had found her. But deep down she knew the walls she would build around her heart could not protect her; they would only seclude her—from feeling, from loving. She couldn't thrive in seclusion. Zack had taught her that.

She had driven a few more hours when she saw the sign, "BROOKSPORT VILLAGE," next exit two miles up the highway. She needed gas.

"Might as well stop here," she reasoned with herself.

Little did she know that this would be the time. This would be the place. This would be her open door.

PART II

Brooksport Village

As Kate drove into Brooksport Village, she caught her breath. Cute little town. Cute little names on store buildings. Lots of tourists walking the streets. Friendly. Why had she never heard of this place? She pulled into the gas station. A young boy about fifteen years of age ran out.

"Can I fill 'er up for you, ma'am?" he asked.

"As a matter of fact, you can. What's your name?" Kate asked.

"My name's Charlie. What's yours?" he replied.

"Kate, my name is Kate," she replied.

Charlie looked at her. "You have a last name?" he questioned.

"I do, but why do you ask?" Kate replied.

"Oh," Charlie began, "Trudy's been teachin' me some manners." He continued as he began pumping gas into her car, "She told me I needed to address older women as Mrs. or Ms. And with their last name, not their first."

Kate smiled and said, "I see."

"So what is your last name?" Charlie questioned again.

"It's Clarke, Kate Clarke. But why don't you call me Miss Kate?" she replied.

Charlie looked at her, studied her for a moment, cocked his head, and finally answered, "Well, I guess I could."

He finished pumping her gas and walked over to clean her windshield.

"But I think I better ask Trudy if that is proper and all. I don't want to get on the wrong side of Trudy! Nobody in this town ever wants to get on her bad side!" he exclaimed.

Kate asked, "Well, Trudy must be pretty important in your town. Why do you call her by her first name?"

Charlie answered, "Oh, she's important, all right. She's like a landmark in our town. She came up from the south and brought a lot of her tradition with her. Nobody ever crosses Trudy. We all know better!"

Charlie finished cleaning Kate's windshield, looked up at her, and continued, "I like her. She's kind of taken me on as a son since my mom died. I was only four years old when it happened."

Kate flinched. It did not go unnoticed by Charlie.

He asked, "Ever have somebody die, Miss Kate?"

Kate did not answer. Instead, she asked, "How much do I owe you?"

"Just follow me inside, Miss Kate, and I'll ring you up," Charlie answered.

As Kate followed Charlie inside the gas station, she quickly changed the subject. "So you've known Trudy a long time, Charlie?"

"Just about all my life. That's why she said it was okay for me to call her by her first name. She said it was okay for me to not be so formal with her," Charlie explained.

Kate continued, "What does Trudy do around here?"

"She does hair," Charlie answered.

Kate looked at him questioningly.

Charlie continued, "She fixes hair. You know—fluffs it up—she makes women look prettier. She owns the hair salon down the street."

Kate paid her bill while Charlie continued talking. "You just turn right outta here and you'll see it. Can't miss it—it's purple."

"Purple?" Kate questioned.

"Yeah," Charlie answered. "The mailbox, the building, and everything about her—purple."

Kate asked, "What's the name of the salon, Charlie? I may stop in and let her 'fix' my hair."

Charlie looked at her. "Don't see anything wrong with your hair. Don't think it needs fixin'."

Kate smiled. He had won over her heart. "Well, thank you, Charlie."

Charlie put the money in the cash drawer and said, "The name of her salon is Trudy's Tresses & Tootsies."

Well, what did she expect? Cute little town. Cute little store names. It only stood to reason, and Charlie was so serious. As Kate turned to leave, Charlie asked, "Think you'll be stayin' here awhile, Miss Kate? We could use another pretty face around here."

Kate had to admit he was quite the charmer at the ripe age of fifteen. Years from now, she thought he would make some girl a fine husband.

"It's something to think about, Charlie," she answered.

As she started the engine to her car, she whispered to herself, "I'll know when I find it. I'll know where I'm going."

She pulled out of the gas station and ventured into town.

8

The first thing she saw was the purple lipstick. It matched her purple skirt, flowered blouse, and scarf tied around her hair. Really? Yes, really. That was the first time Kate set eyes on Trudy, owner of Trudy's Tresses & Tootsies.

Kate questioned why she had set foot in this salon. She began to wonder what her hair would look like when she left. It was because Charlie had won her over and she was curious, plus she felt she just needed a break. She needed to relax. She needed some foolishness, she guessed. She needed a scotch and water. God only knew what she needed.

So now, she was standing in this salon, waiting for this "purple people eater" to make her a new woman. She needed a change. She needed to accept the new hand she had been dealt and having her hair "fixed" by a woman she didn't know seemed like a good start for a new beginning. All she knew was that this woman that "did hair," as Charlie described her, this woman at Trudy's Tresses & Tootsies liked purple—a lot.

"Haven't seen you around these parts," Trudy began.

That was Kate's welcome as Trudy motioned for her to sit in the shampoo chair. She draped the salon cape around her shoulders.

"Thinking I might move here," Kate replied.

"Well, you came to the right place," Trudy answered.

"How so?" Kate questioned.

"You can hide here, and people keep your secrets," Trudy replied.

"I have no secrets," Kate lied.

"Sugar, *everybody* has secrets. What's your name?" Trudy questioned.

"It's not Sugar," Kate replied.

Trudy exclaimed, "Oh my, a little sassy one has come to our town! A cute little thing that dares to talk back to Miss Trudy!"

"Never thought of myself as being sassy," Kate answered.

Trudy kept tousling Kate's hair as she continued to size her up, just like Charlie had done.

"You from the city?" Trudy asked.

"Why do you ask?"

Trudy replied, "You just look forlorn. Most city folk look that way when they come here. Seems they are always lookin' for some kind of an escape—like they're runnin' away from somethin'. That's why I thought you were from the city. But people always leave with smiles on their faces. Some of 'em even come back."

"Is that so?" Kate asked.

"Yep," Trudy replied.

Trudy kept looking at Kate. "I ask a lot of questions, so get used to it. I figure how am I goin' to ever learn about people if I don't ask questions?" She quickly added, "Plus, I'm curious."

"I've heard it said that curiosity killed the cat," Kate said with a mocking smile.

Trudy took a deep breath. "It would take a lot to kill me, sugar. I've risen from the ashes so many times in my life. I'll continue to rise."

With that, she quickly changed the subject. Trudy didn't like people asking her questions, and she felt she had just opened herself up for a bundle of them to come at her from this cute little stranger.

"So what you want me to do with this marvelous head of hair?" she questioned.

"Just fix it. Charlie said that's what you do," Kate replied.

"So you've met Charlie?" Trudy asked.

"Yes, and he is the reason I'm sitting here, even though he said my hair didn't need fixin'," Kate replied.

Trudy smiled. "Well, I'll have to give him a free haircut for finding you."

She looked at Kate and repeated her question. "So how do you want me to 'fix' your hair? Do you have somethin' in mind?"

Kate looked her straight in the eye and said, "Make me look sassy since you already think I am. Might as well look the part."

"I can do that," Trudy said.

Kate couldn't help herself. Suddenly, it just came out. *You know what they say about hairdressers*, she thought, *they are the best therapists.*

"And while you're at it, fix my life."

"Can't do that, honey. Only you can fix your life. But I am the best hair 'fixer' up here north of the Mason Dixon line!"

"Then fix it. That's a start. My name is Kate," she replied.

Trudy looked at her. "That's a good, strong name—Kate. It reminds me of that movie John Wayne was in. But—I think she was a redhead—would you like to change your hair color to red?"

"Gracious, no!" Kate replied emphatically.

She gave Trudy a look of "Don't you dare" and changed the subject.

"So Charlie said you came up from the South. Where bouts?" Kate asked.

"Down in peach country, sugar, South Carolina. I thought I had lost a lot of my accent. Been up here for thirty years."

"What brought you here?" Kate asked.

"Oh, that's a long story, sugar. Let's just say I found this little spot when some friends asked me to visit. I decided I didn't want to leave," Trudy replied.

"I just came into town to buy gas. I met Charlie. Now I'm here. Where would you suggest I have lunch after you 'fix' me up?" Kate questioned.

"The Stumble In," Trudy replied.

"The what?" Kate asked.

"The Stumble In. It's just down the street. Really good food. Best burgers you'll ever have, and if you decide to spend the night, there's a hotel across the street. We used to have a bed and breakfast on the edge of town, but now it's up for sale."

Kate's interest was noticeable to Trudy, so she continued, "Oh, it's a pretty place with flower gardens, and it overlooks the lake. Those flower gardens have a few weeds in 'em right now, though. It's a shame that place is vacant. Some highfalutin' doctor decided he didn't want to be bothered with it anymore."

"Not all doctors are highfalutin', Trudy. The ones I've met have been perfectly sincere and caring," Kate interjected.

"There she goes sassin' me again!" Trudy exclaimed.

But Kate felt the weight of a question forthcoming from Trudy, and she shifted slightly in her chair. She had left herself wide open for Trudy's cross-examination.

Trudy did not let her down.

"So you've had experiences with doctors, eh?" Trudy asked.

"No more questions," Kate stubbornly said. She attempted to change the direction of the conversation. "After you've given me my new do, how about a mani/pedi, too?"

Trudy looked at Kate out of the corner of her eye and asked, "You just get divorced, sugar?"

Kate made a face, stared at her, and firmly said, "No."

Trudy persisted. "Somebody die?"

Without blinking, Kate replied, "Yes."

"I'm sorry, sugar. Now I even have to admit I'm gettin' too personal. It's just that when somebody comes in here wantin' all three of my services on the same day, either they just got divorced or somebody died," Trudy compassionately said.

It was Trudy that shifted the conversation. "Well, I'm goin' to fix you up. You won't even know the old you when you walk out of here!"

"Tell me a little more about the bed and breakfast Trudy," Kate said.

"Well, as I said before, it needs some work, but it can be done. Beautiful view too. Tourists used to flock to that place! You may want to take a look at it, if you're lookin' at startin' your own kind of business, that is. I'll bet you could turn it into an escape of sorts for all those city people I told you about—you know the ones with the forlorn faces?"

Kate kept looking in the mirror watching Trudy work her miracles. But she was thinking that she would, definitely, go take a look at that bed and breakfast located at the end of town. Good things always seemed to be found at the "end of the street." Good things like Zack.

9

When the hairdo was done, Trudy stood back to admire her sassy creation.

She gave Kate a mirror to view it as she swiveled the chair around for her to view from all sides.

"Not bad. What do 'ya think, sugar?" Trudy asked. "Is it sassy enough for you?"

Kate did not answer immediately. Trudy exclaimed, "You're makin' me nervous, sugar! Do you like it or not? I blossom when I get compliments!"

"I think I like it a lot. And yes, it is sassy enough," Kate answered with a smile.

Relieved, Trudy asked, "Ready for that mani/pedi now?"

"I think I'll come back another time for that," Kate replied.

"Does that mean you're goin' to stick around for a while?" Trudy asked.

"We'll see," Kate replied.

"One other thing I have to tell you, sugar. When I was washin' your hair, I noticed you have a big knot in your neck. You need a massage too," Trudy told Kate.

"Anybody in town give massages?" Kate asked.

"Nope," Trudy replied.

"Guess I'll have to deal with it myself," Kate replied.

"No, darlin', you just need a good man with big hands," Trudy exclaimed.

Kate had to admit it was a "done deal." She liked Trudy. She would try her best not to "talk back" to her anymore.

Kate paid Trudy and said, "Think I'll just go on down to the Stumble In and get one of those burgers you were raving about, but I'll be back, Trudy."

"Yes, you will, Miss Kate. I think you're goin' to like it here."

Kate left the salon, murmuring to herself, "Right—a good man with big hands and skinny legs."

10

Kate wished she could be as sure as Trudy about her staying in Brooksport Village. She did like what she was seeing. It was good that she had met Charlie who hooked her up with Trudy. What would Zack have said to her?

God ordained, missy, God ordained.

Yes, that's what he would have said. If she decided to stay, she somehow knew she would be seeing a lot of Trudy. She needed Trudy's flamboyant personality that was larger than life itself. You could see her coming toward you from a mile away, dressed in all that purple. Kate couldn't help but smile as she walked toward the Stumble In. That's what she was doing these days, stumbling through, getting a lot of scratches along the way, along with bruises as blue as the Brooksport Village sky.

Yes, perhaps this is exactly what she needed—this place and someone like Trudy to help wipe that forlorn look off her face. Again, Kate smiled as she made her way to the Stumble In. Suddenly, she was very hungry.

"*Kadima,*" she whispered as she stepped inside "*Kadima…*"

11

Trudy watched Kate walk toward the Stumble In.

Wonder what her story is? Trudy asked herself. She looked and felt perplexed. *Don't know what it is,* Trudy continued, *but there's something about her I just can't put my finger on.*

She decided she would think about that later. She had to close up shop and get to the grocery store. Buddy, her favorite man-cat was just about out of his low-fat cat food, and she was running low on her favorite crackers.

She knew it was going to be another mind-blowing experience once she passed the pickle aisle and headed for that cracker aisle—it always was. She knew today would be no different. It was the beginning of summer, and all the summer help had to be "trained." She took a deep breath and entered the store. The first thing that assaulted her ears was the loudspeaker. "Clean up in aisle six! Clean up in aisle six!"

She sighed as she walked the cracker aisle.

"I knew it! I knew it!" she exclaimed, her eyes scanning the shelves. "Low sodium. Baked. No salt!"

She called for the aisle stocker. She didn't wait for him to arrive; she sauntered around the corner and saw him walking lazily toward her.

"You!" she exclaimed, pointing a finger at him. "You new around here?"

His eyes widened as he stared at the woman in purple. He finally managed a slight whisper, "Yes, ma'am."

"Well, Mr. Here-for-the-Summer, I'm goin' to teach you something today. I came up fresh from the south about thirty years ago, but I still want lard!"

He looked confused, like an alien in a strange land, gazing at Trudy in disbelief.

Trudy continued, "I mean there's no 'original' crackers here—no fat, no grease. A southerner up here gets real edgy when they don't get their lard and salt. So run along in the back and get me some 'original' Chicken in a Biskit crackers!"

"Yes, ma'am," he said as he literally ran to the back room. He ran head-on into the manager of the store as he went flying through the double doors.

"Some crazy woman out there wants the original Chicken in a Biskit crackers," he exclaimed to the manager.

"Oh, that's Trudy. We order 'em up just for her. She gets real edgy when her fat level runs low. When you see her comin', just put a couple of boxes out on the shelf where she can see 'em. She thinks she gets the last two boxes every time. Makes her day."

The manager walked over to the overstock and handed him two boxes of crackers.

"I have to go back out there?" Mr. Here-for-the-Summer aisle stocker asked.

"Go!" was all the manager had to say.

Trudy was waiting in the cracker aisle, leaning on her cart. "Oh, I see you found 'em," she exclaimed.

"Yes, ma'am," he humbly replied.

"Well, see that you have 'em here next time!" Trudy exclaimed.

"I understand," the aisle stocker answered. "You need your lard."

Trudy couldn't help but smile. "Yes, I do, young man, and don't forget it!"

Trudy gave him a friendly pat on the shoulder and added, "I do, however, need low-fat cat food," as she scurried off to the pet food aisle.

"I take better care of my cat than I do myself!"

Trudy saw Gordy, owner of Gordy's Stable, as she turned the corner, noticing the cleanup had been done in aisle six.

"Hey, Gordy! How's that writer wife of yours doin'?"

"Mighty fine, Trudy! Mighty fine! I see you got your Chiken in a Biskit originals!" Gordy shouted back.

"Yep, just have to keep trainin' the newbies every summer!" she exclaimed and continued her shopping.

Gordy couldn't help smiling. He walked up to the young stock boy, flung his arm around him, and said, "The world with all its health labels may be leaving Trudy behind, but this grocery store never will. She wants lard, she'll always have lard. Don't let her get to you. She's really harmless. Learn from this experience. What's your name?" Gordy asked.

"Seth, sir," he answered.

"Well, Seth, the next time you see her coming—and believe me, you'll see her coming—make sure you have a spot on the top shelf of the cracker aisle that no one else will ever reach for reserved for Trudy."

"Is that her name?" Seth asked.

Gordy nodded, gave Seth a friendly slap on his back, and turned to leave.

Seth learned a valuable lesson that day—how to handle people 101, especially southern women with purple scarves in their hair. They needed lard.

12

Trudy had been right. Stumble In had the best burgers she had ever tasted. All the goo from that burger ran out the bottom of the bun. Kate thought she may need a shower by the time she finished, but, boy oh boy, it was worth forgetting your manners for a while.

Kate looked around and saw everybody else licking their fingers, so she joined in the fun. She was feeling like a kid in this village town. She ordered another glass of wine, leaned back in her chair, and looked out the window. She saw that purple scarf yet again, walking out the door of Brooksport Grocery. Trudy was waving to everyone who passed her on the street and saying who knew what to each person that walked by.

"How is it that I have only met two people in this town but feel so at home?" she whispered to herself.

Still looking out the window of the Stumble In, Kate took her final sip of wine.

"I've lived with 'untils' all my life." She began to reflect.

She thought of all the "untils" she had waited on, been disappointed in, and yet had survived. Wait *until* morning, wait *until* you go to high school, wait *until* graduation. Oh, it'll get better, you just have to wait *until* the grief is gone. Wait *until* the betrayal is not so raw. One day, you'll forget, but *until* then, try to muddle through. Only one person in her life never said *until* to her. He had said *kadima*.

"Is this one of those times, Zack?" she asked herself.

What would he be saying to her now?

He would say, *Take a walk, missy, take a walk to the end of the street.*

That's exactly what she decided to do. She paid her bill and began to walk toward only God knew what. She saw it from a distance, and that was almost all it took. To her, it was magnificent. But she had trained her mind not to be too impulsive. Was she hearing "until" in her mind? But this was a major decision. Yes, it needed a little 'fixin' up' just like Trudy said. Until? Until what? No, she would not let the *until* make her run away.

She walked to the backyard and took in the breathtaking view of the lake. Once again, Trudy had been right. It was what she saw next that began to convince her she was soon to be done with all her "untils." She walked over to the flower garden and gently touched the petals of a flower she had only seen pictures of in a magazine. Weeds seemed to be taking over, but this little flower had burst through all the thickets.

"How appropriate," she whispered, "so fragile and yet so strong, a little shape of a tear at its base, a heart that had survived the storm, still trying to breathe. Bleeding Hearts." They spoke to her. In her own way, she could identify with those fragile flowers.

There was a wooded area beyond the flowers. She walked over to where the woods began and discovered a small bench on which she sat. She sat for a while before she heard a scurrying sound in the trees. She looked up and saw them—two sweet squirrels running and jumping from branch to branch. She nearly jumped from the bench with delight as she thought of Zack and what she imagined he would have said about those squirrels they had set free.

Oh, those squirrels have probably had babies. They're runnin' free, eatin' out of people's birdfeeders and playin' in their bird baths, driving bird lovers crazy.

That was what finally did it. She was going to buy this place. She would make it into a home for weary travelers—from the city—travelers with those forlorn looks. Travelers who just wanted some peace and a little quiet place to land for a day or two—maybe a week or two. She would make it even better than it had been before. She rose from the bench, walked a little distance ahead, and looked back.

"The first thing I will buy is a bird feeder and a bird bath—for the squirrels," she said aloud.

She would place them next to the bench where her decision had been made.

She turned to go. She was going to pay a visit to the realtor. She whispered, "No more 'untils.' Now is the time for *kadima*."

As she walked back into town, she thought about the name she would give her very own bed and breakfast. It was going to be a new life, a new chapter.

14

After the highfalutin' doctor had been notified and the legal documents had been signed, Kate made her way to Trudy's salon. She burst through the door and nearly shouted, "Are you ever wrong, Trudy?"

Without turning around, Trudy answered, "Very rarely."

Kate smiled, saying nothing, while Trudy busied herself around the salon, preparing for her first client. Finally, she turned and said, "Okay! Tell me! Tell me! What am I right about this time?"

"I was waiting until I had your full attention," Kate exclaimed.

"You have it, now tell me!" Trudy shouted.

Kate walked over, looked Trudy straight in the eyes, and said, "I'm staying."

"Does that mean we're friends and I can call you sugar now and again?" Trudy questioned, giving Kate a big hug.

Even to Kate's surprise, she hugged Trudy back and exclaimed, "I just bought the bed and breakfast at the edge of town!"

The barrier had been broken, and Trudy didn't think twice in offering another big hug to Kate. "You're goin' to love it here, sugar, and you're goin' to love being in business for yourself! Have you thought of a name for your new place?" Trudy asked.

"I have," Kate said.

"Something catchy like *moi*?" Trudy fanned her hands in the air and breathed in all her purple.

"Maybe not quite as catchy as your salon," Kate answered.

"Do tell, sugar, what is the name?"

"Open Door, Trudy. it's going to be called Open Door."

It wasn't long before all of Brooksport Village locals knew of the bed and breakfast purchase and the person who bought it. Trudy made sure of that. The renovations began. Everybody stopped by Open Door to see how they could help Kate get settled in.

Charlie was the most interested of all. He arrived on Kate's doorstep one afternoon and began his sales pitch. "Good afternoon, Miss Kate," he said.

"Good afternoon, Charlie," Kate replied.

"I see you got your hair fixed at Trudy's salon, it looks good. But I still think it really didn't need fixin'," Charlie began.

Kate laughed, saying, "I like my new sassy look, though! It's a new me!"

"Well," Charlie said, "the old you was nice too."

"Come on in, Charlie," Kate said, stepping aside to allow Charlie's entrance.

"Let's go in the kitchen," Kate said. "I have some fresh sweet tea just ready to drink."

They sat at the table while Kate poured two tall glasses.

Charlie began the conversation. "I was just thinkin' now that you're the new owner of this place, you're goin' to have a lot of guests that are goin' to want to read the newspaper, even if they are on vacation."

"That's true," Kate replied and took a sip of her tea.

"Well, I was thinkin' I could make you a deal. You see, I not only pump gas at the other end of town, I also deliver newspapers," Charlie continued.

Kate smiled and said, "I see."

"Well, would you, being a businesswoman and all, would you like to order twelve papers to be delivered to your front door every morning for your guests and all?"

Kate looked at him when he quickly added, "I could give you what Belle down at Belle's Bakery calls a baker's dozen if you want to order twelve. She makes really good crispy fried doughnuts, just to let you know. Trudy kind of brought that up here as one of her southern traditions too. A baker's dozen means you could get one free—a newspaper in my case."

Kate poured another glass of tea.

Charlie asked, "Did you learn this sweet tea thing from Trudy?"

Kate laughed and said, "I've learned a lot of things from Trudy since I've been here, but no, I've always liked sweet tea."

"Oh, I thought that was another Trudy-ism," Charlie replied. "That's what she told me, anyway. She was determined to have sweet tea in the coffeehouse in the middle of town when she came up here years ago."

Kate smiled again before saying, "And what Trudy wants, Trudy gets."

"That's right," Charlie said. "You know, it's amazin' how many people order that down at the café. Sarah likes it too."

"Who's Sarah?" Kate asked.

"Oh, she's Wes and Reva's daughter."

Charlie shuffled in his seat and moved the glass of tea around in his hands before saying, "I kind of like her."

"Well, if you like her, I want to meet her, especially if she likes sweet tea." Kate laughed.

Charlie managed to choke down the last of his second glass of tea and said, "I don't think men are supposed to like this stuff."

Quickly, he remembered his mission and asked, "Would you like to order twelve newspapers to be delivered by me every morning, Miss Kate?"

Kate put her elbows on the kitchen table, looked at Charlie, and answered, "Yes, Charlie, I think I would."

"Oh, thank you, Miss Kate!" he exclaimed as he ran out the door.

Kate chuckled as she watched Charlie hop on his bike and head for the Brooksport Village Gazette.

"You're one fine businessman, Charlie, and you've just proven a salesperson will do anything for an order—even if it's choking down sweet tea."

*"Patriotism consists not in waving the flag,
but in striving that our country shall be righteous
as well as strong."* (James Bryce)

16

The spring days went by, lazily, in Brooksport Village as Memorial Day weekend was approaching. It was just another day of roaming free in "God's country," enjoying the warmth, and preparing for the big balloon launch in memory of all the vets of long-ago wars.

Brooksport Village was a patriotic town, and two of their very own vets, Gordy and Wes, helped plan the yearly celebration that also served as the entrance of summer. But most importantly, it was a time of remembering the ones who had died for their country and the freedom that had made America great.

Romance was beginning to bloom as tourist teens, holding hands, made their way to the lake after a stop at Belle's Bakery. Tourist teens were always fun to watch. Summer love—ah, nothing like it.

You could hear a guitar strumming through the doors of the coffeehouse. Chip, the area singer/songwriter, began to rehearse for the crowd that would begin gathering around three o'clock, and Crabby's Bar was open for people who needed their morning Bloody Mary fix.

Gordy was tending to his horses, and Jessie, his wife, was writing in her own quiet little getaway. A novel about life, she said. Something she had always wanted to do.

The Stumble In would soon be preparing to open for lunch, and Trudy was busy fixin' a lot of hair. All was well in Brooksport Village.

Kate was making her way to Trudy's salon after serving her guests their breakfast. Time to make good on the mani/pedi she had promised Trudy upon her arrival to Brooksport Village.

Yes, it promised to be just another ordinary day, but those ordinary days were about to end. What they didn't know was that somewhere in New York City, there was a man named Jake Arbor. And Jake Arbor was the kind of man that once you met him, you never forgot him.

17

Jake Arbor had it all. His home was New York City, but he loved cowboy hats, and he wore his well. Sometimes, he put on boots and added a little swagger to his step. He knew just how to smile that crooked grin, and tipping that hat to pretty women was one of his specialties. He was handsome, very handsome, and he knew it. He owned his own company, Arbor Global, "Tree Maintenance, Clean Up, and Restoration."

He had so much money he couldn't fold it fast enough, and he spent a lot of it on women. It seemed they loved it too—the money—and his good looks only added to his charm. He knew the effect he had on women, and he didn't hesitate to use all that charm and charisma to woo them over to his way of thinking.

No woman ever gave him a chase, so there was never really ever a "catch," thus causing the interest he may have had in the beginning with redheads, blondes, or brunettes to wane rather quickly. He had never met a woman who would even think of giving him a challenge. He didn't really know how he would react if he ever did meet one of those. He was well acquainted with the "familiar" in his life; he knew how to handle the ones who fell at his feet, and he settled for that. It was enough. Besides that, he didn't like to think too deeply about stuff. That was his MO.

Memorial Weekend was quickly approaching when he decided it was time to vacate the city for a few days. He needed peace; he wanted quiet. The corporate world was getting to him. He wanted to be alone. And yet leaving the city and going to his home in rural New York seemed too lonely for him this year. He wasn't the type to buy a case of beer, settle himself in front of the TV with a remote in his hand, and go comatose over the long weekend. Yet he didn't know exactly what he wanted.

He walked out of his private office and nodded to his assistant. "Why don't you take off early today, Sandra? Enjoy your weekend."

Sandra looked up from her desk, gave him a look from the corner of her eye, and replied, "Who is she this time, Jake?" She looked straight at Jake. "Oh, never mind! I don't want to know! Do you still want me to finish this project before I leave?"

Jake sat down on the corner of her desk, focused his blue eyes on her face, and looked as innocently as he could while he replied, "There's no one."

He continued, "No need to finish the project. It'll be waiting for you Tuesday morning. Now go on, get out of here, and enjoy your family."

Sandra didn't hesitate. She blew him a kiss and said, "Be wise, Jake Arbor, don't get yourself into any trouble, and watch out for redheads. You might as well watch out for the blondes and brunettes too!" With that she was out the door.

Jake smiled as he watched her go. The last woman in his life had been a redhead, and he had told Sandra all about her. Sandra was his confidant. She knew him well and had been a loyal employee for many years. She was like a little sister to him.

He had a special place in his heart for Sandra. She was like family to him, and she could sure handle all those men that worked for him with all their foolishness and kidding around. She could think quickly on her feet, she was adorable with her humor, and he couldn't run the business without her. She deserved to leave early once in a while and so much more.

Jake went back into his office, picked up the phone, and called his main man. Butch always picked up on the first ring.

"Hey, Butch, I'm heading out of town for the long weekend. Can you keep the home fires burning here?"

"Sure thing, Chief, where 'ya goin'?" Butch questioned.

"Not sure," Jake replied. "I may be gone longer than the weekend, though. Take the weekend off and then hit the road running Tuesday morning. I'll be in touch."

"I'll call 'ya only if there's an emergency, Jake," Butch replied.

Both men knew they could depend on one another. One thing Jake always demanded of his employees was loyalty, and they gave it to him. He was good to them, he was loyal to them, he respected them, and he paid them well. No one would ever betray Jake. No one.

Jake called his driver and walked out the front door of the office building. The driver was waiting.

"Where to, boss?" he asked.

"My house," Jake replied.

Jake's driver was a man of few words, and today Jake was glad. He wanted to do something different; he didn't know what, and the driver asked no questions. He merely followed orders.

They pulled up to Jake's house.

"I won't be in need of a driver for a while. Enjoy your time off. I'll call you when I return," Jake said.

His driver nodded.

"Oh, you will be paid in the interim," Jake said while exiting the car.

Again, the driver nodded, but this time there was a smile behind the nod.

18

Jake walked through his front door and yelled, "Hello! Anybody home?"

Only an echo came back as his answer against his hardwood floors.

He shrugged his shoulders, walked into the kitchen, and poured a glass of orange juice.

"Nobody home," he said to himself.

He looked around his empty kitchen and said, "I need a dog."

He knew he wouldn't get a dog because he had no time for one; dogs needed attention. They needed playtime. They needed somebody throwing them Frisbees. They needed walks and exercise. They needed love and lots of it. He wasn't capable of doing any of that. It wouldn't be fair to the dog, but at this particular moment, he needed a dog.

"I wonder if they rent out dogs?" he questioned himself.

He downed his juice, got up from the chair, and said, "I gotta get out of here!"

He walked to the bedroom, pulled out a travel bag, and began to pack.

"Just the essentials," he said to himself. "If I stay some place longer, I'll buy what I need."

He looked out the window one last time before locking up and making sure everything was secure in his house. He walked to his car, got in, turned the ignition, and backed out of his driveway.

"Let the adventure begin!" he shouted as he pulled onto the street. His radio was tuned to oldies but goodies. As he drove to the ramp to merge onto the highway, he began to sing along with the music.

"Up, up, and away in my beautiful balloon…" He was good at sweeping the loneliness under the carpet, really good. He continued to sing. "The world's a nicer place in my beautiful balloon. Up, up, and away!"

Jake was on his way, although he knew not where.

He drove for hours, or so it seemed. His eyes were beginning to glaze over when he saw them. Hundreds of balloons were drifting toward the sky—red, white, and blue balloons.

"What the…?" He didn't finish the sentence. He saw the next exit, Brooksport Village. That's where all those balloons were coming from. He had to go into this town. He simply could not resist. Hadn't he just been singing a song about balloons when he left his driveway? A beacon of hope? He decided that yes, yes, it was.

He took the exit and drove into Brooksport Village.

19

As he pulled into town, everyone seemed to be in a frenzy. He parked his car, got out, and started walking down the street. The first person he saw was Charlie.

"What's goin' on?" Jake asked.

"Oh, somebody's goin' to have hell to pay," Charlie explained. "They just let all the balloons go that were supposed to go up on Memorial Day!"

Sarah came running up to Charlie. "What happened?" she hollered.

"The net holding the balloons wasn't secure, and there they go!" Charlie exclaimed, pointing to the sky, as every balloon began disappearing, going higher and higher.

"What are we goin' to do now?" Sarah questioned.

Charlie shrugged.

Jake watched as everyone in this little village became more and more exasperated.

"Man, do you know how long it took us to get all those balloons heliumed up for Memorial Day?" Charlie asked.

"Can't say that I do," Jake replied.

"Well, it took a long time," Charlie answered.

"The day won't be the same without that launch," Sarah said, her big eyes brimming with tears.

Jake felt badly for them. They were so concerned. All it would take for him to do was make one phone call to solve the problem. And those tears threatening to fall from Sarah's eyes made him react quickly. He never could stand to see a woman cry no matter how old she was. He even gave candy to baby girls crying in the grocery store. He just couldn't stand seeing girls cry. He had made too many redheads, blondes, and brunettes cry in his lifetime already. Now it seemed a personal mission to put smiles on their faces instead of tears in their eyes.

"We'll handle it," Jake said, looking at both Charlie and Sarah.

"How?" Charlie questioned.

"Trust me," Jake replied. "We'll handle it."

As he walked away from the two teens, he pulled his cell phone from his pocket and dialed.

Butch answered on the first ring, "Hey, boss."

"Butch, I want you to ship three hundred each helium red, white, and blue balloons to Brooksport Village by Monday morning," Jake said.

"Have you just met a redhead, boss?" Butch laughed. "I know how crazy they make you."

"No, no redheads, Butch, just send them." Jake appreciated Butch's humor.

"Any address?" Butch asked as he picked up a pencil.

"Chamber of Commerce," Jake replied and hung up.

Problem solved. That's what Jake did, he solved problems, and obviously this was a problem for these townspeople.

He wished all his problems were that simple. He took a deep breath and walked toward the Chamber of Commerce to let them know about the delivery that would be happening on Memorial Day.

Those kids and this town would have their balloons in honor of the red, white, and blue on Memorial Day. He didn't know it at the time, but he had not only found a patriotic town, he had also found a righteous village.

20

The next morning, Jake awakened in his hotel room and decided he wanted to know more about Brooksport Village. He splashed water on his face, dressed, put on his boots, shook the cobwebs out of his head from the previous night, placed his cowboy hat on his head, and walked down the street.

That was when he saw her—he saw the big purple scarf in her hair before he heard the voice.

"This town has more than a problem with their balloons," he murmured to himself. "Lordy mercy," was all he could say.

She was in a frenzy all her own. As Jake watched her hurry into Belle's Bakery, he surmised that she seemed a little 'left of center,' but his curiosity was piqued. He decided to follow this purple-clad lady. He could not let her disappear. And besides that, he had to make absolutely sure his mind wasn't playing tricks on him—he had to make sure that he was completely sober from last night's binge at Crabby's Bar.

When he stepped inside the bakery, he heard the voice—so sweet—even in her frenzy. This was the voice his dad had always warned him about when he made his many travels to the south on business. The voice that oozed of Southern charm.

You'll come home married, son. Won't even know what hit you. Be careful of those Southern women!

Jake smiled as he remembered his dad's words.

Been there, done that—no more marriages for me, Dad, Jake thought in his own mind.

Trudy's voice burst into his thoughts.

"Did 'ya see those balloons go up yesterday, Belle?" Trudy exclaimed.

"Sure did," Belle answered. "The whole town did."

"What in the world happened? It won't be the same without our launch on Monday!"

Shaking her head, she repeated, "Just won't be the same. Been livin' here many years. Just won't be the same." She kept repeating it.

She pointed to the hot oil. "I need a doughnut—extra crispy— with chocolate frosting."

"Got this oil hot just for you, Trudy. Glad you showed up," Belle said.

"Then give me two," Trudy replied as she filled her coffee cup at the end of the counter.

Jake continued to watch Trudy from a safe distance. He was trying to decide if he should take a table close to the nearest exit. He couldn't help but wonder how this woman clad in so much purple had found her way to rural New York. She had said that her home was here. The more questions he silently asked himself, the more curious he became. He got the impression that she was her own woman, a determined one who always got her way. She didn't need a Southern accent to get what she wanted. Her very demeanor alone got her wherever she wanted to go.

Belle handed Trudy the doughnuts on a plate. "Extra crispy with chocolate frosting," she said.

Trudy smiled and turned to find a table. It was then that she spotted the newcomer in town for the first time.

"Lordy mercy, look what's standin' here in the middle of Belle's Bakery!"

She looked Jake up and down.

She continued, "Are my eyes deceivin' me, or are you my future husband? I've been waitin' for someone like you all my life!" Again, she looked him up and down.

"Now, Trudy, don't go scarin' our new visitor," Belle began. "We'd like him to enjoy his visit with us before he goes back to that city he ran away from."

Trudy kept looking at Jake. "Um, um, um," she said while balancing her doughnut plate with one hand and her coffee cup with the other. She spotted his boots.

"Those boots 'specially made for runnin', darlin'?" she questioned.

She didn't wait for an answer. He couldn't think of an answer, anyway. He was still stunned that a woman like her existed in the first place. But he had to admit, she had a charm all her own. And he was convinced nobody else in the world could carry off that big purple scarf in their hair like she did.

"Hey, cowboy," Trudy exclaimed pointing to a table in the corner. "Let's go over there and sit ourselves down. Let's get cozy. My name's Trudy, in case you missed it."

Trudy patted the seat of the chair next to her and continued, "Oh, don't be scared. Come join me, I'm really harmless."

She took a bite of her doughnut.

"Get one of these first, though. They simply will melt in your mouth. Nothing sold like this north of the Mason Dixon line until I came up here and made this town my very own little corner of the world. Everybody tries to resist 'em, but one bite tells 'em they can't."

She took another bite of the doughnut and practically swooned.

All he could say to Trudy was, "My name's Jake."

Trudy looked at him, smiled, and kept munching her doughnut.

Jake had to admit he was amused, very amused. He made a decision to do exactly what she had commanded.

"Give me one of those too," Jake said as he winked at Belle.

"Extra crispy," Jake added.

"Chocolate frosting?" Belle asked, returning his wink.

"No frosting," he answered.

"Sure thing," Belle said. "You know she has that way about her. She attracts, like steel to a magnet. Before you leave here, she'll know your entire life history. Consider yourself warned."

Jake smiled and took his extra crispy doughnut over to the table where Trudy was sitting.

"Glad you decided to join me, cowboy. I'm not goin' to ask 'ya too many questions because I don't care where you're from or what secrets you're holdin' in your mind. I just wanna know where you're goin' and how 'ya plan on breaking those chains behind that handsome face of yours that hold you captive."

She took another bite of her doughnut and continued, "I don't say it like that Cal Farley guy, all proper, but 'ya get my meanin', don't 'ya, cowboy?"

Jake bit into his extra crispy doughnut and looked her straight in the eye. She was right, it did melt in your mouth. She was right about that captive thing too. He wondered how she knew so much about him. He had never set eyes on her before. Did he wear some kind of sign on his forehead? A sign that screamed, "Warning! I'm mixed up and confused! Get to know me at your own risk!"

Trudy licked her fingers, found the very last crumb of sugar, and said, "Jake, I like that name. So where do you come from, Jake?"

Jake laughed. "The city," he answered.

"Oh, one of those?" Trudy replied.

"Meaning?" he questioned.

"A runner—running from all the horns, crazy drivers, and racket. Runnin' from the jungle," she replied.

Again she was right. He had been running all his life—from east to west, north to south, and now to this place, Brooksport Village. Years of running. It seemed that's all he knew how to do. Running was familiar territory. He knew how to react in new terrain. He knew the basic questions to ask when getting to know people. Those "first impression" meetings. But he couldn't communicate when it got into the deep stuff—the inward emotional stuff—and he didn't want to learn. So every time he became befuddled about a person, at the first glimpse of something deeper happening, he would run. He didn't always know where he was going; he just ran.

"Why did you just get that faraway, forlorn look in your eyes, Mr. Jake?" Trudy asked, interrupting his thoughts. She snapped her fingers. "Come back to me, cowboy!"

"Oh, I was just thinking about something," Jake replied.

"You're probably askin' yourself what in the world you're doin' here in this bakery talkin' to a woman named Trudy, dressed in all her purple, right?"

Again he laughed. "Maybe that is exactly what I was thinking!"

"I own the salon in the middle of town," Trudy said, wondering if she was bold enough to run her fingers through his hair and tell him he needed a haircut. She determined that she wasn't quite that bold—yet.

Jake finished his doughnut. "Do you cut men's hair?" he asked.

Trudy almost blushed, thinking he had read her thoughts because that's what cowboys do. But she gathered herself quickly. "Of course, I cut men's hair. There's not been a head of hair on this planet that I couldn't cut. Ever since my daddy bought me one of those pretend hair blowers and tons of stylin' products when I was a little girl, I've had a passion to make this world a prettier place in fixin' people's hair. Come on by some day and see for yourself."

She looked at him and decided she had suddenly become bold enough to say, "I'd like to get my fingers in your hair!"

"Do you always say outrageous, spontaneous things to people you just meet, Trudy?" He quickly added, "I like it."

"Well, I have to admit, cowboy, that I had to build up my courage to say that to you, but just look at yourself—do you ever look in the mirror?" Trudy asked.

"You do make me laugh, Trudy! I think I'm going to enjoy being around you while I'm here!" Jake exclaimed.

"I hope so, cowboy, I'd like to get you in my salon chair, surrounded by those mirrors to show you just how good-lookin' you really are!" Trudy exclaimed. "But you probably already know that," she said.

"I'll drop by soon for my haircut," Jake replied. "But for now, I'm going to be thinking about lunch at the Stumble In."

"Oh, you've made your rounds, I see. Stumble In has the best burgers anywhere!"

"Especially after a hangover and a night out at Crabby's," Jake replied. "You know when the gallbladder says to you the next morning, 'Send down grease.'"

"You've been to Crabby's too?" she questioned.

"Yes, I have," he replied. "I helped close down the place last night with a man named Phil."

"Now don't you tell me you're goin' to be a drinkin' buddy of Phil's! It's best you become a mentor to that man," Trudy exclaimed. "Teach him how to wear boots and cowboy hats instead. Teach him that real cowboys don't have to drink to be real men. Teach him that even cowboys have to learn one day to forgive themselves."

Jake had that "deer in the headlight" look as if Trudy had just opened a door to his own secret self.

"Hope you stick around for a while, Jake," Trudy said as she stood to leave. "Been real nice meetin' ya."

She decided she just couldn't resist. She rumpled Jake's hair as she walked by his chair and walked toward the door.

Before she reached the door, Jake stopped her with his question. "Trudy, how did you see so much in me that others have never seen? How do you seem to know so much about me?"

Trudy turned to face him and replied, "It's all in your eyes, cowboy. It's all in those sad eyes of yours."

With that, she was gone.

Jake had made a friend for life. He didn't know at the time just how much his life would change from this chance meeting with Trudy. No, he didn't know how much a crispy-on-the-outside fried doughnut would impact not only his taste buds but also his future. He could not have possibly known how this bakery located in a small town called Brooksport Village would alter his path.

If he had known, he told himself much later, he would have come to this village by the water a lot sooner—much sooner—before his life had become so complicated with so much racket, before the "jungle" had led him down so many twisted paths he didn't think he would ever find his way out.

Oh yes, a change was in the making.

21

Trudy saw the young teens standing in front of her salon, and she knew what all the giggles were about. If she turned to look where their fingers were pointing, she would bet dollars to Belle's doughnuts that Jake was somewhere in sight.

Trudy had to prove it to herself, so she turned. Sure enough, there stood a cowboy, tipping his hat to those giggling girls.

Trudy exclaimed, "Now you girls get through that door and settle yourselves down before I douse you with the water hose instead of my shampoo nozzle!"

"Well, Trudy, you have to admit he is about the most handsome man that ever walked the streets of our little village town," one of the girls exclaimed as she reluctantly took her eyes away from Jake to step into the salon.

"Yep, that's for sure," her friend said, following Trudy through the door.

Trudy studied both girls and rolled her eyes. "Come on, girls, stop jabberin' about the masked man and let's get started."

"I didn't see a mask," one of the girls quipped as she sat down in the shampoo chair.

"I didn't either," her friend chided in.

"Oh, dearies, everybody who comes to our town has a mask of some kind. And believe you me, he has on a mask," Trudy replied.

"Oh, he's the type that just passes through like the Lone Ranger, Trudy?" one of the girls asked.

"That's right," Trudy said. "And he's not goin' to carry you away on his white horse to live happily ever after!"

"I didn't see a horse," one of the girls said.

"Oh, sit down!" Trudy commanded. "And besides that, he's too old for you two girls."

Trudy knew of which she spoke—one partner being too old for another. She quickly put that thought far away from her mind, looked at both girls, and asked, "Who's first?"

As the girls settled in for their do, one of them quipped, "If he's too old for us, then he's too young for you, right, Trudy?"

"Sadly, yes," Trudy answered as she began the shampoo process.

The girls laughed their girlish laugh and became silent. Trudy was simply glad they had finished their senseless jabbering.

Trudy glanced out the window as the girls were preparing to leave. Kate was approaching the salon just as Jake was coming out of Stumble In. Trudy took a deep breath as she watched the pair come alongside each other.

"Okay, cowboy," Trudy said to herself, "let me see you do your stuff."

It was at that exact moment Jake looked at Kate and tipped that cowboy hat of his.

"I knew it! I knew it! He's trouble," Trudy exclaimed again to herself.

Kate looked his way and gave him a little smile as she continued walking toward Trudy's Tresses & Tootsies. That smile was all he needed to give her more than a second look.

The girls paid Trudy for her services and headed out the door just as Kate entered.

Trudy gave Kate a look that was full of questions, like, *Well, what do you think of our new arrival to Brooksport Village?*

"Stop it, Trudy!" Kate exclaimed, as if she had read Trudy's mind.

"Stop what?" Trudy innocently asked.

"Matchmaking in your mind. I saw you looking out the window when I came alongside whoever that was!" Kate said a little too nonchalantly.

"I wouldn't do that, sugar, not to you. That cowboy is trouble with a capital T."

Kate went immediately to the shampoo chair and sat down. Trudy wrapped the cape around her shoulders and said, "I've already met him—he has secrets."

"Oh, Trudy, you said something similar to me when we met! What is this secret fixation with you, anyway?" Kate asked.

"He has a saunter," Trudy continued. "Lord help you if you ever feel a quiver when he's around!"

"What in the world are you talking about?" Kate asked.

"You'll find out soon enough, sugar. Something tells me that since he has seen you, he's curious, and he's goin' to be around our little summer place longer than he expected to be."

"Just fix my hair and be quiet," Kate replied.

"Yep," Trudy said. "He's goin' to be around for a while. You two have sparks a-flyin'."

Kate rolled her eyes and gave Trudy a warning look.

"You don't know it yet, but you do," Trudy replied and gave Kate a look of her own.

Jake decided to go to Crabby's Bar. He was hoping Phil would be there. He wanted to know more about this little town, especially the woman he had just passed on the corner. Maybe he would follow up with what Trudy had said—"Teach Phil how to be a cowboy"—that he could do. What he couldn't do was teach him about forgiving himself.

He almost laughed when he thought about teaching someone else about life and forgiveness. Damn, he couldn't take care of his own life much less teach someone else about what they should or should not do. In no way could he ever teach someone when, where, or how they should forgive. He was a mastermind when it came to business matters. But the truth be told, he was a complete idiot when it came to personal matters. With those thoughts banging around in Jake's mind, he decided that being Phil's drinking buddy was the best option.

Jake walked into Crabby's and spotted Phil sitting on his favorite stool in front of the bar.

Phil looked up and shouted, "Hey, 'ole buddy, you back for more after helpin' me close the joint last night?"

"Yep," Jake replied. "Back for more."

"Good! I've been savin' this bar stool right beside me for you! I was hopin' you'd be back!"

Phil ordered another drink. "And one for my buddy too!"

Phil continued, "Decided to stay a while, did 'ya? Who knows? I may tell you my story tonight if I get drunk enough!" Phil exclaimed.

"Maybe I'll tell you mine too," Jake replied and slapped Phil on the shoulder.

"Countin' on it," Phil said as he took a swallow of his drink.

The bartender, Leon, looked at Phil and said, "I'm watchin' you tonight, Phil."

"Countin' on it," Phil answered. "Good 'ole Jake here will see me home, don't worry." He looked over at Jake. "Won't 'ya, buddy?"

Jake looked at Leon and said, "Sure enough. You can depend on me."

He gave Phil a slap on the back.

Leon looked at both men and walked away mumbling to himself.

"He worries about me," Phil whispered to Jake.

"I heard that," Leon shouted back at him.

"The whole village worries about you, Phil," Leon continued to shout, staring Phil down.

That was a look Jake didn't miss. He suddenly knew that he might be forced to become more than a drinking buddy to Phil. There was something hidden here. He refused to let his mind go there. He refused to go deep with whatever this was; things that were hidden rubbed him raw when they came to the surface.

Jake thought, *The whole town worries. Why?*

Phil leaned in to Jake and boldly asked, "You been here long enough to meet my son yet?"

Jake merely lifted his drink and asked, "Who's your son?"

"Charlie. Charlie's my son," Phil answered and took another swig.

Jake thought for a minute and realized Charlie was the young teen he had talked to about the balloons, but he said nothing.

"That's why we worry," Leon said. "We worry for Charlie."

Phil excused himself, walking toward the restroom.

Leon took the opportunity to continue talking while looking Jake straight in the eye. "You're new in town, you don't understand. But you will if you stick around. The last thing that man needs is a drinking buddy."

Jake swallowed the last of his drink, looked at Leon, and said, "Tell Phil I had to go."

With that, he walked out the door. Hadn't Trudy said the same thing? This was getting far too deep than he wanted to deal with. He had come to this *getaway* to do just that—get away. He was determined not to get into the middle of its problems nor its secrets.

He shifted his mind to that woman he had been walking alongside just a few hours ago. Against his better judgment, he decided he would stay a little longer. And besides that, the balloons would be arriving Monday. He had to stay for that launch that everyone had been talking about. He felt more comfortable thinking on these things—women and balloons.

Brooksport Village had accepted the fact they would not have a balloon launch this year. Then a truck pulled up in front of the Chamber of Commerce. Charlie was the first to see it. His eyes widened as he witnessed the nets of balloons being taken off the truck. Trudy saw them next. Jake was standing in the distance. Trudy walked up to Charlie.

She poked him on the shoulder and said, "Where'd those come from?"

Charlie replied, "Not sure, but if I were a bettin' man, I'd say those balloons are from him," he continued while pointing to Jake.

"The cowboy?" Trudy asked.

"Yep!" Charlie exclaimed and ran off to find Sarah. He gave Jake the thumbs-up sign as he ran past.

And so it was, Brooksport Village had the most spectacular launch of balloons the town had ever seen. Gordy and Wes led the salute to the flag in memory of the fallen soldiers of past wars. And the standing ovation could be heard into the next town. It was all due to Jake Arbor.

Trudy just kept asking, "Exactly who is that masked man?" She was determined to dig deeper into that mind of his. One thing was for sure, Brooksport Village had, indeed, acquired its very own personal Lone Ranger, mask and all, and that man made everything good and right.

24

Trudy was standing next to Kate when Kate looked across the crowd and saw Jake.

"He's still here, I see," Kate said.

"Yep, sure is. I think I've caught his eye again. Met him in Belle's the other day before he saw you," Trudy replied, while fluffing her hair and waving to Jake.

"Stop it, Trudy! He's going to walk over here!" Kate exclaimed.

"That's what I'm hopin' for, sugar. Why else would I be fluffin' my hair?"

Trudy looked at Kate.

"But sad to say, it's not me he's lookin' at. I'm sure of that," Trudy said.

"Whatever do you mean, Trudy?" Kate asked innocently.

"Don't give me that innocent look, sugar. It's you he's lookin' at!" Trudy laughed.

Kate shrugged her off and said, "Here he comes, I'm leaving. Enjoy yourself."

"Oh, I will, sugar, I will," Trudy said as she watched Jake make his way toward them.

Kate had already fled the scene when Jake walked up to Trudy. He put his arm around her and asked, "You goin' to the fireworks tonight, beautiful?"

"You're my fireworks, cowboy! I think I just fell a little in love with you for what you did for our town this special day," Trudy exclaimed with a little gleam in her eye.

"I fell in love with you the first day we met," Jake, jokingly, said.

He looked in the direction Kate had walked only moments earlier.

"Who was that lady you were just standing with?" he asked.

"Oh, you mean the one that just ran away like her pants were on fire?" Trudy laughed.

"That would be the one," Jake replied.

"That's Kate," Trudy said.

"Does she live here?" Jake continued his questions.

"Sure does," Trudy replied. "Stick around and you'll learn a lot more!" She winked at Jake, turned, and walked, swiftly, toward Belle's.

"Where you goin', Trudy?" Jake asked. "I'm not used to a woman walkin' away from me, and especially not two of 'em in the same day within minutes of each other!" Jake laughed.

Trudy looked over her shoulder. "Get over yourself, cowboy. There's always a first time! And for your information, I'm goin' to Belle's for my daily fix," Trudy yelled back to him.

"Oh, of course, you need lard," Jake exclaimed.

Trudy kept walking, dismissing him with the wave of her hand. He didn't see her smile.

She whispered to herself, "There's goin' to be fireworks all right, and I'm not talkin' about the fire in the sky ones. I'm talkin' 'bout the ones between you and sweet Kate."

Trudy walked into Belle's, ordered her doughnut, extra crispy, took it and sat down at a table near the window. She watched Jake as he walked toward the hotel he'd been staying in since he had arrived in town.

"Got to get him over to 'Open Door,'" she said out loud.

She took a bite of her doughnut, swooned as only Trudy could, and watched Jake walk through the hotel door.

"Those two have caught each other's eye, no denying it. Kind of like that 'stranger across a crowded room' stuff. Yes, sir, I saw the sparks between those two. Shoot, they don't even know they've been hit yet! They're goin' to need a little nudge, though, and I'm just the one to get this party rockin'!"

With that, she licked her fingers, gave Belle a thumbs-up, and walked back to the salon.

25

Trudy was busy preparing how she was going to get the party rockin' between Kate and Jake. She could hardly wait for Kate to walk through the door of the salon.

"He may be trouble," Trudy said to herself, "but not with a capital *T*. Maybe he's just a cowboy full of himself—that's trouble with a little *t*. That's okay. And besides, perhaps that is exactly what Kate needs in her life right now—a little *t* of trouble."

Kate walked into the salon with a bag of extra crispy doughnuts.

"Well, what do you think of him?" Trudy asked.

"Who?" Kate asked.

Trudy exclaimed, "Who, she asks. Who? Indeed, who? The cowboy for heaven's sake!"

"You're continuing with this, really?" Kate replied.

Trudy began dancing in place. "You've both caught each other's eye, sugar. You may as well admit it, kiss him, and get it over with!"

"Oh, if it were that simple, Trudy," Kate said.

"Oh, I forgot, you're the kiss and run type," Trudy murmured.

"Tryin' not to be—anymore—the runnin' type, anyway," Kate replied. "I've found my place here in Brooksport, and I don't want any complications that would make me run somewhere else. Thank you very much!"

Kate opened the bag of doughnuts and began to munch on one before continuing, "He's just a tourist who will probably be traveling back to where he came from in a week or two."

Trudy replied, "Maybe, maybe not. You know, some people— like you and me—decide to stay."

Trudy took a doughnut for herself, bit into it, and continued, "Maybe I can find a building for him to buy where he can set up shop—like I did with you."

Kate rolled her eyes.

"Well, it worked with you," Trudy continued.

Trudy motioned for Kate to sit in the shampoo chair.

"Don't know much of what he does back there in the big city, but rumor has it he owns some business internationally, not just here in the good 'ole USA but international."

She began to shampoo Kate's hair. "I hear he's got money and plenty of it." Trudy kept talking. "He'd be a mighty fine catch for you, sugar."

"I don't need his money. Trudy, please, just do what you do best and fix my hair!" Kate exclaimed.

"Well, sugar, if you remember, there was a time when you asked me to fix your life," Trudy replied. "I do believe it was the first time that we met," Trudy concluded.

Kate sighed.

"Just tryin' to oblige," Trudy said with a shrug.

Then she mumbled to herself, "Gotta get this party rockin'!"

26

Kate caught her breath when she opened the door. There he stood, the cowboy—hat, boots, and everything else she would only admit to herself that she wondered about. He was just as surprised to see her.

"You work here?" Jake asked.

"You might say that. I work hard here. I own this place," Kate answered.

"Oh," was all he was able to say.

Kate smiled and invited him in. "I've never seen a cowboy tongue-tied before," she said to him as they walked into the living quarters.

He pretended not to hear her because he refused to admit that, indeed, he had no clue of what to say to her. He didn't like surprises, and he was going to talk to Trudy about it when he saw her. Yes, he was sure going to talk to her and get a few things straight. She should have told him who owned this place. He could have planned something intelligent to say if he had known or, at least, something cute. Now he found himself acting like an idiot with a schoolboy crush. This wasn't like him at all. Well, at least, she wasn't a redhead. Sandra would be proud of him.

Kate motioned for him to sit down. "Did someone send you here?" Kate asked. "Someone who likes purple, maybe?"

He laughed, and with that laugh, the ice was broken. She liked the sound of his laugh. She liked the way he walked, and she liked the way he looked at her. What was she feeling? No! No! She blocked it from her mind—she refused to let even a flicker of a flutter Trudy had talked about run across her mind. This man who had tipped his hat, this man who caught her eye, this man that stared at her when all those balloons went up was sitting in her living room, and she was beginning to feel what Trudy had so expertly talked about. Kate surmised Trudy must have felt a quiver at some time in her life to know so much about it.

"Trudy has a way about her that reels you in, if you know what I mean," Kate said.

"I think I do," he replied. "I think she sizes people up in a mere second. And that, my dear, is faster than a New York minute."

Kate was silent as she questioned to herself, *Did he just call me 'my dear'?*

What did he just call her? he asked himself. He quickly continued, "To answer your question, yes, Trudy sent me here."

"I see," was all Kate managed to say.

"She told me she cut men's hair when I first came to town, so I decided to pay her a visit—just about an hour ago. That's when she told me if I was going to have an extended visit here, I might as well get out of that hotel I was staying in and check out a place with a woman's touch. I liked the name Open Door so here I am."

In all your glory, Kate thought.

"What she failed to tell me was that the woman who has definitely caught my eye was the owner of this place."

Jake had finally found his groove again; he knew how to woo. He added, "I would have come sooner if I had known."

Now Kate was speechless. Heaven forbid, she felt it. It began as a flicker. When he asked that she show him a room that he might like to extend his stay, it had turned into a full-fledged flutter.

She took a key to the only vacant room available. It happened to be the one right next to her private quarters. As she turned the key, she, privately, thanked God this flutter was not a quiver. Not yet, anyway.

"Can a man stay here alone? I mean, is it one of those honeymoon places just for couples?" he asked Kate as they walked back into the living room.

"I have an open door here, but I need to know your name. I can't register you as cowboy," Kate said.

"I see the name Trudy has given me has stuck with everybody." Jake smiled. "My name is Jake Arbor. It's good to meet you." He held out his hand. "My name is Kate, Kate Clarke," she replied, reaching out for a handshake. Instead, Jake took the hand he had been offered and kissed it.

Charlie saw it all. He had come to visit with Kate and cut her grass, pull some weeds, and be tender with the "bleeding hearts." Charlie watched from the corner of the house as Jake turned halfway down the sidewalk and said, "I'll be back with my suitcase." Then he tipped his hat.

Kate turned and walked back into the kitchen. She took a deep breath. God help her. Trudy was right. She didn't know how long she had been denying it, probably since Jake had come to town. It was that instantaneous chemistry. She was in dangerous territory. She had felt a flicker/flutter at the same time. The quiver was in hot pursuit of the former two.

Thankfully, her thoughts were interrupted when she saw Charlie from the kitchen window gearing up the lawn mower. He waved to her.

"Want something to drink before you start, Charlie?" she asked.

"How about after I'm finished?" Charlie asked. Oh, how he dreaded that sweet tea, but after he was done mowing the grass, he knew he would drink anything that promised the slightest refreshment, even sweet tea.

Kate was ready. She knew Trudy would be full of questions on this particular day of her pedicure. She knew the questions would come at her like a wave as soon as she walked into the salon. But surprisingly, Trudy said nothing. Neither did Kate. Kate merely walked over to the footbath, took off her shoes, and slipped her feet into the warm water.

Trudy walked to the corner of the salon, picked out a pretty pink towel, and walked over to Kate, not even glancing up to look at her.

Kate began to relax while soaking her feet in the warm footbath, preparing herself for a morning of pampering, but she couldn't resist.

"Get that smug look off your face, Trudy." Kate broke the silence.

"Whatever do you mean?" Trudy asked even more smugly than the look on her face.

"He showed up—I'll tell you before you ask," Kate said.

"Who?" Trudy asked.

"You know who!" Kate exclaimed.

Trudy looked at her, smiled, and said, "Well done, Trudy, well done. Did you give him a good room?"

Kate did not answer.

"Just for your information, I did not send him. I nudged him, and he took the bait," Trudy said. "So answer my question, did you give him a good room?"

"Yes, I did," Kate replied, moving slightly in her chair.

"So have you felt the quiver yet?" Trudy innocently asked, pointing to the well-positioned heart ornament hanging next to Kate's chair that read, *What makes your heart flutter?*

"Oh, Trudy, would you please stop this stuff about flutters and quivers!" Kate exclaimed, taking the heart and throwing it in the chair next to her.

Trudy kept working on Kate's toes. "I know you have," she said.

Kate rolled her eyes and decided to change the subject. She looked at Trudy and asked, "Tell me something, Trudy, I've known you long enough to ask, why do you love purple so much—I mean"— she pointed around the salon and finally to the purple bow in Trudy's hair—"I mean you really *love* purple!"

Trudy's face clouded over, suddenly going from a gleeful side to a serious side, which was very rare. Kate felt as if she had overstepped her bounds and apologized. "Trudy, I'm sorry, I didn't mean to pry."

"You read me too well. It's okay, sugar. Nobody's ever asked me why." She continued, "People have always looked at me and said, 'Oh, she's that looney woman up from the South.' I know those who meet me for the first time have something to talk about over dinner when their day is done. But those people are mostly the tourists and that newbie teenager down at the grocery store."

She laughed and continued talking. "I think I put the fear of God into him over my Chicken in a Biskit crackers!"

Trudy's faraway look came again; it was a look that was no stranger to Kate. She saw that same look on her own face in the mirror, especially mornings of dates she had circled on the calendar that she would never forget. Sometimes anniversary dates were just too hard to face. Kate had concluded there should be a different word for that type of dreaded anniversary, when tragedy had struck.

Trudy continued, "Once people get to know me, they look past the purple. They accept it."

Kate smiled.

"But since you asked, I'll tell you. I wear it, I surround myself with it. I sleep with it. Yes, I have purple sheets. I just plain and simple love purple because it reminds me of royalty—the kind that never betrays you."

Trudy finished Kate's pedicure, looked her straight in the eye, and said, "One day, sugar, one day, when the time is right for me, I'll tell you more. But for now, just settle for this. Some people wear crosses, I wear purple."

28

Charlie was resting. He had thoughts to ponder, and the bench in the middle of Kate's flower garden seemed to be the proper place to do just that—ponder. He had seen Kate there many times. Sitting there seemed to work for her. She always walked away with a smile on her face, so he figured he would try it too.

Kate was with Jake—no threat of sweet tea coming his way. He sighed.

"Well, Trudy, you sure did do some matchmaking this time!" Charlie said out loud. "Sparks fly when those two are together. Everybody sees it."

Charlie walked over to the bleeding hearts, touching them gently. "Sure hope I can be like Jake one day," he whispered, remembering the night before when Phil had stormed through the house, angry and drunk. "It's for sure I don't want to be like Phil."

Switching back to more pleasant thoughts, he continued thinking of Jake and Kate. "I wonder if they know they have sparks flyin' all over this town. Trudy said they just don't want to admit it, but Kate is always fanning herself when Jake is around. Yep, those two are together a lot."

Charlie looked out at the lake. "They go boat ridin' together, picnicking together, but she can't get him to go to church with her. I wondered why, so I asked him. He said the ceiling would fall in if he went to church—that it was a long story."

He stooped down to pull at some weeds that had grown, seemingly, overnight. "Trudy said Jake can't keep his hands to himself when Kate's around. He's always touchin' her on her shoulder or her hand."

Charlie continued to walk around the garden before beginning his grass mowing, remembering the day he stood on that very corner of the house and watched Jake take Kate's hand in his and kissed it. He saw them through the window. Kate was expectin' a handshake.

"Oh, I knew then those two should be together—even though they didn't have an inklin' what was happening. I think Trudy always knew it too. Oh, is he ever more fallin' for her—oh yes, he is!"

Charlie walked to the nearby shed to get the lawn mower. It was at that moment he thought life was good. He liked Jake. Charlie had to believe now that Jake and Kate were an item and that the "cowboy" would stay in their little town forever.

He was wrong. Little did he know that Jake was getting restless; things were getting too deep for him, and he didn't know how to handle deep. He was a man with emotional limitations.

29

Kate had to talk to Trudy. She hoped this was not a busy day at the salon. She stopped by Belle's first for Trudy's favorite treat and then made her way to the salon. She saw Jake going into Crabby's. Something was off center; something wasn't right. He was becoming distant, and she didn't know why. Trudy would know, she reasoned to herself. Trudy knew everything. Trudy was "royalty."

"Hey, sugar." Trudy welcomed her when she walked through the door.

"Busy day today?" Kate asked.

"No, just washin' some towels and lookin' at my finances. Why?"

Kate held up the bag holding the doughnuts. "Wanna take a walk down to the lake?"

Trudy saw the concerned look on Kate's face and said, "I knew he was trouble with a capital T, but I convinced myself he was merely mixed up and was trouble with a little t. What's he done to make you look so forlorn? You're in Brooksport Village, not the city."

"Let's walk," Kate replied.

Trudy opened the door to the salon and took the bag of dough-nuts. "Let's go," she said.

"Wonder what it is about men and balloons?" Kate asked.

"Huh?" Trudy asked.

"It seems all the men who come into my life with the most impact have something to do with balloons," Kate said with a big sigh. "Zack carried balloons to my hospital room after my collapse, and Jake made sure we had our balloon launch Memorial Day."

"Oh, don't read too much into that, sugar. Balloons are nice, but go for the big hands." Trudy tried to lighten the conversation.

"Remember when you said I had a big knot in my neck that first day we met?" Kate questioned.

"I remember," Trudy replied. "I told you that a man with big hands could take care of that."

"Well, Jake has big hands, but he has knots of his own," Kate almost whispered.

"He's all tangled up inside?" Trudy asked.

"He can't untangle his own knots, much less help me with mine." Kate admitted. "I should have known better. The first time he tipped his hat, the first time he kissed my hand. I should have known better. He's one of those cowboys that ride in, steal your heart, water their horse, and ride out of your life as if nothing ever happened. I've been there and experienced that before. I should have known better. I'm supposed to be older and wiser now."

Trudy motioned to the empty chairs along the beach area of the lake. "Let's sit," she said.

"He won't talk to me about 'heart' things, Trudy. He doesn't want to share feelings that are deep. Do you think he's been hurt before?"

"Oh, sugar, we've all been hurt before. Anybody who has lived as many years as we have has been hurt in some way, maybe different degrees, but with the same common denominator—pain. Some of us talk about it, some of us, like Jake, keep it inside until one day it bursts out, hopefully, in the right direction," Trudy said.

Trudy thought for a long moment before she spoke again. "It's true, Jake is the restless kind. I knew that the first time I saw him. Those sad eyes of his told me that. He's always runnin' somewhere. I think it's because of his pain—the kind you can't touch or put a name to. But let me tell you somethin', I wouldn't give up on him, not yet anyway." She took another doughnut from the bag and bit into it.

Kate looked at her, wanting her to continue, but Trudy was silent.

Kate broke the silence. "Can I trust him, Trudy?"

"Oh, sugar, if there's any man you can trust, I believe it's him—warts and all. He doesn't realize it yet, but oh, how he loves you. Maybe that's what he's runnin' from. Men do that, you know?" Trudy said.

Kate smiled.

Trudy continued, "Believe me, Jake has to find his way. He has secrets. I told you that the first time I talked to you about him. It's those eyes of his. He tries to hide behind his humor, he can't fool me. But he's also the type that once his wings are clipped, it's for good."

Kate remained silent. Trudy took her hand. "Oh, sugar, I should have told you—flutters aren't dangerous—it's the 'quiver' that gets you in trouble, and you're in a heap of it. But, I don't believe in my heart of hearts that your heart is going to be broken."

Trudy saw the tears forming in Kate's eyes. It was then she cupped Kate's face in her hands and whispered, "You know someone once said when a man falls in love with Jesus, it makes a difference how he falls in love with you. Maybe that's what Jake needs to do first."

The two women got up from their chairs and began to walk back into town.

Trudy was thinking to herself as they walked back toward town, *I'm goin' to have a talk with Jake Arbor, a real serious talk.*

When she got those two together, she only wanted the rockin'. She hadn't counted on the hurtin'. Yes, siree, she was going to have a real serious talk with Mr. Jake Arbor.

30

Jake was perplexed. He thought he needed a walk. He needed fresh air. He needed to visit Crabby's. When he walked through the door, he saw his old drinking buddy. In spite of Trudy and Leon's warnings not to cozy up to Phil at the bar, he liked the old guy. So he was glad to see Phil sitting there on his favorite stool. Jake walked over to the seat next to him and sat down. Phil looked up and exclaimed, "Well, well, good to see 'ya, Jake! Been savin' this seat for you!" He slapped the seat of the stool and continued, "Sit down!"

Jake sat down.

Phil looked at him from the corner of his eye and asked, "Where in the world have 'ya been all these weeks?"

"With a woman," Jake replied.

"That figures," Phil answered. "You better watch out, 'ole boy. Women can take you on quite a ride if you let 'em."

"Tell me about it." Jake agreed.

Phil motioned to Leon for another drink. "Bring one for my buddy too." He instructed. Leon gave Phil a warning look. "Don't worry, Leon, I've got a way home now that good 'ole Jake is here," Phil said, pointing to Jake.

Jake nodded to Leon, but Leon still didn't like it.

Jake looked at Phil and asked, "What do you do when a woman gets in your head and you can't get her out?"

"You get drunk," Phil answered without hesitation. "Drink up!" he finished saying.

Jake looked at Phil. "You got a woman in your head too, 'ole buddy?" he asked.

"Had one," Phil replied. "She's gone."

"Where'd she go?" Jake asked.

"Died," Phil said to his drink more than to Jake.

"I'm sorry, Phil," was all Jake could muster out of what he considered his big mouth.

"It's okay. How would you know unless Trudy told you?" he concluded.

Jake shook his head. "No, Trudy's told me nothin'."

Phil smiled. "Well, that's Trudy. She can sure be the Brooksport News around here, but when it comes to personal things—really personal things—she becomes a mute."

Jake ordered another drink. "She keeps secrets?" he questioned.

"Oh yeah, she knows when to talk and when not to talk. She's seen firsthand what happened to me when my Iris died."

"Tell me about her," Jake managed to say.

"Iris was Charlie's mother. She was my wife," Phil began. "She was a petite little thing. I loved her with all my heart. We had it all, we surely did."

Tears were forming in Phil's eyes when he hollered for Leon to bring him another.

Jake began staring at the bottles behind the bar. He didn't know where else to look. He felt uncomfortable, but he had asked for it. Why did he do that? He wasn't a good one for listening to all this 'deep' stuff. Perhaps that's what scared him about Kate. He was beginning to think everybody in this town was too deep for him.

Phil sighed before continuing, "My world fell apart when Iris left me. Oh, I know she didn't want to. God just took her—real sudden and all—he just took her."

Jake did not want to ask questions; he didn't know if he wanted to know the answers, but Phil told him anyway.

"She had this swollen leg," Phil said as he gulped down his final swallow and motioned for another. Jake nodded to the bartender.

"We thought it was because she was on her feet a lot. She loved doin' volunteer work at the hospital," Phil continued.

Jake shifted on his stool.

"I told her to get that leg of hers checked out when she went to volunteer the next day, and she promised she would," Phil began.

"Well, she got there all right. She was walkin' down the hall to the doctor's office and boom!" Phil slapped his hand on the bar.

Leon gave him another warning look.

"Sorry, Leon," Phil said and quietened down.

Jake needed another drink and motioned for one.

"Boom, she was gone," Phil whispered, looking Jake straight in the eyes.

Leon brought Jake's drink, turned his back to Phil, and whispered, "Blood clot straight to the brain."

Phil took a deep breath, got up from the bar stool, pulled his wallet from his back pocket, and paid for his tab. He looked at Jake, patted him on the shoulder, and walked out the door.

Leon motioned for Jake to follow Phil. "You promised," was all he had to say.

Jake left his drink and caught up with Phil. "I made a promise to get you home safely," Jake began.

"And you're a man of your word, eh?" Phil asked.

"Yep, I may be many other things, but I am a man of my word. Let's get you home," was Jake's final reply.

31

Charlie was home when Phil stumbled through the door. Jake wasn't far behind; he just wasn't stumbling.

Charlie looked at Jake. "Thanks for bringin' Phil home," he said. "One time, he ended up sleepin' behind Belle's 'cause he couldn't find his way."

"I'll help you get him to bed, Charlie," Jake said.

When Phil was safely in his room, Jake turned to Charlie. "Are you going to be okay here tonight?" Jake asked.

"Oh yeah, I'm used to it," Charlie replied. "Would you like some sweet tea before you go?"

"Sweet tea?" Jake asked, making a face.

"Yeah, I've seen you and Miss Kate drinkin' that stuff in her garden. You like it?"

"Not really," Jake laughed.

"Me neither," Charlie said. "How about a cup of coffee?"

"You need to talk, Charlie?" Jake asked.

Charlie nodded.

Oh, dear, was all Jake could think of in his own mind. More "deep" conversations. He was beginning to think he should never have stepped foot in this town, much less Crabby's, on this particular night.

"I wanna talk about girls," Charlie told Jake as he went to the kitchen to make a cup of instant coffee for Jake.

Jake was relieved. He could talk about girls. He didn't have to dig deep to talk about girls; it was women he didn't know what to do with, especially a woman like Kate. Charlie returned with two cups of coffee. Jake smiled as Charlie sat down facing Jake.

"What do you want to know about girls, Charlie?" Jake asked.

"What makes them tick," Charlie answered and took a sip of his coffee. He nearly spit it out. "This is awful! Don't feel like you have to be polite and drink it!" Charlie exclaimed. "First time I ever made it!"

He looked at Jake and reasoned, "Is that what we are, Jake? Polite around girls like Miss Kate and Sarah—drinkin' all that sweet tea, gaggin' all the time, tryin' not to let them know how much we really don't want to drink that stuff?"

"Probably so, Charlie," Jake answered.

"You ever met a girl that looks straight through you, Jake?" Charlie asked.

Jake thought for a moment and had to admit that, indeed, he had. She lived right up the street.

It was as if Charlie had read his mind when he asked, "Does Miss Kate do that to you?"

Jake said nothing.

"Sarah has this way of doing that—like she knows what I'm thinkin' before I say it. It kind of creeps me out, to tell 'ya the truth." Charlie admitted.

"I know what you mean, Charlie. It creeps me out too," Jake answered.

Jake took a sip of his own coffee and agreed with Charlie. "This is awful! How did you make this?" Jake asked.

"With a teaspoon of instant coffee and hot water," Charlie replied. "There was some weenie water left over from when I boiled my hot dog, and I thought that would be quick enough to use 'cause I was in a hurry to talk to you about girls."

Jake looked at Charlie and ran for the kitchen. After pouring the weenie water coffee into the sink, he exclaimed, "Come in here, Charlie, and let me show you how to make a good cup of coffee."

When Charlie entered, Jake flung his arm around his innocent shoulders and led him over to the sink, saying, "First, you pour *fresh* water into the pan."

32

"Tell me something, Charlie," Jake began as the two sat down at the kitchen table to drink their good coffee. "Why do you call your dad Phil?"

"That's his name," Charlie answered and took a sip of coffee, nodding that it tasted much better when made with *fresh* water.

"But he's your dad," Jake said.

"In name only," Charlie replied. "He hasn't been a dad to me since my mom died."

"How old were you when she died, Charlie?" Jake asked.

Charlie took another sip of coffee, "I was four."

"You were young," Jake said. "Do you remember your mom?"

Charlie thought for a moment and replied, "I don't remember much." He set his coffee cup down. "But there is one thing I do remember."

"What's that?" Jake asked.

"I remember the apron she used to wear when she baked cookies in this kitchen. It was white with yellow irises on it. She always wore it when she made my favorite cookies," Charlie replied.

"What kind of cookies are your favorite?" Jake continued to ask his questions.

"Sugar cookies," Charlie sighed as he answered. "I do remember that."

"That's a nice memory," Jake replied.

"Sometimes I feel I can still smell 'em bakin' when I sit in here by myself," Charlie continued sharing.

"I can understand that," Jake replied.

"You ever have anybody die, Jake?" Charlie asked.

"No, no, I haven't," Jake replied.

"It's a sad thing," Charlie confessed.

He looked around the kitchen where his mom had once walked. His focus turned to the phone.

"That's an old phone over there," Charlie began, pointing to the wall.

Jake looked at the phone hanging on the wall—a landline with a dial. "Yes, it is," Jake said.

"We keep it for a reason," Charlie began.

"Why is that?" Jake asked.

"Mom always talked on that phone when she was baking my cookies, and Phil said he would keep that phone until the day he died," Charlie began.

He looked off into the distance and suddenly exclaimed, "I do remember something else about my mom."

Jake sat still, not saying a word. He could only imagine the forlorn look he had on his face. He felt so badly for Charlie.

"I remember running over to her when she was on that phone. I ran over to her and hugged her legs. She had told me they were hurting, and I wanted to make them feel better. I remember that," Charlie exclaimed.

Jake didn't move a muscle. He wanted Charlie to keep talking. Somehow, he knew Charlie had a lot of stuff inside he needed to get out. Perhaps Kate was rubbing off on him as well as running through his head all the time. Perhaps he was developing a listening ear after all.

"It didn't work." Charlie took another sip of his coffee.

"What do you mean?" Jake asked.

"She died the next day," Charlie replied.

Jake sat motionless.

"You know," Charlie added, "I never knew what happened to that apron after she died. It just plain disappeared."

33

Phil caught up with Jake the next morning as he was coming out of Belle's.

"Hey, 'ole buddy!" Phil greeted him. "Thanks for gettin' me home last night!"

Jake nodded as he kept remembering what Trudy had told him, "The last thing that man needs is a drinkin' buddy." After his talk with Charlie last night, he believed it. He vowed not to be a drinkin' buddy, not anymore.

He wanted to help Charlie, but he was no damn child psychologist either. He didn't know how to handle his own problems, much less Charlie's or Phil's. Hell, he'd probably end up causin' more harm than good anyway. And the most harm would be to himself, especially if he got too close; he always ended up losing.

His shoulders were too weighed down with his own baggage. He couldn't carry even a small knapsack stuffed with somebody else's problems, and he wasn't going to. Still, he felt sorry for Charlie.

"You comin' down to Crabby's later, ole buddy?" Phil interrupted Jake's own private conversation with himself.

"Don't think so," Jake replied.

"Why not?" Phil asked.

"I may be leavin' town soon. I gotta get back to the city and get some work done," Jake replied.

It seemed like a viable excuse to flee this town.

Phil walked another distance with him, shrugged his shoulders, and said, "Ah, that woman again. Has you all wrapped up in knots.

Who is it, Jake? Who is that woman that has you runnin' in circles of your own makin'?"

Jake said nothing. He kept walking toward Open Door. It was time to leave. He was going back to the familiar. He knew how to handle that. Nothing was going to hold him back—not even Kate's eyes that seemed to sear right through him. Charlie was right—it creeped him out.

Phil walked into Crabby's.

"The only thing you're gettin' to drink in here this early, Phil, is a ginger ale," Leon began. "So don't bother to order anything else."

Phil looked at Leon and said, "For once, I agree with you. At least for now," Phil replied. "I kind of remember Jake gettin' me home last night, but that's all."

Phil sat down on the bar stool. Leon brought him his ginger ale.

I vaguely remember talkin' to Charlie about something after Jake left, but for the life of me, I can't remember what it was, Phil said to himself.

Phil shrugged his shoulders. *Charlie seemed pretty upset this morning.*

Phil began drumming his fingers on the counter. "How much longer 'til noon, Leon? I'm ready for a drink."

Leon ignored him and went on about his preparation for the day's events. He sure wished he could find a singer like they had down at that coffeehouse. He really brought in the crowds—Chip was his name.

34

Kate and Trudy were overlooking the lake when Kate looked up at the sky. "Well, I'll be damned," Kate said.

"I can't believe it!" Trudy exclaimed. "Did you just say a cuss word?"

"I did," Kate answered, pointing to the sky. "There it is, look up there. Do you see it?"

Trudy looked up, rolled her eyes, and said, "You are obsessed with hidden meanings when it comes to balloons."

"Yes, I am!" Kate exclaimed. "Something is going to happen, I just know it is!"

Trudy picked up a stone and threw it into the lake. "I think you need some lard," Trudy began. "Let's go back to Belle's and get some doughnuts. Nothin' is goin' to happen—except me gainin' more weight if I give in to this temptation! I can smell 'em from here!"

Kate was having none of it. She sighed and sat down on the nearest chair. "I don't know how to love him. He's different." Kate confessed.

Trudy decided it was no use talking about doughnuts to the lovelorn and sat down beside Kate.

"I know, sugar," Trudy replied.

"What should I do?" Kate questioned again.

"Just hug him once in a while, sugar, and place those lovely lips of yours on his. Have you ever thought about getting those lips of yours insured?" Trudy tried to lighten the mood.

Kate looked at Trudy so pitifully, she had to become serious.
"He's a questioning man, sugar. Just love him the best you can. Those
who question are being prepared for the answers."

Trudy sighed.

"Lovin's your middle name. You take care of people. You just
don't want to be hurt, betrayed, or left behind anymore. That's what
you're afraid of. Can't blame you for that," Trudy said.

Trudy was right. That was exactly what she was afraid of. Being
hurt. Being left behind again. Being betrayed. Once bitten, twice shy.
Isn't that what people say? Was that what she was, "twice shy"?

Trudy took Kate by the shoulders and said, "Sugar, let me tell
you something. That cowboy is a wild man that needs tamin'. If any
woman can do that, it's you."

Kate looked at her, wanting to believe her.

Trudy continued, "One thing is for sure, and I believe this with
my whole heart." Trudy pointed to her chest. "I've told you before,
and I'll tell you again, he'll never fly again once his wings are clipped.
Trust me."

That being said, Trudy got up from the beach chair and turned
to leave. Halfway up the stairs, she realized she had to also tell Kate
a truth she might not want to hear, so she turned and walked back
to that beach chair. Trudy faced Kate once again and repeated, "I do
believe he's got it bad for you. He just doesn't know how to handle it
yet. He thinks he's in way over his head," Trudy began.

"What aren't you telling me, Trudy?" Kate asked.

Trudy took a deep breath, looked at Kate, and said, "He was
born to run. I knew that the first time I saw him—even asked him
if those boots he had on were made for runnin'. You have to accept
the fact that he could also be a heartbreak just waitin' to happen. Just
know what you're dealin' with and God help you."

She gave Kate a hug and said, "Got work to do."

She turned back to the steps and continued her climb up and
away from the lake.

Trudy reached the top of that hill where the flowers were
blooming and looked back at Kate sitting there, looking out at the
water. Trudy looked up at the sky. The balloon had long since disap-

peared, but she was feeling the same thing Kate had confessed earlier. Something kept haunting Trudy. What was it about Kate she couldn't quite put her finger on?

She shrugged it off and headed to the coffeehouse. Charlie had called her earlier. There was something he needed to talk to her about.

When in the world did that child start drinkin' coffee? she asked herself.

Trudy was in for a big surprise. Something was happening, all right, and how she handled it would determine either a boy's broken heart or a new lease on life.

Charlie was waiting for Trudy in the coffeehouse when she arrived. Chip was strumming a ballad on his guitar as Trudy walked by, giving him a high-five. She walked over to Charlie and sat down.

"Are you sick?" Trudy asked. "You look pale as a ghost!"

"Did you know?" Charlie asked.

"Know what?" Trudy asked.

"The biggest secret that everybody in town knows—everybody but me—that I'm adopted," Charlie asked, looking her straight in the eyes.

Trudy took a deep breath before she answered.

"Charlie, I've never lied to you, and I never will," she began. "Yes, I knew."

"Why didn't you tell me, Trudy?" Charlie nearly screamed.

"It wasn't my place to tell you," Trudy answered. She took another deep breath and said, "It was your dad's place."

"Well, he did tell me—last night," Charlie said.

"Was he drunk?" she asked, exasperated.

"Of course, he was," Charlie exclaimed. "He's always drunk."

"He hasn't been much of a dad to you, Charlie, that's for sure. He's had his issues since your mom died," Trudy began.

"He's not my dad," Charlie said with vehemence. "And Iris was not my mom!" he shouted.

Trudy nearly jumped from her chair. "Now you listen to me, young man, and you listen good! That woman you claim was not your mom was one of the best things that ever happened to you! She loved you as her son! You were her son! She chose you! You were precious to her! What you just said out loud are fightin' words, boy!"

Charlie shrank back from Trudy. He admitted to himself he should have known better than to say something like that, especially to Trudy.

He looked down at his hands, tears forming in his eyes. He couldn't help himself. He had loved his mom too. He didn't want her to be gone, especially now. He didn't care if he was fiffteen years old; he wanted his mom's arms around him again.

Trudy calmed herself and took Charlie's face in her hands. "You've had a hard life since your mom died. I've tried to fill in whenever I could. Phil has not made it easy for you, but, Charlie, you're a good boy. You work hard. Your dad—"

Charlie interrupted her, "Not my dad."

Trudy reminded him. "He was a good dad for four years, Charlie."

"I can't remember any of that, Trudy," Charlie added.

"Well, take it from me, he was. He was so happy when they placed you as a baby in Iris's arms. They both beamed."

"You were there?" Charlie asked.

"I was. I loved your mom, Charlie. She was a special friend. I knew your mom and dad long before they came to live here. I knew them before Brooksport Village. They were a good pair. They loved each other. You were raised here, Charlie, but you were placed in their arms in another state, another city. The 'whole town' does not know 'your secret'—as you put it."

She took a breath.

"And it never should have been a secret, if that sweet Iris friend of mine—your mother—had lived. She was so proud of you! She would have told you and everybody else in this town—"

"If only she had lived," Charlie finished her sentence for her.

"Your four years with Phil and Iris were special years, loving years," Trudy took Charlie's hands in hers. "They gave you a chance, Charlie, a second chance."

Trudy looked around the coffeehouse before continuing, "In a way, they gave me my second chance too.

Charlie looked at Trudy, saying nothing.

Trudy continued, "I was runnin' from a past I was tryin' to forget. I was grievin'. They convinced me to visit them here. I decided to stay."

"Is that why you took such a shinin' to me? Tryin' to teach me manners and all?" Charlie managed to question.

"I've always loved you, Charlie. You're as much a part of me as Iris and Phil."

"That's why Phil trusts you like nobody else in this town, right?"

"Probably so."

"Is there anything else I don't know, Trudy?"

"No."

After what seemed a long silence, Trudy said, "Your mom would have told you in a gentle way, Charlie. She was going to tell you when you were old enough to understand."

Trudy looked directly at Charlie before continuing, "She wanted to make it real clear to you that you were 'chosen.' They *chose* you. They *picked you out* of all the rest. And I'm tellin' you now exactly what she would be sayin' to you if she were sittin' here! Do you hear me?" Trudy questioned.

She took his face in her hands once again. "I asked you a question!" Trudy exclaimed.

Charlie nodded his head.

"I want more than a nod, Charlie. I want you to hear me loud and clear with not only your ears but with your heart. So I'll ask you again, do you hear me?"

Tears were streaming down Charlie's face when he answered, "Yes, I hear you. I miss my mom! I want her back!"

Chip stopped playing his guitar and looked at Trudy. Trudy gave him an okay sign. Chip decided it was time to give them a little more privacy, took his guitar, and walked to the other room.

"I know you do, Charlie, and let me tell you that if she had her way, she would still be here with you. But God wanted her home. She had finished her job here," Trudy tried to explain.

"No, she hadn't finished her job here, Trudy! Her job was to stay here and be with me and Phil!" Charlie cried.

Trudy was at a loss for words. She didn't understand all this herself. How could she possibly explain it to a fifteen-year-old who had finally allowed the dam of tears to burst after all these years? How indeed?

All she could think of doing was hug him and love him the best she could. Wasn't that just what she had said to Kate a few hours earlier? Little did she know at that time she would have to follow her own advice. Suddenly, she was questioning, just as Kate had questioned, *How do I do that?*

Trudy left the coffeehouse and walked up the street to Open Door.

"I have to talk to you," she said to Kate as she walked through the back door of the kitchen.

Kate finished putting the final touches on the table for breakfast the next morning and motioned for Trudy to join her outside. They walked over to the bench and sat down.

"You're scaring me," Kate said, looking at Trudy.

"I'm scaring myself," Trudy replied.

"What's wrong?" Kate asked.

"It's Charlie," Trudy began. "I'm thinkin' he's goin' to come lookin' for you, and you need to be prepared."

Kate waited for Trudy to continue.

"Lord, help me," Trudy began. "I swore to Phil I would not tell a soul until, well, until he told Charlie. So I'm guessin' it's okay to tell somebody now."

"What is it, Trudy?" Kate asked.

"Charlie's adopted," Trudy said. "Not that it's a bad thing, it's not. It's a good thing. At least, it was a good thing for a while, and then Iris died, and Phil started drinkin', and oh, I'm rambling—" Trudy stopped talking and took a breath.

Kate remained silent, waiting for Trudy to continue.

"Iris wanted to tell Charlie when he was old enough to understand—in her own gentle way. I'm the only one in town that knew. They moved here right after Charlie was placed in her arms—I was in on it from the start. Iris and I had been friends before their move here. They couldn't have children, and I knew some people, and well, it's a long story—the fact is both of them swore me to secrecy until they saw it fittin' to tell Charlie," Trudy said, taking another deep breath.

"I take it that Charlie knows now," Kate said. "Who told him?"

Trudy looked like she could strangle somebody when she answered, "Phil."

This time, it was Kate who took a breath.

"Phil told him last night after he had spent a few hours at Crabby's," Trudy said.

"Oh no," Kate began. "He told Charlie the truth when he was drunk?"

"That's the bottom line. That's why Charlie wanted to meet with me when I left you down at the lake earlier," Trudy exclaimed.

"How is Charlie now?" Kate asked.

"I did what I could and said what I could to soothe him, but I think it was more the way he was told than the fact that he was told," Trudy said. "Anyway, I think he may come here to talk to you about it. He said you always told him he could come here and make it his peaceful place when he had to think about things. I think he's goin' to take you up on your offer—when—I don't know," Trudy concluded.

Both women sat in silence for some time. Kate couldn't move. She began to think back over her own life, almost sixteen years ago. She pictured the nursery her mom and she had painted and decorated together. She pictured the crib that had been assembled and awaited a baby that never came. She pictured the paintbrushes she had thrown out by the side of the road where Zack had found her that fateful day. She pictured the man who had betrayed her. It all came flooding back. Eventually, the mighty do fall from their pedestals, and oh, the noise they make when they do—the pieces they leave behind for you to clean up. And Charlie had a lot of pieces to pick up.

Trudy interrupted her thoughts. "Kate?" she asked, bringing Kate back to the present moment.

She looked up as Trudy continued, "It's just that he's always said how easy it is to talk to you that you have this peaceful way about you, and he's comfortable around you."

"I think the world of Charlie too," Kate replied.

Trudy got up to leave. "So it makes me think he's goin' to come here for sure. I want you to know it's for an important reason. He trusts you. I want you to be prepared."

Trudy walked to the edge of the garden. "I hope you can give that boy some peace, Kate. He's one torn-up mess right now."

Kate nodded because she still couldn't move. Finally, she managed to say, "I'll be here for Charlie. I'll be here for him."

35

Kate was restless. How could she help Charlie? She kept walking around the kitchen, opening and closing cabinets.

Jake watched from the doorway.

"Why do you look lost in your own kitchen?" he asked.

She turned to face him. "I didn't know you were there," she managed to say.

The look on her face did not escape Jake. "What time is it?" he asked.

"Four thirty," Kate replied.

Jake walked to the cabinet, took two glasses from the shelf, grabbed the whisky, and walked to the table.

"Sit," he commanded as he poured a shot of whisky into both glasses.

They both sat opposite each other, "Talk to me," he said.

"I'm going to tell you something," Kate began.

"It's not one of those 'woman' things, is it?" Jake asked. "Because if it is, I'm goin' to get Trudy."

Kate couldn't help but smile. He could forever deny the fact that he couldn't handle anything deep, but she knew the truth about him. They were 'like' spirits. He was also a runner. She had sadly admitted that fact after leaving Trudy on the beach earlier that day. It takes one to know one.

Still he was the one she needed to tell, the one she wanted to tell. Her past was catching up with her. Everyone's past ran them over eventually. And if he ran, well, he would just run.

"I've had a lot of regrets in my life," Kate began, "and I've lost a lot of people I've loved."

Jake shifted in his chair.

Kate took a sip of her drink.

"What I'm going to tell you is the biggest regret in my life and the loss I cannot get over," Kate said.

Jake listened as she continued, "I had a baby, Jake." Tears were forming in her eyes. "I was barely nineteen years old." She looked out over the garden. "My mom thought that Frank, my dream man, was a charmer. But she also thought he was nice, and no one could deny that he was very handsome. My dad would have kicked him out of the house at their first meeting—looking back on everything, of that I am sure." Kate leaned in toward Jake. "My dad always used to say, 'Men know men.'"

Jake couldn't help wondering what her dad would have thought of him. Would he have kicked Jake off the porch as soon as he stood at her front door on that summer day?

"You say 'would have.' Where was your dad?" Jake asked.

Fresh tears pooled in Kate's eyes as she replied, "My dad died suddenly before this man entered my life. Mom and I were devastated. A massive heart attack caught us both off guard."

Once again, she looked out over the garden.

"This man caught me midair after my dad's death. I was young and vulnerable. I had this big empty space that I had to fill, and Frank did that. So I fell hard."

She got up and walked to the kitchen window.

"I wanted his child. He had made a lot of promises, and I believed him. My mom was determined to help me raise the baby. She stood lovingly beside me, and our neighbors kept pretty much to themselves, leading their own private lives. No one knew what was going on behind closed doors unless information was volunteered. It seemed everyone had their own lives to live. They minded their own business. It was as simple as that."

Jake poured himself another drink.

"Mom began knitting a baby blanket. She prayed over every stitch that the baby would be healthy. And she promised God that she would always be there, that no harm would ever come to this baby or to her only child, me, as long as she was around. She accepted the reality of my pregnancy and loved me through it. She said we would manage as best we could. She was strong."

Jake walked over to her and took her hands in his. His arms went around her instinctively.

"I've only told one other person this story, Jake. You're the second."

He held her tighter. They stood there in silence. He didn't know how to break the silence. He was scared. He had never been this close with anyone before. She was different. He didn't know if he would be able to handle her honesty, her openness. He had never been intimate like this with any woman—a woman sharing her heart, her well-kept secrets until now. It was always the "other kind." He knew what to do with the lusty stuff, but this? This was different. This was deep, and he was wading out far beyond his comfort zone. So he just kept holding her; he didn't know what else to do. Shoot, he had walked back to Open Door to sneak in the back door, pack, and head out of town. Now he was holding a woman in his arms with tears streaming down her face. He couldn't go anywhere, at least not right this minute.

Kate broke the silence. "When I told you I had lost so much in my life, well, sometimes I still cannot understand or comprehend why it all happened. Two months before my baby was born, my mom died."

Jake could not hide his shock. He had to question, "This man, this man, where was he? You did tell him about the baby, didn't you?"

"Oh yes, he knew. That's when everything hit the fan, so to speak. That's when I discovered he was a married man. It was as if someone had kicked the very breath out of me. I never heard from him or saw him again after I told him."

"I need some fresh air," Jake said.

"I don't know about you, Kate, but I could use another big swig of this stuff," he said, pointing to the whisky. "I'll bring it out to you—you go sit," Jake said, pointing to the bench.

He brought both glasses and the bottle with him and sat beside her, pouring the whisky as he sat.

"What happened after your mom died?"

She sighed, taking a sip of whisky. "I felt totally lost. Just barely nineteen years old, I didn't know what to do or where to turn. I disappeared for a while to have my baby. When I returned, Zack came into my life."

"Zack?" Jake asked, feeling a tinge of jealousy.

"Yes, Zack, he was older. He became my saving grace. He lived at the end of the street. A widower. No children. You might say he adopted me. I know he treated me as his own."

Jake continued to listen.

"He helped me overcome some of the guilt I had from the decision I had to make—a decision that although I knew was the right thing to do all those years ago, it's still a decision that I struggle with."

"What was that decision, Kate?"

She poured herself another swig and drank it. She didn't care if she did get looped at this point. If the pattern in her life remained true, after confessing all to Jake, he would be packing and walking out the door anyway.

She put the glass down, looked directly at him, and replied, "I gave up my baby. They took the blanket my mom had begun to knit—the one I finished after her death—and they wrapped that sweet little thing in it. I handed my baby over to the adoption agency."

Kate touched a nearby flower. "I didn't just cry that day. I wept that day as I watched them walk away with my precious child. Some days I still do, even after all these years. But I knew I couldn't raise a child on my own at my young age, and I felt that child needed a running start in life with two parents in a good home."

Again they sat in silence until Kate spoke. "Zack was my lifeline, and I grabbed it. We were good for each other, he and I. He saw me through a lot of thunder in my life. He was the first and only person I told, until you, until now."

Before Jake asked the obvious question, he took another swig. "What happened to Zack?"

She looked at him and replied, "He died."

She stood then to walk back into the house. She turned before walking through the door. "If I were you, Jake, I wouldn't just walk away from me, I would run. I don't have a very good track record when it comes to those I love."

Well, now she had done it. The four-letter word had come out. She blamed the whisky. If her story had not scared Jake into leaving, she was sure *that* word had done the trick.

She dared to turn and face his "forlorn" look, as Trudy would say. "I've been a mess most of my life, Jake. I admit that. Some of my decisions have been wrong and most of them not very well thought out. But I'm here in Brooksport Village, trying to make a new start, and for the most part, I've been pretty successful in doing just that."

Jake kept staring at her, trying to forget the word *love* had just been used.

Kate continued, "This town called out to me when my gas gauge read empty. Truth be told, I was pretty much empty myself. I met Charlie at that gas station."

She remembered that day with fondness and smiled.

"I've heard it said that some of the seemingly most inconsequential meetings in our lives are the ones that change us forever. I think that was true when I met Charlie," Kate said.

"It was Charlie who told me about Trudy's Tresses & Tootsies." She laughed. "So I decided to go see for myself what that purple salon looked like. Little did I know at the time that more than my hairstyle would be changed when I walked out of her salon."

Kate took Jake by the arm with one hand and the empty whisky bottle by the other. "Let's go back inside," she said.

"Trudy told me about this place. I talked to the realtor, and before I knew it, Open Door was mine. I've worked hard not only with my B and B, tearing down some of its walls and rebuilding, but with tearing down my own walls too—the ones I've built around myself. I used to think they were walls of protection, not letting anyone get too close, because I didn't think I would be able to survive one more person leaving me."

Kate took his hands in hers. The whisky had made her quite brave, she admitted to herself. She continued, "But life doesn't work that way. Someday, whether it be rainy or sunny, God sends a sandal-clad traveler across your path, and the walls come tumbling down."

"Who was your traveler, Kate?" Jake asked.

"The only one who can tear down the walls one brick at a time," she replied.

"Who's that?" Jake asked, hoping it was not him of which she spoke.

"Jesus Christ," Kate replied. "He's the reason I'm not a bitter woman. There's always a reason to keep hope in your heart."

Jake looked at her, thankful it wasn't him who had torn down her walls. If he had done something so demonstrative in someone's life—something that good—he sure as hell wanted to remember it. Besides that, he wore cowboy boots, not sandals.

She continued, "I don't know why I felt I had to tell you my story. Perhaps it's because I see walls you have built around yourself."

She walked over to the window, looking out on the lake. "You see, once someone admits they're a mess, they can spot another person who is a mess a mile away."

She turned back to him. "And, Jake, you're a mess."

He sat there, saying nothing, trying to take in everything this gentle, tipsy soul continued to share with him. She had quite suddenly turned the spotlight on him.

She kept looking at him, not expecting a reply. "I know you'll be going away. Trudy saw it first when you walked through town in those boots of yours," she said, pointing to his feet. "You'll be leaving not because of the story I've told you but because of your own story, your own bricks and mortar. Find the one who can tear that wall down, Jake. And when you do, turn that car of yours around and get back here. Only you can figure out what you're running from or what you're running to."

Jake got up to leave.

"I've never thought I needed savin', but if I do—and I'm not admitting I do—who do you think can save me, Kate?" Jake asked. "I mean really, if a woman like you can't, I don't know who can."

It seemed the whisky had made him pathetically honest too.

Kate looked at him, gave him a kiss on the cheek, and answered, "Believe me, you'll know exactly who that is when you arrive at your safe place to land. When you arrive at your own Jericho."

As Jake left her doorstep, she was grateful that Trudy had given her a warning just a few days ago at the beach. Somehow it had helped her say the things she needed to say to Jake—that and the whisky. She had to give some credit to the whisky.

She could hear Trudy's voice, even now, in her mind, saying, "*He could be a heartbreak just waitin' to happen.*" But what else had she said? "*If any woman can tame that cowboy, it's you.*"

Kate watched Jake walk away. He hadn't packed his bags— yet—but she knew he would. It was only a matter of time.

She walked back into her living room and out to her garden; she sat beside the bleeding hearts. Touching them gently, she whispered, "Tame you, Jake? Oh yes, I think I could, but free you? No, that's not up to me."

PART III

The Storm

36

"I am not the settling down kind," Jake kept telling himself while walking away from Open Door. And to top it all off, she had said *that* word, that four-letter word, and it made him nervous as hell.

He kicked a stone at his feet as he continued to walk back into town, hands in his pockets.

"And besides that, I don't deserve her," he said out loud.

She was way beyond his league. He had to admit he was way over his head with this one.

By the time he reached town, he had made his decision. No more vacillating. He had to get out while the getting was good. It was time to go back to New York. Time to go back to all the racket he was used to. Too much "quiet" in this village had allowed him to think. That was bad for him. He didn't like to think. Time to tell Butch to go on an extended vacation the way he had. Time to tell Sandra that no, he had not met a redhead. (Thank God Trudy had not dyed Kate's hair red!) Time to get his groove back on. And he would not look back. Time to go get a dog.

For Charlie, the next few days were spent processing all the things that had been told to him, beginning with Phil's drunken blunder. At least, that is what Phil told him later when he apologized. But truth was truth, and the truth hurt.

Today would not be just another ordinary day. His schedule would be just as ordinary as yesterday, but his thoughts were running rampant. He had to quieten his mind. The rest of his days would be different because he was different. He wasn't who he thought he was. He didn't know exactly who he was anymore. Now he knew about the secret that had been hidden all these years, a secret that wasn't meant to be a secret at all. If only his mom had lived.

When Phil came to apologize to Charlie, he thought that perhaps Phil had made up the whole story in his drunken state. That's why he went to Trudy; that's why he met her in the coffee house. But she had confirmed it.

"Another day in paradise," Charlie said to himself as he rode his bike, delivering his papers. "Another morning of sunshine, water, and fried doughnuts, extra crispy."

He delivered his papers to the local businesses, all except for Crabby's. Leon never needed newspapers. Trudy had told him not to bother selling papers there. The people who visited Crabby's in the mornings didn't want to read the newspaper; they only wanted a Bloody Mary and for nobody to slam any doors, so that was one potential customer he had marked off his list. He did take a moment to peek inside. He saw him—Phil.

Grabbing his bike, he jumped on it and pedaled like a crazy person to Open Door. He liked Miss Kate. He liked talking to her. She was kind and inviting. He always left her place as his final destination to deliver the papers because he liked looking out over the lake in hopes of seeing her. But today was different. He didn't want to see anybody. He felt that not even Miss Kate could soothe the ache that had parked itself smack dab in the middle of his heart.

He parked his bike next to the house and walked around to the back of Open Door to look out over the lake.

He murmured to himself, "Peaceful, at least that's what I heard one of Miss Kate's guests say."

He kicked at the grass. "Should be mowed soon," he said to himself.

"Those tourists just drive into town, stay awhile, do some shopping, eat some food, sleep, and move on. I wonder if they keep the peace they find here out there in the real world?" he questioned himself. He wondered if he would have peace when he left this town. He had made up his mind he was going to do just that, and he couldn't wait to put on some cowboy boots and be just like Jake. He was already looking at cowboy hats.

Jake knew things. He knew how to be a man. That's what he wanted to do. He wanted to be just like him. He taught him things about girls and how to make coffee—good coffee.

Charlie walked a short distance to the pond beside Kate's garden of flowers. He could understand why people from the city liked to stay here. He sat down on the bench beside the birdbath and bird feeder and looked at the flowers. Two squirrels scurried in the distance.

"I wonder why Miss Kate laughs every time she sees those squirrels?" he asked himself. "I don't see anything funny about them."

He began to walk slowly among the flowers.

"They sure are beautiful," Charlie said out loud. "I know what this place looked like before Miss Kate got here. That's why I respect it now—I know the story behind it, when that doctor threw it to the wind, and it was neglected. I knew it when the weeds came up. I know how much time it took before it bloomed again. You gotta learn what makes beauty tick, what crooked roads led to what it became. What weeds were there, chokin' the life out of 'em before they were rescued by a lovin' hand."

Charlie understood these things. Wise beyond his years. He began to walk the path of the flowers. He remembered the storms that had come into his young life, especially the one that had cut through his heart when his mom was swept away from him. The torrent of trouble that came into his life was still surging.

Phil never got over Iris's death. Now Charlie had another reason for not calling Phil 'Dad.' Not only because he stopped being a dad when his mom died, but now—well, now—he knew another truth that had knocked him silly.

Charlie was approaching a part of the garden where he had seen Kate sit quietly alone when she thought no one was watching.

"People think Miss Kate has it all together, but I don't think she does. Why else does she sit out here with all these bleedin' hearts? I think she's rememberin' stuff—rememberin' stormy stuff in her life."

Charlie walked back toward where he had left his bike, stopping to look once again at the lake.

"Ah, yes, the perfect little town, but even little towns have big secrets. The behind-closed-doors kind of secrets. Some secrets you try to hide more than others, but they just can't stay hidden. People in small towns know. Sometimes, even the tourists find out. Everybody knows everybody. Word gets around fast. He secretly wondered why anyone in town even needed a newspaper to get the news. But then again, nobody had talked about his own private secret—the one even he didn't know about until a few days ago. So maybe small towns could keep quiet.

Charlie's wounds were deep. His dad had become the yelling kind, and there was no way Charlie could hide the awful yelling and hurtful words that spewed out of Phil's mouth when he was drunk. The whole town heard him when he got on one of his rampages. He was a verbally abusive drunk. His words even had Charlie wondering if Charlie himself had something to do with his mom's death.

The whole town knew Phil was a drunk. Crabby's Bar had become Phil's haunt after Iris had died. Charlie, a mere four-year-old, did not understand the turmoil that left him without his mom, but he was sure feeling the aftereffects of it now. There were people who came to Charlie's rescue, and he knew they meant well, but words from Phil bruised more than hugs from friends helped.

Then suddenly, after years had passed, there was Miss Kate. He would always remember the day she pulled into the gas station. There was something about her. She was now the one he went to when he was troubled. She was a 'like' spirit. She understood. He didn't know her story; he was just glad she was here and only a bike ride away.

He had a feeling that Miss Kate had dealt with some pretty harsh words in her lifetime too. You know the kind, the ones that rip your heart out a piece at a time. The ones that make you bleed inside—kind of like those "bleeding heart" flowers of hers.

He remembered the time he told her about his mom. That had been one of those conversations you label as very private. He remembered going home that evening, wanting desperately to find that apron he had talked to Miss Kate about. He had even talked to Jake about it that fateful night. He still looked everywhere for it. He didn't know what Phil had done with it, and he was afraid to ask.

"I felt so close to Miss Kate that day," Charlie whispered as he bent down to touch the heart-shaped flower. "Like she was a real mom herself."

He remembered asking her, '*You have any children, Miss Kate?*' She hadn't answered.

Charlie sat there for a long time, remembering their conversation.

"*Those bleeding hearts like shade,*" she told him.

"*Kind of like my heart now, all shaded up,*" Charlie had confessed.

"*There's this little teardrop that comes out of the tips of those flowers,*" she had said.

He remembered Sarah had told him they were fragile little things, and I should be careful not to hurt them with the lawn mower.

"People are fragile too," Charlie said quietly. "We should think before we mow through their hearts like a threshing machine."

Well, today was one of those days where Charlie had taken Kate up on her offer to come to Open Door anytime he needed to sit and think about things.

He needed to think about what Phil had told him the night Jake had brought him home. Shortly after Charlie and Jake's conversation about girls, while drinking some good coffee, and Jake had left, Phil came out of the bedroom. Still weaving, still drunk, he sat Charlie down, looked him straight in the eye, and said, "*Charlie, you're adopted.*"

Nothing more, nothing less—three words, '*Charlie, you're adopted.*'

Kate saw Charlie's every move when he came to Open Door that day. She watched him carefully as he walked around the premises. She watched his facial expressions. She wanted desperately to hear what he was saying aloud as he walked. She saw him touch the bleeding hearts tenderly. She saw him sit on the bench where the squirrels ran freely from bird feeder to birdbath. She held herself back from running to him. There was so much she wanted to say to him. So much she understood. She had warned herself long ago about impulsive behavior. She had to wait. She held her heart back and listened to her head.

As he rode his bike away from Open Door, she paced back and forth from her personal quarters to her kitchen, asking herself over and over, "How can I help you, Charlie? How can I help you understand that sometimes life just happens and we have to deal with it the best way we know how?"

Jake was far from her mind. She had bigger fish to fry.

Charlie had to find Jake. He had to tell him, man to man. He wanted to be told everything would be all right. He needed a good, solid man's advice.

He found Jake down by the lake, just looking out on the horizon, and for a short second, Charlie thought he shouldn't disturb him. It looked like he was having a private moment all to himself. But Jake turned and saw Charlie just as he was getting ready to ride away on his bike.

"Charlie!" Jake shouted. "Come on down here and enjoy the lake with me for a spell."

Charlie thought it funny that Jake was saying words like *spell*.

"Seems like we're rubbin' off on you, Mr. Jake," Charlie said.

"How do you mean?" Jake questioned.

"You're pickin' up our kind of language and all," Charlie began, looking a little nervous.

Jake smiled and asked, "What's on your mind, Charlie?"

Charlie shuffled his feet.

"Wanna know more about girls?" Jake asked.

"No, I want to tell 'ya somethin'," Charlie replied.

"I'm listenin'," Jake said. "Let's sit."

Both Charlie and Jake walked to the beach chairs and sat down.

"After you left that night you brought Phil home, he came out to the livin' room and told me somethin'," Charlie began.

Jake gave him a questioning look.

It was then Charlie told Jake the whole story.

Jake sat there for a good long while after Charlie left. Too deep. That was all he could think of. Too deep. He felt badly for Charlie, but he knew himself better than anyone else. He couldn't handle this. He felt a stronghold on his heart. It was as if every fiber in his being was saying, "Get out. Get out now."

He had done one good thing, though. He felt he had told Charlie what he wanted to hear, even though he didn't believe it himself. He had looked Charlie straight in the eye and said, "*Everything's goin' to be all right, Charlie. Everything's goin' to be all right.*"

He thought that was what Charlie wanted to hear—what he needed to hear—so he had said it. Sometimes young boys just needed to be told a little white lie. Was there even a chance of everything turning out all right?

When all the thinking was done, it wasn't Kate Charlie ran to; it was Sarah.

"Please don't offer me sweet tea," was the first thing he said to her.

"What's wrong, Charlie?" Sarah asked.

He said nothing. His look said it all.

"Let's walk," Sarah said as she took his arm.

"Where are we goin'?" Charlie asked.

"My secret place," she answered.

"It seems this town is full of secrets I've known nothing about all my life," Charlie mumbled.

They walked in silence until they reached a small alcove beyond Open Door.

"This is my lovely little place," she began. "No one knows about this place but me. It's my respite."

"Your what?" Charlie questioned.

"My respite, my quiet place, where I come to think," Sarah replied.

She sat down on the ground and patted the space next to her for Charlie to join her.

"Don't you go tellin' anybody about this place." She warned him, pointing her finger at him.

Charlie looked at her and smiled. "I won't," he answered.

"I don't share this place with anybody. You're the first," she said.

They sat in silence for a while.

"That's what this place does to you," she began. "It makes you sit still and not say anything," she concluded.

Charlie found his voice. "I came to you because you're fifteen years old like me."

Sarah did not rush him into talking. She looked at him, straight through him, but this time, it didn't creep him out like it had in other times. In fact, he welcomed it. He knew he had her undivided attention.

"Phil's not my real dad," Charlie blurted out.

"What do you mean by 'real' dad?" she questioned.

"You know, he wasn't responsible for my birth," Charlie answered.

"Are you saying you're adopted?" she asked.

Charlie nodded.

"Wouldn't that bother you if you were me?" Charlie asked after a short silence.

"No," she answered. "It wouldn't bother me at all. You know *adopted* is not a bad word, Charlie," she concluded. "You can say the word."

"It's just that I should have known the truth about myself long before now!" Charlie exclaimed.

"Lots of things happened to you *before now*," Sarah answered.

"You mean, my mom dyin' and all and Phil becomin' the town drunk?" Charlie asked.

"Yes," she said. "Life can take an unexpected turn, and all the best intentions in the world go out the window. I think that's what happened with Phil. He just didn't know how to deal with it after your mom died."

"Maybe," Charlie acquiesced.

"You want to know what I believe, Charlie?" she asked.

"That's why I came to you," Charlie answered.

Sarah took a deep breath. "I believe that anyone can give birth to a child, but it takes a very special person to *choose* a child, bring that child into their home, and raise that child as their own," she said simply and clearly.

"Okay, so they chose me, but..." Charlie began.

"But life threw you a curve," Sarah began. "You have to remember that life also threw Phil a curve," she concluded.

Charlie thought for a moment and had to admit that was true. Why else would he have become a drunk? Shoot, maybe he himself would have become one if he had been older.

Charlie said, "Phil stopped raising me when Mom died."

Sarah nodded in agreement.

Charlie shuffled his feet yet again. "Trudy tried to fill the empty spaces," he said.

"But it wasn't the same," Sarah concluded his sentence.

Charlie told Sarah the whole story—the night Phil told him and *how* he was told.

She did not blink an eye; she kept staring through him. "Charlie, there's lots of second chances we're given in life. Can you look at this new revelation in your life as being just that, a second chance?"

"How so?" he questioned. For the life of him, he couldn't figure out where she was going with this second chance stuff.

"Truth has a tendency to make us move—either forward or backward. Our choice," Sarah said.

She looked up at the sky and said, "You know, someone once said, 'With the devil chasing you from behind and an angel to lead you on, you have got to go somewhere.'"

"Which direction do 'ya think I'm goin' to go?" he asked Sarah.

"Only you can decide that, Charlie," she answered. "But one thing I do know, with the second chances we're fortunate to be given in this life, something good can come out of all this—something even better than you could ever imagine," Sarah said.

Charlie shrugged.

"One day, Phil will realize he has to make things right with you. It's then you'll be called upon to forgive him," Sarah said.

After some thought, Sarah looked out into the distance and asked Charlie, "Can you remember anything at all—something to hold on to that could help you think of Phil in a good way until that day of forgiving comes?"

Charlie doubted that the day of forgiveness would ever come, but he tried hard to remember something, anything. His whole identity was hanging on by a thread at that moment. What did he have to lose?

"I do remember something," Charlie said, not sure of how to explain it to Sarah.

"I remember how my mom laughed and clapped her hands when Phil would come home from work. We would be anxiously awaiting his car coming into the driveway. Phil would come into the house, pick me up, twirl me around, and give me a strong hug before turning to her and doing the same thing. It's funny I just remembered that sittin' here with you," Charlie whispered.

Again, Sarah gave him a look that pierced straight through his heart. "Then that's what you hold on to, Charlie. You hold it tight. You remember that anticipation you had, standing by that window with your mom. You remember the laughter and your dad's hug. You hold on to those memories and don't let them go. Store up the good thoughts now so you'll be able to forgive later."

"Do you really think that day will come?" Charlie asked hopefully.

Sarah smiled and said, "Oh yes, I do believe that, Charlie."

"Why? Why do you believe that? What makes you believe that? How do you hold on to that?" Charlie dared to ask all three questions at once without taking a breath.

"Faith, Charlie, my faith helps me believe in things not yet seen," she answered.

Charlie felt a peacefulness come to his mind. It seemed a long distance from his mind to his heart that he would have to walk, but he was willing to give it a try.

Charlie looked at Sarah for a long time before he did what he had seen Jake do with Kate many times. Without saying a word, he took her hand, raised it to his lips, and kissed it.

He smiled as he thought, *Just like Jake.*

Charlie did eventually go to Open Door, but it wasn't to talk about his now-known secret; it was to cut Kate's grass.

Kate wanted desperately to initiate a conversation with him. She wanted to hear his thoughts about his adoption. She wanted to know what she should do next, what she should say, if anything. She wanted to know how she could help him.

So many parts to this equation, she thought, *especially what had happened four years after the adoption when his quiet, cozy world turned rancid. Ugly word, rancid,* she thought, *ugly circumstances deserved ugly descriptions.*

Charlie was sitting on the bench in the flower garden after mowing the grass when Kate appeared with two glasses of sweet tea.

"Why do all you females like to drink so much sweet tea? Is it some kind of miracle drink for 'ya?" Charlie asked.

Laughing, Kate answered, "No, Charlie, not a miracle drink, but chamomile works wonders, especially at night."

"Huh?" Charlie asked.

"Chamomile is a soothing tea," Kate said, handing him one of the glasses. "Not to worry, this isn't chamomile—that stuff helps you sleep."

He took it, trying not to roll his eyes.

"It's probably a lot better for 'ya too, better than beer." Charlie admitted.

He was thirsty after mowing Kate's grass. That's how he always rationalized drinking sweet tea. One day, he was goin' to have to tell her he liked lemonade better.

Charlie took a sip of his drink and asked, "You ever been through somethin' in your life that was gut-wrenchin', Miss Kate?" he asked.

"Yes, I have, Charlie," she answered.

"Me too," Charlie confessed.

Kate looked at him, expecting the door to open for the conversation Trudy had warned her would come just a few days ago.

"It was gut-wrenchin' when my mom died. Now it's gut-wrenchin' just livin' with Phil. You know he's a drunk, don't you? I mean everybody else in town knows, so I just figured you do too," Charlie said.

Kate nodded.

"Sarah said I should try to hold on to somethin' good I remember about Phil so when the time of forgivin' comes, it would be easier," Charlie said.

"Are you able to do that?" Kate asked.

"I'm sure tryin', Miss Kate," Charlie answered.

Charlie looked out over the lake and said, "There's a storm comin'."

He looked at Miss Kate and asked, "You ever had storms in your life?"

"More than a few, Charlie," she answered.

"I'm not talkin' 'bout the weather kind. I'm talkin' 'bout the heartbreak kind," Charlie said, looking down at his hands. "You ever had storms like that?"

Kate smiled, resisting the urge to tell him her whole story. But she knew you didn't lay stories like hers on young shoulders like his. Some stories were for adults only. So instead, she answered, "Yes, Charlie, I've had the heartbreak kind of storms in my life."

"Is that why you sit out here at night, sometimes in the middle of those bleedin' hearts, and cry?" Charlie asked.

"You've seen me here?"

"Oh yeah, sometimes when I can't sleep, I go ridin' my bike, and I see 'ya up here," he answered.

"I see," Kate replied, promising herself she would not dare let one tear fall from her eyes because she knew she would not be able to stop. And that was the last thing Charlie needed right now—an all-out bawlin' woman.

"Would it be okay if some night you're out here an' all—" He stumbled over his words. "Would it be all right if I came up here and cried with you?"

This time, she wrapped her arms around Charlie and hugged him tight. "I think that would be all right, Charlie. I think that would be just fine."

Looking up at the clouds forming rapidly in the sky, he pulled away from Kate slowly and said, "I better get home before the rain hits. It looks like it's goin' to be a whopper!"

He walked to his bike, turned, and said, "I'm real good at keepin' secrets, Miss Kate, if you ever want to tell me about your gut-wrenchin' times."

With those parting words, he jumped on his bike and pedaled quickly down the road.

"Oh, Charlie," she whispered as she watched him ride away. "I want so much to help piece your heart's questions back together. Secrets need to come out in the open sooner or later. God help me when mine does."

Kate looked at the sky before going inside. A storm was coming.

"See him safely home, Lord, before this 'whopper' hits," she whispered.

Jake had been distancing himself from Kate the past few days. It was easier than he thought it would be. She seemed preoccupied with Charlie. It was like her focus had suddenly shifted, and he wasn't even part of the equation anymore. He didn't quite like this turn of events either. It seemed he never could be quite pleased with anything in his life. All he knew was that he was definitely going back to the city.

Kate frightened him and threatened his way of life. He knew he would have to change if he let her get to him. He didn't like change, and he especially didn't want a woman to be the cause of a change in his life. If he was going to change for anybody or anything, it was going to be on his terms—damn it—not because of a woman who thought she knew how he ticked, and he began to think that maybe she did. Not good.

She understands me, he thought. He wasn't used to that. No woman had ever been like her, and he had known a lot of women in his lifetime. He thought it just might scare her off if he shared some of his stories about his past, but it didn't. She confused him.

She was not at Open Door when he decided to pack his things. It was better that way. He had determined in his own mind that no woman could love him the way he was; no woman would be able to put up with him, especially her type of woman. There were times he couldn't put up with himself.

He had done a lot of things in his life to get to the top of that infamous corporate ladder, and he harbored the guilt to prove it plus a few scars, some deeper than others. That guilt had become a second nature to him. That's what had led him to this little tourist town in the first place. He had hoped he could lay all the 'what ifs' and 'if only's' by the side of the road and never look back. He had not counted on the fact that he would meet a true lady, a woman that literally knocked his socks off.

"I will not allow myself to get all wrapped up in you, Kate. I simply refuse to let that happen," he said as he began throwing clothes into a suitcase.

He had run from a city that was smothering him and entered a village that freed him to breathe. And he was breathing just fine until he met a woman he could not blast out of his mind, so he would do what he had always done in his past—he would run.

"Yes, Trudy, these boots are made for runnin'," he said out loud.

He had one stop to make before leaving Brooksport Village. He had to see Trudy, and he knew where to find her around this time of day. She always told him, "*I need my caffeine blast around three o'clock. So I head on down to the coffeehouse and listen to Chip rehearse before the crowds start comin' in.*"

Yes, one stop. He could not leave without saying goodbye to his first newfound friend he had met that first day he walked down these village streets—Trudy. He didn't count Phil a friend; he was a drinking buddy. Shoot, Phil probably didn't remember half of their conversations anyway. He would miss Charlie, though. He was a good kid. He'd been dealt a bad hand.

As he got in his car, he was also sorry he would never know why Trudy liked purple so much. It just wasn't meant to be.

Jake walked into the coffee shop. Sure enough, Trudy was sitting there with her triple latte "spooning" over Chip as he rehearsed.

"I didn't know I had competition," he said to her, walking to her table.

She looked up. "Hey, cowboy, come join me."

"I believe that was the first thing you said to me the first day I set eyes on you, Trudy."

"Not quite," Trudy replied. "I said um, um, um." She laughed.

"Yes, you did," Jake said, sitting down beside her.

"Then I talked about your hat, boots, and sad eyes." Trudy looked at him sideways.

"I think that is when I fell in love with you, my lovely," Jake replied.

"Oh, and all this time, I thought it was me tousling your hair when I got up to leave," Trudy exclaimed.

Jake laughed.

Trudy looked at him questioningly. "Don't laugh so loud, Jake, it only tells me you're tryin' to hide somethin'," Trudy said.

He looked at her, saying nothing.

Finally, she asked, "Are you tryin' to hide somethin', Jake? What are you up to? When you're troubled about something, you laugh— too loud—it's called comic relief."

"I'm leaving, Trudy. I came to say goodbye." Jake confessed.

"I see," she replied.

"That's all you have to say?" Jake asked.

"Yep," she said.

"I thought you'd have more to say than that," Jake exclaimed.

"Nope," she replied, giving Chip a thumbs-up sign, signaling she loved his newly written song.

"Well, I guess that's it," Jake said. "We'll just be leavin' it at this."

"Yep," Trudy said, looking him straight in the eyes.

Jake got up to leave but Trudy's voice stopped him at the door.

"I do have somethin' to say to you, cowboy. You may as well admit it—you've got a sweet tooth in this town for somethin' more than Belle's doughnuts. You go ahead and go, but the sooner you face one thing, the better off you're goin' to be."

Jake turned to Trudy. "And exactly what is that one thing?" he mimicked.

Undaunted, Trudy said plain and simple, "You can't run away from love forever. It'll always find you."

With that last tidbit of knowledge from Trudy, Jake walked out of the coffee shop his mind intent upon leaving Brooksport Village.

Trudy watched him go, and Chip kept strumming his guitar.

Trudy looked at Chip and said, "Yep, he's afraid of somethin', and I think I know what it is. Maybe it's time for him to hitch up that horse of his, take off his saddle, and hang his hat on the hat rack. Time to put away his gun and stop fightin'."

Chip smiled and replied, "Think I could write a song about that cowboy, Trudy."

With a big sigh, she blew Chip a kiss and walked toward the door. As she left the coffee house, she turned to see Jake's car heading out of town.

"Looks like I was right, eh, Jake? You're afraid. You're very afraid." She walked a short distance before looking back at his car as it began to disappear. "What did you expect me to say? I mean, exactly? Did you expect a standing ovation? You made it simple. You run, I say, 'Yep.'"

Trudy looked up at the sky. The wind was picking up. The phone was ringing as she entered the salon.

"Hello, this is Trudy," she answered.

"Trudy, I'm so sorry, but I'm canceling my appointment today," the client began. "They're predicting a storm coming through, and I'm going to hunker down."

Trudy assured her it was fine and that she could see her tomorrow.

When Trudy looked out at the sky again, she thought it best to go home too. Hearing the first roll of thunder, she thought to herself that something didn't seem right. The sky looked ominous. She thought of Buddy. Yep, that cat of hers was going to freak out for sure. She began to walk swiftly to her house.

"Buddy, baby, I'm on my way. Don't be afraid. Mommy's on her way," she said, picking her pace up.

When she arrived home, she found Buddy hiding under the bed. Hearing Trudy's voice, he slinked into her arms. She carried him into the living room, turned on the TV to get the weather report, and the two of them settled in for a long evening of thunder and lightning.

Kate began closing the windows throughout her house. She stopped in disbelief when she opened the door to Jake's room. It wasn't the already closed windows that caught her unaware; it was the open closet door with no clothes hanging inside that made her stop midstride.

She walked to the dresser and opened each drawer, finding them all empty. She walked to a nearby chair and sat down. All she could do was stare at the emptiness around her. She heard that old familiar sound—like a wounded animal. Her heart was preparing itself for another break.

She thought her heart had far too many scars to ever break again, but she was wrong. After everything she had lost in her lifetime, she thought she was now immune to any more hurt. But again, she was wrong. Hurt seemed to follow her, find her, and push her into those corners she tried so hard to avoid. The silence around her shouted what Jake could not whisper, "Goodbye."

He was gone. She felt that the time was drawing near, but like this? Without a word. Gone. It was at that moment she heard the first heavy drops of rain. The clouds had burst.

There was, indeed, a storm coming, and it was the kind of storm that you didn't want to have fun jumping in puddles with your boots on—like when you were a kid. Oh no, it was a storm of great magnitude. The kind that you better know when it's time to run for shelter. The kind that wreaks havoc. The kind that if you don't have a basement to cower in, you better find a place without a lot of windows. Oh yes, a storm was coming. A storm of the worst kind.

"In prayer you encounter God in the soft breeze, in the distress and joy of your neighbor and in the loneliness of our own heart." (Henri Nouwen)

37

Phil loved storms. He had loved them since he was a toddler. He never ran from them; he ran toward them. He would put on his little boots, run from his doorway right into the middle of the road, and wait for the first puddle to appear. Lightning thrilled him, and thunder never scared him. He often thought he should have been one of those "storm chasers," but when Iris died, he was busy trying to raise a toddler on his own. The years after Iris's death had gone by so quickly, and Charlie would be off to his own future before he knew it. But Phil would still be sitting here in the same living room, putting his blender to good use, making margaritas, and waiting for the next storm.

He walked to the closet. He always walked to that particular closet, even after all these years, because that was where the apron was. It was the one thing of Iris's that he could never give away—the apron she used to wear, the one with all those yellow irises.

"Your favorite flower," Phil whispered as he gently touched the apron.

Oh, how she loved that apron. Phil remembered.

"I wear it when I bake Charlie's favorite cookies," she would say.

"You wear it every time you set foot in the kitchen," Phil would reply with a smile.

She would laugh and continue baking. She loved to bake.

Phil looked at the apron and touched it again. Iris had always been so delicate herself. He never wanted to hurt her. He treated her with kid gloves until one day she exclaimed, "I'm not a porcupine, you know! Neither am I a china doll! Please handle me as the woman I am who is in love with the man of my heart!"

Phil smiled at the memory. Their lovemaking was never quite the same after that but still ever so gentle.

"I wonder what you would think of me today, my dear Iris?" Phil asked himself.

He had placed that apron on a hook in the closet the day of her funeral and never moved it again. He visited it often. Today's visit found him remembering the question he had asked himself all those years ago. *How do you explain to a four-year-old his mommy is gone?*

His heart broke all over again as he remembered.

"Where's Mommy, Daddy? And why are you crying?" Charlie had asked.

"Mommy's gone, son, that's why I'm crying," Phil had answered.

"Gone where? She wouldn't go anywhere without us, Daddy," Charlie had exclaimed.

Charlie had looked so innocent, so troubled, and so sad when he added, "Did we leave her at that place where all those stones were and those little flags were flyin'?"

Cemetery did not seem a word for such a young mind.

"Yes, son," Phil could barely say.

Charlie had run to his room and grabbed his coat; he had run to the front door, turned around, and said, "We better go get her, Daddy! It's getting cold out there!"

That's when Trudy had appeared at their door with those sugar doughnuts on a plate. Charlie saw the doughnuts and, as any typical four-year-old would do, suddenly forgot how cold it was getting. That had been the night Phil had sworn Trudy to silence about the adoption. He wanted to tell Charlie in his own way.

Where, indeed, had the years gone? He thought back on all the mistakes he had made, all the poor choices he had made, and how those choices had dragged Charlie right through the dirt with him. But Charlie hadn't minded getting dirty. At least, he didn't say so anyway.

Phil shrugged, placed the apron back on the hook in the closet, closed its door, and walked to the kitchen to find the blender, Iris's memory still clutching at his heart. He was going to sit in his favorite chair and wait for the impending storm. He was going to forget his failures. He was going to forget his grief one more time. He was going to relax. He was going to get drunk.

"More poor decisions." He admitted. "Oh well, whatever," he concluded.

Phil looked at the sink full of dirty dishes and the disarray of the kitchen. He decided it would take too long to mix up those margaritas. He pulled a near empty bottle of vodka from the cabinet, searched for a full bottle, found it, and carried both of them back into the living room.

"Don't need a glass," he mumbled to himself as he settled himself in his easy chair. He took a swig straight from the bottle and looked out the window. The storm was coming in fast. He wondered where Charlie was. He did worry about him. He admitted he hadn't been much of a father since Iris died. Still, Charlie was his son, and he loved him.

"Charlie knows that." He tried to convince himself. He took another swig of vodka.

"I don't have to tell him that I love him every day of his life," he concluded. After a few more swallows of vodka, he added, "I don't care what Trudy keeps tellin' me—she says, '*That boy needs to be told that you love him every once in a while.*'" He mimicked Trudy.

Phil finished the near empty bottle of vodka and opened the new one when the first flash of lightning hit.

"Damn!" he shouted as he watched the bolt play across the ground and thunder shook the house.

"This ain't no normal lightning!" he exclaimed.

Phil jumped from his chair, realizing that not only was the lightning different, the storm was also different. This was no run-of-the-mill storm. This was the mother of all storms. Mere seconds passed before the next streak of lightning seemed to hit the house. The thunder and wind were not far behind. Phil realized that the wind was something he better run *from* and not *to*.

He heard a roar that sounded like a train coming right at him. He grabbed his vodka and ran across the room just as a tree came crashing through his living room window, striking the chair where he had been sitting only seconds ago.

"Damn!" he yelled. He stood for only a moment before running to the only place he could find that had no windows. The closet. The closet that held the memory. The closet that would become his refuge in the storm. He cowered there on the floor, doubled over in embryonic shape.

All he could hear was the roaring thunder, the shattering of glass, and the wind whipping around the very foundation of his house.

"I'm goin' to die in this closet!" he shouted above the storm.

The wind continued to hammer the house unmercifully, and once again, Phil thought of Charlie.

"My son's in this rain! I should be protecting him! He's in this storm somewhere out there!" Phil kept saying over and over. Yet, fear kept him in the closet. He knew he would be blown away if he dared to leave.

Phil shook his head in disbelief at all the chaos going on around him outside the closet. He heard another loud clap of thunder and a window crashing inside his house. He closed his eyes. Still crouching, he shouted, "Oh, God! I don't want to die! I haven't talked to you in a long time! I've been so mad at you! But I need your help right now! Right this minute! Please say you can hear me!"

It was in that instant something fell from above. It was a soft thing that seemed to flutter down from the ceiling. Even in the worst of the storm, it seemed as if it floated in slow motion. It fell right into his hands. He opened his eyes. The apron lay soft and still there in his palms.

He began to cry, clutching the apron close to his face. The tears ran rampant and fast. Just like the storm, this was no ordinary cry. Phil was weeping. His entire body shook from the sobs that came from the inner core of his body. His Iris was gone. He let his grief flow. His tears had been held captive by the alcohol. Now it was as if a dam had burst, and the tears were rolling freely, joining the storm.

"I'm sorry," he kept saying over and over as the wind and rain increased its strength.

"I've messed up! Oh, God, forgive me! Help me to do better! Help me to be a dad, a real dad! His tears seemed to mingle with the rain that was now seeping its way under the door frame of the closet.

"My heart was with this woman," he cried as he held the apron close to his chest.

"I need you to take my heart, Lord! I need you to come into this closet and pluck me out of here!"

He heard another crash.

"Forgive the choices I have made! Help me make it through this hell!"

Phil sobbed and sobbed in that closet all throughout the storm. His house seemed to be falling down around him. Another tree crashed through the roof of his living room, blocking the closet door.

And then a sudden peace enveloped Phil. He knew he was trapped. The door could not be opened from the inside, but the wind had stopped as well as the thunder. He wasn't scared anymore. With tears still streaming down his face, he continued to hold the apron with a fierce determination that if God did allow him to survive this, he would do better. He would be a father. He would be a neighbor. He would be more than a survivor. He would be the person he was meant to be. He would be the man Iris always believed he was.

Again he thought of Charlie.

And then he almost laughed aloud when he thought, *Just look at me. I'm a mess. Perhaps I was never meant to be a storm chaser after all.*

Phil was a mess, all right, but it was the kind of mess God always liked to clean up. And clean up he would…God looked forward to messes like this.

Charlie did not make it home before the storm hit. He was pedaling his bike as fast as he could. Crabby's Bar was as far as he got.

"Charlie!" Leon cried from the front door of the bar. "Come in here! You're not goin' to make it home!"

Charlie didn't have to think twice.

"Bring your bike in here too!" Leon commanded.

Again, Charlie didn't even think of protesting.

Once inside, Charlie went to a corner, sat down, and looked around.

Some tourists had already gathered to wait out the storm. They were huddled in their own little groups.

Leon went over and joined Charlie at the corner table.

"Thanks, Leon," Charlie managed to say.

"Hey, kid, no problem. Can I get you anything?"

"How about a beer?"

Leon looked at him, aghast.

"Just kiddin' ya, Leon," Charlie said. "Just kiddin' ya."

A bolt of lightning lit up the sky that was soon followed by a thunderous roll.

One of the women screamed as her husband placed his arm around her.

"Everybody, get away from the windows!" Leon bellowed.

They did not have to be persuaded.

It was then that Charlie had a lot of company in his little corner of the world. They all huddled there, forming a human fence around this special fifteen-year-old. And Charlie had never felt so loved, except for his memory of a woman named Iris who always made him his favorite cookies, a woman that had truly been his mom...

No one could believe the devastation when it all ended. People began to come out of the places where they had taken shelter. They began looking for friends and relatives that had not been able to be together during what people were now calling a tornado. Power was out. Only one place was lit up like a neon sign, Open Door. People heard the hum of the generator and began walking through the debris to get to the one place that had electricity. They followed the light.

Charlie ran in another direction. He ran straight to his house. He couldn't believe what he saw when he got there. The house was almost completely destroyed. One tree had fallen through the living room window, another through the roof, blocking the closet door.

He charged through the house, jumping hurdles of debris, shouting, "Dad! Are you in here?"

Charlie heard a feeble knocking from the closet door and ran over to it. "Dad?"

Phil did not answer at first. He was overwhelmed with relief and happy tears. Charlie was okay.

"Dad?" Charlie questioned again, holding his breath.

"Did you just call me Dad?" Phil questioned in a low, loving voice.

"Dad?" Charlie asked again while standing outside the blocked door. He was wondering if it was, indeed, Phil. The voice seemed too tender.

"Yes, it's me, Charlie. Are you okay? Do you have any broken bones or anything?" Phil asked.

Charlie nearly collapsed with relief. "I'm okay, Dad. How about you?"

"Oh, I'm all crunched up in here. I think my arm's broken, but that's all," Phil answered.

"I'll get help!" Charlie shouted. "We'll get 'ya outta there, Dad, don't worry! I'll be back with help!"

Charlie brought help, dozens of people—men, women, children, tourists, residents, and one man with a chainsaw. They all came to free Phil from that closet. They cut and lifted the trunk of that tree, and when they opened the door, Phil walked out.

Charlie knew in an instant that something had changed. He saw it in Phil's eyes. His left arm was hanging limply by his side. His right hand held not a drink but an apron.

Charlie caught Phil's eyes pleading for forgiveness. There comes a time you just don't need words. A look says it all. It was then that Charlie ran to his dad and found the arms he had wanted for so long enfold him and hold him tight—well, at least one arm. The other hung limply by Phil's side. But that one arm was enough. Indeed, Sarah had been right. The time for forgiveness had come.

38

Jake was driving hard and fast. He was driving away from Brooksport Village and all it had to offer. He had made up his mind that not only the town would be gone from his mind but also the smile of a woman he couldn't handle. His life would be simple again. He wouldn't have to try to figure himself out like she kept saying he had to do. He kept trying to convince himself he wasn't a mess, although she said he was. What made her think she was so smart, anyway?

He sighed when he finally pulled into his driveway and walked through the door.

"Still wish I had a dog," he confessed to the empty space.

Tomorrow he would go back to his office to see Sandra, who would ask him a million questions about where he had been, and lead his company into more money and a secure financial future. That's what he was always meant to do. Get more. Spend more. Be more. He didn't have time for picnics with cheese and wine. He didn't want Kate's eyes searing through his brain like a laser—as Charlie had stated so perfectly—making him wonder if maybe she was right. He was done. He was moving on, maybe back to his redheads, although Sandra would not like that in the least. She would most assuredly start charging him for her psychological advice, although she loved to give it.

And then he sat down, put his feet—boots and all—on top of the coffee table, popped a can of beer, and turned on the TV. That was when he learned of the storm that had hit Brooksport Village.

He didn't have to think twice. He was out the door, keys in hand, in less than a minute. No need to pack. He hadn't unpacked! He was on his way back, as if he had never left. He backed his car out of the driveway and headed back to Brooksport Village faster than when he had left that small village in the dust—or so he thought.

"Oh my god," was all he could say.

Halfway down the highway, he picked up his cell phone and called Butch.

As usual, Butch answered on the first ring, "Hey, buddy, you back?"

"I was for about ten minutes. Butch, I need you to get every available truck we have and get down to Brooksport Village. They need us," Jake exclaimed.

"Is this the same town you wanted all those balloons sent to?" Butch asked.

"Yes, same town, different emergency," Jake replied.

"What's happened?" Butch asked.

"A storm, Butch—in my mind, from the news reports, I believe it was a tornado touchdown. Get everybody that we can gather to get down there!" Jake almost shouted.

"You got it, Jake," Butch replied.

With that, Jake put the gas pedal to the floor and headed back to Brooksport Village on a wing and a prayer, continuing to say, "Oh God, oh God, please."

He didn't know what else to pray; he had not prayed for years. He couldn't help but wonder, would God even know who was praying to him? Would God hear his plea? Would God answer the prayer he didn't know how to pray? Could he even bring himself to say the words, "Is she still alive?"

Thoughts kept bombarding Jake's mind as he drove back to Brooksport Village.

"Trouble, trouble, trouble! From the first time I saw you, I knew you were different." He hit the steering wheel, demanding his car to go faster. "And you aren't even a redhead," he exclaimed.

Yes, Kate was different from any redhead he had tangled with. She had a charm all her own—not that the redheads didn't, but Kate had a *following*. Everybody gravitated to her. She lit up a room and didn't know it. That was it, she was humble.

His car sped faster toward Brooksport Village.

"Don't need a collision here." He tried to calm himself, slow the car down. "She's caused enough collisions in my mind, that's for sure." Jake continued to argue with himself.

Jake thought he had been one of the unfortunate men who had a defective gene—you know the kind, a man that leaves a wake of hurt because he never seemed to say the right thing or do what those special women expected him to do. He didn't know why he could never quite measure up. It seemed every woman he walked away from, and even those who walked away from him, always ended up in therapy.

"This one I will not hurt. I will not wound her." He tried convincing himself.

Too many had been wounded already. He had been determined to stay away from this one. His head finally got ahead of his heart with Kate. He got out in time, or had he? Why was he rushing back to Brooksport Village if he didn't care?

No! Kate needed something more than he could ever give her, and he would spend the rest of his life trying to convince himself of that fact if he had to.

"It's everybody in that town I'm rushing back to. They need me. All of them, not just Kate. I care about the people there, especially that woman in purple." He smiled as he thought of Trudy.

"And, Charlie," he said almost in a whisper.

His mind wandered back to the time Kate told him about her baby.

"Oh my god!" he exclaimed. "I wonder if Kate has thought—" Jake almost ran off the road as he dared to say his thoughts out loud. "I wonder if Kate has thought—the time frame is right, the age is right—could Charlie be that baby? Could Charlie be her son?"

Jake's mind continued to run rampant.

He smacked the steering wheel again and again.

He thought he had made his great escape. He had actually made it out of that village town without looking back. Without stopping for gas. Without looking for a rest stop. He had fled—fast and furious.

Now here he was, going back to Brooksport Village. That storm had ripped through their village. It was a storm that took no prisoners, destroying whatever was in its path. News reports kept analyzing wind patterns—tornado or severe crosswinds?

"Dear God, let her be okay," Jake whispered. He looked startled. "Did I just pray again?" he questioned himself.

He looked directly at himself in the rearview mirror. His eyes looked worried. "What was it Trudy had said about his eyes?" he questioned again. "*They're sad, cowboy, it's your sad eyes.*"

That's what she had said. Jake had to admit it. His life had been pretty sad. He wasn't going to make Kate's eyes sad too. He wouldn't do that to her. He could not break her spirit. He would not. His track record had not been good. He doled out hurt wherever he went.

"Did you hear that prayer, God?" Jake almost pleaded.

"Of course, you didn't. Why would you want to listen to me, anyway?"

The last memory Jake had of God was when he was so angry with the Almighty one he questioned his existence.

"Perhaps I'm still angry," Jake said. "Why else am I so mixed up in my head about everything? And why in the world would God bring him face-to-face with a woman like Kate and not allow him to really have her?"

Jake was silent then, watching the miles add up as he kept driving.

"Maybe I have it all backwards," Jake said. "Maybe God's angry with me."

With that, Jake put the pedal to the floor, and not even a speeding bullet could stop him. It took a storm to make him turn around and go back to Brooksport Village.

Little did Jake realize that another storm had arrived. It came as a gentle breeze. It announced its arrival with his whispered prayers. God heard it all.

And the wind began to blow against the walls he had built around his heart so very long ago…he was on his very own trip to his very own personal Jericho.

State police allowed Jake entrance into Brooksport Village through the back roads due to his corporation sending trucks to help clear age-old trees from roadways and intersections. The trucks he had previously had Butch send to the village were entering now directly behind him. To the townspeople, it looked like a convoy—a very welcomed convoy.

The devastation made Jake's eyes widen. Roads were closed, power was out, and people were walking the streets, shaking their heads in disbelief. He wanted every building to still be standing. He saw roofs blown off and windows shattered. The little town he had come to know so well still stood—as a skeleton, but it had survived.

He heard chainsaws being revved up and saw a community get united. He had come into a patriotic town when he first arrived that Memorial Day, and now he was witnessing a righteous town— neighbor helping neighbor, tourists picking up debris, children with plastic bags picking up sticks. His eyes were beginning to sting from tears that were threatening. He had to admit that his heart was sinking into the deep—that scary place, that uncomfortable place he never could quite grasp. But this scene had grabbed a hold of him, and he couldn't swim out of it. And much to his dismay, he didn't want to.

Trudy saw him first. She went running up to him and cried, "Oh, Jake, can you believe this? I'm so glad to see you! You sure left a storm in your wake, literally, when you left!"

Jake put his arm around Trudy, and they began to walk up the street. "Tell me about the damage, Trudy."

"Belle's Bakery lost part of its roof. A tree fell right in the front doorway of my salon. Stumble In lost some windows, and Crabby's Bar—well, Crabby's—has to be rebuilt."

"What about Open Door, Trudy?" Jake almost trembled as he asked the question.

Trudy looked at Jake and replied, "You won't believe this, Jake." Jake's heart sank.

Trudy saw Jake turn pale and quickly said, "Oh no, Jake! Kate is okay! In fact, what you won't believe is that the storm didn't even touch her bed and breakfast! It's almost as if God ordained that house to keep standing, straight and tall. But her flowers—all those beautiful plants and flowers were crushed—a tree missed the house but took out the flowers."

Relieved, Jake asked, "Where is Kate now?"

"She's helping Phil," Trudy replied.

"Phil?" Jake questioned.

"Oh, honey, Phil suffered the worst of the storm—except for Crabby's. A tree fell right through his house while he was runnin' for cover!"

"Is Phil okay? Was he hurt? Is he—" Jake couldn't bring himself to complete his question.

Trudy replied, "He's in shock. Has a broken arm, but that's all."

"Take me to Kate," Jake said.

"They're both at Open Door," Trudy said. "Let's go."

Kate saw Trudy and Jake walking toward Open Door. She wanted desperately to run to him. She didn't know exactly what held her back. Was it her pride? Or was it the fact that he never said goodbye? Or was it a complete and utter feeling of rejection? Of betrayal? She didn't know which, maybe all of the above. She did not move. All she could see in her mind's eye was the fact that he had left and never said goodbye.

Both Trudy and Jake approached her.

"How's Phil doing now?" Trudy asked.

"He's doing okay. I just got him settled in one of the rooms upstairs. Charlie is with him," Kate replied.

"How are you doing, Kate?" Jake asked.

"I was the only one that fared well out of this whole ordeal," Kate answered. "That generator you talked me into buying has sure made our lives around here a lot easier."

Jake nodded.

Trudy could not contain herself. "You two drive me crazy! You've got more to talk about than a frickin' generator! You've got unfinished business, for goodness' sake! Now get to talkin'!"

With that, she turned on her heels and began to walk away. She walked a short distance before turning to Jake and said, "I'm goin' back to the salon and tell those people you sent down here how to remove that tree from my salon's front door," Trudy said. "Now I mean it, you two start talkin'!"

She walked a few more steps away from them and shouted back to Jake, "I thank you for sendin' 'em!"

Jake smiled and shouted back, "You do that, Trudy. Go down there and tell them how to do their job! And you're welcome!"

With the wave of her hand, her back still to those two, she began walking back to the salon, shaking her head as she went.

"I'm glad you're okay, Kate," Jake began. "I was worried about you."

"Well, considering what this town just went through, we are all blessed that not more people were hurt. Everyone took shelter, except Phil. He wanted to watch the storm," Kate said.

"And suffered the consequences," Jake replied.

Kate turned to walk into the house, Jake following close behind. They walked through the kitchen to go outside to what was once Kate's flower garden.

"Some consequences for not taking shelter when you should aren't so bad, Jake. But I'll let Phil tell you his story. All I want to tell you is that things are going to be a lot different now between Charlie and Phil."

"Suffering breaks our world. Like a tree struck by lightning—splintered, shaken, denuded—our world is broken by suffering, and we will never be the same again. What will become of us is a mystery." (Nathan Kollar)

They walked out the back door. Some of the trees had literally been uprooted and were lying across the path that led to Kate's flower garden. Jake stopped midstride when he viewed the damage she had suffered.

"I'm so sorry, Kate," he whispered.

"I know, but it's fixable, Jake. There are some things in life that aren't, but this is one of those things that is," Kate said.

Jake looked at her. All he wanted to do was hold her, but he could not find the emotional strength to open his arms. Those emotional limitations of his were kicking in full throttle. He had made a fast getaway, at least, for a few hours. He could make another one, although he wanted to stay. He was so confused.

It was then she stood tiptoe and kissed his cheek. "Let's go inside," she whispered.

She took his hand, and they walked into the kitchen. They could hear the generator humming in the backyard as they walked inside. Trudy's parting words echoed throughout both their minds. *You two have more to talk about than a frickin' generator! You've got unfinished business!*

Kate made a path to the cabinet that held the whisky.

"I have more people coming to help." Jake broke the silence.

"Thank you," Kate replied as she lifted her glass. "A toast—to you and your crew."

They clinked glasses and sat in silence for what seemed hours before Jake spoke.

"I won't be staying," he began. "I'll be goin' as soon as we get the roads cleared."

"I know," Kate said. "Anyone who leaves without saying good-bye never plans to stay if they come back for whatever reasons."

"You deserve some answers." Jake stumbled over his words. "I just don't have them."

Kate merely smiled, patted his hand, and put the whisky back in the cabinet.

She turned and said, "I know you don't have answers. One day you will."

She looked him straight in the eye and continued, "Until then, don't come back."

"I understand," Jake whispered as he got up to leave.

Kate watched him walk out the door, sighed, and went outside once again to look at the mess she had to clean up. Charlie was already there.

"They're strong," he said, looking up at Kate. "Those bleedin' hearts have lost their bloom, but you just wait. They'll bounce back after some tender care."

Without saying a word, Kate joined Charlie, kneeling beside him, trying to salvage what was left.

Charlie was thinking, but didn't dare ask because he thought he had eavesdropped a little when he left his dad upstairs to rest and saw Kate and Jake in the kitchen talking. Still, he questioned in his own mind, *Wonder why Jake didn't kiss Miss Kate's hand today of all days when she needed it most.*

Jake sat on the front porch steps of Open Door for a while before walking into town to join his crew to help with reopening the roads. The cleanup seemed a daunting task, but it would get done, and it would be done right. This town and its people deserved only the best.

As he left, he saw Kate and Charlie both on their knees, working around those bleeding hearts. He saw the closeness the two of them shared, kind of like a mother would have for a son. Again he thought, *Could it be? Could Charlie be her son?*

"Impossible odds set the stage for amazing miracles."
(Author Unknown)

There was never a prettier sight when the town saw the rest of Jake's convoy from New York pull into their little village town. ARBOR INTERNATIONAL—Tree Maintenance, Cleanup, and Restoration took on a brand-new meaning for all who lived in this small town. Once again, Jake had come to the rescue, but this was a far cry from the launch of hundreds of balloons.

Trudy decided that the children must be included in the cleanup. After all, they had suffered loss, too, just like the adults, and most of those young ones were still scared out of their wits. She thought that busy hands would help them forget their fear. She was determined to make them a part of the restoration.

Charlie and Sarah watched as she gathered the children together.

"She's somethin' else, isn't she, Sarah?" Charlie said.

Sarah replied, "Sure is. She understands. She knows. She's got a special gift, gatherin' all those young 'uns together—just like a hen gathers her chicks—and put 'em all to work."

Both Charlie and Sarah watched as Trudy gave the children instructions on what to do. Charlie looked contemplative.

"What are you thinkin', Charlie?" Sarah asked.

"Just wonderin' why Trudy never had a young 'un of her own. She loves 'em so much. Probably somethin' to do with her past," Charlie replied.

"Some people can't have babies of their own," Sarah began. "That's why you're so special, remember?" Sarah smiled, looking at Charlie.

Right then and there, Charlie decided he wanted to hug Sarah, and he did, nearly taking her breath away. Charlie thought that kissing her hand in public was not the right thing to do. That should be saved for more private moments—after serious conversations. Everybody was always hugging in Brooksport Village, they were neighborly like that. Nobody would think it odd, him giving her a hug. No one would ever guess about the feelings Charlie had for Sarah. Only he knew.

But he was wrong; Sarah knew too. That hug was much more than a friendly gesture, and she smiled all the way home.

The town became energized and began to get to work. Everyone pitched in, including the tourists. Trudy took all those young 'uns under her wing. There she was, bigger than life, leading those little ones through the village all the way to the cemetery with little American flags in their hands. There were no trucks or chainsaws in the cemetery; they were safe there from falling debris. She had instructed them that their job was to pick up sticks not much bigger than themselves and to place American flags straight on those graves. She made sure that those little ones were feeling good about helping, and the whole town was touched, watching them out there in that cemetery.

"Children have to be included in all of life, the good, the bad, and the downright ugly," she told the parents.

"This is the spirit of America," she kept telling those little ones. "It's the spirit of America to help each other! And we must always remember with respect the ones who have gone before us!"

And they just kept picking up sticks, placing them in their little plastic bags and sticking those flags in the wet earth. One little girl looked up at Trudy and exclaimed, "God just did a big sneeze, didn't he, Miss Trudy?"

"Yes," Trudy answered. "A really big sneeze."

Those kids helped, those kids cried, and Trudy hugged them all, held them close, and somehow even the children knew the town would survive.

Electrical companies arrived from all over the country. People needing people. People getting to know people. It seemed to Charlie that it was another example of how God turns all things for good for those who love him. And all of the townspeople had sure been loving him a lot lately. No one had been killed in that storm, and that was good.

Jake worked hard. It seemed strange to Charlie that he never once saw Kate and Jake together during the ordeal. He just guessed that Jake didn't have time to kiss anybody's hand; he was too busy.

There was a big sigh when Jake's trucks turned the corner with Jake right behind them. He was gone again.

"Why's Jake leavin'?" Charlie asked Trudy while they both stood on the corner watching them go.

"He's searchin'—he's just searchin," Trudy answered.

"Whatever that means," Charlie replied. "Doesn't make much sense to me," he concluded.

"Me neither," Trudy said.

"Searchin' for what?" Charlie questioned her.

"Himself," Trudy said and turned to walk back to her salon that had been repaired temporarily until a new door could be installed.

Charlie shrugged and said again, "Whatever that means."

All he knew was that Miss Kate looked forlorn when Jake had left the first time. Now he was leaving again. Charlie felt bad for her. Only city folk were supposed to have forlorn faces. Trudy said so. Kate lived here now; she was one of them. She shouldn't look forlorn. He thought maybe Jake didn't understand women as much as he thought.

He began to walk toward Open Door. He thought that maybe he could put a smile on Miss Kate's face. At least, he was going to try.

Still, he was perplexed. He kicked at a stone in his path and finally said aloud, "Is that what love does? Does love just keep walkin' away?"

Phil lost weight after the storm and shaved off his beard. One hardly recognized Phil after that storm. It was like he came out of a cocoon...a handsome monarch butterfly taking flight.

He never touched another drop of alcohol. He didn't even gargle with Listerine. Trudy would see him in the grocery store, reading every label in the health aisle to make sure no alcohol was in the ingredients.

"Readin' those labels like me, Phil?" Trudy would ask.

"Sure thing, Trudy, but I'm not lookin' for lard!" Phil would reply.

They both would laugh. Trudy was mighty proud of Phil after that storm, and she eased up on Charlie a little too with the manners thing. She told Charlie that Phil could take over from here, and she was right.

Phil gave up cussing and started exercising. Everybody just kept watching him. He became quite a phenomenon in Brooksport Village. He wasn't lifting weights or going to a workout center. There wasn't one in their village, anyway. Trudy said people on vacation didn't want to exercise; they just wanted to eat extra crispy doughnuts and relax.

No, the kind of exercising that Phil did was found in riding his bike—the kind with the big wheels that plow through sand on a lake beach. Yes, siree, you could see him every morning, his belly hanging over his belt, his heart pumping, and his breath coming out in little gasps. But he persevered, and that's how he lost his weight.

He didn't go to Crabby's anymore once it was rebuilt, and he traded his potato chips for crackers—the low-fat kind—and cottage cheese. He skipped the ice cream aisle too.

Phil became a man during that storm. A man that Charlie came to admire. A man Charlie was finally able to call Dad and mean it. He was proud that Phil had *chosen* him. Real proud.

Oh, there were times Charlie wondered if the shoe would drop, thinking Phil just might go back to his old ways, but he never did. Trudy said that Phil had to go back while sitting in that closet. Sometimes you have to do that in order to go forward, and sometimes the road back takes a little longer than we would like. It was only important that Phil knew where he was going now.

Charlie often thought of his conversation with Sarah—that day he kissed her hand. She was right. Sometimes you have to go back and remember the good stuff in order to forgive, especially when it comes time to forgiving yourself. Phil had done just that. He had gone back, way back. What happened in that closet was between him and God, and Charlie was sure glad that God had shown up.

Charlie had a story of his own during that storm. It seemed odd to him that God would put him inside Crabby's Bar, of all places, when the winds hit, but there he was.

Leon had a secret. He had a little hideaway underneath that bar of his. When the storm hit, he made a snap decision.

"Downstairs!" he shouted to all who had huddled inside. Everyone looked at each other and thought, *There's no downstairs!*

"Follow me!" Leon had ordered.

The group was in no bargaining position as the storm came bearing down. Leon rushed behind the bar, lifted a small carpet from the floor, and opened a trapdoor. Nobody asked questions. They were all going down those stairs two at a time when Leon commanded. He was the last to come into his underground cave of sorts. He shut the trapdoor, and everyone stood there, saying nothing, just waiting.

Leon lit a kerosene lamp, and everyone looked around the dirt room. Stockpiles of water, canned food, and a few cots were scattered around.

"Make yourself at home," Leon said. "You'll be safe here until all this hell breakin' loose subsides." Leon motioned for people to try to get comfortable before continuing, "It's not the Ritz, but it's sure goin' to save your ass."

Everyone was wide-eyed and knew that Leon was right. They were grateful, and nobody cared that he had said ass.

Leon walked to one of the cots and sat down.

"My safety net," he began. "I've always been a planner. Plan for the worst and expect the best, I've always said. This little secret of mine has been here a long time. Finally, it's comin' to some good use."

One of the male tourists came over, slapped Leon on the back, and said, "Hey, man, this is by far the nicest four-star hotel I have ever been in!"

"I'll book it for next year!" another tourist exclaimed.

That being said, the people who had surrounded Charlie in the corner of Crabby's encircled him once again. They grasped hands, and someone said, "I've never really prayed before, but someone told me once that's what you do when you have nobody else to turn to. I really think we should pray right now!"

And that is exactly what they did. They did a lot of praying in that earth-bound cave. Somebody once said that God sometimes puts us on our back and forces us to look up. That's what he did that day. They were looking up as the entire building above them blew away.

PART IV

Young Love in a Small Town

40

Things went back to normal eventually after the storm, but the one that Brooksport Village had grown to love was missing—Jake.

Charlie didn't know what to do to help Miss Kate. He kept seeing her sitting out there in her garden. Those bleeding hearts had come back up just as Charlie had predicted, and the cleanup around her bed and breakfast had left everything beautiful once again minus a few trees, but Kate looked so sad. Charlie thought that every bit of life had been drained out of her. He knew she was tired—everybody was—so one day, he decided to take her a glass of sweet tea.

Charlie would never forget that day, the day Miss Kate cried in front of him. There was just something about an adult crying in front of a young 'un, especially a woman. He didn't know what to say, but he somehow knew she needed more than sweet tea that day.

She looked at Charlie through those big eyes of hers with tears rolling down her cheeks and said, "Charlie, always remember you can't share your life with anyone else until you take care of your own stuff—your own personal messes. I'm an expert with messes. I know a mess when I see one, and Jake is a mess. In fact, I told him that."

Charlie was silent. He had never looked at Jake as being a mess. Shoot, Jake was everybody's hero in Brooksport Village, and it all started with a bunch of balloons. But Miss Kate was a smart woman, and Charlie wasn't going to start doubting her now. He just nodded, shuffled his feet, and kept drinking his sweet tea, even though he couldn't stand the stuff. He didn't rightly know what else to do.

When Miss Kate went back into the house, he prayed that Jake would straighten out his mess, whatever it was. Charlie didn't know who wanted him to come back to Brooksport more, Miss Kate or himself.

"I've got a whole lot more to learn about women." Charlie confessed, looking up at the sky, "And I need Jake tellin' me how to handle 'em," he said to God.

"Jake, you better get your sorry you-know-what back here and fast!"

He knew better than to say the *a* word. Phil would have a fit if he heard him, especially now that he talked to God a lot.

Phil had begun the lesson in Manners 201 for Charlie. Charlie supposed he had graduated from Trudy's instruction, but tonight Phil was teaching Charlie how to dance, of all things. He couldn't help but smile as he looked back at a new memory he had recollected in recent days—Iris and Phil, his mom and dad, dancing in the kitchen. Sometimes memories come back like that at a moment's notice.

"Women love to dance," Phil had told him that morning. "When you get home tonight, I'm goin' to teach you how to do just that."

Charlie couldn't help but think he better close the kitchen curtains when the lesson began. He was thinking it would seem a little weird to be dancing with his dad in the kitchen. But then again, maybe not. He had waited for moments such as these for a long, long time. The closeness of a father and a son. And just maybe, the village had waited for this too.

Shoot, Charlie thought, *we may even hear applause.*

Charlie started thinking about people's messes and how they were supposed to bring all their secrets out into the light. So he decided to tell Miss Kate his secret—well, it wasn't really a secret anymore, but it wasn't a mess either. He just felt she should hear it from him, them being so close and all.

It was early September when he sauntered over to Open Door and asked her if they could talk. He guessed he was trying to walk like Jake. She dropped everything she was doing and gave him her full attention. That was one of the many things he loved about Miss Kate. She always cared about what he had to say. She made him feel important.

They walked around to the flower garden that had been fixed by the touch of her hand and the help of all the neighbors. They sat down on her garden bench, and he remembered thinking and being grateful that there was no sweet tea on the table.

No sooner had they sat down that Charlie blurted out, "I'm adopted."

Kate looked at him, saying nothing.

So he kept on blurting out, "Phil told me one night when he was drunk."

Kate shifted herself on the bench, remaining silent.

"Jake had brought him home that night, but it wasn't until Jake left that my dad stumbled out into the hallway, sat me down, and told me it was time I knew."

Still, Kate remained silent, but her mind was in a whirl.

Charlie continued, "Oh, I'm glad I was *chosen*. It took me a while to accept that, but comin' from Trudy and Sarah, I figured I should, at least, try. I guess it's the *way* I found out that bothered me."

Charlie looked at Kate's hand that now held his.

"You don't need to say anything, Miss Kate," Charlie began. "Thank you for always being here for me. I'm so glad you decided you needed your hair fixed and you met Trudy. You know she takes all the credit for you stayin' here."

Kate didn't know what to say to Charlie. She squeezed his hand, and that was obviously enough for him.

After Charlie left, Kate continued to sit on the bench in a stupor.

"Oh, Charlie," she said to herself, "you have accepted this new chapter in your life. You've proven yourself much stronger than I. Why can't I accept my own new chapters as quickly as you?"

Kate's mind was exploding. She didn't have time to think about Jake anymore. What would Trudy be saying right now, *"You've got bigger fish to fry, darlin'."* Yes, she did.

That night, her heart flew back to the day she spoke with the lady at the agency—the one who made a promise to her young nineteen-year-old heart.

Yes, sometimes you have to go back, way back, and find a way to forgive yourself. Even after all these years, tears were forming in her eyes as she remembered.

Kate thought about how she had prepared herself for the grief that would follow when she handed over her baby. She had prepared everything else. She had been staring at the locket she held in her hand when the social worker had walked into the room for any final questions.

"I have a request," Kate had said, stumbling over her words.

She walked over to a nearby chair and picked up the baby blanket that both she and her mother had made.

"Promise me you will wrap that sweet child in this blanket and pin this locket to the blanket with this note I have written for the child's adoptive parents," Kate said.

The social worker stared at her, shaking her head. "I can't—"

She saw the tears flowing down Kate's face—the very face of a broken heart, a shattered heart.

"This soft spot in my heart is goin' to get me in trouble," the social worker replied, walking over to Kate and taking the blanket, locket, and note from her hand. She squeezed Kate's hand, hugged her, and whispered, "I promise."

Kate had cried all the way home. She was returning to an empty house with a grief upon her shoulders she would never be able to shake.

Way back, way back she had gone in her mind. She remembered it as if it were yesterday—watching her baby go to a new home in the arms of a new mother with a proud dad walking beside her. Both smiling. That sweet child was wrapped in the blanket, and the man was holding a note with a locket dangling from his right hand. The promise had been kept.

Kate was brought back into the present when she looked up and saw the tiny carved squirrels on her fireplace mantle.

"Oh, Zack, I was a mess when you scooped me up from the street. In many ways, I still am," she whispered, walking over to those carved figures. She touched them affectionately. A lone tear rolled down her cheek.

"You never get over a grief such as this," Kate said to herself. "You learn to live with it, but how do you ever get over it?"

"Rhizoo—it means to be rooted, strengthened, and firmly fixed."

No doubt about it. Phil had been smack dab in the middle of a crisis that stormy day in that particular closet. He could have been at Crabby's Bar, but he wasn't. God had invited Phil to his own miracle party, and nothing was going to stop it from happening.

The invitation was threefold. God invited; Phil ran for cover. Phil invited. But it was not the miracle that would be forgotten when times became better. Oh no. Phil invited God into everything he did and everywhere he went—his meals, his bike rides, his grocery store visits, and the curbside where he got rid of all his bottles.

Trudy told Charlie that Phil had rhizoo. Charlie didn't know what that meant, but it sounded good because Trudy looked up at the sky and smiled when she said it. Charlie went to the library and looked up that word. When he walked out of the library, he too looked up at the sky and smiled.

Rhizoo. Phil was rooted, firmly fixed. He would remain constant in his quest. He would remain true and steadfast.

Charlie suddenly remembered that tonight was going to be an unusual night.

Sure hope God shows up in the kitchen tonight, Charlie thought. *Teachin' me to dance is goin' to have to be another miracle.*

He thought of Sarah, her being a girl and all—he was sure his dad was right. She probably liked to dance.

"It'll be worth it," Charlie whispered to himself. "This learnin' how to dance thing."

But he still kept wondering if he should close the kitchen curtains when the lesson began.

The days rolled by, and Charlie kept trying to assure Kate of one fact. "He'll be back, you know," he said to Kate one day while they worked in the flower garden.

"Who?" Kate asked.

Charlie gave her that look she had come to cherish in his oh so innocent eyes before answering her.

"Jake," Charlie replied.

"How can you be so sure, Charlie?" she asked.

"I know men," he answered.

Kate couldn't help but smile while standing to go into the kitchen. Charlie thought, *Oh no, here comes that sweet tea.*

Kate watched Charlie from the kitchen window. She watched how gently he pushed the flowers away from the weeds before pulling the root of the weed up and out. She wondered how long it would be before she could do the same—before she could pull the weeds in her heart up and out.

"He's so young," she commented to herself. "How does he know so much? How did he surpass me on this journey of life?" She wondered how he had coped with the sadness at the young age of four when his mother had died. "I could learn a lot about living from Charlie." She sighed.

Someone else entered the garden, silently creeping up behind Charlie. She made him jump.

"Sarah! You just scared the livin' daylights 'outta me!" Charlie exclaimed.

Kate continued to watch from the window.

"Young love," she said. "And they don't even know it yet."

She walked to the table to pour one more glass of sweet tea. "Ah, they will know soon enough," Kate said.

She knew Sarah loved sweet tea; Charlie had told her in his own comical way one afternoon in the garden. She poured a lemonade for Charlie, placing it on the tray with the sweet tea, and walked out to a very nervous Charlie and a smiling Sarah with gleaming blue eyes.

Charlie looked at the lemonade with a questioning glance.

"Yes, the lemonade is for you, Charlie. I think I have finally learned," Kate said.

"No more sweet tea?" Charlie questioned.

"Only lemonade," Kate replied.

Labor Day passed. The school year had begun, but Charlie had more than studies on his mind. He regretted that Jake wasn't around so he could ask him more questions about girls. Jake was the expert. His dad had taught him to dance, and it wasn't as hard as he thought it would be. But he really wanted a man like Jake to talk to him about girls. Sometimes Charlie figured you couldn't talk to your own dad about certain things. You needed a cowboy.

Charlie shrugged his shoulders and thought, *Well, Miss Kate's the next best person to talk to about the subject.*

Charlie had just finished mowing the grass at the bed and breakfast and took a seat beside Kate on the bench where she loved to watch those squirrels. He still couldn't figure out what fascinated her so much about an animal with bushy tails.

Charlie sighed.

"What's on your mind, Charlie?" Kate asked.

Charlie shuffled his feet before replying, "So I was wonderin', what do you think about young love? Do 'ya think it really exists?"

"I think it's wonderful, Charlie, and yes, I do believe it exists. Why do you ask?" Kate responded.

Kate smiled at Charlie and continued, "Are you in love, Charlie?"

"Maybe," he replied.

"Sarah?" Kate asked.

"Maybe," he replied again. It seemed that's all he could say. He thought that was quite a stupid answer to her question.

He quickly added, "I know a couple who survived young love to live another day."

"You do?" Kate asked. "Who might that be?"

"Well, there's really four," Charlie answered.

"Really?" Kate asked. She was enjoying this interchange with him.

"Yep, they survived all the ups and downs," he continued.

"Tell me about them," Kate said.

"Trudy told me the story about all our 'lovebirds' when I was growing up," Charlie began. "She thought I needed a fairy tale, I guess because of the life I was leadin' with Phil—I mean my dad—at the time."

"Shall I go get us some sweet tea, Charlie?" Kate laughingly questioned.

Charlie rolled his eyes.

Kate questioned again, "How about lemonade?"

"That's better," Charlie answered.

When Kate returned, handing him the drink, Charlie began.

"Trudy always used to tell me that small town boys grow up with small town girls and fall in love," Charlie said, taking a sip of his lemonade.

"That's what happened with Gordy, Jessie, Wes, and Reva. They had been friends since kindergarten. They grew up in Brooksport Village and were inseparable. They swam in the lake, had picnics in the town square, shot off fireworks every Fourth of July, and helped decorate the huge Christmas tree in the center of town every December."

Charlie looked out, glancing at the lake.

"Trudy said that our town had its very own Cinderella for girls and John Wayne for boys. When we heard these stories, all of us wanted to grow up just like Gordy and Jessie and their best friends, Wes and Reva. Trudy kept saying that one day we would build our own picket fences around our own little pieces of land and live happily ever after."

Charlie shrugged. "Trudy's a great storyteller who loves happy endings. Have you noticed?"

Somehow Kate thought Charlie was right about that. Trudy just seemed to take the long road home to happiness. She hid so much of herself. Kate was sure there were things about Trudy she might never know. Still, she would like to try to pull some of those purple things out into the open.

Charlie suddenly laughed before continuing, "The first boy that ever kissed Jessie was Gordy. They were in the third grade when they were chosen to be king and queen of the Fall Festival. Trudy said that Jessie cried—happy tears—but Gordy thought she was sad and tried to console her by giving her a kiss on the cheek. Jessie was so embarrassed she slapped him. Trudy said Jessie was just overcome with emotion at the time and didn't really mean to hurt Gordy's feelings."

Charlie continued to drink his lemonade.

"Anyway, those two did have their moment regardless of the kiss and the slap. They walked down the school's aisle in front of the entire community to be crowned as king and queen of their grammar school. Gordy's look was very serious from all the photographs everyone giggled over. And his hands kept to themselves—one by his side, the other folded over his middle—so Jessie could hold on as they walked their own little golden mile. She was smiling, and he wasn't. He knew better to not be anything but serious."

Kate questioned, "They were only eight years old then?"

Charlie nodded. "Young love," he answered.

Charlie spotted a weed in the flowers and walked over to pluck it from the ground.

He looked up at Kate and continued, "But then suddenly, Jessie took a likin' to Gordy in the ninth grade. Trudy said there's something that takes over a girl about that age."

"Hormones?" Kate questioned.

"Yep, that was it, hormones," Charlie replied.

"Both Gordy and Jessie were seen ridin' their bikes through town side by side, stopping at the end of town, talking about who knows what."

Charlie laughed. "I guess they were too busy to study algebra because they both flunked it and had to go to summer school. From what I hear, they barely passed it then."

Charlie walked back to the bench and sat down beside Kate.

"Rumor has it that Jessie finally let Gordy kiss her and, this time, not on the cheek. Yes, they were an item, all right—all the way through high school right on up until college."

"What happened then?" Kate questioned.

"Gordy stayed local. Jessie went in an opposite direction. Oh, they met up on holidays when all those who had left our village for college came back, however brief it was. Everyone hoped there would be a weddin' one day. Those two just seemed to fit together ever since way back in third grade."

Kate said, "They're married now!"

Charlie replied, "Oh yes, the weddin' did take place but not until years later after time and circumstance finally forced Jessie to take off her rose-colored glasses."

Charlie took another sip of his drink. "Jessie's heart was in her writing. Gordy confided to Wes that she had told him she wanted to write a bestseller one day. He didn't take her seriously until one day she announced she was leaving Brooksport Village."

"She left?" Kate interjected.

"Yep," Charlie answered. "Trudy said she packed her bags, and much to the dismay of her parents and her three best friends, she left them standing bewildered at the airport. She just flew away like some lone bird, hoping to find a flock of her own. At least, that's what Trudy thought."

Kate kept looking at Charlie.

"Can I have some more lemonade, Miss Kate?" Charlie asked.

"Of course," Kate answered, taking the empty glass. She walked back into the kitchen.

When she returned, Charlie continued, "From what Trudy said, Jessie tried her best to get Reva to go with her to that dream city she called New York, but Reva stayed. Reva was the quiet one, the homebody. All she wanted was to marry Wes, settle down, and have a house full of children. She wanted to bandage skinned knees and make macaroni and cheese and cookies with sprinkles on top. She wanted to be a mom, and that suited Wes just fine. That's what he wanted too."

"I've never really talked with Wes and Reva since I moved here," Kate said. "But I hear they are a real fine couple. They've overcome many struggles, especially Wes being blind and all."

"Oh, they are," Charlie said. "Sarah's their daughter—you know, the one I think I'm in love with."

Kate smiled and answered, "I see."

"Well," Charlie continued, "when Jessie left, Gordy joined the military, and Wes was right beside him. We have always considered our town patriotic and righteous—Trudy said so—and everybody around here always talked about those two being true to their calling. When they returned from their patriotic service, Wes and Reva were married. Gordy wanted that marriage of his own with his impulsive Jessie, but he couldn't have stopped her from leaving, and he was smart enough not to try."

"Did Trudy tell you that too?" Kate asked.

Charlie nodded.

"Trudy's pretty smart," Kate exclaimed.

"Well, Gordy put all his energy into taking care of his horses and making his stable a welcoming place for the children of tourists who flocked there to take riding lessons, feed, and brush down those beautiful creatures. Still, he seemed lost without Jessie."

"Wes and Reva moved away for a while. They said they needed a change—a new environment. I don't understand how people keep leavin' places they love."

Kate gave Charlie an empathetic look as he continued.

"Well, they didn't much like their new environment because after almost two years, they came back to Brooksport. And, boy oh boy, did they have a surprise for everybody!"

"What was that?" Kate asked.

"They came back with a baby."

Charlie took a breath before continuing.

"Then Granada happened."

"How do you remember so much of this story? You were so very young." Kate asked.

"Trudy told it so much to all of us kids I think I memorized it," Charlie replied.

"Sounds like Trudy had her own little story hour with all you kids," Kate said.

"Oh, she did, and we loved it. I'll bet I'm not the only one of us kids that tells this story to people who want to hear it."

Kate wanted to know more about Charlie's true fairy tale, but it was getting late. She decided to ask him if he wanted to go to Stumble In for a burger.

As they began their walk into town, Charlie suddenly asked, "Do you miss Jake?"

Kate stopped midstride. Just the name of Jake made her heart seem to stop.

"Yes, Charlie, I do," she replied.

"Me too," Charlie said.

Kate thought, *End of conversation. End of Jake. Once again. Goodbye, Jake.*

They reached the Stumble In, found a table, and ordered their burgers. Kate had a fleeting thought that this was exactly what a mother and son would do when the subject of young love came up and answers were needed. She was there for him, and it made her feel good. She felt a certain peace as she settled herself down to listen to the rest of Charlie's story.

"Both Gordy and Wes were called to serve in Granada, and they did not hesitate."

Kate took a sip of her water.

"It proved to be a short war, but Wes returned home with injuries he would endure for a lifetime," Charlie said, looking at Kate.

"Wait a minute, Charlie," Kate began. "Wes's blindness—was it due to Granada?"

Charlie nodded.

Kate took a deep breath, not knowing what to say.

"It was the bombing of the US barracks. Out of nowhere and just like that, his life changed forever," Charlie exclaimed.

"Oh, he had his days of strugglin'," Charlie continued. "But Gordy was there. He *leaned in* when Wes *leaned out.* It was Gordy who kept calming both Wes and Reva's fears. Wes wondered how he was going to manage in helping Reva raise a daughter because of his blindness. He needed a job to support his family, and he wondered who in the world would hire a blind man. Decisions had to be made. Life demanded adjustments. Can you imagine losing your eyesight?"

Kate replied, "It would be like learning a new language in a foreign land with new customs and a separate culture. Most things familiar but seeming so foreign."

The server brought their burgers, and the two of them ate in silence for a short time before Charlie continued.

"Gordy stood with them through it all. He was their rock of strength. To him, they would always be indebted. Their friendship grew stronger. They often thought of Jessie, missing her all the more during that crisis they were facing. I guess the three just needed to be four again."

Charlie nodded.

"Good friends grieve when one moves away," Charlie said. "Especially when you've grown up together."

Charlie thought for a moment and looked at Kate.

"I guess there's different kinds of grief. Do you believe that's true, Miss Kate?"

"I do," Kate replied.

"Kind of like you greivin' Jake? I mean, he's not dead and all, but he's not here either."

Those words hit hard, but then again, the truth has a tendency to do that—hurt.

"Mid pleasures and palaces though we may roam, be it ever so humble, there's no place like home." (John Howard Payne)

All that Charlie had shared with Kate was true. Since childhood's first kiss through high school and into college, it seemed Gordy had always been saying goodbye and hello to Jessie and then goodbye again. But he was ever so patient. He knew what he wanted in the end, and it was still that little third grade girl he had first kissed, even if she had smacked the tar out of him.

Gordy was drifting while he waited. Somehow, he always thought she'd wander back to Brooksport. You could see him walking the lakefront always alone. Oh, lots of ladies tried to get close to him— the tourist ladies, that is. He was quite a looker and still was. At least, that's what Trudy always kept saying. Trudy had always been one to build up a person's ego. Everyone who lived in Brooksport knew better than to try to hook up with him. The natives of Brooksport knew that his heart beat with Jessie, so all the ones from other parts of the country who came to visit for the summer could only shrug their shoulders, put their cover-ups over their bikinis, and walk away when he didn't give them the time of day.

Phil had said that Gordy attracted women like bees were attracted to honey. But he paid them no mind. His eyes were only meant for Jessie. People tried to get him to move on and forget her.

Phil had told him once while in one of his drunken stupors, "She ain't never comin' back here, boy. Forget her! Just look at all these women around here that are after you! You can just reach out and take your pick!"

But Gordy didn't. In his own mind, he stayed with Jessie, and his porch light was always on as soon as dusk began to fall. Everybody guessed that was his way of letting her know his door remained open for her and only her.

There are a lot of things in life one can never be sure of, but Gordy was always sure of Jessie. And then one day, quite unexpectedly, there she was—chopping wood, of all things.

It was autumn, and most of the tourists had made their way back to the city. One would have thought that after all that waiting, Gordy would have run up to her, spun her around, and given her a big kiss—and not on the cheek.

Instead, he sauntered over to her, using that slow walk of his, and merely asked, "What are you doing?"

She looked at him as if he were crazy—kind of like she had done in the third grade. "Picking blueberries. Really? Seriously, Gordy, what does it look like I'm doing?"

"Still sassy, eh?" Gordy grinned. "Some things never change."

"I want a fire tonight. In case you haven't noticed, the nights around here in the fall can get quite chilly," Jessie replied as she continued to chop wood.

"Oh," Gordy replied.

That's all he said, "Oh."

Then he merely turned around to leave.

Jessie stopped chopping and yelled, "Hey, Gordy!"

Gordy turned and faced the one who always made his heart skip a beat, still wondering how a little thing like that could chop wood with such strength.

"Wanna join me tonight by the fire?" Jessie asked.

"Only if you give me that ax and let me chop the rest of that wood," he answered.

She walked over to him and put the ax in his hand.

Gordy winked at her and said, "No, I haven't forgotten how cool it can get here on crisp autumn nights. I remember those bonfires down by the lake."

Sometimes it happens like that— the falling leaves vibrant with color—while you're sharing wood chopping. And later, a cup of coffee by firelight with an extra crispy doughnut from Belle's Bakery. Add it all up and you're a goner.

At least, that's where Gordy and Jessie began again, and this time it would be forever.

Jessie had been a dream chaser, penning words to paper that never came to life. The rejections had sent her back home where everyone thought she belonged in the first place, and Gordy was a happy man once again. The whole town was glad she was back. Those people out there in the wide world didn't know what they had missed—rejecting Jessie and pushing her aside—but Brooksport

Village knew. They missed her so much that they literally loved her all the way back home—especially, Gordy.

She remembered that love, and as it turned out, Brooksport Village was where her real success was forged. All of Charlie's bedtime stories about the lovebirds always ended with what happened by the fire that night when Gordy spoke. "I was drifting through the days without you here to the stable and back, to the lakefront and back, to Trudy's purple salon just to pester her and back home again. But one thing I never did, I never drifted away from you, Jessie. You were always on my mind and in my heart."

It was then and only then that he kissed her, welcoming her home. And this time, glory be, she didn't smack him. Oh no, she kissed him back.

And then he said, cupping her face in his hands, "All those rejection letters you got, well, did you ever think it was because you didn't have the right story, yet?"

And so it was that Gordy and Jessie began their dual dream of loving each other. They were married, finally. They were planning their future, rescuing their horses, and giving birth to their son—the very story Jessie had been waiting for was appearing before her in panoramic vision.

Brooksport Village would see her sitting in her little attic office in front of that window that Gordy had built for her right above the stable. She had made it her own. That is where she did all of her writing. That is where she created a story that Gordy believed would one day be published. And as he encouraged her, she wrote and wrote and wrote.

Life was good. Life was very good. She was home, at last, to stay. Gordy was happy, and the stable flourished. The soulmates were together—a happy ending to Brooksport's very own little fairy tale. Yes, sometimes happy endings do come along. Sometimes they stay, and sometimes…

PART V

'Life' Strikes

42

It was five o'clock when Jessie walked into the kitchen, opened the cabinet, and grabbed the chocolate chip cookies.

Gordy and their son, little Sam, looked at her.

"Cookies before dinner?" Gordy questioned.

"Yep!" Jessie exclaimed, giving one to Sam, who yelped with glee.

"This can be dinner for me, Mom!" Sam exclaimed.

"What brings on this sudden impulse to change the rule of no cookies before dinner?" Gordy asked, playfully grabbing a cookie for himself.

Jessie sat across from her two guys and announced, "I'm going to New York—but not to stay—I'll be back."

"Can't help feeling a little déjà vu, my dear," Gordy replied.

Jessie took a deep breath and said, "I finished the book."

Gordy smiled.

She smiled back at Gordy and continued, "I think it's pretty good."

"I'm sure it is," Gordy replied. "Now what?"

"I told you I'm going to New York."

"Oh, I see, you're just going to stroll into a publisher's office and say, 'Here's my book'?" Gordy asked.

"Pretty much," Jessie said, taking another cookie from the bag.

She handed a second cookie to Sam. "And I'm taking you with me, little man! It's going to be your first plane ride!"

"What about me?" Gordy questioned.

"You have to stay here and take care of the horses, my darling," she replied.

She walked to the kitchen window and looked out at the pasture.

"Just look at him, would you? My sweet pride and joy," she said, pointing to the white horse she and Gordy had rescued and brought back to life.

"That's my horse, always will be," she whispered, walking back to the table and plopping down on Gordy's lap. "Promise me something," she said.

"Anything, my lovely," Gordy replied.

"Promise you will tie a red bow around that white horse of mine before I walk through this very door when I get back here. Have 'Star Bright' welcome me back with a red bow around his neck."

"A red bow it is with some roses tucked inside." Gordy laughed.

He knew if anyone would come back to Brooksport with a success story, it would be Jessie.

Little Sam walked to the refrigerator, poured a glass of milk, spilling more than went into the glass, turned to his parents, and asked, "Do they have cookies on plane rides?"

Jessie had been in New York almost two weeks when Gordy came running into Belle's with a printed e-mail message in his hands. Trudy was there, getting her extra crunchy fried doughnut along with Kate.

"I told her before she left to go to New York to get the job done and get back home as fast as she could!" Gordy exclaimed.

He was frantically waving the e-mail around in his hand.

"Well, she did it!" Gordy shouted. "She found herself a publisher!"

He ran over to Trudy and planted a big kiss on her cheek and began dancing with Kate.

"You know, ladies, that's really unheard of. I mean who can just walk into a publishing firm, hand over a manuscript, and ask them to read it?" Gordy was beyond joyful.

"I think her charm helped her a bit," Trudy interjected. "I don't think those powers-that-be even had time to blink when the whirlwind known as Jessie walked into their leather-chaired offices."

The three of them, including Belle, had their own private celebration right then and there.

But it wasn't long before the whole town knew. Trudy filled them in. She was good at that; she was better spreading news than the local newspaper. But no one ever forgot—she knew how to keep secrets too. That was her *other* side.

Yes, siree, Jessie was coming back. She had made that perfectly clear before she left. Brooksport Village was her home, and it was there she would stay and write. She would never leave again. And the town looked forward to watching her continue her newfound career. They could hardly wait until their "very own" came home.

The town had never seen such excitement, and the entire population of Brooksport Village began decorating its streets for the homecoming celebration. Gordy's wife was coming home with their five-year-old son. Everybody in town was hoping Jessie would come back home a successful author after finding a publisher. She had always been famous in their minds; now it looked like she was well on her way with more books to write.

She had been working on that first book of hers for years. People would wave to her as they walked by her attic studio, and Gordy could be seen bringing her coffee, along with pastry from Belle's.

Midafternoon surprise, he called it. Jessie loved sugar. Everybody loves something. Just like Trudy and her lard thing.

During those writing days, Jessie had gazed out at the horses she and Gordy had rescued and told all of her friends they gave her inspiration, especially her very own, 'Star Bright.' Oh, how she loved that white horse! She had brought it back to health with her gentle touch. At least, that's what Trudy said, and that's what Gordy knew. It was sure a fine specimen of a stud now and was spoiled beyond belief by all the children who visited and lived in Brooksport Village.

No doubt about it, that book may have taken years to write, but then one day, boom, it was finished. And Jessie's adventure was about to begin, and the people of Brooksport Village would be walking right alongside her, celebrating all the way.

Banners of welcome went up all over town, bordered by ribbons of all colors. The town was decorated up like Christmas in September. Stores put tables outside their doors and gave stuff away. Belle made cookies and cakes from real lard, and everyone grabbed at least one cookie as they walked by.

Lard was pretty popular that day—nobody cared about it being bad for you. Trudy announced that it didn't matter on days of celebration, everything was free, including the calories.

Brooksport Village had never been so alive with enthusiasm and pride for Gordy's famous wife. And, boy oh boy, had Gordy decorated their home with banners. All the horses had flowers around their necks. After all, they had inspired her, especially that special white one that loved her as much as she loved him. He knew her touch, he knew her voice, and he was the one with the red bow around his neck with roses tucked into each fold, just as Gordy had promised Jessie before she left.

The town and everyone in it, including the animals, was ready for Jessie's return. That sweet, little tired town, from all its activity, turned out the lights and went to sleep with anticipation of the celebration yet to come—everyone except for Gordy. Every light in his house was on. Jessie and little Sam would be home by noon the next day. Gordy was just too excited to sleep.

Gordy had always been a man of surprises, and Jessie loved every "Aha!" moment of their life together. One of the things Gordy loved most was surprising her. This celebration would be no different. Gordy could picture the look on Jessie's face when she saw what the town had done for their elect one. She never disappointed him with her gratitude. And so it was that one surprise built upon another, and their marriage was never boring. It was filled with humor, respect, and love. Those were the thoughts going through Gordy's mind that morning she and little Sam were to return.

He pulled on his jeans, put on his boots, and grabbed his cowboy hat. Yes, that would be another surprise for Jessie. Jake had convinced him of that fact before he blew out of town. Jake had said that anyone who owned a horse stable should be a real cowboy.

He remembered the conversation well. Jake had looked at him and said, "Hey, man, you need a cowboy hat if you're goin' to call yourself a dude."

"I never called myself a dude," Gordy had answered.

"Isn't this a dude ranch?" Jake had retorted.

Gordy had walked away after flashing a smile at Jake.

"Only you, Jake, only you," he had said, shaking his head. "What in the world ever brought you into my life, anyway?"

"You wouldn't know what to do without me, you may as well admit it."

"Never," Gordy had hollered over his shoulder and continued walking.

"Go get a hat!" Jake exclaimed.

"Don't wear hats, don't like hats."

As Jake had walked away, Gordy heard him mumble, "You're goin' to get a cowboy hat. I know you will."

And Gordy had done just that. Today he had it on. Too bad Jake wasn't here to witness it.

Yes, he remembered that conversation warmly. He liked Jake. Everybody liked Jake, and he had to admit that he missed the sun of a gun.

Gordy looked in the mirror, this way and that, and finally admitted something else.

"I do look pretty good in it."

He left his house singing that Mac Davis song, "*Oh, it's hard to be humble when you're perfect in every way.*"

He looked up at the promising sky and said, "Just kidding, God, just kidding."

As Gordy walked into town, he felt an overflow of thankfulness. Again, he looked up at the clear, blue sky and whispered, "Thank you for a clear day to travel. Thank you that my sweet Jessie will be home today with my son."

Gordy was halfway down the road, whistling, kicking rocks with his boots, and thinking about how good he looked in his cowboy hat when his phone began to ring back at the ranch. The message machine picked up.

That message would become like an echo that would reverberate through the empty hallways of his home for months to come.

It was one of those moments. You know the kind, when you remember exactly where you were, who you were with, and what you were doing. Timeless—that's all anyone could think of that day. The day time stopped. The day the world stood still.

Charlie remembered. He was on his bike, delivering papers and murmuring about how he would never understand women. Yes, that's what he was doing—and then—when it all came down to the bottom line, he realized that understanding women was not so important anymore.

Brooksport Village would never be the same as silence enveloped the town—neither would America, ever again.

It seemed the whole town had gathered in Belle's Bakery, even some of the tourists who remained after Labor Day. People didn't want to be secluded in their rooms watching in horror what the TV was conveying. They wanted to be holding someone's hand, even if it was a total stranger. All eyes were riveted on the tiny TV in the corner. A plane had hit the World Trade Center.

The main question on the minds of the Brooksport community was, where were Jessie and little Sam? Were they safe? Were they just stuck in an airport somewhere and not in the air?

Gordy kept staring at the TV. Trudy walked over to him, placing her hand on his shoulder, saying nothing but looking very worried.

It was one of the tourists who broke the silence.

"How in the name of hell could someone fly a plane into a building—the World Trade Center, for heaven's sake!"

It was at that moment another plane crashed into the second tower of New York's tallest buildings. Everyone gasped as the town witnessed an event so horrific they could not express themselves in any other way.

"America is under attack," the news anchor announced, trying desperately to keep his composure.

Looking back, that moment would be remembered as being the quietest anyone had ever seen that little village town.

Gordy stood stunned for one minute that seemed like hours. Then he walked to the door. Before walking out of Belle's, he turned and answered the question that had been on everyone's mind.

"No! They're not on those planes! Jessie is flying out of New York with our son—not Boston!"

Trudy said, "Of course, they're not on those planes! They're in the airport, stuck on the ground. We'll hear from her soon."

For one last solid moment in time, everyone believed that to be true. That solid moment would soon turn to sand, running through the fingers of those who waited. There was a sense of heaviness, like a dark cloud descending.

Another storm was rising, and it was not the kind that tears down trees, like before, but the kind that shatters hearts.

That tourist had missed the question somewhat. Instead of *how* could someone fly a plane into a building, it should have been *who* would fly a plane into a building. Evil personified, that's who—pure evil personified.

Gordy felt a sense of impending doom. He couldn't shake the feeling as he walked back to his ranch. He held his cowboy hat in his hand as he kicked stones out of pure frustration. No whistling, no singing. He was trying to remain calm, but he felt something was not right in his own corner of the world. He couldn't shake the feeling. He opened the front door and walked in. His gaze went immediately to the flashing red light on his message machine.

"*You have two messages.*"

He pushed the button.

"Hi, honey, it's me."

Gordy felt a sudden sense of relief. Jessie's voice. And then. "I've decided to take Sam to the west coast to meet my aunt, you know the one I talk about all the time?"

Without taking a breath, which was so typically his impulsive Jessie, she continued with her message. "So, my trip home will be delayed a bit. Hey, why don't you take a break and fly out to California and meet us there? It's time you meet this feisty aunt of mine—the one I get all my good traits after! Wes can take care of the horses. Will call you when we get there!"

Finally, she took a deep breath before saying, "Oh, I'll be leaving out of Boston instead of New York. Thank goodness it's a nonstop flight! Sam is excited! They've promised him chocolate chip cookies. Love you, babe!"

Gordy's knees buckled as he fell to the floor. The second message was short, much too short.

"Oh my God, Gordy…"

Gordy could hear the chaos in the background.

"Sam's holding tight. He's my brave little man—he takes after you…We love you."

And then there was total silence.

The streets of that small village town had been readying for a celebration—the successful homecoming of Jessie and Sam. Instead, they found themselves caught in a fragment of time in which the whole picture could not possibly be imagined. They waited for word of the whereabouts of Jessie and Sam. They were bracing themselves as they sought for the good but feared the bad.

Little did they know at the time that Gordy was the only one who knew the truth. They would know that truth themselves very soon.

Gordy had disappeared. Nobody knew what to do, not even Trudy. It was Wes who finally said he was going in search of Gordy.

"He shouldn't be alone, not knowing—I'm going to find him," Wes said, patting his leader dog, Jeb, on his head. "Come on, boy, let's go. You know the way."

"We should go with you," Trudy exclaimed.

"No, I'm going alone," Wes replied adamantly.

With that, Wes left Belle's, whispered something to Jeb, and began walking toward Gordy's ranch.

He found Gordy crumbled on the living room floor. As Wes waded through all the streamers and banners that Gordy had so carefully placed on walls and furniture now lying on the floor in torn pieces, he could hear Gordy sobbing.

Gordy heard Wes approaching him.

"I tore them all down, Wes, I tore them all down. 'Welcome Home' they said. She won't be coming home, Wes, neither will Sam," Gordy cried.

"What have you heard?" Wes questioned.

Wes sat down in the middle of all the debris, along with Jeb. He grabbed Gordy and held on to him for dear life.

They had been buddies for a long, long time. They had grown up together. They had double-dated together. They had suffered through wars together. They were military. They were strong for one another.

Gordy had been strong for Wes when he had returned home—blind. Now it was his turn. He continued to hold Gordy, saying over and over, "Leave no man behind, leave no man behind. I've got you, Gordy. I've got you."

Both those men sat in the middle of that floor and cried for everything that had been lost in their lifetime because of evil, pure evil, and this day was the worst of the worst.

Innocence lost. No, America would never be the same, and neither would Gordy. Even Jeb knew it. He walked over to the two men. He lay down beside them and ever so gently began to lick the hands of the trembling men. Yes, it was a dog but not *just* a dog; it was a kiss of comfort—a kiss from a most unlikely source who knew more than any human could ever imagine—unconditional love.

Nobody knew how all those streamers, banners, and posters disappeared overnight on the streets of Brooksport, but they did. Community effort. Everybody just grabbed somebody else's weak corner and held it up.

"There's strength in numbers," Trudy kept saying. Rumor had it that she was the one who organized the whole thing. That was

Trudy—getting the job done, even with tears streaming down her face.

Yes, community effort led by one who came up fresh from the South and loved lard. Brooksport Village saw it firsthand when tragedy hit that little town with a mighty sucker punch.

"Into the nebulous, ongoing mystery of life I welcome, as if through an open door, the continuing spirit of the one I have loved…keep the door to her life open." (Martha Whitmore Hickman, Edith Fogg Hickman)

The air was heavy the day of the memorial. The clouds were low and dark. Hearts were shattered. There was doubt that the pieces could ever be put back together. The town had cried when that terrible storm of the physical kind had hit, but roofs could be fixed, trees could be removed and replaced, and roads could be reopened, but this—this was a tragedy of the heart.

Recovery would take much longer. This kind of grief was a longer mile to walk. The streets were flooded not with rain but with tears. Two of their very own had died in a tragedy too incomprehensible to ever understand. They wept. Not only did tears flood the streets of America, but this town's homes were also filled with them. Indeed, what more could the town take?

But as Trudy had said, there was strength in numbers, and everybody gathered, relying on each other. Even in their weakness, there was a wind of a strong spirit enveloping each one of them.

Yes, it was true that tragedy had hit their town. But truth was there to comfort and guide, and the hand that soothed their aches was the same hand that said they would never be left in the middle—they would be loved safely back. Oh, no doubt they would be changed forever, and they would have to put new pictures in old frames. But the community held on to the promise that each day they would become a little stronger, a little wiser, and a lot more loving.

They put their arms around Gordy—each in their own way—even the little ones. Those little ones that had picked up sticks in the cemetery after the storm were now carrying little flags once again to place on graves. Trudy saw to it.

Three of those young ones—Kelli, Natalia, and little Nate—all walked beside Trudy after the memorial. Leaving the cemetery, Kelli was the first to speak. "We feel sad for Gordy."

Trudy replied, "I know you do. Come sit with me for a while."

Trudy led them to a nearby bench, and they sat down together.

Trudy, forever the strong one, forever the one in control, prayed to find the right words.

"It's like a black hole," she began. "Gordy has to see a path through it."

All three of the children looked at her, wanting more, but the lump in her throat would not let her continue. She, of all people, was at a loss for words.

"Hurt hearts that mean well are always speechless." Trudy reminded herself silently.

The only thing she could think of at a time such as this was to grab those three children with their big eyes full of questions and hug them. That's exactly what she did.

Driving home, Trudy continued talking to herself. "It's goin' to be a long night. Those kids are full of questions, questions no one can really answer. Not me. Not their parents, not anyone."

It seemed that one-word questions were always the hardest to answer. Why?

Trudy wished she knew the answers, but right now all she could do was cry as the rain came pouring down.

* * *

Phil headed straight for Crabby's right after the memorial. He seemed a man on a mission as he practically marched into the bar, ignoring the "Closed" sign. His march did not go unnoticed. Trudy saw him storming down the street.

"Oh no, no, no! This ain't goin' to happen, Phil!" Trudy exclaimed.

She began a march of her own, running to catch up with Phil.

Leon looked at Phil when he walked through the door and announced, "We're not open."

"Oh yes, you are," Gordy called from the doorway.

He, too, had followed Phil. He wasn't going to allow Phil to take one sip of anything that even resembled alcohol.

Phil looked at Gordy.

"It's goin' to be busier than usual. Everybody in this town is goin' to need a drink after what's happened here," Phil exclaimed.

Both Leon and Gordy looked at one another. Leon began wiping down the counters, looking at both men from the corner of his eye.

Trudy burst through the door.

"Phil, what are you doing?" she shouted.

Phil looked at her, shrugged his shoulders, and said, "Right now, just sittin' here."

Trudy walked over to the bar and sat down on the stool to Phil's left while Gordy took the stool to his right.

"Well, lookey here, would ya? I have two guardian angels makin' sure I don't mess up!" Phil shouted, looking at both of them.

Leon was standing directly in front of Phil when he added, "And another one standin' right smack dab in front of me!"

Very calmly, Phil looked directly at Leon and ordered his drink. "I'll have a coke," he said.

Gordy ordered orange juice, and Trudy sat there with her mouth open. It was then they heard another voice from the doorway.

"I'll have the vodka that was going to go in the orange juice—straight up."

It was Jake.

Jake walked over to the group and sat down next to Gordy.

"Gordy," he began, "I don't know what to say. I've been out of the country, like to never got back in. I just found out about your wife and son. I am so, so sorry."

"Thanks for coming, Jake. There's not a whole lot anybody can say, really, but I do appreciate you coming. I really do," Gordy replied.

They all sat in silence—Phil with his coke, Gordy with his orange juice, and Jake with his vodka. Trudy sat there, speechless, watching all three men handling grief in their own way.

It was Phil who broke the silence when he got up from the stool, walked over to the door, and put up the "Closed" sign. He walked back to the group and said, "I don't want any interruptions."

Phil sat down and looked directly at Gordy. "I know you're a Christian man," he began.

"Yes, I am," Gordy replied.

"I am too, as you know—became one during that awful storm," Phil said.

Trudy decided it was time to order a coke. Jake ordered another vodka.

"God's blessed us both, hasn't he, Phil?" Gordy said after a brief silence.

Phil nodded and ordered another coke.

Jake looked perplexed, downed his second drink, and exclaimed, "How in the world can you two sit there and say you are blessed?"

Jake ordered another vodka, straight up, and kept talking. "This is no blessing, man! Gordy, you just lost your wife and son! Phil, you lost your wife when Charlie was a mere four-year-old! I got news for you fellas—you ain't blessed!"

Jake's words hit both Gordy and Phil hard. Trudy gave Jake the "evil eye," warning him he better start thinking about shutting up. Leon also gave Jake a warning glance.

Jake ordered the whole bottle as his mouth got bigger and bigger. He didn't care.

"I don't understand how a loving God can allow something like this to happen! Or how a caring God can take such a sweet girl and such a small boy with so much potential away from you." Jake continued his tirade.

Leon leaned into Jake and whispered, "I thought you came back here to soothe the bereaved, not to question their faith."

Jake poured himself another drink from the bottle. Taking the bottle from Jake, Leon shook his head and said, "You're cut off."

Jake continued, looking straight at Gordy, "Your God better be good and strong when the tears come bustin' through—when you face the night, realizing you're not blessed at all. Yes, siree, your God better have mighty big shoulders then because he's goin' to need 'em to hold a big man like you up."

Jake looked at Leon. "I do believe I want that entire bottle you have in your hand sittin' right here in front of me!"

"No more, you're done. Go back to New York," Leon exclaimed.

Trudy rose from her seat and walked over to Jake, took his arm, and stood him on his feet. "You're comin' with me, cowboy."

"Where are we goin', Trudy?" Jake asked. "You're not takin' me to Open Door. I don't wanna go to Open Door!"

"No, I'm takin' you to the hotel where you stayed the first time you made your presence known in this town. When you saved our Memorial Day celebration. When you were our hero. That's where I'm takin' you."

She walked a stumbling Jake out the door.

"This isn't like you, Jake." She looked him straight in the eye. "Somethin's eatin' you up inside. You gotta find out what that somethin' is. You gotta let it go, cowboy. You need what those two back at Crabby's have."

They walked across the street and into the lobby of the hotel.

"He needs a room," Trudy said to the clerk. The clerk looked suspiciously at Jake.

"Don't worry," Trudy said. "I'll tuck him in. He's not goin' to cause any trouble."

Trudy did just that. She tucked him in, but before she left, she said, "Those guys you just lit into down at Crabby's, they've both got grievin' to do. I have a sneakin' feeling so do you. You just can't touch that grief that you're battlin' right now. You will one day, and when that day comes, heaven help you, cowboy."

"Trudy, what do I need those fellas back at Crabby's have?" Jake slurred.

"Faith," she replied, giving him a farewell kiss on the cheek.

Trudy walked to the door to leave. She had learned long ago never to try to talk to a drunk. You couldn't win. They wouldn't remember the next day, anyway. She turned around, looked at Jake all tucked in, and said, "You're welcome."

She closed the door behind her and began her walk home. It had been a long day, and it just got longer with the appearance of Jake. Everyone was on edge. Still, she could smile through her tears. There had been a victory today. She looked inside Crabby's as she walked by. She didn't have to go in. Phil had ordered another coke, and Gordy was drinking orange juice. They were okay. They had their faith.

As Gordy walked home to his ranch, he thought it strange—the things people say to you when somebody dies. It was even stranger the things people give you. Tourists were giving him breath mints at

212

the cemetery. What in the world did that mean? He guessed they just didn't know what else to do. Just give him something. Dig in your pockets and just give him something. And that's what they did. He wasn't going to try to figure it out. They meant well, and that was enough.

Then there was Jake. He meant well too. He just had a big mouth when he drank too much. Gordy didn't know whether to feel sorry for him or hit him. One thing was for certain, Gordy would never forget that night. Jake's words would ring true. "*God better have big shoulders to hold you when the tears come bustin' through.*"

The next morning, Jake walked, gingerly, into Belle's Bakery. That's where he knew he would find Trudy. Trudy was sitting at the corner table with her extra crispy doughnut.

"You need some grease, Jake?" Belle asked.

"Yep, gall bladder's sayin' send down grease." Jake admitted.

Belle handed him two extra crispy doughnuts, and he walked over to join Trudy.

"Do I need to apologize to anyone this morning?" Jake asked.

Trudy nodded and answered, "Gordy, Phil, and maybe Leon too."

"How about you?" Jake asked.

"No apology needed. I just gave you a lecture after I tucked you in. You probably don't remember," Trudy answered.

There was silence for a moment, and then Trudy asked, "Does it take a storm to get you back here? Because if it does, we don't want you back. We can't take much more. This town has been rocked to its core. The last thing we need is a cowboy stirin' things up again."

She got up to leave. At the doorway, she turned, "Leave Kate alone. Don't go to Open Door. She can't take much more either."

And then she was gone.

Jake sat there looking at those greasy doughnuts. What Trudy didn't realize was that he did remember. He remembered every word of her lecture last night, and he was going to do exactly what she had told him not to do. He was going to walk right up the street to Open Door. He would see Kate. He had to see Kate. He had to tell her the truth about himself and why he would not be back ever again. Trudy was right—he did have a grief he couldn't touch. A grief so raw he didn't want to go near it, much less touch it.

But Kate deserved an answer, and by god, he was going to give her one. Sometimes Trudy made sense, sometimes she didn't, and he was going to come as close as he could to this grief of his by talking to Kate. Yes, he would come close, but he was not going to touch it.

Kate opened the door. Once again, she was caught unaware. There he stood as if he had never gone away—Jake.

"Back again?" she questioned."

"May I come in?" he asked.

Lord, help me, Kate thought. *Why can I not tell this man no?*

She stood aside for him to enter. He walked straight to the kitchen, pulled open the cabinet, and retrieved their infamous bottle of whisky along with two glasses.

Jake walked to the table, pulled out a chair, and sat down. He felt like a crumbled man. The last thing he needed was a drink, and yet it was the only thing that would get him through what he had to say. He poured the shots and handed her one.

"The first time we did this, I was telling you all my secrets," Kate began.

"I remember," Jake replied.

"The second time, we were cleaning up a mess the storm had made. What is it this time, Jake?"

They both swallowed hard before he began, "You're not the only one with a past, Kate. You live long enough, we all have 'em."

He poured himself another shot and continued, "That's why we all run around with guilt on our shoulders heavy as boulders. I've disguised my guilt behind my humor and by keeping myself busy all the time."

Kate took another shot.

"I'm listening," she replied.

"When your burden is heaviest, you can always lighten a little some other burden. At the times when you cannot see God, there is still open to you this sacred possibility, to show God; for it is the love and kindness of human hearts through which the divine reality comes home to men, whether they name it or not. Let this thought then, stay with you: there may be times when you cannot find help, but there is no time when you cannot give help." (George S. Merriam)

Gordy was sitting on the steps of his front porch when he saw the three of them coming toward the ranch. They were holding hands—two sisters and their brother, little Nate, Sam's playmate. Not saying a word, they walked up to him and sat on the steps next to him. Little Nate kept shuffling his feet.

It was Natalia, the oldest of the three, who spoke first. "Hi, Mr. Gordy."

Gordy cleared his throat, trying to ignore the lump that had formed deep inside his gut.

"Hey, girls."

Looking at little Nate, he forced himself to hold out his hand. "Give me five, Nate!"

Little Nate obliged and then quickly looked down.

Kelli, the younger sister, said, "We brought you a flashlight, Mr. Gordy."

Gordy looked at it and said, "That's a mighty big flashlight."

Natalia replied, "It was Nate's idea, but we knew you would need a big one. And this was the biggest one we could find down at the hardware store."

"Why do I need a big flashlight?" Gordy asked.

Kelli replied, "Miss Trudy told us that you had to find your way out of a dark hole."

Gordy nodded. "I see."

Little Nate looked at Gordy and began nodding his head.

Gordy looked at Nate's big eyes filled with questions, knowing even though he was the adult and supposed to know all the answers, he couldn't find them this time. So he just patted Nate on the shoulder.

Gordy felt the lump in his throat getting bigger.

He finally said, "Trudy's right—about finding my way out of a dark hole."

Natalia said, "Kelli, Nate, and I want you to find your way out soon."

Little Nate spoke next. "That's why we looked high and low for the biggest one we could find. We want you to get out of that hole fast!"

Gordy took all three of those youngsters and held them close. That was his way of saying thank you. He couldn't speak, and he refused to allow the tears to fall while they were sitting next to him. There was just something about an adult crying in front of children.

Nothing more was said. The three stood up, almost simultaneously, and began to walk down the path.

They turned to wave when suddenly, little Nate came running back to Gordy, threw his arms around his neck, leaned in close to Gordy's ear, and whispered, "I miss them, too."

Just as suddenly, he ran back to his sisters who were waiting.

It was only then that Gordy's tears escaped. He gripped the flashlight as if it were a lifeline and walked inside.

"Can I do this?" he asked himself.

He was determined.

"A little child shall lead them," he whispered as he continued to walk.

He forced himself to go into the bedroom he and Jessie had shared. He placed the flashlight on the empty pillow next to his own. It was beginning to get dark. He flicked it on. He took off his shoes and lay down on his side of the bed—the first time he had stepped foot into the room since the news had broken his heart.

"At least, it's a start," he said to himself.

He couldn't continue facing the pillow where Jessie's face had once smiled up at him; he turned his back to the light and looked across the room.

There they were, right where she had left them not so long ago—her shoes. It was then he remembered Jake's words, and they were ringing ever true.

He remembered, *"Your God better be good and strong when the tears come bustin' through—when you face the night, realizing you're not blessed at all. Yes, siree, your God better have mighty big shoulders then because he's goin' to need 'em to hold a big man like you up."*

Gordy lay there and cried out, "I hope you're strong, God! I hope you have big shoulders 'cause I sure need to be held up!"

And the tears came like a torrent.

44

"As you know, I've been very successful in my life," Jake began. "I own my own business. I ploughed my way to the top. I didn't care who I stepped on to get there, and I didn't care how many women I slept with along the way. I used them, but in a way, they used me, too."

He swallowed hard before continuing, "I guess I was a lot like your mystery man you told me about. I betrayed a lot of people in my life, Kate. I'm not proud of that, especially since I've known you."

He took her hands in his. Kate looked at him, knowingly, but not anticipating what might come next.

Jake looked at Kate so intensely she thought she would become a little pool of water on the floor. It was like a laser when he said, "Kate, I had a wife that I betrayed."

Kate didn't blink. Her eyes looked right through him.

Jake knew that look well. The one he and Charlie had talked about often. He remembered very vividly the talks he had shared with Charlie about understanding girls.

Jake continued, "The best thing that ever happened to me was finding this little town," Jake said, still holding her hands in his.

Kate answered, "I feel the same. I came upon this place quite by accident. Best thing I ever did was take that exit to fill my empty gas tank."

Jake looked down before continuing. "I want to tell you about my ex-wife," he said. "I let her down."

Kate did not interrupt with her own questions. She dared not do that. She had waited too long for him to open himself to her. This was his door. He had to walk through it.

"She was a petite little thing. She was religious like you," Jake began.

Kate smiled. She found it almost amusing how people tossed out the word *religious*. They hadn't learned yet that it wasn't religion. It was all about relationship. She kept listening.

"She was good to me. She was good for me—I just didn't see it at the time. She wanted a baby more than anything in the world, but I wasn't sure I did, so I kept putting her off. She kept pushing and pushing for me to agree with her, and the more she pushed, the more I ran the other way."

Jake shifted in his chair.

"I've learned that nothing is easy about confessing things about our past," Kate said. "I've also learned once it's confessed, it's a lot easier to move on."

She encouraged Jake to keep talking.

Again he shifted in his chair.

"Well, one evening, I came home from work, and she was happier than usual. Dinner was cooking in the oven, and she welcomed me home with a kiss," Jake continued. "She led me to the living room and announced she was going to have a baby."

Jake got up from his chair and walked over to the window.

"I was shocked. I thought we had agreed not to have any children. I did not react well to her news, and I'm not proud of it to this day. I felt she had betrayed me by stopping all her birth control pills. I felt she had tricked me. I was not happy."

Kate turned to look at him. "Go on," Kate said.

"Well, she thought I would be happy—once I got used to the idea. I wasn't, and I wasn't going to get used to the idea—ever. I told her so. I wanted a career—a career that would allow me to go on vacations and buy my own toys, not kids toys. I wanted all of her attention. I didn't want to share her with anyone, especially a baby that would definitely take up all her time. She had this fantasy that I would twirl her around the room and start picking out baby wallpaper."

Kate walked over to him. They both looked out the window.

"I said the unthinkable to my wife, Kate." Jake confessed.

"What was that?" Kate asked.

"I demanded she get an abortion."

Jake looked down and then back at Kate. "I will never forget the look on her face. I betrayed my wife in the worst way I could have ever done to any woman, especially the woman I married. I walked out then. I just plain disappeared for three weeks. She didn't know where I was. I didn't call her. I didn't want to talk to her. I had a three-week bachelor party of my own—mostly with redheads. To this day, she never knew where I was or what I was doing."

Kate said nothing; she only stared at him. She refused to ask questions. He had to tell her; he had to say it out loud.

Jake walked to the table and poured another shot. He gulped it down, turned to Kate, and said, "She did. She had the abortion."

"Our marriage went downhill rapidly after that," Jake continued.

Kate kept standing at the window, tears forming in her eyes. Should she turn around? Jake sat down at the table once again.

"I blamed her for tricking me; she blamed me for telling her to do such a thing. She started drinking, and I started staying more and more evenings at the office with my 'then' secretary. It was a mess."

Kate began to feel she couldn't breathe. It all came back. It was still raw. She had made the opposite decision with her baby, but she experienced a parallel guilt of her own. She too had given up her child in a different way. Still, there was the giving up of something precious. She turned and faced Jake.

"What happened next?"

Jake answered, "It didn't last. Her parents showed up, called me every name in the book, and took their daughter home with them. Divorce papers arrived a few months later. I didn't try to fight it. Too many bridges had been burned. Too much hurt had been caused. I signed the papers with no contest, and it was done. She ended up in therapy. The door was closed."

Jake walked over to Kate, looked at her, and asked, "I know you think I am an awful person, don't you? You are probably thinking, 'What a jerk.'"

Kate looked at him and took his face in her hands before answering, "No, Jake, I love you. It's what you did that I don't like."

Jake turned and left the kitchen. He walked outside. Turning back to Kate, he said, "Well, now you know why I run. I'm not cut out for these deep things—these love things. Now you know why settling down is just not for me. I've learned the hard way. I came back this time for Gordy. I had to pay my respects. I don't think I helped him much last night at the bar. In fact, I made a fool of myself."

"So you're leaving again," Kate managed to ask.

"Yes, but this time I won't be back."

Kate walked up to him and said, "I can't help you, Jake. You've built bricks and mortar around yourself. Only you can seek out why the wall was built in the first place, and only you can discover how to tear it down. You just may have to walk around your own personal Jericho."

He looked puzzled as she continued, "One day, you'll know. One day, you'll discover the answers. Until then, don't come back."

He did not speak.

She touched his cheek and tenderly said, "Do me a favor."

He could only nod.

"I've heard too many goodbyes in my life. I've stood at too many graves. I've promised myself I wouldn't paint myself in a corner ever again. And then you showed up, tipping that cowboy hat of yours. Frankly, it scared me to death, and now I know why. You always seemed to show up when I needed you. There you were after the storm. Here you are coming back to give your condolences to Gordy, so my favor is, please don't say goodbye. Just give me a sign to close this out. Just don't say goodbye."

Jake could only nod as he turned to go. Then he turned around and left her as he had seen her that very first time. He tipped his hat while she stood there in the distance.

The place she had vowed never to return all those years ago. Her corner. There was one lone tear that ran down her cheek. She didn't know it, but Jake escaped before she could see a tear, very much like hers, leave his own eyes.

Jake walked toward town. He had one more stop to make. He had to see Trudy. The first time he came back after the storm, he had a job to do. He had repairs to make, messes to clean, trees to clear, branches to break, and roads to make passable again. He could clear the messes left behind by storms he could touch and throw into bags and press into wood chippers. He was familiar with that kind of debris. But this? This was so different.

He didn't know why, but he felt an irresistible force to see the woman clad in purple, the one he met the first time he came to this town. The one who loved lard. He had to say goodbye to Trudy. She was special. He couldn't leave until he saw her.

Kate stood on her porch and watched Jake walk away.

"One of those photo moments you never forget," she said to herself. She knew that only God could tear down his walls. She had to lean on her faith. She had to turn him over to God.

"I will never stop praying for you, Jake," she whispered as he walked out of her sight. He never looked back. In a way, she was glad, but in another way, she couldn't help but wonder—if he had—would he have changed his mind? Would she have run to him?

Before Kate turned to go back into Open Door, she whispered to herself, "I've promised myself many things in my lifetime, but this promise shatters my heart. I promise to let you go."

It was that time of day when Jake knew Trudy would be at the coffeehouse listening to Chip, the ever-so-popular-singer/songwriter who would be rehearsing, preparing for the evening crowd.

Trudy knew Jake would see Kate before he left. She wondered what he would say to her; she didn't have to wonder long. Jake walked through the door, spotted Trudy, and joined her at her table.

Trudy looked up at him.

"What's on your mind, cowboy?"

"I'm leaving."

"Where are you goin'?"

"Back to the city."

"I see," she replied.

"Is that all you have to say?"

"Yep."

"Remember when I first met you?" Jake asked.

Trudy laughed, as she remembered.

"Remember? Are you kidding? You had every head turnin' and spinnin' when you first set foot in this town!"

"Remember what you did?"

"Yep. I came over to you with my extra crispy fried doughnut, invited you to sit down with me at my table, and asked you what you were runnin' from."

Jake nodded.

"And now here we sit and—"

"And what, cowboy? What's on your mind? Or is it your heart you're battlin' with?"

Jake did not reply. Trudy knew how to cut right to the bottom line, always leaving him speechless.

"I just figured I had to say goodbye to you. Any parting words of advice for me, Trudy?"

"Well, since you asked, you remind me of Chip in a way."

She nodded toward Chip who gave her a sincere smile.

She continued, "I've known Chip a long time. Met him when he first came to town. He was a youngster in college at the time looking for summer work."

She took a sip of coffee.

"He didn't really know how much talent he had in that voice of his nor in his guitar strummin'."

Jake looked up at Chip as he continued to play.

Trudy continued, "Yep, you remind me of him in a way."

"How so? I can't sing. I don't play a guitar," Jake replied.

"No, but you both have calluses," Trudy almost whispered.

Jake looked down at his hands, not really understanding.

Trudy continued, "Chip's got calluses on his fingers from all his guitar playin', and you've got 'em all over your heart."

She looked at Jake and said in a low voice, "I'm goin' to let you in on a secret, Jake."

Jake leaned into her, looking her straight in the eye.

"What's that, Miss Trudy? You are so wise in so many things."

"Don't mock me, cowboy. That hat of yours doesn't turn me on or off in any way, but I know who does that to you."

She looked him right back straight in the eyes and said, "Runners are not bulletproof, Jake, and you're a runner. Told you that the first day I saw you in those cowboy boots."

Jake knew exactly what she was talking about. She cut right to the chase. The bullet she sent between his eyes was filled with truth that he refused to admit.

"Hey, Miss Trudy," Chip interrupted. "Wanna hear my new song I just wrote for all these city folk with forlorn faces who have come to our little town? I wanna give you a special preview."

Trudy turned her gaze from Jake, looking at Chip. "Of course I do. Jake here would like to hear it too before he hits the road."

Jake was grateful for the interruption. Trudy was getting too close to his head. And once Trudy spoke, well, you just didn't forget what she ever had to say. It stayed with you like indigestion. He had heard about that poor grocery store clerk who made a special section in the store for her Chicken in a Biskit crackers.

Chip said, "This is a song I just wrote. Need your opinion before I sing it for the first time tonight."

Trudy gave him the thumbs-up sign.

Chip began to sing "Hometown Girl."

Somewhere in the middle of the song, Jake began to listen to the words that hit straight to his heart.

"Flew out of Laguardia, the New York city lights could sweep you away, up speeding through the sky, but I'm just writing—how it's the heavens that made you. I wouldn't change you at all. You're the arms that have saved me. Love you for who you are. 'Cause you're my home, you're my small-town girl. You're the reason I'm the man that I am. The look in your eyes, holding on tight, staying up all night our silhouettes in the firelight, my whole world, my hometown girl…"

"Well, well," Trudy exclaimed when the song was done. "Perfect song, I would say."

She looked at Jake.

"Made some memories here, eh, Jake? Sometimes those memories make you dance at night—other times they make you cry—but there ain't nothin' like the real thing."

"Why don't you spell it out, Trudy?"

"I will. It's time to let the whisky-breathin' mornin' breath women go, Jake. It's time for the real deal, and you know who the real deal is. This is your one time to get it right, Jake. Don't blow it."

"Speaking from experience, Trudy? Have you ever been in love?"

"Once."

"What happened?"

"Nobody knows but me, cowboy, and I'm not goin' to start sharing my secrets with someone who has their own head on crooked."

She looked at him and continued, "Maybe it's time for you to leave, Jake. Better go get some pharmacon."

Trudy stood to leave.

"What in the world is pharmacon?" Jake asked.

Trudy gave Chip another thumbs-up sign. "Great song, Chip. It reminds me of someone we know, don't you think?"

Chip gave her a salute and replied, "Would you be thinkin' of the cowboy from New York City with the forlorn look?"

He looked at Jake.

"I like writin' true life stories," Chip said.

Trudy looked over her shoulder as she left the coffeehouse.

"Pharmacon, Jake, is God's healing salve. It's best if you go find it."

And then she was gone, leaving Chip with the calloused fingers. Leaving Jake with the calloused heart.

Jake walked out of the coffeehouse and took one last look at the town that had tried its best to hold him, walked to his car, and began his drive out of town.

Trudy was halfway to her salon when she turned and saw him go. Charlie saw it too.

"Hey, Miss Trudy, where's Jake goin'? Is he leavin', again?"

Trudy answered, "I hope he's goin' in search of healing salve."

"Huh?" Charlie questioned.

"He'll be back. Too much unfinished business here to take care of. He's full of questions, and a questioning man always finds his answers."

It was cloudy on the day Jake left, and when the rain came, it didn't want to stop. Kate stayed inside. That's where Charlie found her when he showed up sopping wet on her front porch.

"Come in this house, Charlie," Kate exclaimed.

"I thought you might need some company," Charlie said. "Got any sweet tea?"

45

Charlie was sitting on one of the beach chairs, looking out at the lake. He was helping to store the outdoor furniture to prepare for winter that seemed just around the corner. He had to think. It seemed to him that sometimes you could only sit back and watch while a person grieved. He was thinking of Gordy and how he kept working through the loss of his Jessie and little Sam.

Charlie kept looking out at the lake.

Soon it'll be frozen, he thought.

He remembered how little Sam used to play on the water's edge, Jessie close by his side, the two splashing each other, laughing and hugging each other. Those two were special all right.

Charlie's thoughts took him back not so long ago. He missed them too.

Jessie lived in her own little castle world—all sparkly and glittery. Everyone wanted to spend time with her. She radiated promise and hope. People wanted to rub shoulders alongside her, hoping to get some of that glitter on themselves. A person always felt lighthearted after a visit with Jessie. She was the type who attracted people—the inviting type. When she looked at you, you just couldn't help but walk up to her. Even conversations about the weather seemed an important topic to talk about. She always cared about you, and she was never in a hurry to get away from you. She took her time, kind of like grandmas do with their grandkids, always smiling and walking slow, looking at plants, bugs, and things.

That's how Charlie best described Jessie. He questioned, "Is it any wonder how much she's missed? It's as if a light's been turned off in this town."

Charlie got up from his chair and walked toward the water. There was a slight breeze. He pulled his collar closer to his neck. He wished he had brought his scarf that Sarah had knitted for him. He wondered when she had learned to knit. It seemed she was always full of surprises.

His thoughts went to little Sam. That boy had a zest for life that was contagious. He was special. He was the type of young one that entered a room, and that very room lit up. He was a ray of sunshine that permeated every corner, nook, and cranny. He was a young child that had already developed a sense of humor that no one could resist. Both adults and children laughed with little Sam and all his antics.

Charlie remembered the very day he had decided little Sam also had a certain gentleness about him. He had watched that moment when he had leaped with joy when he saw Kelli walking toward his house. She was struggling as she tried to walk down the hill that led to his yard. He scurried up that hill to help her. Charlie watched him as he took her hand, and his other arm went around her waist to keep her from stumbling.

The whole town saw that gentleness, and yet he was *all* boy. He skinned his knees and banged his elbows. He fell on his nose and got back up again. He attempted to ride old metal trucks down his driveway—much to the horror of Trudy. But he didn't mean to scare people; it was the thrill of the ride for little Sam. Charlie figured that Trudy was just old and could see accidents in her mind before they happened.

Charlie walked along the water's edge and continued to think of little Sam.

He remembered his love of singing. Charlie could still see him running around town with a pretend microphone in the form of his mom's hairbrush, singing to the top of his lungs. Little Sam always looked up to Chip. Chip had taught him a lot of songs—little ditties he had written just for Sam to sing. He even had Sam come up to the platform one night in the coffee shop and sing one of those ditties with him. Needless to say, he brought the house down. And when he took a bow, the crowd clapped even louder.

Trudy believed he was destined for great things.

"He's goin' to make our town famous one day!" Trudy would proclaim.

No one knew where little Sam got all his talent to gather an audience. Gordy was such a quiet man, never seeking the limelight. Trudy said it was from Jessie. Charlie guessed that was true—her being a writer and all—you know the creative type. *Oh, and let us not forget her spunkiness*, Charlie thought. Sam was sure that, and more.

He ran everywhere he went. Little 'Mr. Man' people began to call him. Charlie remembered one Sunday when he came out to the middle of his front yard, dressed up with his little bow tie, pressed pants, and jacket, announcing to the whole village, "I'm goin' to church!"

Trudy proclaimed, "That boy is goin' to be a pastor one day!"

Someone else chided in, "A singin' pastor!"

Little Sam told his dad he wanted a guitar for Christmas, and Chip had already told Gordy he would give him lessons—for free— he said little Sam had a talent that was unheard of in others at his young age.

So Gordy bought the guitar and hid it in Jessie's writing room, anticipating little Sam's excitement that Christmas morning.

It was a plan to develop little Sam's love of singing. Gordy's plan. Jessie's plan. Chip's plan. Our town's plan.

God's plan was quite different from our plan, Charlie thought, picking up a stone and skipping it across the lake.

He looked up at the sky. "Sorry, God, but I question your plan right now," he said.

So many 'whys' continued to echo through the hallways of the homes in Brooksport Village.

People were shaking their fists at God.

Charlie remembered what Trudy had told him one day. She had said that God is okay with all the questions and fist-flingin'. She said God's shoulders were big enough to take it.

Charlie took one last look at the lake and went back to retrieve the summer chairs one at a time, storing them for the winter season.

"Guess I'm just goin' to cling to the promise that God makes all things good for those who love him," Charlie began.

"Sorry, God," he said out loud. "Right now, I'm findin' it very difficult to love. I'm mad, good and mad. I'm mad at you too, God. And one thing I know is that 'good' and 'mad' just don't mix at times like these."

"*Let it not be death but completeness. Let love melt into memory and pain into songs. Let the flight through the sky end in the folding of the wings over the nest. Let the last touch of your hands be gentle like the flower of the night. Stand still, o beautiful end, for a moment, and say your last words in silence. I bow to you and hold up my lamp to light you on your way.*" (Rabindranath Tagore)

46

Gordy knew it was time. It was dusk when he made the decision. He had to go to Jessie's writing room, Jessie's quiet place. He had to sit in her chair. He had to stare at her computer. He had to look out at the horses that had inspired her. He had to follow her footsteps in his mind. He had to. He simply had to.

He looked at the nightstand beside the bed where the flashlight stood upright.

He walked over to it. "Maybe this will help," he said to himself. "It's goin' to be dark soon. You need lights in a dark hole to find your way out of," Gordy whispered, remembering his conversation with Natalia, Kelli, and little Nate.

He took the flashlight and walked outside.

"Looks like a full moon tonight," Gordy said aloud.

He walked slowly toward Jessie's attic getaway writing room.

It took his breath away when he opened the door.

It was as if he could smell her presence.

"How could someone so full of life one day be gone the next?" he questioned.

He walked over to her desk and sat down, staring at the computer he dared not touch. She had given him an ultimatum not to go near the keyboard where once she herself had spilled water. No liquids were allowed at her desk after that. Gordy remembered it had been a mess. Thankfully, all her files had been safe, but it set her back in time for the completion of her book.

Maybe, just maybe, if she hadn't worked so hard to finish the manuscript, she would have been delayed and on another plane—not the one *that...*Gordy shook the question from his mind. He wouldn't allow himself to think about the what-ifs in this whole sad, tragic story. It only gave him the feeling of being one step closer to going stark raving mad. He had to be calm for his own good.

His eyes scanned the entire room and fell upon a photo of Jessie and little Sam in the snow. He had snapped that picture the previous winter. He had captured all her spunkiness with the push of a button on his camera as she ran through the snow, tongue sticking out, catching snowflakes with little Sam.

Right beside that picture frame was another where she had posed beside a pile of wood, leaning on the very ax she had given to Gordy that day they had been brought back together after so many years. He walked over to the picture and picked it up.

He smiled when he remembered her slinging that ax around, chopping that wood because she "wanted a fire that night." He held the picture close to his chest. Oh yes, that was the day she had returned, and that time it was forever—until—he kept picturing those planes hitting those buildings over and over again.

He shook his head, demanding the memory to flee. He thought of the woman she had been. The wife that she was—the mother that she was...She was afraid of nothing. She would just as soon pick up an ax as place a bow in her hair. She was daring and, simply, loved adventure. And oh, how she loved horses.

He walked to the window, gazing out at the one she loved most, Star Bright.

He remembered her quiet side and how she needed to be alone at times. He had asked her why she needed all that quiet around her. He confessed to her that he thought something was wrong when she retreated into a room and closed the door. She had looked at him and whispered, "To write, Gordy, I need quiet time to write."

That was the moment he decided to build her a quiet place right there on their land amid the horses—her very own respite, her very own oasis.

"I just fell in love with you all over again!" she had exclaimed to him, flinging her arms around him and kissing him wildly all over his face.

"I would marry you over and over again, Gordy, my man." She had gone on and on. Made him feel like a million bucks. She was so grateful for everything that he had ever done for her.

Gordy turned from the window and walked to the middle of the room.

He had always wanted their home to be a safe place, a shelter of peace, and a palace of protection. He had told her that. He remembered how they had worked together to make their stable a safe haven not only for themselves and for their son but also for their horses. That's what they did, and they did it well.

Again he walked to the window, looking out at the horses.

"We sure rescued a lot of horses and brought them back to life, didn't we, Jess?" he asked as if she could hear him. "Those horses out there—they're the ones that everyone else seemed to have forgotten. Well, they're not forgotten anymore."

Those horses gave a lot of children who visited their village town a lot of pleasure as they gathered to ride, feed, and water those once forgotten ones who had now been nursed back to health by tender loving hands of husband and wife working together.

He walked to yet another picture. It was a white horse. It was Star Bright. Gordy would never forget the day he brought that horse of unbelievable needs to their stable. Jessie fell in love with that white horse. She saw restoration for that horse. Diligently, she worked with it and literally loved him back to health. Gordy had found her one night sleeping there in the stable beside the horse she had made her own. He had walked over to the sleeping pair and saw a note Jessie had written. He had saved it.

He walked to the bookcase, took a book from the shelf, flipped through the pages, and found the note she had written. He knew the special place where she had tucked that note. She had read it often. He walked to the nearest chair because he knew his legs would not hold him upright. Tears formed in his eyes as he read aloud.

"Star Bright—that's the name I give to you. You will survive this. Do you hear me? You are so good and so strong. You will be great in stature. I will love you and make you strong again. Love is powerful, and so is prayer. I pray for you. Star Bright, do you hear me? You will survive."

Gordy spent all of the evening in Jessie's private place. He didn't want to leave. He wanted to hold on. She was everywhere. The scarf she had left behind was still on the chair. He picked up her pens, just wanting to hold what she had touched. He opened drawers and shut them. He walked to her refrigerator and saw her stash of sweet tea that she only allowed herself to drink—outside. It was when he touched her Bible on the table next to her favorite chair that he knew it was time to go. The evening had turned dark.

With tears in his eyes and the note in his hands, he left Jessie's quiet place and walked outside to the gate where Star Bright stood as if watching and waiting for a woman who would never return.

Gordy stood in silence for a long time. He looked up at the sky, and there were stars everywhere along with that full moon. It was as if the whole earth was lit up.

Gordy walked over to Star Bright. "I need you to walk with me, buddy," he said to the horse. "They're gone, buddy, both of them."

He patted Star Bright's head. "You miss her too, don't you?"

Star Bright spoke his own language to Gordy at that exact moment. His neigh proved it.

"I know you do." Gordy choked on his own words.

They stopped walking at the gate as Gordy continued, "You were hers. I'm glad you knew how much you were loved. She nursed you back to health."

Gordy led the horse into the corral. "I know how much I was loved too. She had my baby. It took us a while to get where we were, but we got there. Oh yes, we did," Gordy said. He continued talking. "And little Sam, he knew he was loved too."

That marvelous white horse looked at Gordy. "You know there was a bedtime story Jessie always told Sam at night. It was called, 'Baby Star.'"

Gordy had memorized that bedtime story himself. He had stood outside Sam's bedroom door when Jessie was tucking him in. Sam always listened so intently to her gentle voice.

Gordy rubbed Star Bright's mane and began.

"I'm going to tell you that story," Gordy said.

Gordy put his arm around Star Bright's neck.

"Here goes. It's called 'Bedtime for Baby Star.'"

Gordy convinced himself he was going to do this. Grief made him do it. He would get through it.

He coughed. He choked on his words, but he began.

"*Once there was a little star. He lived up near the sun. And every night at bedtime, that baby star wanted to have some fun.*"

He rubbed Star Bright's nose.

"*He would shine and shine and fall and shoot and twinkle oh so bright, and he said, 'Mommy, I'll run away if you make me say goodnight.'*"

Gordy took a breath. Then he continued, "*And then his Mommy kissed him on his sparkly nose and said, 'No matter where you go, no matter where you are, no matter how big you grow, and even if you stray far, I'll love you forever because you'll always be my baby star.'*"

Gordy looked straight into Star Bright's eyes as tears filled his own.

And at that very moment, Star Bright blinked as if he understood.

It was near dawn when Gordy's tears stopped falling upon the soft nose of the one his Jessie had loved so well.

47

The miles kept adding up as Jake pushed the gas pedal to the floor. Why was he asking himself the question? Over and over it kept coming back to his mind. *Why am I fighting this feeling I have for Kate? How am I going to live without her? Could I be good to her? Could I be true to her? Could I not damage her beyond repair?*

He felt it wasn't fair to her. He couldn't hurt her. She was such a tender soul.

Suddenly, he thought of those bleeding heart flowers in her garden. They were fragile like Kate, but they had survived the storm that had ravaged Brooksport Village. Yet they could be crushed so easily. It was that little teardrop at the tip of that fragile heart that got him every time. He simply could not and would not be the cause of that final tear falling to the ground from Kate's eyes.

He thought of Trudy.

He exclaimed as if she were sitting right next to him, "What's so wrong with whisky-breathin'-mornin'-breath women, anyway?"

They were easy to walk away from, and he was good at that. He liked the familiar.

With that resolved in his mind, he kept driving to the city while "Hometown Girl" kept spinning through his mind.

And the miles between them just kept growing.

What he didn't realize was that someone was in hot pursuit.

Charlie thought that at any given moment, he would see Jake coming back into town. He kept watching for him to turn the corner. He figured he would suddenly stop that car of his and come to his senses. Charlie thought he would stop for gas or for lunch, take a breath, and ask himself, "*How can I leave a woman like Kate?*" Charlie thought that was the craziest thing he had ever seen any man in his right mind do—leave Kate. Maybe Jake wasn't in his right mind. Maybe Kate was right—Jake was a mess.

Trudy and Charlie had both watched him go. No wave goodbye. And the traffic light that had just turned red when he approached it didn't stop him either. He ran right through it. Charlie half-wished there had been a cop there to stop him. They never seemed to be around when you really needed them at times like when Jake left.

Charlie thought that Jake was one of those people who came into your life and you were never quite the same, especially when they left. It's always the good ones who seem to go, and Charlie was of the belief that everyone who loved Jake Arbor would keep on trying to walk in, around, and beside the footprints he had left behind.

Charlie felt sad for Kate. She went into a sort of seclusion. You know the kind people can do when a memory beckons. They put on a mask of "dealing with life," and some do it quite well, like Kate. They smile a little too much, they hug a little too tightly, they say nice things with lots of adjectives, and then at night, they look at themselves in the mirror. They finally allow the tears to stream down their faces, cracking the mask before taking it off for the dark night to unfold.

Charlie concluded that was how Kate was. Nobody knew her like he did, and nobody knew Charlie like Miss Kate except for, maybe, Jake. After all, he did teach Charlie all about girls after they threw out the coffee made with wennie water.

Charlie had watched Kate go out to that flower garden of hers, and it almost seemed like she was waiting for those bleeding hearts to bloom again. Charlie guessed she wanted to prove their strength to survive, and she could be like them too.

Charlie felt her sadness, and yet he knew he couldn't touch what she was feeling. It was a private matter. He understood. He had private matters of his own. Disturbing someone with private matters was not a good idea. He supposed Trudy was right. People like that with those private matters needed pharmacon.

Charlie finally decided that Jake was gone for good. He quit looking for him to reappear. But he still couldn't understand Jake Arbor and how he could not only leave Kate but also a town that was still in mourning for Jessie and little Sam. Charlie had to reconcile himself to the thought that Jake had his reasons, so he, along with all the other townspeople, kept muddling through, trying their best to help Gordy in any way they could.

"There's a price to becoming involved in the struggles of others (David Mccasland), but we find to our amazement that we have power to keep wonderfully poised in the center of it all." (Oswald Chambers)

The first thing Gordy saw while sitting on the steps of his front porch was the purple scarf tied in a bow around her head. She walked up to him and said, "Now don't you think I have designs on you, handsome. I don't."

Trudy showed him the basket. "I brought you a casserole."

She walked right up those porch steps, stared directly at him, and said, "You know what they say about women bringing casseroles to men in bereavement—you better beware—but I'm not most women. Oh, I will return because this casserole is not in a throwaway container. I'm comin' back for it because you need to talk not because I think you're the best-lookin' thing that ever came into this little village town of ours, and that includes that cowboy that just absconded from our town. You just get yourself up from there and follow me into the kitchen."

Gordy had to smile because he couldn't believe Trudy had said all that with only one breath.

He knew there was no use fighting or making excuses to Trudy. It was going to be her way today, and that was the bottom line. You didn't argue with Trudy, especially when she wore purple bows in her hair. That was her signature. She only wore purple bows when she meant business. And today she had one in her hair. So he obediently followed her into the kitchen. He watched her busying herself around the room, and just like a busy honeybee, she kept talking.

"I call it my special spaghetti casserole."

She looked at him, sighed, and said, "Come on, sugar, you need to eat."

She took his arm and sat him down at the table.

"Okay," she began, "I'm ready to listen."

"Trudy, you? You listen?" Gordy asked.

"Yes, I can listen. Now start talkin' while I give you somethin' to eat."

Gordy sat down at the table and watched as she kept walking in circles around the kitchen.

"It's too early for spaghetti." Gordy protested.

"Who said I was goin' to spoon out spaghetti? Where's a plate?"

"In the cabinet over the sink."

She retrieved a small plate and opened the basket. She took out a small bag and put a doughnut on the plate in front of Gordy, sat down, and said, "Extra crispy, just like you like it, sugar. Eat up. I'll join you."

Trudy took a breath. "You talk only when you're ready. Let's enjoy these doughnuts for now."

They ate in total silence.

"See," she said. "I can listen, even though you're not talkin'."

They kept taking one bite after another and kept looking at each other.

Suddenly, Trudy spotted the flashlight—the *big* flashlight.

"What's that, do you think it's big enough?"

"For what it's meant to do, yes, it's big enough."

Trudy looked at him with an unspoken question.

"It's mine because of your wise words to three little sweet ones at the cemetery."

Trudy remained silent and waited.

"Kelli, Natalia, and little Nate came over to my house with it."

Trudy sat back down.

"Go on," she urged.

"Those kids sat there with me on my front steps and told me why I needed it," Gordy said.

Trudy remained quiet.

"It was to help me see my way out of the black hole."

Trudy smiled as she remembered what she had told the three youngsters that fateful day.

"Oh," was all she could say.

And then she began, "Gordy, I understand why sometimes you have to be alone while you find yourself in this broken space of your life, and that's okay. I understand you have to get a grip on what has happened. And sometimes you can only find that in the privacy of your own home with the doors closed and the blinds down. Grief is untouchable. You don't want intrusions. But just know this—you don't have to go through it alone. I think Kelli, Natalia, and little Nate told you that in their own special way. There are others of us who want to help you too."

With that, she kissed him on the cheek and walked toward the door.

"I have to get back to the salon," she said.

Gordy watched her go. The last thing he saw was the purple scarf flying in the wind. Yes, that was Trudy. She knew darn well that scarf blew off her head. She probably untied it so it would blow off. She was making sure she had a reason to return to Gordy's front porch. He appreciated that. He loved her for it.

He smiled as he walked to the edge of the road where the scarf had landed, retrieved it, and slowly walked back to his house.

Gordy looked at the basket Trudy had brought when he walked back into the kitchen. There was another small bag. He opened it. A note inside said, "For tomorrow morning, extra crispy." He smiled and put it next to the coffeepot.

He took the spaghetti casserole dish from the basket. As he removed the little purple towel, he saw the Bible with another note, Psalm 119:105. He turned to the verse: "Thy word is a lamp to my feet and a light to my path."

That night, after he forced himself to eat the dinner Trudy had brought, he took the flashlight and the Bible to his bedroom. He placed them both on the empty pillow beside him, pushed the on button of the flashlight, and pointed it toward the open Bible of the verse he had read earlier.

It was that night that Gordy finally came to the truth that Trudy had spoken of earlier that day. He couldn't do this alone. He couldn't walk this trail of tears by himself. He had a whole village of people out there. They needed each other. And he finally realized that they all needed to cry together before they would ever be able to laugh again. He fell asleep—the first time he had slept through the night since 9/11.

"In desperate hope I go and search for her in all the corners of my house. I find her not. My house is small and what once has gone from it can never be regained. But infinite is thy mansion, my lord, and seeking her I have come to thy door." (Rabindranath Tagore)

49

Trudy and Gordy were sitting facing one another in the coffee shop.

"I don't know who I am anymore, Trudy," Gordy began.

Trudy gave him an understanding look, saying nothing.

He sighed and continued as he let his finger follow the coffee circle his cup had left on the table.

"Server's a little shaky today," Trudy replied.

It was her feeble attempt to say something, anything.

"People are nervous around me these days, Trudy. They just don't know what to say to me anymore after all that has happened," Gordy began. "Even you."

He took his napkin and wiped the table free of the coffee stain.

"Shoot, I don't even know what to say to myself," he continued. "I don't know the man in the mirror anymore. I seem to have lost my identity. My world centered around Jessie and Sam."

Trudy took his hand in hers and squeezed it.

He wanted her to feel comfortable.

"Trudy, it's okay you not knowing what to say. You just meeting me here and listening is enough."

Again, Trudy only smiled but did not let go of his hand.

"A lot of people don't know how to act around me, so they don't bother to come around. Friends I thought I had, well, I don't see them much now. It's as if they're afraid to mention Jessie and Sam, like, they're goin' to catch some kind of virus that they want to avoid."

Trudy finally said, "Oh, Gordy, this has hit so close to home, maybe they're afraid."

"Of what?"

"That something like this could happen to them."

Gordy looked at her as she continued, "I think people go into denial. They hide in any corner of their mind that they can find and pretend something like this didn't happen. They think if they don't acknowledge it, it will go away and not come so close to their own house."

She patted his hand and continued, "What they don't realize is they need to not only look at it but also stare it down."

She sighed before adding, "Don't be so hard on 'em, sugar. They are just at a loss. They're afraid your grief will spill over into their own lives, and they want to avoid that at all costs. It's part of bein' human."

She motioned to the server for a refill of coffee before continuing.

"But there's plenty of us who are strong enough to hold up what they can't for now."

Gordy replied, "I know, Wes has been a strong arm for me. You know he was the one who found me on my living room floor after I heard that recording."

Trudy nodded. "I know," she answered.

"He proved to me just how strong he was that day. After all he's been through, I imagine he could feel my own heart breaking."

Trudy took a sip of coffee.

Chip could be heard in the distance strumming his guitar.

"Chip must be writing a song back there," Trudy said.

Gordy smiled. "He is. He's memorializing little Sam. You know how much Sam looked up to Chip."

"Oh yes, I do," Trudy answered.

"He asked my permission to write a song about him."

Suddenly, the conversation shifted.

"Do you remember when I hired Wes?" Gordy asked.

"I do," Trudy replied.

"That was when he told me he may not have his eyes but that he had strong arms and legs that could still work. If I was willing to give him a chance, he could show me."

Again Trudy took his hand.

"Seems all I can do is keep grabbin' your hand, handsome. Somebody's goin' to think we got a thing goin' on, especially since I brought you that casserole," Trudy whispered.

"Yeah," Gordy replied. "You gotta watch out for women bringin' casseroles."

Trudy straightened up in her chair. "That's right, and don't you forget it!"

"But back to Wes," she said, "You gave him that chance."

Gordy nodded and took a sip of his coffee.

"Well, as I was saying, that day he found me on the floor, I found out just how strong those arms of his were. We sat there in the middle of that floor, and he held me while I cried like a baby."

Gordy motioned for the server.

"It's okay for men to cry, don't you think, Trudy? I mean, it doesn't make us less of a man, do you think?"

Trudy let go of his hand and exclaimed, "Yes, it's okay for men to cry! I think it's the sign of a hurt so deep that the pain has to come out, or the heart will explode! Kind of like a pressure cooker. Women don't have the market on cryin', Gordy. And you, my friend, are one of the manliest men I have ever known! So don't you think twice about shedding those tears of yours. It's the most natural thing you can do when you have loved someone so intensely and have had to let them go."

She took a sip of coffee.

"I hope I just made some sense to you because I cannot, for the life of me, remember a thing I just said!"

"That's what happens when the spirit takes over, Trudy. I really believe that God just spoke through you," Gordy replied.

"Do you have somewhere you have to be right now, Trudy? I don't want to keep you from where you're supposed to be."

"I have all day and all night if you need me to be here, sugar. I'm not goin' anywhere."

Gordy shifted the conversation back to Jessie.

"I find myself constantly staring at Jessie's shoes."

Trudy looked at him with compassion, grabbing his hand again. The speechless side of Trudy had resurfaced. People who had experienced their own torn heart knew when to be quiet.

"And I cannot even walk in little Sam's room," Gordy continued. Trudy shifted in her chair.

"Am I making you uncomfortable?" he asked.

"Oh no, Gordy, you need to talk," she replied. "I told you when I came over with all that stuff in my basket, remember?"

Gordy smiled and said, "I do. Oh yes, I remember."

"I'm glad," she replied.

"And I have to tell those sweet kids that their flashlight helped more than they will ever know," Gordy said." He continued, "That flashlight actually got me back in our bedroom. I was determined to sleep on the couch for the rest of my life."

They looked at each other, both in silence, both with a broken heart.

When Gordy got up to leave, he said his parting words to Trudy. "Thank you, Trudy. Little Nate is comin' by to ride one of the horses. It's time to go saddle up."

He stood, gave Trudy a kiss on the forehead, and walked out the door. Suddenly, he had switched gears. Trudy understood. Grieving people did that a lot. They wandered around. Sometimes their conversations didn't make sense, but that was okay. He had talked. He had shared. Today, that was enough.

Trudy watched him go.

"Sometimes you just gotta stare things down. Only Gordy can walk this rocky, winding, and thistle bound path."

She choked back her tears. She knew all too well that it was when the doors were closed and the blinds were drawn—well, that was where the biggest battles of grief were fought.

She stood up from the table. As she walked to the door, she said, "Well, Gordy, saddling up the horses is a start."

"It is important, when dealing with all aspects of grief, to keep the process moving. The temptation is to freeze, to stay perpetually recoiled against so terrible a blow." (Martha Hickman)

50

They say that time heals all wounds, and Brooksport Village had a gaping wound that would take a lot of salve to cover. They went through many months of minutes turning to hours and hours marching into days until the townspeople felt like becoming themselves again.

The town had to get to a point of accepting the fact they would never be the same again, especially Gordy. The status quo had been tinkered with. The old way of living was gone, and each of Gordy's friends had to go through different kinds of birthing pains to be reborn. But somehow, they did. They managed. Trudy said it was all because of an unseen hand that reached down and dried the town's tears.

Charlie believed her. God does mighty things, and the town got to a point where they weren't mad at God anymore. They needed him too much. They needed his strength. They needed his shoulders. So the town started leaning into his grace instead of fighting it.

The town had its memories, and life went on.

Charlie kept watching Gordy walk through his grief. He thought one of the turning points for Gordy came after all his talks with Trudy. He had heard about her casserole talk with him, along with their meetings at the coffeehouse. But Charlie kept wondering about the flashlight that Gordy kept carrying around, even in the daylight hours. Trudy told him there was a story behind that flashlight, but Gordy would have to tell him when the time was right for Charlie to know. She said Charlie would have to wait for that answer and when the time came that Gordy would tell him. And then he would have to sit quietly and listen. Gordy still needed to talk about things, so Charlie had made a promise to himself that he would do just that—listen when the time came. He was getting pretty good at listening. Trudy had also told Charlie that grieving people do things and say things that people might not understand at times, but that was just the way it was, and everybody needed to understand it. So that's what Charlie was going to do. He was going to understand Gordy—whatever he did and whatever he said. He felt that was the best way he could help him.

Gordy began to reach out to his friends. They were able to walk through their own grief with him, and Charlie thought that, in itself, helped Gordy a lot. Charlie hoped that he would never have to know the feeling of a loss like that. But Trudy had said Gordy was blessed beyond measure to have loved someone so deeply. She told Charlie he should pray that he would have a love like that one day. Charlie guessed that when he was a little older, he would understand more of Trudy's truths.

Trudy said that everyone had to take one step at a time. She said a lot to Charlie during those grieving days. She told him that adults sometimes don't know what to do or say. They just try to manage with what they have been given to work with. They try to do their best.

Charlie believed that to be true. All he had to do was look at Phil, his dad. He had done his best too. He had been thrown a boulder that had brought him to his knees when Charlie's mom died. He just couldn't handle it. Trudy told Charlie that he self-medicated with alcohol. That was true. Both Charlie and Phil had the emotional bruises to prove it. But a second chance came for Charlie and his dad—just like it would come for Gordy. Trudy said God always opens a door.

And that is what Charlie and the town clung to as they watched Gordy move forward. One thing was for sure, he would never ever find himself another Jessie, although healing would come.

Brooksport Village would never have another Jessie either. It would take a long, long time to get over this.

Charlie was so glad Trudy was a part of his life. She knew so much—more than a lot of people gave her credit for. Charlie just bet she had a story of her own—one that he didn't think he would ever come to know. But that was okay. Charlie respected privacy, but if the time ever came, he would be ready to listen.

51

Time marched on. Belle continued to make her extra crispy dough-nuts. Trudy continued to fix hair in that purple salon of hers, getting to know about all the tourists that came through those doors. Wes showed up at Gordy's stable, caring for the horses and just talking to Gordy on the porch when all the work was done. Phil stayed on the 'wagon.' Charlie was worried about him falling off when tragedy hit their town, but he remained true to his promise, never to drink again. And, the apron that had been Charlie's moms had come out of the closet for good. It continued to hang in the kitchen. Both Charlie and Phil received tremendous peace from that little yellow iris design every time they looked at it. Kate and Sarah continued to drink that awful sweet tea, understanding that Charlie's choice was now lemonade.

One day, Charlie and Kate were sitting on the bench near the flower garden when Sarah just appeared out of nowhere. Both Charlie and Kate laughed a lot when Sarah was around. Sarah just had a way about her that was inviting. Those two were alike in a lot of ways too. Phil said it was because they were both females, and he swore they all thought alike and that men would never understand them. Charlie just liked being around them. He always felt better after being with Kate. And when Sarah would show up—well, that was a double whammy—a good double whammy for Charlie.

Gordy had told him it was a blessing to be around two lovelies and that he should enjoy it. He said that years later, Charlie would cherish those moments, and then he had a far-off, sad look in his eyes.

Charlie thought he was thinking of Jessie and little Sam. Sometimes you couldn't get them off your mind. That's what you do when someone touches your heart the way they did. Once with you, now gone.

All in all, everything seemed to be balancing itself out. But there was someone missing—Jake. Charlie guessed that Jake really meant it when he told Kate he wouldn't be back. All his friends tried to erase him from their minds, especially Kate, but every once in a while, someone would mention his name.

Memories of Jake made the people who knew him smile, laugh, and cry at the same time. But that's what Jake did—he caused a myriad of emotions whether near or far, whether he stood in front of you or was running around in your mind. One thing remained constant in Brooksport Village. Every time someone saw a balloon making its lazy pathway through the sky, they always thought of Jake. There seemed to be more of those balloons showing up lately. It seemed to be a message of hope, thinking, just maybe…one day he would be back.

But a person needs to keep going forward. Some things you just have to keep forcing yourself to forget. Jake was one of them.

"At every point in the human journey, we find that we have to let go in order to move forward; and letting go means dying a little. In the process, we are being created anew, awakened afresh to the source of our being." (Kathleen R. Fischer)

PART VI

Memories Come Calling

52

Trudy had an itch. She wasn't even sure she wanted to scratch it. Her life was good. Maybe she could just take a deep breath and look the other way, pretend she didn't have the itch.

But when she sat straight up in bed at two o'clock in the morning, she knew. There was no doubt. Slowly, she planted both feet on the floor and walked over to her secret place. She found the key, unlocked the drawer, and stared at the box that held her untold past—a past she resented and yet held close. Could it be? She retrieved a metal box from the drawer and walked back to her bed. She set it in front of her and stared at it.

"I need a shot of whisky," she said to Buddy sleeping soundly on the pillow next to her own.

She walked to the kitchen, opened the cabinet, and pulled out a bottle.

"I never drink this stuff. I've had it forever—probably has sediment in the bottom," she said out loud with a sigh. She unscrewed the top and poured some in a glass. As she walked down the hallway, she murmured to herself, "But before I open that box, I need a drink—sediment or not."

Buddy was purring beside her as she settled herself back under the covers. She was procrastinating opening that box. She knew it. She fiddled with the latch in its center, remembering the night she had shut it, vowing never to open it again. But here she sat, now at two thirty in the morning, getting ready to release the contents of her very own personal Pandora's box.

In her hands was a container whose contents would bring back a part of her past she desperately had tried to forget. But it had to be done.

She swallowed the shot of whisky in an instant, opened the box, and allowed the past to spill out upon her bed. She looked at all the contents. She read every note. She looked at every picture. And when she had turned everything inside out and upside down, she cried.

It was true—the itch she didn't want to scratch. The itch she couldn't scratch. The itch she didn't want to recognize was there.

"Everything eventually comes back around," she whispered. She would have to deal with it once and for all. Just how she would approach it or when the door would open for her to go through it, only God knew.

It was then she fell to her knees and surrendered it all to the throne of God.

The next morning, Trudy awakened with that metal box still on her bed beside her. She sat up, rubbed her eyes, and looked over at Buddy.

"Still with me, 'eh, Buddy?" she asked as she patted his head.

Buddy looked up at her, stretched, and laid back down.

"Well, we sure went through a lot last night together," Trudy said as she pulled back the covers and put both feet on the floor.

"This act of forgiving is hard work," she said as she walked to her kitchen.

The day was going to be a bright one. The sun was appearing, and a slight breeze could be felt when she walked out onto her patio.

Buddy faithfully followed her. She reached down and patted his head. "You're always with me, aren't you? Thank you, my friend, thank you."

Buddy responded with his loud purr as he rubbed alongside her legs.

Trudy looked up at the sky and asked, "What now, God? What do I do now?"

She heard God's whisper to her. *"Maybe an itch isn't so bad, Trudy. It means you've got more healing to do."*

Kate had a busy day ahead. First stop was Trudy's salon. As she approached Tresses & Tootsies, she saw the sign on the door: "CLOSED."

Kate was puzzled. Why would Trudy be closed? Perhaps she was merely running late. But that too was not like Trudy. She would have called to let her know.

Kate looked at her watch and decided to grab one of those doughnuts at Belle's.

"Do you know why Trudy's late opening the salon?" Kate asked Belle.

Belle answered, "Saw her leaving in her car real early this morning."

"It's not like her to forget my appointment," Kate said. "I hope nothing is wrong."

"All I know is she was leaving town pretty fast," Belle answered.

Kate had a disconcerting feeling. She said, "That's not like Trudy." She turned to face Belle. "These are the best of the best, Belle!" she said, holding up her doughnut as she left the bakery.

53

Trudy was halfway to the city before she let up on the gas. It was when she pulled into the rest stop that she thought of her appointments that morning. Kate. Kate was the only appointment.

"That's okay," she said to herself. "She'll understand once she knows. She'll understand why I had to leave just for a short while."

Trudy's short while became more than a long week. Everybody asked where she was. Nobody knew. And then suddenly, there she was walking up the street with her cat—Trudy didn't go anywhere without her cat—no way, no how. That Buddy of hers was family, and where she went, Buddy went. Yep, suddenly, there she was, just marching up the street like she hadn't disappeared for more than a week with Buddy in her arms.

"What's everybody starin' at?" she asked as she passed them on the way to open her salon.

Kate saw her and began running to her. They both came to the salon door at the same time.

"I don't know whether to hug you or smack you!" Kate exclaimed.

Trudy looked at her and said, "Sugar, your hair needs fixin'!"

Kate followed Trudy into the salon, bewildered and fuming.

"You had all of us frightened to death, Trudy!" Kate exclaimed. "Where in the world have you been?"

Trudy sighed, turned to Kate, and said, "Your hair looks like a pack of birds just flew through it. Sit down, sugar, take Buddy here on your lap. I've got some work to do!"

"Trudy!"

Trudy held her hand up for Kate to stop demanding where she had been. Kate looked at her, knowing her protests would get her nowhere. She sighed, gave Trudy a look of disdain, and sat down obediently.

"Now that's better," Trudy said.

She put the cape around Kate's shoulders and simply said, "I've been to the city."

"The city?" Kate questioned.

"Yes, sugar, as in New York City."

"For heaven's sake, why? You don't like crowds. You said so yourself. That's why you moved here. You ran from a city! Why in the world would you go back to another one—even for a visit?"

Kate fidgeted in the shampoo chair. "You didn't go back there looking for Jake, please say you didn't!"

"No," Trudy answered. "I had to go face some of the racket."

Kate had no answer, so she looked at Trudy and finally said, "You're weird."

Trudy laughed. "I've been told that before, sugar."

Kate shook her head and said, "Well, I'm glad you're back."

"Me too, sweet girl, me too. Another week gone, I would not have been able to fix this tangled mess on top of your head!"

When Kate left the salon, Trudy watched her go. She whispered to herself, "I had to get rid of my own racket rattling around in my head. And the city seemed the best place to go."

She secretly whispered, "Thank God I did not come back with a forlorn look on my face."

Trudy looked toward Belle's and suddenly realized how much she had missed those doughnuts. She put her purple visor over her eyes, walked out the door, and made a dash for the bakery.

"Scars only show us where we've been. They do not dictate where we're going." (Heather Flannery)

54

"Good mornin', Belle, give me one of those deep-fried doughnuts with chocolate frosting. Extra crispy."

Belle looked up.

"Hey, Trudy, got the oil hot just for you. Saw you walkin' down the street with that cat of yours in your arms. Where in the world have 'ya been? We were startin' to get worried about you," Belle said.

"Away, just away," Trudy answered her.

"Well, welcome back," Belle said. "I've missed your flair."

Another week went by before Trudy decided it was time—time to put some pharmacon on that itch of hers. It was time to talk to Kate.

Kate had settled herself into the shampoo chair.

Trudy put the cape around her shoulders and asked, "Ever heard that Southern girls are always daddy's girls?" she asked.

"I've heard that Southern daughters really know how to wrap their daddies around their little finger," Kate replied.

"I think that goes for most daughters and daddies," Trudy added. "Same style, sugar?" she asked.

Kate nodded.

"I was a daddy's girl," Trudy confessed. "No finer man could ever be found, no siree."

Trudy began to shampoo Kate's hair and continued, "I trusted my daddy with every fiber of my being. He was true. He was faithful, he was a provider, and he loved my mama with every breath he ever took."

She poured the conditioner into the palm of her hands and began combing it through Kate's hair.

"Both Mama and I were his girls, and everybody in town knew that if anyone messed with us, they would have daddy to fight."

Kate enjoyed listening to Trudy tell about her growing-up stories.

"My granddaddy was right there too—protecting me the way those Southern men do. Granddaddy was retired, and he loved sittin' on the front porch cleaning his gun," Trudy said with a smile on her face.

She retrieved a towel from the shelf and placed it around Kate's head. She stopped talking and thought for a moment.

"In fact, I think somebody wrote a country song about that."

She motioned for Kate to go to the styling chair.

"Seemed he was always sittin' there when one of our neighborhood boys came around. They didn't tarry once they saw him. They just kind of waved, mumbled something, and moved on down the street."

Trudy plugged in the hair dryer.

"We lived right next door to my grandparents. It was a good life when I was growing up. Shoot, I thought Norman Rockwell painted his pictures with our little family in mind! At least, that's what my grandma always told me."

Trudy didn't say any more as she began to dry Kate's hair.

When she was finished, she asked, "Did I ever tell you how glad I am you bought that Bed and Breakfast, sugar?"

Kate smiled and replied, "I believe you have, more than once actually."

Trudy was trying to distract Kate as she stuck a little purple bow in her hair.

"Really? Seriously? Come on, Trudy, take that out of my hair!"

Trudy shrugged, did as she was commanded, and continued talking. "You have a green thumb. Those flowers of yours never cease to amaze me, sugar."

Again, Kate smiled as Trudy continued, "And that's not all you have. You have an 'art.' Not too many people take the time to listen these days, but you do, and I thank you."

Completely out of the blue, Kate asked, "Why did you leave South Carolina, Trudy?"

She looked at Kate for a long time before she answered, "Oh, that's quite a long story, sugar, not for the tellin' today."

But Kate was determined to keep the conversation going. She felt Trudy was on the edge of telling her about some of her own personal mysterious past.

"That must have been hard, coming from the south to New York," Kate said.

"Rural New York, sugar—that's a big difference from the city. Look at me, though, I would have fit right in," Trudy added as she swept her hands around all her purple. "But I could not have handled all those horns blowin' all the time."

Trudy walked over to the cash drawer. "I just wanted to get as far away from South Carolina as I could. I was runnin', I guess, just like you were when you first came here and sat in this very chair. Remember that day, sugar?"

"I sure do. I couldn't decide if I was going to like you or not." Kate laughed.

"And now?"

"You're my best friend, Trudy."

Trudy smiled, but Kate saw a faraway look cloud over her face.

"Want to talk about what's on your mind, Trudy?"

"Maybe."

"I'm listening."

The ringing of the phone broke the train of conversation and gave Kate a chance to hold on for the ride. She knew something big was coming from Trudy when she hung up the phone. Trudy walked back to Kate.

"Where was I?" Trudy asked.

"One curl to the left, two steps to the phone, and questioning if you really want to talk about whatever is on your mind," Kate replied.

Trudy smiled. "I think I've rubbed off on you since first you said you wanted a 'sassy' hair style."

"I think you have too." Kate admitted. "I've sure learned to love purple—but not bows in my hair!"

"Well, what I'm goin' to tell 'ya is all about that color, sugar. It's kind of a symbol with me. Come on, let's get outta here. I need some air," Trudy exclaimed.

As Trudy placed the 'closed' sign in the salon window, she asked Kate, "Ever had a hero?"

Kate thought for a moment and answered, "I'm glad to say that yes, I have."

"Who was your hero, sugar?"

"Zack."

"I'm glad you didn't say Jake."

"Well, he's gone."

The two began to walk toward the lake.

"Let's not brush him off so easily," Trudy said.

"Oh, it hasn't been easy." Kate admitted.

She took Trudy by the arm and whispered, "You see, I felt the quiver."

Trudy smiled. "Mark my words, baby doll, you haven't seen the last of Jake Arbor. But I'm glad he's not your hero. He's your man."

They kept walking arm in arm.

Trudy continued, "Hero's fall and you can't put them back together. Men make mistakes, but the pieces go back together, and a man becomes stronger than ever. With a hero, you only remember the fall. With a man, you accept the vulnerability and help him rebuild."

They were getting closer to the lake.

"Did Zack ever disappoint you?"

"No. He was my rock, my lifeline, my second chance. He was the reason I found Brooksport Village—my 'open door.'"

Kate had learned long ago that Trudy was an expert at changing the subject quickly, so it didn't surprise her when Trudy spun around and said, "Hey, let's go back and get a bag of those doughnuts and then come sit by the lake and eat 'em. You game?"

Kate nodded and thought, *Those doughnuts are going to be the death of me.*

But if that's what it was going to take to help Trudy be free of something she had never told anyone before, then she would eat them and smile as she chewed. And besides that, she had Zantac in her pocket.

Doughnuts in hand, the two women settled into two beach chairs by that beautiful lake. Trudy looked out at the water, a sailing lesson in progress in the distance. It was too early for many tourists to gather, but some husbands with ADD were up and running with towels to save the seats for their family later in the day.

"Nobody follows the rules on a beach, do they?" Trudy questioned as she pointed to the sign, "PLEASE, NO SAVING SEATS."

Kate replied as she bit into her first doughnut, "Maybe if we took the word *please* off."

She was silent then, giving Trudy an opening to continue her sharing.

"It's goin' to be a beautiful day," Trudy began. "Reminds me of the day I left South Carolina."

Trudy retrieved a doughnut for herself before saying, "My daddy was my hero when I was growing up. I was surrounded by 'knights.' And oh, how their armor did shine. Those 'would-be princes' who came to my door didn't get too far if daddy was home, especially if he didn't like their looks."

Trudy took another bite of her doughnut.

She continued, "He wanted shirttails inside the pants, no long hair, and heaven forbid if they had an earring in their ear! Those boys didn't even make it to the porch. Daddy would be at the door, saying, 'No need to come any further, boy. She's not here.'"

Trudy laughed.

"Of course, I was home, in my room, studying the latest movie magazine. That's what girls did in the South, they studied—movie stars and the way they fixed their hair—and boys washed their cars and tried their best to get as far as the porch."

Kate asked, "Didn't that make you upset? I mean if you really wanted to be with the boy?"

"Oh no, sugar, I felt protected and loved by someone who guarded over me with all of the best intentions."

Again, Trudy shifted gears. She motioned for Kate to have another doughnut. Kate hesitated and then rationalized. "Okay, they're small."

Trudy said, "That's how Belle gets them extra crispy. They have to be small."

Kate had to admit they were very tasty and reminded herself that Trudy wasn't herself without her daily dose of grease.

Trudy exclaimed, "Lard's the best, you know?"

"Lard?" Kate questioned.

"That's what we cooked with in the south—lard and lots of it."

Kate looked at Trudy out of the corner of her eye.

"I know, I know, I'm changin' the subject. It's just that I'm not so sure I want to talk about this right now."

Trudy folded the top of the bag of doughnuts and handed it to Kate.

"Have one tonight for a midnight snack," she said.

Again Kate dared to ask, "Why did you leave South Carolina, Trudy?"

Trudy took a deep breath and stood up to leave. She began walking back toward town. After walking a short distance, she turned and said to Kate, "Betrayal, Kate. It was all about betrayal."

Kate sat in that chair for a long time after Trudy left. One word was what it came down to. She knew all about betrayal.

It was close to midnight when Kate heard the knock on her kitchen door. She opened the door to see Trudy standing there.

"I came for my midnight snack," Trudy said.

Kate opened the door, motioned for Trudy to sit down at the table, walked across the room, and retrieved the leftover bag of doughnuts. She sat down across from Trudy and calmly said, "Talk to me."

"My daddy hung the moon, you know?" Trudy began. Kate kept listening. "Do you think it's crazy? I mean, I'm an old woman, so to speak, and I still call my daddy 'Daddy.'"

Kate replied, "I don't think it's crazy at all. I think that someone who had a daddy like yours should always be called Daddy."

"Thank you for that," Trudy replied.

"I really don't want a doughnut," Trudy said. "But don't tell Belle. I love 'em most of the time but not tonight. I would prefer a glass of wine."

Kate smiled, stood up, went to the refrigerator, and pulled out both red and white. "Which one?" she asked.

"White," Trudy replied. "And lots of it."

With the first sip, Trudy began to talk. "Nobody in this town knows why I left the south and stumbled upon this little town, but I'm going to tell you."

She took a bigger sip of wine.

"I discovered not all men were like my daddy."

"So your daddy didn't fall like other heroes?" Kate asked.

"Oh no, he didn't fall, but because he was my ultimate role model, I went in search of a man just like my daddy," Trudy began.

"Did you find him?" Kate asked.

"Oh yes, I found him," Trudy answered.

"How did you know he was the one?" Kate asked.

Trudy smiled and took another sip of her wine. "I felt the quiver," Trudy answered.

Kate rolled her eyes, took a sip of her own wine, and said, "Seriously, Trudy, how did you know? Was it the first time you saw him? Or weeks later?"

Trudy laughed and said, "I think it was when I felt a flutter alongside the quiver."

"Enough talk about flutters and quivers!" Kate exclaimed.

"You felt it with Jake."

Trudy poured herself another glass of wine.

Kate gave her a look of "*This is not about Jake and me.*"

"Oh, never mind, you've already confessed that you did," Trudy concluded.

Kate got up from the chair and walked to the kitchen window, not facing Trudy.

"Why are you runnin' from your feelins', Kate?" Trudy asked. "Honestly, you and Jake are enough to drive a sane person crazy! Both of you are runners! I do wish one of you would just stop and let the other one run smack dab into you. That's what you two need to do—just knock each other down and don't get up off the ground until you settle some things!"

Kate turned and asked, "Are you done? Trudy, this midnight talk is not about Jake and me. If I recall, you just showed up at my back door, sat yourself down with a glass of wine that you requested, and began to tell me the story of how you went in search of a man like your daddy."

Trudy shrugged her shoulders, shook her head back and forth, and said, "Okay, okay, sugar, settle down. You're right."

Kate gave Trudy a warning look, walked back to the table, and sat down. She looked straight through Trudy and said, "I'm listening. Talk to me."

"I told you it was betrayal that had me flee South Carolina," Trudy began, betrayal of my husband. Because of that betrayal, it took me a long time to trust again. I mean you're supposed to trust your husband. If you can't do that, who can you trust?"

Trudy shifted in her chair.

"My husband, my hero, the one who had built me my own white picket fence, proved not to be so trustworthy."

"He was your hero that fell?" Kate asked.

"With a mighty crash," Trudy confessed. "Turned out to be nothing like my daddy."

"I understand," Kate replied.

"I know you do, sugar. I knew that the first time I met you. We who have been wounded by betrayal can spot others a mile away."

"It's a long road back to trust, isn't it, Trudy?"

"Oh yes, it is, but you take little victories one day at a time. Sooner or later, we romantics have to stop 'romancing' our grudges, our hurts, and our pains. We have to give up revenge and let it go, or we'll end up all dried up and hollow."

Trudy continued, "He didn't play around—well, I guess it depends on how you define 'playin' around,'" Trudy said. I give him credit for that."

Trudy looked directly at Kate and continued, "But there was one that came along, a special one for him that he just couldn't get over."

Trudy continued, "I saw regret in his eyes every time I looked at him. I thought he regretted having married me. I was older than him, and he looked a lot younger than he really was. I thought the age difference was startin' to bother him. I started thinkin' that was one of the reasons he had searched for and found her—the other woman. When I couldn't stand seein' all that regret every day after he met her, I started runnin'. I had to face the fact that my marriage was over. She, plain and simple, got into his head, and there was no pushin' her out. I had to get as far away from South Carolina as I possibly could. He never asked for his freedom. I just handed it to him and left."

"How did you know? I mean, how did you know for sure this was going on with him?" Kate asked.

"Oh, I had no visible proof at the time, but a woman can tell—almost like a sixth sense—when somethin' is a little left of center in her marriage," Trudy said.

Trudy got up from her chair, took her wine glass to the sink, and rinsed it out. She walked to the door, opened it, turned around, and faced Kate.

"It wasn't until he died and I discovered a black metal box in his closet that I knew for sure what he had done, where he had been, and with whom."

That being said, Trudy turned and walked out the door.

Trudy walked around the corner of Open Door and saw Kate sitting on the bench in her flower garden. She watched her from a distance and studied her. What was it Jake had said to her once? "Kate shouldn't try to study me, she won't graduate." Yes, that was it.

"Well," Trudy said to herself as she climbed the hill to Kate's flower garden. "That cowboy's not smart enough to come up with a quote like that."

That quote was from "Scorpio" and Trudy knew it. She just let Jake think he was smarter than he really was. Still, she liked that son of a gun and wondered what he had been up to since he left their little town.

She walked up to Kate, sat down beside her on that bench, and said, "Thought I'd find you here."

Kate looked at her suspiciously and asked, "No doughnuts?"

"No, that wine last night did me in," Trudy answered.

"You only had two glasses," Kate replied.

"Well, sugar, you didn't follow me home. You didn't know I had two more when I got home. Yes, sir, me and Buddy had us a grand time last night!"

Kate didn't know whether to believe Trudy or not, but from the looks of her this fine morning, she decided it was the truth.

Trudy continued, "I learned this morning that the older I get, I can't shake a hangover as fast the next morning."

She took a deep breath, looked at Kate and said, "I tried shakin' it like that female judge on *American Idol* used to do. What was her name?"

Kate replied, "Jennifer Lopez."

"That's her! Well, like I said, I tried to shake it off like her, and Buddy ran out of the bedroom."

Kate couldn't help but laugh.

"What's so funny about that?" Trudy asked.

"Did Buddy bow his back and run sideways out the door?" Kate asked through her laughter.

"As a matter of fact, he did," Trudy replied.

And then they were both silent.

"What's wrong, sugar?" Trudy asked.

"Oh, I was just thinking about our midnight talk last night," Kate replied.

"I see," Trudy said.

"That must have been awful for you, that whole ordeal," Kate exclaimed.

"It was," Trudy replied.

"How long did it take you to get over it?" Kate asked.

"I learned to forgive, sugar, but to be honest, I still have trouble forgetting."

Again they fell into silence.

"Come on," Trudy said. "Let's walk down to the lake. It's beautiful this time of day."

She tried shaking her body like Jennifer Lopez.

"I need to fill my lungs with good fresh oxygen after last night," Trudy said with a wink.

They began to walk toward the lake.

"You know, I thought about going into the dentist office to see if I could bribe him into giving me some of his pure oxygen this morning. You know, the kind he gave you after your sedation when he did your root canal," Trudy said with a mimicking smile on her face.

"How did you know that?" Kate asked.

"Word gets around in a town like ours. You should know that by now. But it's okay. There's a lot of folks that fear those drills in the dental office, and I know 'em all, includin' me!"

They arrived at the lake and sat at one of the beach tables. Trudy looked at Kate and said, "Go ahead, ask me what you're wondering. I've gone too far into my past with you to stop now."

Kate looked at her and said, "You actually forgave him—to his face?"

Trudy answered, "Yes, when he showed up at my salon right here in Brooksport Village."

"We had been divorced for quite some time when he just walked in like he owned the place, sat down, and said, 'We have to talk.'"

Trudy sighed and continued, "It's funny now that I think about it. I thought only women said that to their husbands—not the other way around."

She laughed before continuing, "Yes, sir, when a woman says that, a man gets all antsy. They wanna run away."

Kate encouraged her to go on.

"I told him I had nothing to say to him. He laughed at me and told me he had never known me to be speechless."

Trudy's face clouded over.

She turned to face Kate and said, "I told him he had not witnessed the tears I had cried in total silence. Those tears blended with the water from the shower and disappeared down the drain many a night. I told him he had not seen the many dinners I had eaten alone in silence. I told him he didn't know about how loud that ticking clock in our living room was as I waited for him to walk through the door on those nights I had no idea where he was or who he was with. I told him about the nights I reached out for him and he wasn't there. I was totally silent then. I had been very speechless during that awful dark time in my life."

Trudy took a breath and added, "Then I told him that yes, I could be speechless."

Kate asked, "What did he say to all of that?"

"He did something I didn't expect," Trudy answered. "He jumped up from the chair, grabbed me, and held me tighter than he had ever done in our entire married life together."

Trudy stood up from her chair.

She continued, "And then he asked me to dinner."

"I was so shocked by the hug he gave me that I let him do just that—take me to dinner," Trudy said. I saw a crushed man sittin' across from me that night. I guess guilt can do that to 'ya if you let it."

Trudy looked out upon the lake.

"And that particular night I really felt sorry for him. It was a godly sorrow. I was ripe for forgiveness—enough time had passed that my desire for revenge had weakened and had all but disappeared."

Both women began to walk along the shore.

"I didn't know it at the time, but that dinner was his 'making amends' dinner. He told me about the affair. He confessed it all, and I didn't flinch or move a muscle," Trudy whispered.

Trudy picked up a stone and threw it into the lake.

"He looked at me and said, 'You knew all along, didn't you? How did you know?'"

Kate looked at Trudy; she was feeling the hurt that Trudy had felt. She understood how forgetting would be a hard thing to do.

Trudy continued, "I told him a woman always knows. And then I took a deep breath and asked him if he had married her."

They walked in silence for a long time before Kate asked, "Did he?"

"No," Trudy replied. "He said he never saw her again after our divorce."

"And you believed him?" Kate asked.

"I had no reason not to. He was no longer my husband. I guess I just didn't care anymore. Believe me, he was not looking for reconciliation. Too much time had passed. I had moved on quite successfully. Well, moneywise, anyway. It was the trust issues I had to deal with."

"To forgive oneself? No, that doesn't work; we have to be forgiven. But we can only believe this is possible if we ourselves can forgive." (Dag Hammarskjold)

55

The two walked to the picnic grounds, found two empty chairs, and sat down.

"It wasn't all bad—our marriage," Trudy exclaimed to Kate. "He brought a certain light into my life during those early years. He made me remember those good years when he came here to see me one last time."

Kate could hear the break in Trudy's voice.

"He took me over to that rickety old chair that no one dares sit in at the salon—that is, except for you. You sit in it from time to time."

Kate knew that chair. And yes, she had sat in it many times. She wasn't afraid of it.

"He put his hands on my shoulders and gently pushed me down in that chair—and for the record, I will never part with that chair."

"What happened next?" Kate asked.

Trudy answered, "He got down on his knees, put my face in his hands, and asked me to forgive him."

"That is when you did forgive him," Kate whispered.

"You know, there's something about an ex-husband gettin' down on his knees in front of his ex-wife and askin' for forgiveness. This man that I had once adored, looked up to, and placed on a pedestal was bowing down to me. I had always thought I could never forgive him for what he had done to me, but there was somethin' about that moment when I knew I could."

Kate asked, "Did you look him in the eyes and say yes?"

Trudy smiled. "I looked straight into his eyes and said, 'I do forgive you.'"

Trudy looked relieved that she was telling her story to Kate.

"And then it was as if a dam had burst and all the hurt came flowin' out of both of us. There was no reason to belabor the past. It was time to tie it up and move on."

Kate smiled. "I'm glad," she said.

Trudy stood up, straightened her skirt, and began walking back toward town.

She turned around and said, "Kate, I thank you for not asking me questions about his betrayal."

"It only matters that you made things right with him," Kate answered.

Trudy took a deep breath and said, "I might as well tell you all of it."

She cleared her throat and continued, "I've never told anyone as much as I've told you, but I trust you with my past and with my truths, blemishes and all. He betrayed me in the worst way a man can betray a wife."

Kate held her gaze. A slight breeze ruffled her hair. She braced herself for what would come next. Little did she know just how much Trudy's secret would impact her. She dared not move.

"You see, Kate," she began, "he not only had an affair but also sired a child. I guess you could call the baby a 'love' child."

Trudy confessed. "I was crushed. I had a long talk with God after I found out about the baby. Oh, he didn't tell me about the baby that night at dinner. I discovered that tidbit of information after he died. I found the complete truth in a little black box in his closet."

Kate exclaimed, "I can only imagine how long that talk was."

"I went away for a while—I do that when things surprise me— you know, when that right ball comes out of left field, knocks 'ya down, and 'ya don't think you'll ever be able to get up again."

Kate understood. She had been knocked down a time or two in her life.

"Well, God took me to a quiet place and reminded me just who I was. I was *his*," Trudy said, pointing to the sky. "After much cryin' and wailin', after my temper tantrums and a lot of slammin' doors, God convinced me I didn't need a white picket fence or a knight in shining armor. I belonged to the one who would never betray me, and there will never be a day that goes by that I don't acknowledge that truth."

Kate continued to look at Trudy. It was as if a glow had come over her face as she continued.

"Nothing and no one can ever steal my royal heritage. That's a fact, that's truth. It's real—not a fantasy."

Trudy took Kate's hands in her own, looked her straight in the eyes, and said, "That, my dear, is why I wear purple. God convinced me that I am royalty."

They began to walk back into town. The tourists were starting to gather around the lake. As they walked, Trudy admitted. "He wasn't a bad person. He was just mixed up in his head, and it wasn't because he was a man. We all get mixed up in the head at one time or another, even women."

As they came closer to town, Trudy said, "Honestly, I think he fell in love with two women at the same time. He couldn't help himself. Kind of like that Dr. Zhivago type, you know?"

"Was the other woman's name Laura?" Kate smiled as she asked.

"No," Trudy replied. "And I don't know if she wore those furry hats either."

"Funny you should ask about her name," Trudy said as they stood in front of her salon.

"Why?" Kate asked.

"I came to know a lot about her, but I never knew her name. He protected her. He never shared her name. I guess in a way he was a lot like my daddy, after all. He protected her name and honored her in the only way he could. I discovered all that later after he died," Trudy said.

"You mean there's more to the story?" Kate asked, almost aghast.

Trudy took the 'closed' sign out of the window of the salon, turned and said, "Oh, sugar, there's much more."

"My husband had quite a charisma about him," Trudy said as she began to style Kate's hair. "Everybody liked being around him. He made people laugh. Young girls especially gravitated toward him."

Kate wasn't sure that she wanted to hear any more of the story. Her mind was beginning to short-circuit.

"I had been caught up in all his charisma too, and he did love the attention. He liked to flirt, but then what man doesn't?" He travelled a lot—being a salesman and all."

"He was a salesman?" Kate asked. She was beginning to feel uncomfortable.

"Yep, and a mighty good one," Trudy answered.

She walked to the cash drawer, opened it, and said, "I think he betrayed the young girl too, the one he had the ongoing affair with. Through the years, I've always wondered what happened to her."

Trudy sighed and sat down in the rickety old chair whose past had been poured out upon the floor.

"He never knew either. He told me he was so confused and torn back then. He ran back to me, but all he found when he got home were divorce papers and an empty house. There was no salvaging our marriage. I knew that this girl would forever be on his mind."

Kate got up and walked over to Trudy.

"Don't know about you, sugar, but there's no way I'm goin' to be with a man whose mind is always thinkin' of somebody else. No way!"

Kate could hardly breathe.

She managed to say, "I couldn't do that either."

"I had to ask myself, how long could I allow myself to drown in my hurt? I knew that sooner or later it would drive me crazy. There comes a time of lettin' go, and that's what I decided to do. I let it go."

There was a silence then between the two friends.

Kate paid Trudy for her services.

"I have to go," Kate said. "Need to run some errands for tomorrow's menu."

She walked toward the door, while Trudy got up from the chair and began preparing for her next client.

"Trudy?" Kate turned and asked.

Trudy stopped what she was doing and looked at Kate.

"May I ask your husband's name?" Kate asked.

"Sure can. His name was Frank, Kate. His name was Frank."

"When we allow God to change the way we see our past, the power of our past changes dramatically." (Beth Moore)

56

Kate didn't have errands to run; she just wanted to run. She found herself stunned to the core while making her way to that bench in her flower garden.

Trudy was right. There was much more to the story. A lot more.

"Could it possibly be?" she asked herself. "Her Frank?"

She rose from the bench, went into her kitchen, and recovered the whisky from the top cabinet. The sweet tea sat in the middle of the table—she needed something more today, much more.

That night, Kate went to her private quarters and locked the door. She was in search of an old photograph album she had packed secretly away. There was one picture she had to hold in her hands one more time. She remembered how Frank had put up a fuss about having his picture taken, but she had insisted, and he had finally relented.

She found it quickly. She had especially marked it back then with little red hearts and the promise notes he had left behind each time he had to leave again.

"It's my job," one note said.

"Until next time," another one read.

And then one day, "next time" never came. That was after she had told him about the baby.

She touched the photograph. Frank. A face she remembered so well, looking up at her from the photograph. She had been young, but she had loved this man. Now she seemed closer to him than ever.

Trudy was her best friend. Frank had been Trudy's husband.

There was no belaboring what she had to do, what she must do.

Kate slept with that photograph, and the next morning, after feeding her guests, she quickly left her house. She was walking straight to the salon with the photograph album cradled in her arms.

Trudy's night had been rather peaceful. She had a much lighter heart than she had expected. Her wine remained corked. No need for it. Forgiveness had taken over.

She had forgiven her husband, and now there was a forgiveness yet to be known by the other.

"The other," Trudy whispered as she unlocked the door to her salon. If she knew Kate like she thought she knew her, she would be walking through that door very soon.

"Help me, Lord," Trudy whispered as she began to prepare for her day.

"Maybe you're right, God. Perhaps an itch isn't so bad. It proves I'm healing," Trudy said over and over again.

Trudy continued to look out the window, and then she saw her.

"Good," was all she said.

She busied herself, waiting for the door to open, and when it did, she was ready.

"You don't have an appointment today, do you?" Trudy questioned.

"No, I was just here yesterday, remember?" Kate replied.

"Oh, that's right," Trudy replied.

Kate looked at Trudy.

"What's wrong with you? You look as pale as a ghost!" Trudy exclaimed.

Kate burst into tears.

All the well-rehearsed lines from the previous sleepless night had gone astray. All Kate could do was cry. And the first chair she collapsed in was the old, rickety one that Frank had sat in years ago.

She opened the photo album and pointed to Frank's picture.

"Is this your ex-husband?" she asked.

Trudy came across the room and looked at the picture.

"Yes, it is—a much younger version, I must say. But I'd know that crooked grin anywhere. That's what got all the girls' minds messed up—that crooked grin of his. Sure messed mine up."

Kate couldn't believe Trudy was being so nonchalant.

Kate said, "I didn't know."

"You didn't know what, sugar?"

"I didn't know he was married. I didn't know he had a wife. I didn't know, I just didn't know."

Trudy looked at her. She didn't try to interrupt the flow of emotions.

"Oh, Trudy, I was that girl! I was the one your husband had an affair with. I didn't know I was in the middle of an affair. If I had known, I would never have done what I did! You have to believe me!"

Saying nothing, Trudy walked over to the desk and pulled out a picture she had kept for many years.

She walked back to Kate, bowed down on her knees, just like her ex-husband had done years ago, looked at Kate, and handed her the picture.

Kate took it, looked at it, and exclaimed, "That's me! A much younger me—but me."

"So it is," Trudy said. "So it is."

"I don't understand," Kate began.

Then she remembered that day the picture was taken. Frank had insisted he take a picture of her, even though he hadn't wanted his own picture taken.

She remembered what Frank had said—he wanted to have her with him when he was away, and he snapped the picture.

Trudy pulled out a note that was tucked behind the photograph and said, "He also wrote this. I found it in the infamous metal box he had hidden in his closet after he died. I want you to have it."

Kate took the note and began to read.

"My dear, dear one, I don't know what to do. I am a coward, I guess. I am so sorry to leave you like this. Please know that I meant you no harm. The one thing that I want you to know is that I did love you. No matter what others may say or what others may do, I loved you. Someday I will seek your forgiveness, but for now, I must be absent from your life. Perhaps one day, you'll understand when you know the whole truth about me. And then again, maybe you won't."

"Just knowing that God's good can come from life's bad is one of the most liberating concepts in the entire Word of God."
(Beth Moore)

57

Trudy broke the silence.

"He did love you, you know. The years between you were many, but I've come to learn that love has no boundaries. He was mixed up. He betrayed you by not telling you about me, and he betrayed me by being with you, but, Kate, it wasn't your fault."

Kate looked at Trudy, tears still streaming down her face.

Trudy continued, "You were caught in a web of deceit, and I'm so sorry he did that to you."

Trudy rose from her knees and walked to the refrigerator for some water. She went back to Kate and poured it into a glass. Then she sat down on the floor at Kate's feet.

"There was always somethin' about you I couldn't put my finger on ever since you first stepped into my salon. There was a familiarity that I couldn't explain. I didn't connect the dots until that morning at two o'clock when it suddenly hit me. I got that black box of my ex-husband's out of my closet and looked at it real close, and I knew. I knew it was you. I had seen that face of yours before—a young you."

Kate stared at Trudy and took a sip of the water.

"It took me this long to figure it out. Oh, sugar"—she took Kate's hands in her own—"please tell me you had the baby."

Kate looked directly at Trudy. "Yes, I had the baby. I gave my baby up for adoption."

"Then let's not waste any more time. Let's find that baby. Let's find that child together."

"That child is all grown-up now," Kate stammered, continuing to stare at Trudy.

"I know you're thinkin', how can she be so kind and understandin' after all that happened between her husband and me—"

Trudy took a breath.

"Let me tell you. Remember that day when I put the 'Closed' sign on my salon door? Well, I have to admit the truth put me in a tailspin for a while. I pert near went through a bottle of whisky that night truth hit me between the eyes. I needed to get away. That's when I went to the city and lost myself for a spell. You remember?"

"I remember," Kate replied. "The whole town was getting worried about you."

"Well, I got myself together while I was hailin' down cabs in that city, shoppin,' and eatin' lots of comfort food in fancy restaurants. When it was nighttime, I went back to my hotel room and thought about Frank. And it was in that hotel room that I realized he was just a man—I had made him out to be something he could never be. I had set my hopes on a hero. I had made my expectations of him too high. There was no way he was goin' to measure up. So when he fell, he fell hard."

Trudy went to the refrigerator and got a bottle of water for herself.

"He was able to put some pieces back together for both him and me when he came here. I realized that it takes a real strong man to come to someone and ask forgiveness. And it takes a real strong woman to give him that forgiveness. We made our amends."

Trudy walked to the salon door and put the "Closed" sign in the window. She did not want any interruptions now.

She walked back to Kate and sat herself back on the floor.

"He told me where to find his little black box. He had come clean with everything. I was with him when he died."

Kate continued to cry, and Trudy continued to soothe her.

"I've known you for a long time now. You are a good person, a kind person, and a loving person. We're both older and wiser. When I left that hotel room and came back here, I had reached a very important conclusion. I can honestly say I know why Frank fell in love with you."

After the tears had stopped, both women looked at each other in total silence and yet with an understanding that only two who had suffered much, loved much.

"We've got a child to find," Trudy said again.

She helped Kate to her feet, walked to the door, and changed the "Closed" sign back to "Open."

"I think it's Charlie," Trudy told Kate.

"No, even though I would love for it to be Charlie, it's not," Kate replied adamantly.

"You don't know that!" Trudy exclaimed. "Or do you? What are you not tellin' me?"

"For now, I just want to tell you it's not Charlie," Kate replied.

"Let's walk," Trudy continued.

Trudy continued, "There's something about Charlie. You two like the same things—"

"It's not Charlie!" Kate exclaimed once again. "I understand Charlie and I are kindred spirits, but it's not Charlie. He was adopted. I gave up my child. Both of us have parallel hurts that run deep. We understand that about each other, but that is it. I promise you, it is not Charlie."

They had reached the lake. Both women took off their shoes and began to wade in the water.

"Well, if you are so sure it is not Charlie, and I respect your opinion—don't understand how you can be so sure—but I have to ask you, are you willin' to go out into the deep with me, sugar?" Trudy asked.

Kate stared at her.

"By deep," Trudy continued, "I mean out on a limb?"

She kicked the water with her feet.

Kate said, "I'm listening."

"I'm no computer whiz, but in my research, I found a techy in Detroit," Trudy said.

"What on earth are you talking about?" Kate asked.

"Someone who can move his way around computers that could lead us straight to your baby—grownup by now—but still you would know who that child is," Trudy said. "I have references that say this guy is really good at findin' people."

Kate and Trudy stared at each other, standing in ankle-deep water.

Kate looked at her and said, "Do it."

Trudy made contact with that computer geek. She nicknamed him Techy Ted, and they had lengthy conversations. They vowed to meet one day. He would come to Brooksport Village and give her a report. She had aroused his curiosity with her wit and most unusual way of communicating at all hours of the day and night. That woman was on a mission. He wondered if she ever slept.

Techy Ted was going to do everything he possibly could to help her and her friend, Kate. He made her that promise one night around midnight when he could not get her off his mind. He thought that odd. He hadn't even met the woman, and he thought he was in love. Well, Trudy was Trudy. How could anyone not fall in love with her, even over the phone?

What Kate and Trudy didn't know was that no computer geek was going to give them answers, although he had vowed to do his best to try.

God had this, and he was taking them on a journey straight to that child in his own timing. It would happen sooner than either woman could ever imagine. The script had been written, and the stage had been set many years before.

PART VII

Dawn

58

Funny how forgiveness frees the spirit to go in search of truths still unknown. Kate and Trudy's friendship grew stronger as they began their search together for the child—now all grown-up. Neither of them knew exactly what they would find, but both were more than willing to take the journey.

"So, Trudy, have you felt the flutter yet?" Kate asked her as Trudy was finishing up her 'do.'

"What on earth are you talkin' about?" Trudy asked.

"You know exactly what I'm talking about!" Kate exclaimed.

"Don't be silly. Techy Ted lives in Detroit, and I'm in Brooksport Village—not plannin' to move anywhere else!" And then she added, "He's geographically undesirable!"

Before Kate left the salon, she couldn't help herself—she turned and hollered over her shoulder, "Lord help you if you feel the quiver!"

Trudy playfully threw the most recent edition of hairdo at Kate, which had Kate laughing all the way home.

Kate loved planning parties, and Open Door was the perfect place to host birthday parties, weddings, and joyous occasions. Reva and Wes had asked Kate if she would share the premises of her place for Sarah's special birthday party. She had readily agreed and had planned to meet Charlie and Sarah that afternoon in the flower garden to discuss all the details.

Kate saw the two of them from a distance as they made their way to Open Door. She could hear their lively conversation about the party and who was to attend. Kate walked into the kitchen and began preparing their cold drinks.

She looked from the window at the two of them. She smiled as she remembered the talk she and Charlie had shared about young love. She watched as Sarah began chatting and Charlie looked at her, totally mesmerized by whatever she was saying. Sarah was fortunate to have found a guy who listened. He was good at that—listening. Kate knew that firsthand from all the times they had spent in the garden. Trudy had taught him how to listen. Again, she smiled as she remembered some of those conversations.

"Don't just lookin' at those bleedin' heart flowers make you sad, Miss Kate?" Charlie had asked.

"Sometimes, Charlie," she had replied. *"They have me remembering many of the blessings I once had and lost. They look so fragile, and yet they are so strong to survive our harsh winters."*

"They survive storms just like we do, don't they, Miss Kate?" he had asked.

"Yes, they do, Charlie," she had replied. She had wondered how anyone so young could be so wise.

Sarah's laughter interrupted her thoughts as she went out to greet them both.

"Hey, you two, ready for the big party this weekend?"

"Oh yes, Miss Kate," Sarah replied.

Sarah took a small box from her pocket and said, "I got an early birthday present today from my mom."

"Oh, let's see," Kate said.

Sarah opened the box and showed Charlie and Kate the locket. It was heart-shaped with one word, "Beloved," engraved on the back.

Kate caught her breath when the contents of that small box was revealed.

She managed to say, "It's lovely," before excusing herself.

Kate heard Charlie exclaim as she opened the back door leading to the kitchen, "Remember, Miss Kate, no sweet tea for me!"

When Kate entered the kitchen, she felt as if she were going to faint. She grabbed the counter and forced herself to stand. She looked out the window and witnessed Charlie helping Sarah clasp the locket around her neck.

"It's really pretty," she heard Charlie say.

"It's special," Sarah replied.

"How so?" Charlie asked.

"Just know that it is," Sarah replied. "It's a long story."

Charlie didn't ask again. He had learned a lot of lessons in his life, and one was not to ask too many questions. He knew that when she was ready to share something that seemed very important to her, she would. Right now, all he really wanted to do was kiss her. A birthday kiss—and not on the hand.

Kate watched the happy duo from her bedroom window. She couldn't speak; she could barely think. That locket. That locket, she had seen before. She had bought it, she had carefully wrapped it and tied it with a bow, and then she had wept. She wept as she gave it to the head nurse at the adoption agency. She wept when she walked to her car without turning around. Oh, she wanted to. She wanted to run back in there, grab her baby, and run out the door, but she knew she couldn't. She knew this precious baby needed a running start in life, and she was unable to give it to her.

She remembered the day she had the locket engraved, "Beloved." Oh, how she had loved that child from the very beginning. Loved her enough to give her life. Loved her enough to let her go. Loved her enough to think of her every minute of every given day.

She would hear a laugh and think of her. She would see a smile and think of her. Every birthday she would imagine what she looked like.

And now there she stood in that garden of flowers. Why hadn't she noticed it before? Even Charlie had noticed how much they were alike.

It was the eyes. Why hadn't she seen it before this? The eyes of Frank. The eyes she had loved. The eyes that had loved her in his own way. The eyes that had deceived her, but she had loved them, anyway. The eyes that had asked Trudy for forgiveness. The eyes that had given her a most precious baby. The eyes—just like his.

"*I loved you,*" he had said in his note to her. "*One day, you'll understand.*"

She had been hurt back then. She was young. She was vulnerable back then. Traveling in and out of her life, he had given her a baby—and left her. The flood of memories came back like a wave while she stood watching Sarah and Charlie. What was she to do now? She had to gather herself. She had to think. She had to sleep on this.

Her mind was spinning, and sleep was not on her list of priorities at two o'clock in the morning.

"Two o'clock in the morning," she whispered. "The hour of truth."

That was when Trudy had reached her truth. What had she done? Gone to the city.

"I'm not doing that!" Kate exclaimed.

She thought of Jake. "He's in the city."

"No! I'm not going to the city!" she repeated.

She grabbed her robe, tied it quickly around her waist, put on her slippers, and headed for the patio door that bordered her garden.

She took so much pride in this garden. She only hoped it brought as much peace to her guests as it did to her.

Charlie loved it, and so did Sarah. All three of them gravitated to it. It was like a sanctuary to them, especially after its very own comeback from the storm.

Gardens bring peace, and they all needed peace. The answers to all her searching had been found within the contents of a small box opened on that day before a nineteenth birthday in her very presence. She had to process this newfound truth in her heart and mind before she shared it with anyone else.

She made her way to the bench in the middle of all those "bleedin' hearts," as Charlie would say.

She sat down and stared. That's all she could do after such a revelation that had come to her. She could hear the night sounds of the surrounding area, and the lake seemed calm. The lighthouse at the end of the pier was in clear view as the moment of truth hit her once again. It was the locket.

"Oh, my God," she whispered. "I've found my baby, my grown-up daughter."

Morning light found her still on that bench in the garden. The time had come to visit Wes and Reva.

Kate was glad she had a full house that morning. She would prepare their breakfast, clean the kitchen, and try to clear her mind. She needed clarity before speaking to Wes and Reva.

After the last guests left for their day at the beach, she went to her bedroom and opened her closet door. Quietly, she reached for the heart-shaped box on the top shelf.

She went to a nearby chair, sat down, and opened the box. She found the envelope with its contents and gently slipped it into her pocket. She was ready. She walked out of Open Door not knowing exactly what she would say to the pair who had no clue what was about to happen. Things like this you couldn't rehearse. She only hoped what she had to say wouldn't turn everyone's world upside down.

As she approached the end of the street, Kate changed her direction. She had to see Trudy first. She turned toward the salon.

59

Wes could feel Reva's restlessness from across the room.

"What's wrong, Reva?" he questioned. "Why are you pacing?"

"Oh, Wes, I don't think we should have given that locket to Sarah!" she exclaimed.

"Reva, we promised ourselves that we would remain true to the mother's wish when we brought that precious child home," he answered.

"But that was a long time ago," Reva began.

Wes interrupted her. "No second thoughts now. We did what we promised we would do. I don't understand why you are so uneasy about it," Wes said.

Reva walked over to Wes and placed her hand on his chest.

"Just listening to my heart," she replied. "I just feel something dreadful is going to happen. I don't know why."

Wes smiled and took her in his arms.

"It's going to be just fine," he said. "Everything is going to be okay."

"It's just that Sarah was holding on to that locket when she left here like it was a lifeline to a drowning person," Reva whispered. "She didn't put it on. She clutched it, looked at it, and put it back in the box. She put it in her pocket and walked out the door."

Wes tried to comfort Reva.

"Where do you think she was going?" Reva asked.

"Probably somewhere to think, honey, probably just somewhere to think," Wes replied. "That girl has a good head on her shoulders. Don't ever doubt that."

Kate found Trudy putting the "Closed" sign on the salon window but ran through the door, anyway.

"Hey, I'm not open today, little missy! In case you haven't heard, Techy Ted has come to our village, and I'm in the entertainin' mood," Trudy exclaimed.

She stopped midsentence when she saw Kate's face.

"You look like a crazy woman! What on earth is wrong?"

"It's Sarah," Kate began as she walked to the rickety chair to sit down.

That chair had its own special forgiving memories. Kate gravitated to that chair because she felt that was the only place she should sit on that particular day.

"What's happened to Sarah?" Trudy questioned. "Has somethin' happened to Sarah?"

A sound of alarm could be heard in Trudy's voice.

Kate sat there, still stunned.

"What is it, Kate?" Trudy almost screamed.

"It's Sarah," Kate said.

Trudy stood in front of Kate and then fell to her knees, shaking Kate's shoulders. Taking Kate's face in her hands, she asked again, "What has happened to Sarah?"

"Nothing has happened to her! She's my daughter, Trudy, the baby I gave away!" Kate exclaimed.

Trudy looked at Kate and backed away.

"Are you sure?" Trudy questioned.

"I am," Kate replied.

"Let's go talk." Trudy grabbed Kate by the arm and walked her to the door.

"My place now," Trudy said.

When they arrived, Trudy went to her kitchen cabinet, got the whisky bottle, went back to the living room, and poured both of them a shot. Buddy sat on the couch, looking at them, stretched lazily, laid back down, and went to sleep.

"I'm not sure about this, but you are," Trudy said to Kate. "So I trust your instincts, and I know you are going to tell me why you are so sure."

Trudy swallowed her drink in one gulp and continued, "Start talkin'."

Kate began to tell Trudy the whole story. When she was done, she motioned for another drink.

Trudy sat motionless, decided another drink was definitely in order, and poured them both another shot.

"Well, I'll be," was all Trudy could say.

Thoughts of Techy Ted would have to wait.

Trudy walked over to Buddy, picked him up, went back to the chair she had been sitting on, and said, "My cat calms me. He helps me make decisions."

"What's he saying now?"

"Nothing."

"Well," Kate began, "I know what God is telling me."

"What?" Trudy questioned.

"I have to talk to Wes and Reva," Kate answered.

"I know." Trudy agreed.

Kate looked out the window, tilted her head, and looked back at Trudy.

"You weren't kidding," Kate said. "Techy Ted is here."

Trudy gathered herself, put Buddy back on the couch, and walked to the door with Kate. Kate hugged Trudy and said, "Thanks for the drink. Tell Ted we don't need his services any longer."

As Kate walked past the techy from Detroit, she smiled, especially when he tipped his chapeau hat. Trudy stood in the doorway, thinking, *Well, he's sure no cowboy, but that purple chapeau sure turns my head.*

No boots either, but he had a swagger all his own. A techy swagger.

She invited him in. No, his services were no longer needed, but he sure had nice shoulders and big hands. He might just be able to rub that knot out of her lower neck—the one that had just formed a mere ten minutes ago.

Buddy looked up from his pillow on the couch, yawned, and went back to sleep. It was as if he were asking what all the commotion was about. So many people coming and going in what used to be his quiet little home.

Yep, just another day in paradise...

What, indeed, was she going to say to Wes and Reva? Those high school sweethearts that had fallen in love, gone through their life together in Brooksport Village, trudged through their ups and downs, ended up on their feet after so many tragedies—was she going to turn their world upside down again?

Maybe she should turn around and forget the whole thing.

No, she couldn't do that. Secrets always put you in chains, a bondage of the worst kind. She had to tell them. She was Sarah's natural mother.

They would want proof, and she had it. Oh, boy, did she have it—not only tucked away in her own heart but a little piece of fabric that had been hidden in a drawer, now safely secure in an envelope inside her pocket.

Determined, she began her walk to Wes and Reva's house.

Reva saw Kate walking up the sidewalk.

"We have a visitor coming," she said to Wes. "Kate is coming up our sidewalk."

"Oh, it's probably about the birthday party," Wes replied.

And then the doorbell rang.

Reva opened the door.

"We have to talk," Kate said, walking into their house.

Reva felt a sense of dread.

"About the birthday party this weekend?" Wes questioned.

"No, about something much more serious," Kate replied.

Kate sat down. Reva took a seat next to Wes.

"There's no easy way to say this," Kate began. "I have to come right out and say it."

"What?" Reva asked.

"Wes, Reva," Kate began.

"Say it, woman! What?" Wes found his voice.

"First of all, I want to thank you."

"For what?"

"For raising my daughter. Sarah is my daughter."

After Reva got over the shock of Kate's statement, she could not help herself when she nearly screamed.

"What are you saying? I don't believe you!"

Wes took hold of Reva's arm, trying to calm her.

Kate reached in her pocket and retrieved the envelope.

She asked, "Do you still have the blanket? I would like to see it."

"You gave the blanket up when you gave her up!" Reva shouted.

She suddenly realized who else would know about the blanket. Who else but Sarah's natural mother?

Wes intervened. "Reva, go get the blanket. Let's all calm down a bit."

Reva took a deep breath to calm herself and went into the bedroom to get the blanket.

"Here it is!"

She handed the blanket to Kate.

Kate gave Reva an understanding look, took the blanket, and removed the contents of the envelope now sitting in her lap. It was a triangular corner of the exact material of the blanket.

As gently as she could, Kate began, "Before I wrapped my baby girl in this blanket, I cut a piece of it away. Someday I wanted her to know how my heart broke—I cut a piece of my heart away from her that day—when I handed her over."

Reva had turned pale. Wes could feel her body shaking beneath the arm he had placed around her shoulders.

Kate continued, "I'm not here to cause you stress or to disturb your life. Whatever decision you make, I will honor. It is not up to me to tell Sarah. It is up to you. Sarah will not hear this from me."

Kate stood to leave, and with her leaving, she proved one more thing. She proved her promise was true. She left the tiny triangle remnant there—her last tangible memory of Sarah. The remnant she had held on to all these years. No more proof. Wes and Reva could do whatever they chose to do.

Wes heard the door close. Reva began to cry. The blanket still on the table with that tiny triangle of a piece of cloth, staring back at them. Reva calmed her tears, rose from the couch, picked up that piece of cloth, walked to a nearby table, and put it in a drawer.

Reva walked back to Wes and sat down beside him.

"What just happened?" Reva questioned. She kept her hands in her lap.

"We kept our promise from all those years ago, and now we have to do the right thing," Wes replied.

Reva's tears came once again like a torrent.

They both knew what the right thing was.

60

Trudy and Techy Ted were planning dinner when the phone rang. It was Kate.

"It's done," she said.

Trudy didn't know what to do. That was it. A mere "It's done." And then Kate hung up, not waiting for a reply.

Trudy turned to Techy Ted and said, "Where were we?"

"We were planning where to go for dinner," Ted responded.

"Oh yeah," Trudy replied as she scurried around the room looking for her purple scarf.

"Let's go to the Stumble In. They have great burgers."

"You want a burger?" Ted questioned. "I thought I would take you some place nice."

"Oh, burgers are fine with me," she replied as she tied her purple scarf around her hair.

"You sure do like purple, don't you?" Ted asked.

"Oh yes, I do, darlin', but it's a long story. You must like it too, judgin' from that purple chapeau you have on your head," she replied, pointing to the chapeau and giving his cheek a little tweak before walking out the door.

He watched her walk down the sidewalk and whispered to himself, "I like her. She has a swagger all her own."

Trudy thought to herself with a smile. Techy Ted probably didn't know that his particular hat was a mark of dignity. After all, he was a techy. Trudy surmised that was as close to an engineer as you could get, but it didn't bother her. She could handle engineers.

Then she said out loud, "Yep, royalty and dignity might just go real good together."

Sarah should be home soon. Reva walked to the window, tears still streaming down her face. Wes continued sitting on the couch.

"I don't know what to do!" Reva almost screamed.

Wes continued to sit quietly.

She walked into the kitchen and poured herself a tall glass of Dr. Pepper.

"Having a Dr. Pepper?" Wes asked from the couch.

"How do you know?"

"You used to tell me that Dr. Pepper was the only doctor you trusted, remember?"

Reva smiled. "Yes, I remember. It was the day you came home from Granada."

Wes patted the place next to him on the couch, inviting her to come sit with him.

She sat down beside him and said, "I didn't think any doctor could fix you. And then here came Trudy with a Dr. Pepper in her hand. She didn't know what else to give me, I guess. She looked so pitiful, especially in all that purple she was wearing."

Wes smiled as he remembered the story and said, "She was new to our little village then."

"Yes, she was. We didn't know how to take her at first."

Again, Wes smiled. "And then what happened?" he asked.

"Sarah looked at her and giggled—she was a wee babe, had been with us right before Granada. We were so afraid then, remember?" Reva questioned.

"I do, we were in the middle of the trial period with Sarah, and we were so afraid the agency would consider us not fit to raise her because of my blindness," Wes said.

"Then there was Trudy, standing in our living room, saying Sarah looked just like you," Reva whispered.

"We smiled at her comment. We knew Sarah didn't look like either one of us, but Trudy thought so. We never did tell her she was adopted, did we?"

"No, in fact, I don't think anyone in this town knows. We had moved away for a while—that's when we got Sarah."

She took a sip of her Dr. Pepper.

"Come to think about it, Gordy is the only one who knows and, of course, Sarah," Wes continued.

Reva brought the conversation back to Trudy.

"It wasn't long before everybody in town loved Trudy."

Wes crossed his legs and patted Reva on the knee.

"I remember when 'ole Phil called Trudy from Crabby's Bar," Wes said.

"Who could ever forget that night?" Reva asked.

"He was so drunk he couldn't walk home," Wes replied.

Reva couldn't help but laugh even as her tears continued to fall.

"He said the only person that would understand what he needed was the 'purple people eater.' Everybody thought he was talking about some alien he had read about in one of those science fiction books of his until poor Charlie told us it was Trudy he wanted."

"I'll never forget that little guy. Charlie could have never gotten his dad home that night," Wes said.

"Somebody said, 'Well, go get her,' and off Charlie ran," Reva replied.

"And then do you remember what happened?" Wes asked.

"I do! Trudy came in that bar and laid the law down to Phil. All Phil could say was, 'Trudy, I thought you would be the one person in this town who would understand.'"

Reva finished her Dr. Pepper before continuing.

"She kept wagging her finger at him, saying, "You want a second chance, you gotta choose to take it, Phil. You can't keep comin' down here makin' an ass of yourself. And that is what you're doin' night after night. Believe me, Phil, you don't get smarter the more you drink. You get louder and dumber! I'm goin' to get you home, and Charlie's goin' to help me, but you better start straightening yourself up. You've got a son to take care of!"

"She said all of that without takin' a breath!" Wes said. "Rumor has it she didn't let up on him all the way home either. She kept askin' him, 'Do 'ya think you're the only person in the world who ever lost anyone? Do you?'"

"And he kept mumbling something," Reva interjected. "I heard she told Phil he had a hole in his heart, but he had to find some way to mend it up, and Crabby's Bar was not going to fill it for him!"

"Everybody thought it was Trudy's constant lectures that turned 'ole Phil around, but it wasn't." Wes said, "No, it wasn't; that's for sure, but I think it helped."

"How so?" Reva asked.

"I think all that truth Trudy was shouting out actually encouraged that storm to come right into 'ole Phil's house. That's where he really saw his second chance come running down the street in the shape of a tree right through his roof," Wes said.

Reva kept looking at Wes.

"So why are we remembering all of this, especially right now, Wes? I'm beside myself. What are we going to do about this thing we have just found out?"

"It's not a thing, Reva. It's about our daughter. It's about her second chance."

"You know," Wes said, "the first thing that came to my mind when I was injured in Granada was that I had failed you."

"What do you mean? You didn't fail me! I was so glad you survived that attack! I couldn't wait to get you back home!"

Wes held up his hand in protest. "Let me finish, I feared I had failed you because I thought the adoption agency would rescind our acceptance and take Sarah away. I mean I was a man who had lost his eyesight. I kept telling myself that I was only three quarters of a man without my eyes."

Reva shifted on the couch, grabbed Wes's hand, and leaned into him as he continued.

"I had to make up for this injury somehow. I had to make sure they didn't change their mind. I had to be proactive."

"I remember," Reva said.

"Oh, I can't say I never felt sorry for myself. I did. I put on a good act for everybody else. But sorry only gets you so far. I had to pick myself up and figure out a way to keep moving forward. I had to relearn a lot of things I had taken for granted. It was like being in a foreign land in my own living room."

Reva replied, "I remember. I had to guide you and move furniture around to make sure you could find your way."

"Without turning over tables and tripping over shoes," Wes laughed.

"Hey, I made it a point to make sure everything was picked up—"

Wes interrupted, "Yes, you did, and that was one of the blessings in all this—a very clean house. Too bad I couldn't see it!"

"And you kept your sense of humor once you decided to move on."

Reva nudged him on the shoulder.

"We did laugh again, didn't we?" Wes asked as he remembered those days of restoration.

"Yes, we did," Reva answered.

"But," Wes continued, "it wasn't until we got our second chance."

Reva replied, "And we have Gordy to thank for that."

"Yes, we do," he replied.

Yesterday's memories came flooding back.

Wes said, "Gordy must have seen me struggling as I was walking up the path to his house because when I nearly fell on my face, I remember a strong arm coming around my shoulders. It was Gordy. *'Let me help you, buddy,'* he said to me. "And for the first time in my life, I let someone help me—outside of you—and it wasn't a threat to my 'manhood.' He guided me right up to his front porch and over to a chair, where I was extremely grateful to sit."

Reva squeezed his hand, encouraging him to go on. She had not heard this part of the story.

"I don't know where I was looking when I began to talk, but I could feel the sun on my face, and I could sense Gordy moving around to face me. I said to him, 'Gordy, you rescue horses and bring them back to health. Now I'm in need of a rescue.'"

Wes shifted his position on the couch.

"I told him I would never be able to see again, but my legs and arms were strong, and if he could show me around the stable, I could feed, water, and even shoe those horses."

Reva encouraged Wes to continue.

"I could only imagine the look on his face. I was sure he would say no, that he couldn't risk me getting hurt or kicked by one of his horses. But you know what he said?"

Reva moved a little closer to Wes on the couch.

"He said that a rescued horse always knew somehow when their humans were in trouble, and he wasn't worried at all about me getting kicked. He didn't care if I dropped the water bucket or spilled the feed. He said he was willing to hire me and work with me, and he did."

Wes turned toward Reva on the couch.

"I was going to make sure that agency would not take Sarah away. I had to prove I could make a living. I had to prove I could support my family."

"And you did," Reva whispered.

"Before I knew it, Gordy had installed labeled Braille tablets in that stable where I would be doing most of my work. He made sure the water buckets were placed where those tablets said they were, along with all the other tools I needed for a good day's work."

"And then when tourists started flocking to our village, Gordy suggested that I use this voice of mine to tell the children stories after their riding lessons he offered them."

Reva laid her head upon Wes's shoulder.

"That voice of yours. Somebody once told me it sounded like the voice of God," Reva whispered.

She came back to the subject at hand.

Looking at Wes, Reva had to admit. "You're right, I know you are. It's all about second chances."

"Yes, it is," he answered. "That Granada experience of mine was hell to deal with, but what Gordy did for me—and you—when that baby girl was ours forever, I will never forget. I had a job. I proved myself. And that adoption agency knew our Sarah would be in good hands."

Reva asked, "Do you remember what the social worker said to you when their final decision was made?"

"I sure do. As she placed Sarah in my arms, she said I was a wounded warrior but, nevertheless, a warrior. She said she knew that I would protect our child, shield her, love her, and provide for her. There was never any doubt in her mind."

Reva remembered that moment too. Sarah was finally their very own forever. They had cried grateful tears when the social worker had left.

"I remember you holding Sarah on your lap and telling her stories," Reva said.

"So do I. It was then I had purpose again. I vowed I would be the best father and daddy a girl could ever have and the best husband a wife could ever wish for."

Wes turned to Reva on the couch and took her face in his hands.

"Second chances should be passed on, don't you think?"

He could feel the tears on her face as he continued.

"Sarah deserves a second chance, Reva. She deserves to know who her natural mother is—a chance to get to know her. Both Kate and Sarah deserve this."

Reva's tears kept flowing.

"She needs to know. We will move forward through all of this just like we always have. We will have no regrets and no looking back."

"Another chapter?" Reva asked.

"Yes, another chapter," Wes replied.

With his thumbs, he wiped away the tears on Reva's cheeks.

"So are we in agreement?" he asked.

"We're in agreement," Reva whispered. "When Sarah comes home, the three of us will talk."

It was then they heard Sarah coming up the sidewalk.
The next chapter was about to begin.

Sarah burst through the door.
Seeing her parents on the couch, she stopped short.
"What's wrong?" she asked.
"Your mom and I have something to share with you," Wes began.
Sarah sat down on the chair across from her parents.
"Oh no!" she began. "Are you two getting a divorce?"
Reva couldn't help herself. She laughed. Perhaps that's what she needed at that critical moment—comic relief. She decided to go get another glass of Dr. Pepper.
She replied as she walked into the kitchen. "My goodness, no! Why on earth would you think that?"
"My friend at school," she replied.
"Explain, please," Wes chimed in.
"Well, she came home from school, and her parents were sitting on the couch just like you two. They were looking all serious with a pitcher of sweet iced tea in front of them, and then they told her they were getting a divorce."
Reva raised her glass half-filled with Dr. Pepper as she walked back into the room.
"Oh no, sweetheart," Wes began. "We are not getting a divorce. I love your mom more than anything in this world. No divorce on the horizon in this house!"
"So what is making you two so serious right now?" Sarah asked.
Wes patted Jeb on the top of his head and asked, "Would you come over here, Sarah, and sit on my lap for a spell?"
Sarah looked at her mom, questioning the request. Goodness sakes, she was all grown-up now. It had been a long time since she had sat on her dad's lap while he told her stories.
Her mother smiled and nodded.

Wes began, "Sweetheart, we know you're older now, and this seems an odd request, but I just want to relive those times you were a little girl when you wanted me to tell you made-up stories before you turn the magical age of nineteen."

Sarah smiled, got up from her chair, and walked over to Wes. His arms were open as she made herself comfortable on his lap.

"I want you close to me when I tell you this story, sweet Sarah. It's a true story, not a made-up one. It's a love story. It's a story your mom and I have cherished all our lives. It's about you."

"When your mom and I were married, we always wanted a family. As it turned out, we couldn't have a baby," Wes began.

"Dad, you've already had this conversation with me. I know I'm adopted," Sarah interrupted.

"But now, sweet girl, there's more to the story," Wes said.

Sarah's mom got up from the couch and ventured to the window, looking toward Open Door, saying nothing.

"I have to ask you a question, Sarah," Wes said. "I want you to think about it before you answer."

Sarah looked at him, wondering what was coming next.

"Do you ever think about your natural mother?"

Sarah was very quiet, twirling the locket between her fingers.

Wes continued, "I don't want you to worry about hurting our feelings."

He cupped her face in his hands, and she put her head on his shoulder.

"Just tell us," Wes continued.

Sarah took a deep breath and answered, "Yes, Dad, I have, especially when Mom gave me the locket."

"Well, I want you to know that it is okay to think about her and wonder about her."

Sarah took a deep breath.

"Thanks, Dad."

She looked at her mom across the room and saw her smile. The assurance of that smile made her feel more comfortable.

"You don't remember when you came to us, Sarah, because you were just a wee babe in arms," her dad continued. "We fell in love with you the first moment we saw you. We had prepared a place for you and have so many pictures to prove it!"

Sarah smiled. "I've seen the pictures."

"So you know how much we wanted you. I want you to always remember that."

Sarah's mom walked back to the couch and sat down.

"Your mom and I had you in our arms before I was called to Granada." He interrupted himself. "Could I have a little bit of that Dr. Pepper, Reva?"

She handed him the glass.

"We were so worried during the trial period because of my blindness. We were afraid the agency might change their minds."

"But they didn't," Sarah interjected.

"No, thank God they didn't, and I thank the good Lord every day for the blessing of you."

Sarah kissed her dad on the cheek and answered, "Me too, Dad."

"You don't know why they remained true to letting you stay with us, but I'm going to tell you now. This is the rest of the story."

Sarah sat up and looked at her mom. Her mom smiled and motioned for her to keep listening.

"It's because of Gordy, Sarah," he said.

"Gordy?"

"Yes, Gordy."

"You see, I felt I had to prove to your mom, the agency, and to myself I was still worthy of being a dad. God brought me to my knees, and that's when the almighty one led me straight to Gordy."

"I'll never forget putting that harness on old Jeb here and taking that walk straight to Gordy's driveway."

"Neither will I," Reva said. "Your dad walked straight and tall. It was then I knew I had my Wes back."

"Little did I know that Gordy was sitting right there on his swing, watching my every move. I stumbled, walking up that driveway to Gordy's. He was beside me in an instant. Together we walked to his porch."

Wes patted Jeb's head.

"We sat down on that swing of his. Neither of us said a word for a long while, and then I began to talk, oh, boy, did I talk."

Wes took another sip of Reva's Dr. Pepper.

"That was the day Gordy gave me my second chance—the day he gave me my open door."

Sarah sat up and looked at both her mom and dad.

"Is that when you began working for Gordy?"

"It is, my child. That is when Gordy hired me on the spot. I'll never forget what he did for me. He looked at me and said, 'Wes, you may be blind, but you can still do for me something in the stables that I need help with—you can brush those horses and water those horses and feed them. So let's see where we go from here.' He wasn't worried about me being injured either. He said horses knew when humans needed them."

Sarah continued to listen.

"And then Gordy made that stable of horses Braille-ready. He called people in to place plaques on certain walls in that stable so I could read with my fingers, and suddenly 'ole Jeb and I had a new career."

Wes smiled, taking another sip of his drink.

"Gordy and I go back a long way, Sarah. We grew up together. We both served our country in 1983. When that bomb hit our barracks, Gordy made sure I got out of there. He saw firsthand the damage that had been done to me. He didn't run for cover, he shielded me and got me out. He kept whispering in my ear, 'No man left behind, Wes. I've got you.'"

Sarah moved from her dad's lap and knelt down in front of him, holding his hands.

"Dad, your eyes may not see, but your heart sees everything that is important."

"Thank you, my sweet daughter, and now my heart is seeing something that you need to know."

Sarah suddenly realized how important it was for her to be sitting right where she belonged as her dad continued his story. She got back on his lap and wrapped her arms around him.

"Your mom and I have talked, and there is something you should know. We only found out about it a few hours ago. What would you think if I told you that you no longer have to wonder about your natural mother? We know who she is, and we know where she lives."

Sarah nearly jumped from her dad's lap.

"What?" she questioned.

"We know who she is," Wes repeated.

Reva sat so still only she could see her heart lying in pieces on the floor.

"Who?" Sarah asked.

Reva got down on her knees before both Wes and Sarah. She looked straight into those eyes, those beautiful eyes of her daughter.

"Oh, my dear Sarah," Reva said. "Your sweet natural mom lives in this very town."

"What?" Sarah asked again, sitting alert on her dad's lap.

"Yes," Wes said, "my sweet, sweet Sarah, it is Kate."

Sarah suddenly remembered Kate's reaction when she had shown her the locket. It was the locket. It was all about the locket. Her early birthday present. How did her parents have it? Sarah had to talk to Kate. She had to get the rest of her answers.

She ran from her dad's lap to the front door, turned around, and said three words.

"I'll be back," Sarah exclaimed.

With that, she was gone, running up toward the northern end of the street, and straight to Open Door.

61

Kate walked to the window overlooking the flower garden and knew instantly that Wes and Reva had made their decision. They had told Sarah. Kate watched as Sarah seemed to almost be running to Open Door. Then she disappeared.

"Where did she go?" Kate questioned. "Did she change her mind?"

The doorbell rang.

"Not now," Kate murmured to herself. "No check-ins, not now."

She walked through the living room to the door, opened it, and saw Sarah standing there.

Neither spoke. The silence was deafening; neither mother nor child knew exactly what to do or say at that moment.

Sarah spoke first. "I know you as Miss Kate. Somehow I felt I needed to ring the doorbell. I wanted to come through the front door, I guess, because I wanted to introduce myself to you as your daughter."

They stood there for a while.

Kate couldn't find the words to speak, so Sarah once again broke the silence.

"Got any sweet tea?" she asked.

Kate held the door for Sarah to enter, and they walked into the kitchen where a fresh pitcher of tea was always waiting.

"I know you have a lot of questions," Kate began as she poured their tea.

Sarah nodded. "I don't know where to start."

Kate understood.

"Mom and Dad—" she stopped suddenly, looking at Kate.

Kate said, "It's okay, Sarah, I understand. You can talk of your mom and dad, and you can continue calling Reva your mom. Would you like to help me with lunch?"

Sarah smiled as she got up from her chair and walked to the refrigerator. "Salad?" she questioned.

"Sounds good," Kate replied, reaching for a fresh tomato. Kate had learned that when hands were busy, it was easier to talk. And she wanted Sarah to be comfortable.

"Was it the locket?" Sarah asked. "I mean, was it the locket—was that when you knew?"

"Yes," Kate replied. "That's when I knew for sure."

"For sure?" Sarah asked.

"Yes, that's when I was certain beyond any doubt. There were little things I noticed from time to time."

Sarah looked at her glass of sweet tea.

"Things like this?" she questioned, pointing to her glass.

Kate smiled and answered, "It was more like the way you held the glass. Something seemed so familiar about your hands."

Kate held up her own hands. "Now I know why."

Suddenly, the conversation shifted to Charlie. Kate surmised that's what happens sometimes when you're talking with someone about serious matters.

"Do you like Charlie, Kate?" Sarah asked.

"I love Charlie."

"He loves you too. He told me once how he would always see you sometimes sitting on the bench in your flower garden, looking all far away and sad."

"Charlie notices things like that, doesn't he?" Kate added.

The two kept preparing the salad.

Sarah nodded. "Trudy told me that Charlie was very deep. What do you think she meant by that?"

"I think she meant that he is very perceptive, especially when it comes to people's feelings."

Sarah nodded and thought for a while before speaking. "Were you thinking of me in the middle of all those flowers, when you looked all far away and sad?"

Kate began slicing a tomato for the salad.

"Yes, there wasn't a day that went by that I didn't think of you. Those sad times Charlie was speaking of, well, those were the times I kept reliving the day I wrapped you in that blanket, kissed your forehead, and handed you over to the adoption agency. I felt a part of me had been severed—like an amputation I didn't know how I would get over."

There were tears in her eyes, even now, as Sarah looked at her.

Kate put the tomato aside. Sarah forgot the lettuce. They both met at the kitchen table and sat down, looking at one another.

"I didn't want to let you go. I wanted to hold on for dear life. I kept thinking I could put pink bows in your hair. I could wrap you in little pink blankets and have tea parties. We could eat those tiny tea cookies. I could teach you how to look both ways before crossing the street. I could read you bedtime stories and tuck you in. I could push you in the grocery cart and buy you your favorite cereal."

Kate sighed.

"I guess that's when it hit me. I couldn't buy you anything. Oh, I could give you all the love, hugs, and kisses for the rest of your life. But reality told me I couldn't buy you the essentials. I couldn't buy diapers, much less tricycles, bicycles, school clothes, and prom dresses."

Kate stood and walked over to the window, looking out at the bench in the flower garden.

Sarah asked, "Do you want to go sit on the bench?"

"I would like that," Kate replied.

They walked to the bench in silence.

Kate looked directly at Sarah and said, "I guess that was the moment of truth for me."

Kate looked up at the sky.

"You were so beautiful, and when I looked at you, I knew you needed a running start in this life. You needed not only someone to love you but also a mom and dad who would be able to give you the things you needed."

Sarah looked at her with eyes of understanding.

Kate knew Sarah needed to hear more. Before she could even ask, Kate continued, "My mom, your grandmother, died suddenly before you were born, and my dad, your grandfather, was gone before her."

"So you had no one to help you at all?" Sarah asked.

Kate sighed. "I was barely nineteen years old when you were born. I was forced to think in realities, not fantasies. And reality told me you deserved a better life."

They looked out at the water.

"When you were born, I held you and had all those second thoughts. Should I? What if? If only? The thoughts that drive you crazy if you let them."

Sarah nodded.

"But in the end of that decision process, I took the blanket that my mom had begun knitting together as a gift to me, and I finished it. You see, we had decided to raise you together, and then…"

Sarah completed the sentence. "She died."

Kate nodded.

"I wrapped you in that blanket, and I pinned the locket with a note inside it."

Sarah's hand went instinctively to the locket around her neck.

Kate continued, "The note was a note to your future parents, whoever they might be. I wanted them to know how much I loved you and how much I ached with my decision to let you go. I wanted you to have the locket I had purchased upon your nineteenth birthday. I told them that in the note. They remained true to that request."

Again, Sarah nodded, still grasping the locket with her hand.

Kate wanted so desperately to grab Sarah and hug her, but she held back, knowing it would have to be Sarah to make that first move toward reconciliation.

Kate continued, "I don't want to turn your world upside down, Sarah. I want you to continue to live your life with Wes and Reva. They have put their heart and soul into raising you. They love you.

I want you to keep growing and prospering in your home with those two very loving people."

And then she looked directly into the eyes of her daughter and said, "What I would like is to share a part of that life with you. There has always been an open door here for you, even before we came to know the truth. I want that to continue. It's true we will look at each other in a different way now, but the one thing I don't want is for you to feel torn between Reva and me. It takes more than giving birth to someone to be a mom, and Reva has shown you that. She will always be your mom."

Sarah spoke. "I don't know if I can call you Mom."

"That's okay," Kate replied. "Why don't you call me Kate, without the Miss in front of it?"

"I can do that," Sarah replied.

Sarah sighed, looked back at Kate, and said, "I have to ask you something."

Kate encouraged her to continue.

"Has my name always been Sarah?"

"Within my heart, I named you Dawn. I wanted you to have a new life and a fresh chance. Dawn seemed appropriate—each dawn brings a new beginning. Your parents named you Sarah."

It was then that Sarah reached for Kate's hand on that bench in that flower garden and restoration began.

62

Charlie saw Sarah and Kate talking in the garden that day and knew better than to interrupt. They weren't chatting like usual. It was for sure they weren't talking about the birthday party. They were serious—too serious for him to interrupt. Too serious for him to try and fix whatever they looked so pensive over. Charlie had learned from Jake that when it came to girls, sometimes you had to be quiet and not say a word.

Charlie remembered the time Jake had told him that men had a flaw—they always tried to "fix" things. It just came natural to men. He said women just want men to listen and not say anything. Jake had told him that men should grunt once in a while, though, just to prove they were listening.

So this was one of those days when he saw those two talking. He decided to just move on and mind his own business. It was probably best not to listen to them; he didn't think he was too good at grunting. Not yet, anyway. He had a feeling he would learn soon enough what their conversation was all about.

Charlie's only thought was, *I hope it's not about me.*

He remembered what Jake had also told him—that sometimes women can cause a man to get all messed up in their head, especially when you see two of them together in deep conversation. He said that they were always up to something…

"Are you at the window, Reva?" Wes asked.

"Yes."

"Please, honey, come away from the window and take a deep breath. It's going to be all right."

"How do you know that?"

"Because I know."

"Really?" Reva questioned. "What if she decides to move in with Kate?"

She walked over to Wes.

"What if this does not turn into the blessing you said it would?"

She paced back to the window.

"What if we lose our daughter? And all because I remained true to a note pinned in a blanket! I can't help wondering if I did the right thing, Wes!"

"Honey, you did the right thing. You know you did. We are living in a fragment of time right now. We will see the whole picture soon enough."

"Here she comes!" Reva exclaimed to Wes.

"Is she alone?" Wes asked.

"Yes," Reva replied.

Sarah walked through the door and saw Reva's questioning eyes. She walked over to her and gave her a hug.

She turned and asked Wes, "Dad, can I sit on your lap for a while? This time, I want to tell you a story."

Sarah told her parents everything that had happened, every detail—from ringing the doorbell to the talk in the garden and leading right up to the locket that opened the door for all of them.

"It's a new chapter," Wes said.

"I was beginning to question giving you the locket in the first place, especially when Kate appeared at our doorstep this morning," Reva said.

"You did the right thing, mom."

Reva took a deep breath and kept looking at Sarah.

"You know, Kate said when she gave me over to the agency, a piece of her was severed, almost like an amputation," Sarah said.

Reva nodded, as if she could feel the pain herself. When Sarah had left the house to go to Kate's, she felt the stab of letting go. She couldn't help thinking, *After all these years, am I losing my daughter?* But both her what if and her fear were disappearing. A certain peace was enveloping her. Sarah removed herself from her dad's lap and knelt before her mother. She looked straight into her eyes just as Kate had done with her a few short moments earlier. It was as if Sarah had read her mother's mind.

"Mom, I'm not going anywhere. This is my home, and it will remain my home. You and dad have loved me enough that my heart is big enough to love the both of you and have room left over for Kate too."

"I'm grateful for Kate," Reva replied. "She could have made other choices, but she didn't. She gave you life."

Reva gave her daughter a kiss on the forehead and walked over to the small table, opening one of the drawers. She put the remnant in her pocket and walked back to Sarah.

She took the blanket that had been left on the chair near the couch and spread it carefully on the table in front of them.

Sarah looked at it and said, "I never noticed a corner of the blanket missing before."

"Before?" her mom questioned.

"Oh, mom, since we're being real open here today, I must confess I've visited this blanket a lot of times through the years."

"You have?"

"I have."

Sarah fingered the corner of the blanket.

"I saw you one morning holding it as you were looking out the window from your bedroom. I think you were praying, Mom."

Reva remembered that day in particular, and that's exactly what she was doing, thanking God for this most precious one that was now standing with her in this very place, looking at that very blanket she had been so carefully wrapped within. She remembered that prayer, asking God what she should do with that blanket—should she keep it? Should she destroy it? She never could quite bring herself to toss it away. It seemed too special.

"I watched where you placed it, in that drawer of your own private dresser that no one else was supposed to go near."

Reva smiled, and Wes gave a little cough.

"But, I take it you went near?"

"I couldn't resist. It seemed that blanket was somewhat of a mystery. I wanted to look at it closely. I wanted to hug it."

"I see," Reva replied. "When did you start doing that?"

"Oh, when I reached double digits. When I was ten years old. I always went to that drawer when you were out running errands."

Reva looked toward Wes. "Did you know about all of this?"

"Of course, I knew. Our daughter didn't pull anything on me. Even though I couldn't see, my sense of hearing was, and still is, very keen, missy! I knew every time she opened that drawer. But it was okay. It kind of became our own silent secret."

Reva looked at Sarah.

"So this blanket had some sort of magnetic pull for you."

"That's a good way of putting it," Sarah replied. "I didn't know the real significance until today—because of this."

She pointed to the locket.

"That's what started the snowball of the blessing to follow," Sarah said. She brought her gaze back to the missing corner. Again she said, "But I never noticed this." She touched the corner that was missing.

"I didn't either." Reva admitted. "Until today."

She pulled the missing piece, the remnant, from her pocket and handed it to Sarah.

"Kate brought it to your dad and me today as proof. It's true, Sarah, what she told you. She felt a part of her had been cut away, and before she placed the note with the locket inside the blanket with you, she cut the corner and kept it in her own secret place that no one knew about until today."

Sarah looked at the remnant as a lone tear rolled down her cheek.

Reva saw that tear and said, "Let's put it back where it belongs."

"The missing piece," Sarah whispered, "has been found. It's time to stitch it back together."

They both saw the stitching at the same time. They saw in very small letters an embroidered name. They looked at one another. Wes could actually feel the anticipation in the air.

"What is it?" he questioned.

Reva walked over to him, took his hand, and led him to the table.

The three of them stood together.

Reva said, "In tiny letters, Wes, there is a name embroidered in this corner, and the name is Dawn."

"That was the piece of me she kept for herself," Sarah whispered. "That was the name she gave me when I was born. She loved me enough to give me a name, Mom. She loved me enough to stitch that name on this blanket. She loved me enough to let me go. Another dawn," Sarah continued. "A new day."

Wes put those strong arms of his around both mother and daughter, those arms that were steadfast and true.

"Kate gave me life. You and Mom gave me a future," she said to her dad.

And then Wes cupped his daughter's face in his hands and wiped her grateful tears away with his thumbs.

63

"It's not always about you, Charlie," Sarah said.

"Sorry," Charlie replied.

He mentally kicked himself for not following Jake's advice he had received so long ago, or so it seemed. Where was that man, anyway? He had gone and opened his big mouth when he wasn't supposed to.

"You and Kate were so serious," Charlie said, knowing that he was still opening his mouth when he shouldn't.

"And you are so curious?" Sarah asked.

She continued, "Well, thanks for not interrupting us."

"You're welcome."

Charlie looked so pitiful Sarah finally said, "I'll tell you, Charlie." She took his hand and continued, "Because I love you."

Charlie didn't know what stunned him most—Sarah's confession of love for him or the story she told him. His mouth dropped open every time he remembered that day. Who would have ever thought that Sarah's birth mother would have found her way to Brooksport Village and would be living up the street all these years later? And nobody knew until the locket.

After Sarah told Charlie her story, he asked her something really stupid. At least, in his own mind, it was a stupid question. He asked her if he had to call her Dawn.

He decided to pay Trudy a visit and ask her if his question had been stupid. He told Trudy he had asked such a stupid question because Sarah had said she loved him moments before and he was all confused in the head. He wasn't thinking straight. That's when Trudy laughed and gave Charlie a hug. Seemed everything Charlie said to women these days made them laugh and hug him. Everything sure seemed funny to them. The good thing was that he always got hugged in the process. So maybe he wasn't saying anything so stupid after all. Women! He would never understand them. He missed Jake. He needed Jake at times such as these. He needed a cowboy's advice.

It seemed the more he talked to Trudy about Sarah, all she could say was, "What a blessing! What a blessing!" Then she started buying Sarah all these gifts, telling her she was a princess and that she should wear more purple.

Sarah thought she had gone nuts, and so did Charlie, but they decided to let Trudy just be Trudy. Besides that, she had just met a man from Detroit who wore purple chapeaus. That looked silly to Charlie too, but it seemed to make Trudy happy, and that was just fine, mighty fine.

PART VIII

Lost and Found

"One of the most pathetic things about us human beings is our touching belief that there are times when the truth is not good enough for us; that it can and must be improved upon. We have to be utterly broken before we can realize that it is impossible to better the truth. It is the truth that we deny, which so tenderly and forgivingly picks up the fragments and puts them together again." (Laurens van Der Post)

64

It was autumn when he left, and now another year had come and gone. Another new year was beginning. Still, Jake could not get Kate off his mind. He saw her face in the crowd everywhere he went, and his life had suddenly become very crowded again. He had to admit, Trudy was right—too many whisky-breathin'-mornin'-breath women. Is that what he had come back to?

He was seated at his desk, looking out the window at all the high-rise buildings around him. He was remembering too much. Wasn't that what you always did on New Year's Eve? No, some people were happy. They put on crazy hats and blew horns.

It would have been easier if Kate had blasted him with angry words when he left. He knew how to react to bitter. But no, she had to mess his mind up even more with kindness. This was definitely an unfamiliar intruder that had blindsided him, trespassed all over his heart.

"Damn, I think I'm in love with that woman," he finally admitted.

"Damn!"

He walked over to the bookcase. He knew exactly where he had put it—the note she had written. He carefully pulled a book from its shelf and turned to the very middle where the note remained tucked between the pages. He was always reading that note, more often than she would ever know. It was becoming worn around the edges and was filled with truth—Kate's truth—she had written straight from her heart. That's where everything came from with Kate—straight from the heart. She was a straight shooter, he would give her that.

He wondered if she ever thought about that note. The way he left Brooksport in such a hurry, she probably thought he threw it away. He was a man who liked to travel light. Well, he hadn't thrown it away.

He sat down at his desk and began to read.

"Max Lucado, a favorite author of mine, once wrote, 'Whether you are a lamb lost on a craggy ledge or a city slicker alone in a deep jungle, everything changes when your rescuer appears.'"

He read the note in its entirety and questioned himself. "Is that what I am, a city slicker alone in a deep jungle?"

Jake had to admit he kept struggling but not with his business. In fact, it had expanded. He wished the struggle had been with his business. Instead, it was with his emotions. The bottom line was it always came back to Kate. It seemed emotions always spilled over in his mind when it came to that woman.

"I knew she was trouble when I first saw her," he kept telling himself.

He smiled and put the note back in its secret place.

"Yes, she was trouble, but she was also cute," he said to himself. And, she just plain and simply knocked him over.

He wondered what she might be doing this New Year's Eve. Did he have a right to wonder? No, not really.

He looked out the window. It was snowing.

"Forget Kate," he told himself.

He stood up, retrieved the note, once again, put it in his pocket and walked out of his office, telling everyone to have a great New Year's Eve long weekend. He sent them home early with a mini vacation included. They were grateful for the extra days. Jake knew how hard they worked for him. They deserved a few extra days—with pay.

Sandra stayed behind after Jake had told everyone to leave early. She walked into Jake's office, saying nothing. She busied herself, watering Jake's plants throughout his office.

Finally, she turned and exclaimed, "Hey, sweet babe, I know a lovesick fool when I see one, and you are definitely a lovesick fool!"

Jake stared at her.

"What's this?" she asked. "Is it new to your plant family? And when did you start liking plants, anyway? I have enough responsibility around here!"

Sighing, Sandra continued to water the plants.

"That's new, I thought I would try something different," Jake answered as he watched Sandra linger over that one plant in particular.

"I don't think it will live here," Sandra continued, "even though you have it under that special light you bought."

"Why's that?"

"It's not a city flower, it looks too fragile."

Jake kept watching her walking around his plants. Suddenly, she turned back to the one that had become his favorite. She walked over to it and carefully touched the one and only bloom.

"It looks like a tear," she said.

"It is, it's called a bleeding heart."

Sandra sat down in the nearest chair. "Jake, I've known you a long time." She fiddled with her skirt. "You're a smart man, and I admire you and what you've done in your life, but…"

"But what?"

"But you're a fool—a crazy fool. I don't know what or who has you tied up in knots this past year, but I'm assuming it's a woman."

"Why's that?"

"Because it usually is," she answered. "But this foolishness is different."

"How so?" Jake asked, looking away, pretending to file a memo in his desk drawer.

"Because of your sad eyes."

"You remind me of someone," Jake answered with a smile.

"Not a redhead, I hope!"

"No, a woman who loves purple."

"Whatever that means." Sandra rolled her eyes.

"It's a long story," Jake answered.

"Your stories are always long, Jake."

"Do you get tired of hearing my stories?"

"Oh, never. I'm writing a book and need another chapter. Just make it a happy ending."

Jake looked at her and shook his head.

"Jake, go back from wherever it was you ran back here from. Go find her. Go get her. Or go stay with her. Just do something!" She got up to leave. "Just do something. You're driving me and everyone else around here crazy!"

Jake looked at her. Oh yes, she was a lot like Trudy. Maybe that's why he liked Trudy so much. Both ladies told him the truth, and the truth always hit him like a two-by-four between the eyes. Maybe that's what he needed—a two-by-four.

"Sandra," he began, "do you think God ever hits you with two-by-fours?"

"Sometimes he has to," she answered. "Go back, Jake. Sometimes you have to go back in order to go forward."

She closed the door behind her as she left his office.

Moments later, the door opened again, and she poked her perky, pretty head back into his view.

"Happy New Year, Jake."

And then she was gone. Off to her own celebrations, off to her own new chapters. A new year was stretching before them.

He stood from his chair and walked over to the one bloom of that bleeding heart. He touched it briefly. He shook his head. No, he couldn't go back. He wouldn't go back. He had cowboy blood in his veins.

65

He didn't know how long he had been sitting in that bar, but it seemed his lips were getting loose. Jake began to talk.

"Someone told me that bartenders make great therapists. Is that true?" Jake asked, looking at the bartender.

The bartender kept mixing drinks and looked up at Jake.

"Yep, I believe it is."

"And it's all confidential? What we say to 'ya?"

The bartender nodded and said, "What I hear in this bar stays in this bar."

Jake slapped his hand on the counter and said, "Then hit me again! I'm goin' to talk to 'ya!"

The bartender retrieved a bottle from the shelf and poured Jake another drink.

"I would have to be good and drunk to call her," Jake said. "What's your name, anyway?"

"You can call me Bub," the bartender replied.

"Bub, what kind of a name is Bub?"

"It was supposed to be Bud, but they misspelled it on my birth certificate. So Bub it was, is, and always will be."

Jake looked at him, not believing a word he said, but continued his conversation.

"Well, Bub, like I said, I would have to be good and drunk to call her."

"Why?" Bub asked.

"She scares me."

"How?"

"I would only hurt her."

"Why do you think that?"

"We're so different."

"How so?"

"She's so angel-like, and she's religious. She's dainty, but she's strong."

"I see," Bub said.

"She's got these bleedin' heart flowers in her garden. They kind of remind me of her. Fragile. She looked at me one day, and do you know what she said?"

"What did she say?" Bub went right along with Jake's train of thought.

"She said, 'I've lost so much in my life already, I need to be careful with you. You'd be too easy to fall in love with. You're the kind that would kiss me and then disappear one day with no warning.'"

"Was she right?" Bub asked.

"That's why she scares me. I would like to think I wouldn't leave her, but my track record proves otherwise."

Jake took another sip of his drink.

"That's why if I don't have her in my life, then I don't have to leave her."

Bub nodded as if he understood. That was his job—to understand drunks.

Jake took another swallow.

"Bub, I'm confused. Why aren't you confused?" Jake asked.

"I don't get paid to be confused," Bub answered.

"I told her I wouldn't do that to her, and then I did. I hurt her."

Bub asked, "And now? How do you feel about her now?"

"Oh, damn, I loved her then, and I love her now. I'll always love her."

Jake shrugged his shoulders, looking directly at Bub.

"Loving her is natural. It's so easy to do. It's like breathing, you know? You just can't help but love her. I've never had anybody like that in my life before. I didn't know what to do with her. She scared me."

"So you left her?"

"Yep, I left her. Give me another drink."

Bub put one more drink in front of Jake and asked, "Do you think you will ever know what to do with her?"

"Not sure."

"Why don't you find out?"

Bub knew Jake had drunk enough when he kept repeating himself.

"Well," Jake said once again, "I'd have to be stinkin' drunk to call her now. She'd probably hang up on me."

"I doubt that," Bub replied.

"You wanna know another reason she scares me?"

"Sure."

"She had this way of making me look at myself, I mean really inside myself, and I didn't like that. She made me want to run from her on one hand and run to her on another."

"Is that a bad thing, running to her?"

"It was then."

"Why?"

"I knew if I decided to go after her, I would get her. I know how to compete. I like a challenge, but she was more than a challenge— one I couldn't handle because I would have to change who I was. I didn't think I could do that. It seemed she had little halos surrounding her, and I had pitchforks in my hands."

Bub couldn't believe he was going to give this man advice, but any man who started talking about halos and pitchforks needed advice and needed it *now*.

So he said, "If I were you, I would call her—better yet, I would go to her and claim her back. I would drop the pitchfork and claim my own halo."

Bub was amazed. Had he really said that? He looked around to make sure no one had heard him say such a thing. He didn't want anyone to know he was turning into a softy when it came to love. But then if the truth be told, he was a softy. What was it his former girlfriend had called him? Marshmallow. Yes, that was it, marshmallow, and he was, especially around her. That's why he ran from her. Seemed he and this stranger named Jake had a lot in common after all.

Jake interrupted Bub's thoughts. "You would?"

"I would."

"Well, I'd have to be stinkin' drunk to call her."

"I know. You've said that."

Jake looked at Bub and asked, "Ever had a woman with eyes that looked straight through you?"

"Once," Bub answered, "and I don't want another one either. They're trouble with a capital T. We lose our senses when we meet up with the likes of 'em. I take it she was one of 'em?"

Jake nodded.

"Should have shown up here before you met her. I could have warned 'ya, but you're a goner now, so you might as well go to her because something tells me if you don't, you'll be comin' to see me for the next twenty years still talkin' about how drunk you would have to be to call her."

Jake ordered another drink, but Bub said, "You're cut off now, buddy. You need to go home and get your head on straight, and I'm not just talkin' about the alcohol hangover you're goin' to have tomorrow. And it's not even New Year's Eve yet."

Bub couldn't believe his eyes when he looked up. There she was. The very one that had called him a 'marshmallow.' It had been years. But, there she was and all the yesterdays disappeared. He looked at Jake.

"Excuse me, buddy, I've got some fence-mendin' to do." Bub walked over to her. *Might as well follow my own advice*, he thought. "Hello, marshmallow," was all she had to say. And, all the years that had come between them melted away.

Jake paid his bill and got up to leave. As he walked out the door, he mumbled, "Yep, I'd have to be stinkin' drunk to call her now."

From the distance, he heard Bub holler, "Don't call her. Go to her!"

And Bub focused all his attention on the one that almost got away.

The next morning, Jake determined that the bartender, Bub, had been right. He did need to get his head on straight. But at the moment, he needed something to rid him of his terrible headache, and right now, he wished he didn't even have a head.

Well, the good thing about it was he had gotten all his drinking over with before the big night. New Year's Eve was coming, and he promised himself a quiet evening with no alcohol or women. He would go to bed early. The last thing he wanted was a party. He didn't want to hear horns blaring; he didn't want to see the ball drop; and the last thing he wanted was a whisky-breathin' redhead. He wasn't going to be kissing anybody at midnight. Again he thought of getting a dog. Maybe a yorkie. The ones with the perky ears and red bows on their heads. They were cutie pies. Kate would like a dog like that.

He decided to go to upstate New York. He remembered a little town up there that reminded him of Brooksport Village. That's what he was going to do. Go there, find a little hotel, and have a quiet, peaceful New Year's Eve alone. No mess, no fuss.

He packed a few things, took a handful of aspirin for his headache, and walked outside. First, he had to see Bub. He had an apology to make. No one should have had to listen to that story he told last night. Heaven only knew how much he had repeated himself. He didn't know how bartenders could stand it. They could probably write a book.

"Hey, look who's back," Bub said as Jake walked through the door. "Is your head screaming for a Bloody Mary right about now?"

Jake stared at him.

"How did you get in, anyway?" Bub questioned. "We're not open yet."

"The door was unlocked."

"Must have forgotten to lock it last night."

"You should know better. You're goin' to get fired."

"Nope, I own the joint."

"That woman that walked through the door last night—somethin' tells me you knew her once upon a time, she the reason you forgot to lock the door?" Jake asked.

Bub looked at him and merely smiled as he continued to dry freshly washed glasses.

"I came to apologize to you, Bub."

"No need—did you call her?"

"Hell, no!"

"Why not?"

"I was too stinkin' drunk!"

"Well, you kept sayin' over and over you would have to be stinkin' drunk to call her."

"I know what I said, but she deserves more than that—much more."

Bub looked at him.

"I feel sorry for you, fella. You really got it bad. You need to call her, but I think you ought to be sober when you do."

"Give me a Coke, Bub, would you?"

"Sure thing—one for the road?"

"Yep, wherever that road leads."

"I got this sneaky feelin' it's goin' to lead back to her. What's her name, anyway?"

"Kate, her name is Kate."

Jake finished his coke, made his apologies, and affirmed his decision that he couldn't spend New Year's Eve standing on a corner in Times Square with—what did Trudy call them—*a red-lipsticked, heavily perfumed, short-skirted bimbo in search of herself tryin' to latch onto the best-lookin' cowboy who had ever set foot in their little town.* Yep, that's what Trudy had said.

"Well, Trudy," Jake said to thin air, "not this year. Not when I know I have walked away from something I will never—can never—forget."

He didn't feel he had anything he could offer Kate. He felt she deserved so much more than he could ever give. He wasn't talking material things. Oh, that he could definitely give her, but she wasn't a material girl; she was a hometown girl who shot straight from the heart, not the hip. That's what scared him the most. Nobody had been able to see through him like she had. Everything he had told Bub last night was true.

This year, he wanted quiet. He had to think. He felt something was wrong with him that he couldn't put a name to. One thing he did know, he wanted peace—no horn blowing, no funny hats. It seemed nothing about his life was funny anymore. How could anything be funny in the jungle, especially alone?

"When we need these healing times, there is nothing better than a good long walk. It is amazing how the rhythmic movements of the feet and legs are so intimately attached to cobweb cleaners in the brain." (Anne Wilson Schaef)

66

Kate looked out her bedroom window. How long had it been since Jake left? It seemed the clock had stopped ticking. One season had blended into another. Secrets had been brought out into the open. It had been a time of forgiving and being forgiven. The snow was falling, pure and white. The storms were over—at least, for now. A calmness was blanketing the village town.

She wondered if Jake felt the same as she. She missed him. She walked to the closet, put on her coat, and walked out the door. She didn't know where she was going. She needed air.

Walking into town, she saw Trudy's house. Trudy had invited her over for New Year's Eve, but Kate didn't want to be a third wheel. Techy Ted was in town.

Kate smiled as she passed Trudy's house. She saw the two of them scurrying around inside. Who knew what they were doing? After all, it was Trudy and Techy Ted—both in their own world, both happy. Kate was glad. Trudy was her best friend. Nobody else knew their story or how closely they were connected. Only the two of them. They had faced their truths and had become stronger because of it.

Charlie was at Wes and Reva's with Sarah. *The two new lovebirds of the town*, Kate thought with a smile. They had invited her, but she had declined. She thought she had wanted to be alone, but she had to ask herself why she was walking these streets, if that were really true.

She was tempted to knock on their door, but she didn't. She turned instead and walked back to Open Door.

She walked inside and sat down in front of the fireplace, continuing to think of Jake. She walked into the room that had once been his. She opened the drawers and closet doors.

"Still empty," she whispered.

She admitted she was having her own pity party, but she didn't care. Tonight on New Year's Eve, she decided she was going to cry. That crying jag would happen at the stroke of midnight. That was going to be her scheduled party for this special night.

She left Jake's room—yes, she still called it Jake's Room—and walked into her office. She had kept his picture tucked away inside a file drawer. He didn't know she had it. Trudy had captured the photo when he hadn't been looking. He was standing in front of Belle's when she snapped it. She wondered what he was thinking, standing there all by himself. She had captured a look that made both women wonder what was going on in his mind at that exact moment. He was showing his vulnerability without knowing it. He very rarely let his mask down. Trudy had given the picture to Kate.

"*I always knew he wore a mask,*" Trudy had said. "*He looks so forlorn. That's what the city does to you.*"

Kate smiled at the face looking back at her.

Kate took the picture from her file and looked at it. It was New Year's Eve. She sat down, still looking at the picture. She smiled at the face staring back at her.

"Such sad eyes," she whispered.

That's what captured her attention. She wondered about the note she had written him. Did he read it? Did he still have it? Will he ever know what it really says?

She traced his lips with her fingertips.

"Yes, this is going to be a quiet night for me, Jake," she said to his picture.

The town had a lot to think about and remember. This year would be no different.

Kate allowed her fingers to move up the photograph to trace Jake's eyes, and then she placed her entire hand across his face and began to pray for the man she might not ever see again.

"When the businessman steps off the street into the chapel, God listens intently, carefully." (Max Lucado)

67

Jake found a little hotel room far outside the city in a little town he had remembered from his childhood. He thought those memories could fill the empty spaces he felt. He had to admit he was always running away from the city. He was running when he stumbled upon Brooksport Village. Now he was running from the city again. Maybe the city no longer intrigued him. Maybe the city was even bad for him. Maybe he needed a hometown with a hometown girl that lived there. Maybe he needed a drink. Then he remembered that night with Bub and the morning after—no, he did not need a drink.

He looked at the clock—almost midnight. It had been a long time since he had left that little village town, where all those balloons had made their circles in the sky. He should be over it by now. He shouldn't feel like someone had reached into his heart, pulled the cork, and poured him out all over this snow-drenched New Year's Eve.

He had to get out into a wide-open place to breathe. He grabbed his coat and hat, put on his boots, and went out into the streets of rural New York.

He had walked these streets so many times in his life when he was younger. He knew every nook and cranny. If he remembered, there was a church at the end of the street. Yes, there it was. The lights were on. Why was he walking toward it? It was as if a force would not let him rest until his feet touched the first step leading to the door.

He took a deep breath and decided to go inside.

"I'll just find a little corner and see if I can reach the end of myself," he said out loud.

As he slowly opened the door, he was astonished to see the place was packed with people. People everywhere. People with smiles. He guessed there were others in this world who didn't like horns and funny hats, just like him.

He sat down beside a spry little old lady in the back row. She motioned for him to take off his hat. He obeyed her silent command and whispered, "Sorry."

She smiled and nodded. *He looks like a lost, sad little boy*, she thought.

He glanced at her from the corner of his eye, wondering if there was something else he should do. After all, he was in church. He hadn't been in one in quite a while. He questioned why he was sitting in one right at the moment. He was nervous. He looked up at the ceiling, wondering if the roof might collapse because he was sitting there.

He thought about leaving. The door was very near. He could make a quick getaway and spare all these smiling people possible injuries if the ceiling did, indeed, fall.

Jake wished Kate were there in that very moment so she could see him actually sitting in church. He could have leaned on her. He was more than positive that she had a direct link to God and that nothing bad would happen if she were there.

That woman beside him kept smiling and looking at him from time to time. It seemed they had their own little sign language going on between them. He kept nodding his head at her, and she kept on grinning.

Finally, she whispered, "It's been a while for you, 'eh?"

Jake nodded.

"Don't worry, our building has a strong foundation. Nothing bad is going to happen because you walked through the door!"

Jake couldn't believe it. She could read his mind. He tried not to think. He tried to relax but kept fidgeting with his hat on his lap.

He decided to focus his sight and his hearing on the pastor instead of this woman with the constant grin, although it was a loving, caring grin.

He turned toward the pastor and began to listen.

"Some people are afraid. They're afraid to change. They're afraid to let people in. They fear hurt and rejection, so they keep running away from something, and it's not to the future that Christ has promised for all that love him. They're simply afraid to be vulnerable, afraid to say what Jesus tells us every day, 'I love you.'"

Those words hit Jake like a bullet. He swore the pastor looked straight at him. Just picked him out of the crowd to make him fidget in his seat even more. Jake did not disappoint him. He couldn't stop fidgeting. He was still fidgeting when the lady next to him stood to leave.

She grinned one last grin at him as she excused herself. She patted Jake on the shoulder as she brushed past. He became very still.

I may have to spend the night here, he thought. *I don't think I can move.*

As the pastor was walking down the aisle to lock up, he spotted Jake.

"How 'ya doin'?" the pastor asked.

"After your sermon tonight?" Jake questioned.

"That bad, huh?"

Jake looked at him and replied, "I think I'm one of those runners you talked about."

"Oh, I see."

The pastor sat down next to Jake.

"What are you running from?"

"Not sure." Jake shuffled his feet.

The pastor merely nodded.

It seemed to Jake all the people in this church smiled and nodded a lot.

Jake finally replied, "It's like somethin's chasin' me."

"Maybe somethin' is," the pastor replied.

"No, nobody is. I keep lookin' over my shoulder, but nobody's there."

Once again, the pastor nodded, smiled, and said, "Oh, somebody's there. You just can't see him yet."

Jake gave him a confused look that prompted the pastor to ask, "Do you know Jesus?"

"Well, I know his face when I see a picture of him."

The pastor nodded and smiled.

Jake couldn't help himself when he said, "You people sure do nod and smile a lot."

Both men remained silent for a moment before Jake said, "There's this woman."

"And she's not with you tonight?"

"No, she's in a little town called Brooksport Village."

"Never heard of it."

"Me neither until I stumbled upon it one day—looked up in the sky and saw all these balloons."

The pastor looked at him, a little confused as to the quick change in conversation.

"It's a long story," Jake said. "Anyway, that's where I met her."

"I see. She's there, and you're here."

"That's about it. I guess I'm still runnin'."

"Probably."

"I don't understand it. I own my own business. I have so much money I can't fold it fast enough, and I still feel empty. Shouldn't I be happy?"

Jake hesitated a moment and continued, "I'm one of those guys you talked about, you know. I have a hard time saying those three words you mentioned in your sermon."

"What words were those?"

"You know."

"I said a lot of words in my sermon. I saw you come through the door a little late. You have to tell me."

Jake pointed to himself, made a heart with his fingers, and pointed to the pastor.

"I see."

"But this woman, this woman is so filled with love I don't know what to do with her. She's been the only one I couldn't even think of as a 'conquest.' Know what I mean?"

The pastor kept listening as he looked at Jake.

"But maybe you don't know what I'm talkin' about, you bein' a pastor and all."

"I think I do. I've seen a lot, heard a lot, and I am a man as well as a pastor."

"Well, you see, I've had more than my share of women in my life, Pastor, and I've hurt most of them in some way. I've wounded them—" He looked up and quickly added, "Oh, not physically, mind you, but emotionally. Even Kate—that's her name—looked at me once and told me she couldn't allow herself to get involved with me. She said I would be too easy to fall in love with. I don't want to wound her, so I've forced myself to stay away from her. But I can't forget her either. I don't know what to do with her. I guess she's right about my walls."

"Walls around your heart?" the pastor asked.

"She said she couldn't bring them down, and then she started talkin' crazy about a city named Jericho, that I needed to walk my own march around that city…she said she couldn't tear down my walls. She said she wasn't strong enough."

"Smart woman, this Kate of yours," the pastor replied.

"And then there's Trudy," Jake began.

"Who's Trudy?"

"Kate's best friend."

The pastor nodded and let Jake continue.

"She told me I couldn't run forever. She said that love would always find me."

The pastor smiled.

"Sounds like a bunch of wise women in that Brooksport Village of yours."

Jake looked miserable. Brooksport Village could have been a part of him, but he walked away from it.

"I'm interested in the walls you keep talkin' about," the pastor began. "Who do you think can bring down those walls?"

Jake shrugged.

"I think you're here because I think the somethin' you're looking for is the someone who is chasin' you."

Jake looked at him, totally perplexed.

The pastor continued, "He has a way of doin' that, you know. Some call him the Hound of Heaven."

Jake looked at him, sincerely trying his best to understand what the pastor was saying.

The pastor took a deep breath.

"My dear man, Jesus is chasin' you."

"Why would he be chasin' me?" Jake questioned. "I haven't done anything to him."

"One day, you'll know exactly what we've all done to him, but for now, just know that he loves you."

Jake didn't understand. He was trying to. He had reached a point in his life that he knew he needed a lifeline.

"He doesn't want to leave you behind. He's determined that he won't live without you, and you can't stop that determination. He will use every means he has to get to you face-to-face, but you make the final decision from your own free will to let him in."

"Let him in where?" Jake asked.

"Into your heart," the pastor replied.

"Is that possible with all the walls everybody keeps tellin' me I've built around myself?"

"He's the one your Kate was talking about."

"The one to tear down the walls?"

The pastor nodded.

"You think he's here right now with us?" Jake asked.

"Probably sittin' right next to you."

Jake turned quickly to look beside him.

The pastor chuckled and secretly thanked God for bringing this man into his sanctuary on this very special night.

Oh yes, Jesus, the pastor thought. *This one is going to do great things for you.*

Jake turned to face the pastor and asked, "How do I say yes to the one who will tear down my walls, Pastor? Do I have to go to Jericho, wherever that place is? The place Kate told me about?"

"No, you don't have to go to Jericho. You don't have to go anywhere. We simply sit here in this church on New Year's Eve and pray. What is your name?"

"Jake."

"Well, Jake," he said as he placed a hand on Jake's shoulder. "Let's pray."

And pray they did.

"You've turned your back on the noise and sought his voice. You've stepped away from the masses and followed the master as he led you up the winding path to the summit..." (Max Lucado)

68

Midnight had come and gone, and he had survived. He had more than survived; he felt different. He couldn't explain it; he didn't even try. All he knew was that he was thankful, very thankful for the "chase."

The snow was falling. If anyone had seen him catching snow-flakes on his tongue, they would have thought him completely crazy.

"All I need is one of Trudy's purple scarfs around my neck!" he exclaimed.

He ran to a bench nearby, sat down, and looked up at the snow falling around his face.

"Pure as snow," he repeated what the pastor had said. "I am pure as snow. Thank you, God, for the chase. Thank you for catching me. Thank you for giving me what I need most, and thank you—no more walls!"

With that, he jumped from the bench, fell to the ground, and made the biggest snow angel anyone has ever seen.

There was someone watching from a little bedroom window up above—the little old woman who motioned for him to remove his hat in that little rural New York church. The one who sat beside him and assured him everything would be okay. The one who whispered she was glad he was there. She was looking down upon his gleeful play.

"Well, mercy me, something tells me he had a little help tonight to find out where he is goin', and I do believe he just took the hand of the Lord to lead him safely there."

Yes, she was watching, and she didn't think him crazy at all. In fact, she thought she might just join him out there, fall on the ground, and make a snow angel herself. But someone would have to help her get back up. That cowboy probably would have helped her up, but she chose to make a cup of tea and watch the show going on below in the pure white snow. Sometimes people just needed privacy during a 'golden moment'.

"I have been thinking about the change of the seasons. I don't want to miss spring this year. I want to be there on the spot the moment the grass turns green." (Annie Dillard)

69

It took Jake another two days to drive back to his house. The weather hindered his progress, but he looked at snow now in a completely different light.

He kept repeating, "White as snow, white as snow."

Once he pulled into his driveway, he went inside, packed a few things, and thought once again about getting a dog. But this time—this time—his thinking was a little different. This time, a pet—he would love, care for, play with, and walk the beach with. He would take time to breathe and throw balls. Yep, one of those little yorkies with the red bow on its head. Kate would like that.

He was finally packed up, gassed up, and ready to go back. He was loved up, prayed up, and joyous that he had finally shut up and listened.

He may not have known where he was going a few short days ago, but he did now. He knew exactly where he was going, and he knew how to get there. He didn't need an escort. Yes, he knew the way.

He was on his way to that place he learned to love, not only Brooksport Village but Open Door. He was on his way back.

He wasn't sure exactly what he was going to say to Kate; he didn't know the response he would receive, especially from that Trudy gal. She always spoke her mind, and she was not real thrilled with him when he left.

But he knew he was ready—ready to accept the love offered to him. After all, he had just opened his heart to the greatest love of all. He had been set free.

He had one more stop to make before his final drive back to Brooksport. He pulled into the parking lot and ran into the store. When he came out, he was carrying two helium-filled red balloons. He was going to have a launch of his own. He thought that maybe those balloons could talk for him. At the very least, they might help to get him one step inside the door.

70

Trudy saw him first. She was standing in her salon, hovering over one of her clients, carefully placing the foil around segments of hair to be colored. Then she looked up in the mirror. She saw the balloons first. She dropped everything, including the hair color, and ran to the window, forgetting everything else.

"Trudy! What in blazes is wrong with you?"

"Lordy mercy," Trudy exclaimed. "Are my eyes deceivin' me?"

She looked at Jake one more time as he practically marched in the direction of Open Door with those balloons.

"It is him!"

"Who?"

"Jake!"

With that, she ran out the door to watch Jake continue his climb right up the street toward Kate's.

"Don't leave me in here with my half-colored hair, Trudy! You get back here!"

Trudy paid her no mind. She could fix whatever went awry with that woman's hair, and she would fix it for free. This—this was something she was not going to miss. This was history in the making. Jake was back, and this time, from the way he was walking—like a man on a mission—he was back to stay. No, siree, she was not going to miss this!

Jake gathered quite a crowd as he continued his stride. Belle left her hot oil and doughnuts. Wes heard the commotion and left the water buckets for the horses, called Jeb to his side, and started walking toward the crowd. Gordy saluted him as Jake walked by.

Reva and Sarah who were close to Wes in the stables were catching up with him as Jeb led the way. Tourists from all directions joined the pomp and circumstance. They were curious bystanders but somehow knew there was a celebration at hand because of those balloons. Their winter getaway was turning into something they had no clue was going to happen.

But those who knew the history of this small village town did have a clue, and all those tourists were quite pleased that whoever this fellow was that appeared on the scene was someone very special, indeed, and they were going to take their own front row seat.

Charlie and Phil saw him from the window of their living room.

Phil exclaimed, "Charlie, is that who I think it is?"

"It is!" Charlie replied. "It is!"

"Let's join 'em!" Phil nearly hollered. "What's he doin' with those balloons?"

Charlie laughed remembering Phil had been in a stupor when Jake had saved the day that Memorial Day weekend. "I'll tell 'ya later!"

Kate saw the crowd before she saw Jake. She dried her hands at the sink and went outside, mostly curious as to why everyone had gathered. Then she saw him.

There was total silence when those eyes locked onto Jake's. Lordy, the town didn't know if Kate would run back in the house and slam the door behind her, or if Jake would suddenly change his mind again and hightail it out of town.

So the town held its breath—even Trudy.

Then they saw it—a slight smile that began to form on Kate's mouth. It was one of those countdown moments like New York does in Times Square every New Year's Eve.

It must have been the balloons because Kate took off running straight toward Jake. He stood there as if he couldn't believe it. He thought he couldn't have moved if he had wanted to. He was so mesmerized by Kate. The love he had for her was shining all over his face.

Trudy came up beside Charlie and said, "This is like one of those slow-motion movie scenes, don't 'ya think, Charlie?"

Charlie didn't care if it was slow motion or fast. He was so glad to see Jake again he could hardly stand it. He just wished those two lovebirds would finally get together so he could talk to Jake about all the things that had happened since he had left.

Then it was like a hurricane. Everything happened so fast. Kate didn't stop running until she jumped smack dab into Jake's arms, locking her legs around his waist and kissing him in the process.

The whole town started applauding. Trudy started crying. Charlie looked at her, a little confused.

"These are happy tears, Charlie. These are happy tears."

Jake was back to talk to him. Phil was still trying to learn about women too, and he was no help. But that was okay. They were struggling through that together. He was a dad now, and that was enough for Charlie.

Charlie looked up and saw Sarah. She was crying too. So was her mom. He guessed they were happy tears too.

Women, Charlie thought. *I'll never understand 'em.*

Jake lost control of those balloons, and they started floating toward the sky. He swung Kate around in his arms and started to laugh. So did Kate. It was when he put her two feet back on the ground that he saw the tears. He cupped her face in his hands and wiped her eyes with his thumbs.

"Happy tears, I hope," he whispered.

She looked at him very intently before answering.

"Something's happened to you, Jake. You're different somehow."

He held her closely and whispered words only she could hear, and she held him a bit tighter.

Somehow Trudy knew, but then she always knew everything.

"He found his pharmacon," was all she said, looking up at the sky as tears continued to roll down her cheeks. "This time, he's here to stay."

As she began her walk back to the salon, she smiled and said, "I guess Kate's right. Maybe there is something about those balloons..."

"Whatever God opens, no one can close." (Revelation 3:7)

EPILOGUE

CHARLIE

"Guess you're wonderin' what happened in our village town after Jake came back—this time to stay. And I'm goin' to tell 'ya.

"Jake decided he could manage his business out of Anywhere, USA, and what better view than Kate's flower garden overlooking the water? Or sittin' in front of a wood burnin' fire in the winter with the woman he loved?

"Town's never seen such a weddin' than when Jake and Kate tied the knot, lordy mercy, they released hundreds of balloons when Jake kissed his bride. Gordy had the high school band playin', and good 'ole Jeb had this little bow tie around his neck with the weddin' rings tucked inside. That Jeb walked up the path alongside a little yorkie with a red bow on her head. Kate sure loves that dog.

"Jake had that pastor from upstate New York come to our town to marry 'em. He said that pastor was one of the most special persons to inhabit this earth. Well, I guess he is 'cause he's the one that helped Jake find his way back home where he belonged.

"Brenda was there, and Kate cried when she saw her. Both of those women kept saying over and over again, 'Are we clear? Are we clear?' whatever that meant. Things looked pretty clear to me. All I know is that those women were cryin' happy tears. One day, I'll understand about that.

"Sandra came to us on that special day too, and she brought with her all of Jake's closest buddies from his New York office. They had watched their boss come alive again. They promised they would visit our little town that had changed Jake's life. And Sandra, oh, sweet Sandra, was ever so happy that Jake had finally forgotten redheads.

"We had some unexpected visitors that day too—squirrels. I still don't know why Miss Kate laughs every time she sees those squirrels in her bird feeder, but that's okay. Most people would be shooing them away or gettin' out their BB guns.

"After the weddin', we settled down again, well, as much as a town like ours can settle down. Gordy continued to open his horse farm to tourists and neighborhood kids to come learn how to ride. He hired me as an instructor for the summers when I come home from college. I love those kids. Just wanna help give 'em a dream. Want 'em to learn how to 'saddle up' for life's adventures. I talk to 'em about Christ too, mostly when their hands are busy pattin' those horse's manes and their minds are real open and all. That's when they open up the most—when they're busy doin' somethin'. Kate taught me that. She said that's when they talk about what makes 'em happy and sad. They confide their secrets…I think I'm goin' to be a therapist.

"Gordy put his cowboy hat back on but only when he rides Star Bright. Last time we saw him with that hat on his head was when tragedy hit our town on 9/11. Must mean he's roundin' the bend of his healin'. I think there's just somethin' special about that white horse and that cowboy hat, somethin' that keeps him close to Jessie.

"And Phil, ah, Phil, after he found the Lord in that closet, well, he's gettin' ready to go on another one of his missionary trips. Everybody's so happy he no longer cusses and closes Crabby's Bar. They actually give him money so he can go to places that need him most, and I hand it to him. He works, too, at Gordy's horse farm. He washes down those horses and feeds them right alongside Wes. He doesn't wanna ride 'em, though. Maybe one day I'll show him how to 'saddle up' just like he taught me how to dance.

"Chip's still strummin' his guitar and writin' songs. Still bringin' in the crowds at the coffeehouse and lovin' every minute of it. Oh, and 'Hometown Girl' is played on the radio a lot these days. Jake saw to that. Guess that song was pretty special to Jake. He winks at Chip every time he hears it.

"And Trudy, well, she fell in love with Techy Ted. He makes frequent visits to Brooksport. Trudy says he's a 'master of detail,' whatever that means. And it seems he likes purple as much as she does. Only thing that matters is that she loves him and he loves her. Sure to be another weddin' around here soon. Oh, she still wants to know everybody else's business, but she's mellowed. The only time she 'rants' is when she can't find her 'original' Chicken in a Biskit crackers—yep, she still does that, especially when she has to break in the newbies down at the grocery store. Almost forgot the most important thing. Techy Ted is movin' down here. Settin' up shop, just like Jake.

"Wes and Reva are still lovin' and still carin'. Wes took on another responsibility at Gordy's stable. Seems kids love his made-up stories, and he has a story tellin' hour with those tourist kids who are on vacation with their parents. Seems Wes and Reva have become the parents of many. She brings 'em cookies all the time.

"A mystery still remains in my mind. I just can't figure out why Kate laughs every time she looks at Jake's legs. They are so skinny.

"No question about it, our village town has been through a lot, but all our secrets have been spilled out all over the streets. All our tears are mingled with healing and prayers. We're settling in and cozying up to brand-new chapters and second chances.

"Now we're makin' ourselves ready for new strangers that will be comin' from the city with those forlorn looks. We're preparin' to make 'em smile, and if they're wearin' cowboy boots, we're goin' to convince 'em they can't run away from love forever.

"And me? Well, as I said, I'm goin' off to college…and Sarah? She's goin' to follow me next year. After all, small-town boys grow up, fall in love with small-town girls, and marry.

"Well, there you have it—except for one thing. If you ever wanna go somewhere to 'get away,' you may wanna pay us a visit right here in Brooksport Village.

"And remember, we don't care where you've been. We only wanna know where you're goin'. Come on down. We'll be waitin' for 'ya. There's always an open door."

ABOUT THE AUTHOR

Judy Baldwin Lord is a newcomer to the writing community with her debut novel, *Open Door*. She grew up in Tennessee, moved to Connecticut, and was a high school English teacher in Ohio. She is retired from her sales position that was headquartered in New York. She currently lives in Michigan with her husband, Ron, and her six-pound yorkie, Ryder. She has one daughter, Mandi, who is married to Steve, and two grandchildren, Madison, ten years old, and Cole, seven years old. Her favorite hobby is loving on those grandchildren and spoiling them as much as their parents will allow.